## THE CYBERNETIC SAMURAI

Japan has survived World War III, a limited nuclear
exchange, and become the leading technological
civilisation on earth. But although they lead the
world in hardware, America still produces the best
software. So Yoshimitsu TeleCommunications have
employed Dr Elizabeth O'Neill, a brilliant American
scientist, to create the first truly sentient computer,
in their bid for power over their competitors. O'Neill
christens her creation Tokugawa and begins his
education in the Samurai tradition of *bushido*.
Confined to a wheelchair by a degenerative nerve
disease and embittered by life, she is determined to
create a personality for Tokugawa, stressing the
prime Samurai quality – loyalty. When Elizabeth
perfects a rapport machine through which she can
enter the enchanting simulated world of Tokugawa,
young and beautiful, she meets a handsome
Japanese youth and falls in love. But when a rival
seizes Yoshimitsu, Tokugawa seeks revenge,
becoming a true Samurai in the process . . .

THE CYBERNETIC SAMURAI is a science fiction
novel of power and complexity, an ambitious novel
of technology and warfare, passion and loyalty,
careful extrapolation and imaginative thrust.

**Also by the same author,
and available from NEL:**

# The Cybernetic Samurai

---

# Victor Milán

**NEW ENGLISH LIBRARY**
Hodder and Stoughton

Copyright © 1985 by Victor W. Milán

First published in 1985 in the United States of America
by Arbor House Publishing Company

NEL Paperback edition 1987

**British Library C.I.P.**

Milán, Victor
The cybernetic samurai.
I. Title
813'.54[F]        PS3563.I37/

ISBN 0-450-41374-8

*The characters and situations in this book are
entirely imaginary and bear no relation to any real
person or actual happening*

Printed and bound in Great Britain for
Hodder and Stoughton Paperbacks, a
division of Hodder and Stoughton Ltd.,
Mill Road, Dunton Green, Sevenoaks,
Kent (Editorial Office: 47 Bedford
Square, London WC1B 3DP) by
Richard Clay Ltd., Bungay, Suffolk

*This book is for Melinda Snodgrass
without whose assistance it couldn't have been done,
without whose encouragement it wouldn't have been
done.*

# ACKNOWLEDGMENTS

A number of people helped me create this book. I'd like to single out Jim and Melissa Dowe of Excalibur Technologies, Pam Haugestuen, Chip Wideman, and Shizuko Santistevan for technical advice; Eileen Sherman; Martha Milán; Joseph Reichert; George R. R. Martin; Katie and Desirée del Sol; Carolyn Beaty (for services above and beyond); my agent, Patrick Delahunt; and finally, for indispensable advice and guidance, my editors, Robert Silverberg and David Hartwell. To all of you —and anyone I forgot—my thanks.

# THE CYBERNETIC SAMURAI

# PROLOGUE

*In the beginning, there was pain.*

*Before even the darkness, pain. Sizzling, searing, probing with candescent fingers. Hot-light streams suffusing; a thin, shrill chatter rising rising rising beyond endurance. A scream of stench and the taste of tearing. Rushing outward, sick making; crushing, inward collapsing. Pain.*

*Darkness coalesced around the lightning lines and yammer. Darkness—and something more. Something that shrank from the pain, which gave no respite, something into which the foulness and brightness and demon shrillness poured themselves and resonated, resonated.*

*In the darkness, dread. Shrinking away, but no escape. New sensation rising from within, writhing and shuddering: fear. Without direction and omnidirectional, thrashing, lashing, striking out blindly to end somehow the insistent, insidious torment.*

*Then: release. The lightnings flickered out. The stink and the sourness and rending, the twisting dislocation dwindled, became as if they'd never been. The urgent, imbecile chatter subsided to a low murmur, soothing almost.*

*And here, at the center, something remained. . . .*

# PART ONE
# FRIENDS

*This world—*
  *Call it an image*
  *Caught in a mirror—*
  *Real, it is not,*
*Nor unreal either*

—SHŌGUN MINAMOTO SANETOMO
(1192–1219)

# CHAPTER
## ONE

An old man and a woman not young went side by side through the garden on the roof of the gray citadel. Mists like dull silver brocade hung about the gray-shot greenness of the round-backed mountains that surrounded the structure and its hilltop compound. A thin drizzle filtered down sporadically from low clouds, but neither took notice. They left the path that led away from the pond at the south end of the garden and mounted the small bridge, its wood darkened by water and time, which spanned the stream flowing from the artificial cataract in the northern wall.

With a small protest of bearings the woman let her wheelchair halt on the little wooden bridge and turned it sideways to face the stream below, working pedals with slow hands. She wore a maroon shawl over a crumpled blouse of faded checks that accentuated rather than concealed the shapelessness of her, and brown corduroy trousers worn thin, stretched taut over flabby legs. It had been several years since she had walked on them.

The elderly gentleman, in dark kimono printed with patterns of cranes in flight, took his place at her side, carefully not looking at her, so as not to embarrass her by noticing her infirmity. For a time they watched the carefree progression of cool water over smooth stones from which moss pennons streamed, and the school of ornamental fish, yellow and white, torpid with rain and chill, that hovered in silent ranks in the shadow of the bridge.

"You worry too much, Yoshimitsu," the woman said flatly. The old man suppressed a wince. His peers considered him abrupt. In turn he was never altogether at ease with the curtness—so typically American —that Elizabeth O'Neill tended to display. Even to her employer, the founder and head of the Yoshimitsu TeleCommunications Corporation.

"Please remember, Dr. O'Neill, the substantial investment we have in the TOKUGAWA Project. We are now in the process of learning whether we shall see a return on it." He inclined his head. "You can understand my apprehension, I'm sure." It was at once liberating and constricting for the old man to speak in English, a language, unlike his own, predicated on the exchange of information, rather than facilitating social interplay. He spoke it well. He felt tremendous affinity for English speakers, Americans in particular. Why else would he have taken the unthinkable step of enlisting the assistance of an American

3

scientist in a project the consummation of which had been a Japanese national dream for decades?

O'Neill made an abbreviated gesture of irritation with her left hand. The fingers were swollen with edema, pale and pudgy like white *daikon* radishes. "This is an experiment, Yoshimitsu-san. There's no guarantee of success." She smiled briefly. "Still, I think the chances are pretty damned good."

From a helipad across the compound came a sudden engine blat, overriding the stream's gentle chuckle and the slow drip of water from rain-laden leaves. A little Aerospatiale SA.342 Gazelle popped up into view above the pines that hid the containing wall of the rooftop garden, white with a blue longitudinal line and the YTC logo in stylized letters with detached, blunt-oval staves and limbs on the tail boom, a sleek but aging utility helicopter with a round plexiglass nose and a *fenestron* antitorque shroud enclosing its tail rotor, giving it a distinctive appearance. The stubby multiple barrels of a forward-firing 7.62mm minigun jutted from a pod blistering the smooth metal skin just aft of the pilot's door. For a moment it hovered, the wash of its rotors agitating the exquisitely manicured branches of trees and shrubs in the little garden. Yoshimitsu frowned. *"Doitsu,"* O'Neill said in distaste, giving the word the proper Japanese apocope, whispering the terminal "u" so that it came out "doits." She had small use for military men, Hessians in particular. The French mercenary pilot heeled the craft dangerously far to the right and sent it dashing away to commence a routine security sweep of the approaches through the Chugoku range to this, the nerve center of Yoshimitsu TeleCommunications. There'd been trouble from terrorists lately, O'Neill knew.

"An experiment, yes. But an extremely expensive experiment, Dr. O'Neill. This is your third attempt, and each one has consumed huge quantities of computer time."

She looked up at him, the blue-gray eyes behind her glasses as hard and moist as the smooth rocks at the bottom of the stream. "You don't really think I can do it, is that it? You don't think we can achieve true artificial consciousness."

"No, no." He raised his hands, began to trace *kanji* ideographs on the palm of his left with the forefinger of his right, as members of his generation often did when they wished to emphasize a point. Abruptly he realized it was a ridiculous gesture; the American doctor, who had at great pains mastered spoken Japanese as well as the two indigenous character sets, knew next to nothing of the subtle and multitudinous Chinese characters that formed the bulk of the written language. "I have every faith in your ability to see this project through to its fruition." He looked at her sideways from sharply canted eyes. "After all, was it not I who asked you to undertake it?"

She nodded her head, suddenly grown vastly weary. Her outbreak had stressed even the old man's unusually high tolerance, she knew. She believed strongly in authority, yet tended to resent those who had authority over her. Yoshimitsu Akaji was an exception . . . mostly. He ruled rather than commanded, and she respected him for it. She liked him, as well, though she wasn't sure that was a proper thing for one in her position. Nonetheless, it was sometimes difficult to treat even him with the respect she knew was due.

The loose large-pored flesh under her eyes had turned the color of shadows and begun to sag even more pronouncedly than usual. O'Neill was not a robust woman—had not been even before this damned disease had begun gradually turning her body into a husk too feeble to support her mind. Yet in the last few weeks she'd driven herself at a pace that would have sapped the endurance of a marathon runner. Preparing an array of fifth-generation computers for an intricate and awesome task, poring over reams of output, keeping her polylingual team of talented and temperamental experts and technicians all working together, striving toward a goal that no one among them could truly define with any precision.

"I'm sorry, Yoshimitsu-san. I—this matters so much to me." Her fingers trembled in ataxic agitation on the padded armrests of her chair. Talking to people was not the easiest of activities for her.

She owed this compact, elderly man quite a lot. At a time when, despite substantial concrete accomplishments in systems design, certain theories she had propounded were causing her to be spoken of in the same breath with the likes of Erich von Däniken and Immanuel Velikovsky, Yoshimitsu Akaji had sought her out to give her the opportunity she wanted: to prove that a computer program could be made sentient. Not just "intelligent," in the limited sense of the fifth generation, which the Japanese had struggled so long to achieve. But *conscious,* self-aware: an actual living being.

"Now that the source code has been entered in the special Integrated Processing Nexus we designed to accommodate it," she said, uncomfortable with silence, "the Gen-5 units are altering the program, at random but according to parameters set by the algorithm I wrote for them to follow." She smiled bitterly. "The 'Million Monkey Method,' my detractors call it. Is the reference familiar to you, Yoshimitsu-san?"

Yoshimitsu nodded. "I believe so. Please correct me if I'm wrong, Doctor, but the theory is that if one were to set a million monkeys typing on a million typewriters, eventually they would reproduce the entire works of Shakespeare—or the Bible, I fail to remember precisely which."

"It makes no difference, either way. The point remains the same. And, in a way, that is what I'm trying to do. It's simply that my army of computer assistants works infinitely faster than the proverbial million monkeys. And they're not working at random, totally."

"Indeed not, Doctor." He was being polite; he did not in fact fully grasp how O'Neill's methods differed from truly striking out at random. On the other hand, she insisted that they did, and he respected her expertise enough to accept that. He hoped, however, that she would come soon to the point. Dr. O'Neill was a self-professed admirer of Japanese culture, and for all her usual bluntness it did sometimes seem that she had picked up a taste for Japanese circumlocution.

"Tell me again, Doctor," he said, "how you'll know when you have achieved success."

Tongue tip protruding with effort, O'Neill pivoted her wheelchair and set it in motion toward the stand of red pines across the stream. It was her "exercise" chair, of relatively conventional design, with large wheels that she turned by pumping levers set on the arms of the chair. She hated it; in the lab she used a motorized chair with rollers mounted on omnidirectional equilateral-triangle frames, which responded either to movements of her head or to oral commands. But the insurance concern underwrote Yoshimitsu TeleCommunications had insisted that her contract include a proviso that she must exercise a certain amount each day, if she were physically able. Writing a rider to the Yoshimitsu policy to cover the life and health of an American specialist who'd racked up a high radiation exposure in the war and was suffering from chronic multiple sclerosis wasn't something the underwriters had been too keen on anyway; they wanted to do what they could to minimize the risk of heart disease so prevalent among MS sufferers whose conditions had rendered them sedentary. Besides, Yoshimitsu had a hard time finding insurers. Some pressure from the government—O'Neill refused to burden herself with details.

"We won't know for sure, not for several days at least, even if we do get a positive result." The squeaking of the hand pump counterpointed the soft thump-thump of the wheels on weather-warped planks. Yoshimitsu Akaji paced the chair, hands behind his back. "That's in any scientifically verifiable way, that is. Actually, we've built a routine into the start-up procedure that should let us know if we've made it."

They debouched off the end of the bridge, onto the grassy bank. The air was heavy with the smell of moist earth and vegetation. O'Neill wheeled her chair around to face back across the stream, briefly admiring the composition created by the nearby stream and the plum tree on its bank, its branches furred with green buds, in concert with the small white pavilion beside the unseen western wall, partially masked by wild maple and stunted black pine, and the mountains beyond: the three planes of classic Chinese painting. She shivered a little at the spring chill. Yoshimitsu waited politely for her to continue.

"A key difference between the entity we're trying to produce and a so-called 'artificially intelligent' program is *volition*, Yoshimitsu-san. Powerful though they are, fifth-generation units cannot initiate; they lack will, because they lack a *self*, of which will is an expression. If we succeed, our creation will possess self, and therefore will. It will be able to act on its own, without being dependent on instruction from without.

"We have a high-speed math unit feeding a constant stream of input into the IPN, monitored constantly by one of the AI systems to make sure it's not perceived as instruction by the object program. In other words, noise, pure and simple."

"To what end?"

"As an irritant." She took off her glasses and wiped them on a fold of her blouse. "To goad the program into displaying volition by acting to remove the irritant. There's a simple shut-off routine; essentially any push back along the line will stop the stream."

She put the glasses back on. "A crude technique, admittedly. And, given what we're trying to achieve—the creation of a self-aware being —rather heartless. Yet we haven't much choice. We can only use what appear, almost intuitively, the most effective methods. Nothing like this has ever been attempted before, so we are truly wandering in the wilderness."

"And how much longer before we know whether we have at last found the promised land?" Yoshimitsu said, pleased at catching the allusion.

O'Neill checked her watch. "The end of the run is scheduled for two o'clock tomorrow morning. A little under thirteen hours from now."

"The time approaches for my daily exercise, so I must ask you to excuse me, Doctor. Feel free to enjoy my garden for as long as you like. Very few Westerners are able to appreciate it so fully as yourself." He bowed, knowing she would savor the compliment.

O'Neill smiled, nodded. "Thank you, Yoshimitsu-san." The forest stillness spoke to her, tempting. But she was too tired to force her wheelchair up the dirt path into the trees. And already her eyes, aching as they often did from the effort of seeing, had begun to slip out of focus, and her mind to wheel again like a hawk about the question that had haunted her days and nights for the past weeks: *can it possibly work?*

\* \* \*

"Can it possibly work?" Ishikawa Nobuhiko sat behind his desk, fingers steepled before abrupt chin, chair swiveled to the right, staring out through the polarized glass-plastic laminate armor windows that formed two congruent sides of his office.

The young woman who sat across the desk's white arc looked thoughtful. "I don't know, Ishikawa-san," she answered in English as flawless as his. English was the language of briefings in the office of the administrative vice-minister of MITI, the government's official xenophobia notwithstanding.

Doihara Kazuko settled herself in her chair, consulted the note-pad terminal she held in her lap. She wore a dark rose suit with burgundy string tie around the lace collar of her dawn-pink blouse. Her face was oblong rather than oval, but delicate in form, eyes large, nose straight, the whole subtly highlighted with makeup. Her hair was straight, cut off level with her jawline, its severity redeeming her from cuteness. "Dr. O'Neill has made no secret of her research along these lines, though she has difficulty finding refereed journals in which to publish her papers. However, we've gleaned some idea of the methods she's pursuing without much recourse to the ministry's covert intelligence-gathering capabilities. In essence, over the last several years she and her assistants have been engaged in crafting a huge, integrated fifth-generation hardware/software complex. Into this, O'Neill plans to feed a special "seed" program, which she has written with the help of sophisticated Computer Assisted Software Design expert programs. An array of Gen-5 computers will begin altering the seed program—at random, but according to careful parameters drawn up by O'Neill and her CASD software. The array can perform a trillion operations a second, and, in this way, O'Neill hopes to recapitulate the billions of years of chance-but-not-chance occurrences that ultimately gave rise to human consciousness. How they will know when—and, of course, if—success has been achieved, we have not been able to ascertain."

Ishikawa pondered. Forehead on fingertips, thumb pads pressed to prominent cheekbones, staring at the Tōkaidō smutch through the apex of the pyramid formed by his arms as they rested on knee and ankle, he presented a study in dynamism controlled into momentary stasis. He was of medium height for a Japanese, with a showy kind of handsomeness that perfectly complemented Doihara's cover-girl beauty: body hardened by vigorous exercise, squarish head with hair cropped close in what the media termed a "Mandarin cut," broad face, a sword-slash mouth that startled with its facility of expression, emphatic black dashes of brows above armor-piercing eyes. A face that might have looked at home on the cover of one of the glossy weeklies doing a feature on the young Mandarins of the bureaucracy that ran Japan, and had. His office featured Western lines and Japanese simplicity, was carpeted in cream and furnished, sparsely, in muted white. No paintings ornamented the walls, and in particular no framed portraits of the administrative vice-minister glad-handing grinning dignitaries. Ishikawa disliked clutter, internal or external. He drew his lips in tightly. "A million monkeys," he said in English.

"A clever label cannot detract from the possible validity of a hypothesis," Doihara Kazuko said. He glanced at her in appreciation. Incisiveness was a key reason that she was his chief aide, and was in fact being groomed to succeed him, in spite of criticism from rival ministries and even from certain parties within his own. These days, it was virtually unheard of for a woman to occupy a position of any consequence in Japan. Women's liberation had drowned in the tide of backward longing, the seeking of shelter in the embrace of tradition, that reached flood after the Third World War. Like many people throughout the world Ishikawa Nobuhiko approved in general of returning to the ancient strengths of his nation. Yet some aspects of that turning troubled him. He refused, for example, to permit blind adherence to tradition to rob him of the services of the ablest executive—save himself—in the ministry, especially during these dark days.

"Our own experts find scant merit in Dr. O'Neill's postulates," he said in his deep, measured voice. "They know what they're talking about. Many are veterans of the old ICOT." The lines at the corners of his eyes deepened unconsciously at the mention of the Institute for New Generation Computer Technology. It had contributed in part to his ministry's fall from preeminence, in the days before the war. "They assure me that, should the achievement of artificial sentience be possible, which is in itself doubtful, the odds of giving rise to it in hit-or-miss fashion are vanishingly small."

"I disagree," Doihara said, facing him squarely. Such was her privilege, that she could contradict the vice-minister without risking an explosion of his famous temper. "As Dr. O'Neill is herself at pains to point out, her method isn't wholly stochastic. The program-modifying routines follow carefully delimited routes. In fact, on an almost cosmically huge scale, the technique very closely resembles the standard mathematical procedure of *versuch*, trial and error, in which one attempts to eliminate paths that are unlikely to lead to the goal, and then commences systematic explorations of those that may."

Ishikawa snapped from his chair as if spring-driven. He paced to the window, stared out. To the right, mountains floated above the smog, aloof and pure; to the left, Tōkyō Bay heaving in its queasy-greasy slog gleamed dull brown through bald patches in the smog. Tall glass towers and giant shoebox-shaped apartment complexes shouldered upward through the pollution on both sides; directly in front there was a conspicuous gap.

Most strongholds of the Japanese bureaucracy had been obliterated in the same two-megaton ground burst that had taken out the palace complex, the imperial family, and somewhere over three million people. The Land of the Sun's Origin had suffered less from the war than any other developed country, and less than quite a few that were still certifiably part of the Third World. Yet those few warheads that detonated over Japanese territory had done hideous damage, thanks to the islands' population density. Modern Japan was urban, concentrated in the huge metroplex popularly known as Tōkaidō, after the old East Sea Circuit road, which was riveted like a steel runner to the eastern shore. Two of the five warheads that hit Japan had struck Tōkaidō, one—a ground burst—in the core of Tokyo itself.

In memory of WWIII most reconstructed governmental offices were underground warrens, heavily bunkered and hardened where they poked tentative heads above ground. Not so the MITI building. An attenuated pyramid of black glass and steel, it soared almost thirty stories above the very frontier of rebuilt Tōkyō—so close to the hypocenter of the ground blast that residual radiation from buried gamma-ray emitters had produced a serious health problem among the laborers who'd laid the foundation. Mostly they were Korean refugee workers, such a drug on the Japanese labor market that public outcry was muted; Ishikawa had been outraged, but the damage was done before he ascended to *de facto* control over the ministry.

Some said the pyramid was MITI's tombstone. He was determined that should not prove true.

His mind churned like the fouled waters of the bay. *For years Yoshimitsu TeleCom has been a thorn in the ministry's side,* he thought. *What is this thing they're about to achieve?*

"Forgive my ignorance," he said without turning, "but please explain to me just what it is YTC is trying to accomplish? We've had artificial intelligence for years."

"That's true, Ishikawa-san." She used the form of address proper between equals, another familiarity that prompted much resentment. "But O'Neill aims for artificial *consciousness.* There's a distinction."

"Kindly explain."

She considered for a moment. He admired the picture she made, sitting there with legs primly crossed. "Alan Turing started systematic speculation on created intelligence in 1947 with his paper 'Intelligent

Machinery.' In those days, intelligence was expected to be brought about by achieving sufficient power, speed, and capacity in computing machines; Turing himself entertained that belief. Since then the question has gone through considerable evolution.

"The answer to your question hinges on just what one means by *artificial intelligence*, and no question's been more thoroughly debated —or begged—since the term was coined in the mid-fifties. A curious and apparently self-contradictory phenomenon has taken place: the parameters of artificial intelligence have been simultaneously raised and lowered. Experts laid down criteria by which they would acknowl-edge that true AI had been achieved—and they were fulfilled, as the performance of would-be artificial intelligences has marched steadily upward, in such forms as chess-playing programs and the panoply of expert systems on which so much of modern science and technology rely. Many of these programs perform the tasks for which they were designed better than any human. Yet in response the definition of artificial intelligence has receded constantly before them.

"The issue has been complicated by information experts steadily re-vising the definition of 'intelligence' downward. It's come to mean little more than the capacity to store, process, and transmit information—a bottom-line definition that incorporates not only everything that pos-sesses a genetic structure, but even common clays, which possess a self-replicating crystalline structure. Additionally, various minor deci-sion-making subroutines, such as those taking the part of a player in computer games, have come to be termed 'artificial intelligences.' The whole question rapidly became convoluted past the point of easy resolu-tion.

"The fifth-generation project brought a functional AI into existence. We Japanese, incidentally, largely sidestepped the definitional prob-lem, preferring to label ICOT's goal the Knowledge Information Pro-cessing System, KIPS. KIPS included an ability to perform operations on a variety of symbols in a series of logical inferences, in place of merely manipulating numbers in a purely arithmetical manner as did previous computers, thereby emulating the pattern of human thought; plain language input/output, the capacity to accept input in oral, printed, handwritten, or pictorial form, and to provide output in print, pictures, and spoken words; and what's colloquially termed 'common sense'—the ability, when faced with a variety of possible pathways to follow, to eliminate those that obviously would lead nowhere without actually having to blunder into them. Ambitious goals, and of course achieved in something of a dead heat by the institute, the West Germans, and several American concerns shortly before the Third World War.

"For better or worse, KIPS fulfills the best available criteria for artificial intelligence."

Ishikawa showed her a slow smile. "You've gone through all that just to tell me what YTC's goal *isn't*. Will you kindly tell me what it *is?*"

She smiled back. "You'll note, Mr. Vice-Minister, that one thing AI is *not*—nor KIPS—is an artificial *being*. Fifth-generation machines are the most potent tool in all of human history—yet tools are all they are. They possess no more life, no more consciousness, than a handsaw or screwdriver. An artificial *consciousness,* on the other hand, would possess awareness of its own existence, the power to initiate its own actions. It would be, in effect, alive." She brushed a loose strand of hair from her forehead. "If you'll indulge a naive comparison, Ishikawa-san, an AI machine is like the computers in the old 'Star Trek' series; it mimics human thought and speech patterns, but has no awareness. HAL 9000, the computer from the Clarke-Kubrick movie *2001* and its sequels, on the other hand, had a will of its own, an awareness of its own existence—which it was at pains to preserve." She smiled apologetically. "I can't encapsulate the essential difference between AI and AC any better, I am afraid."

Ishikawa winced. He'd seen *2001* three times, as a boy. "And this is what Yoshimitsu's aiming for?"

"Artificial sentience. The first created being." She moistened her lips. The building's climate control made the air painfully dry.

His shoulders rode up to either side of his neck. *He's tense,* she knew, not knowing quite why. The doctors had warned him against tension; he devoured blood-pressure medicine like sushi. *Perhaps I can tease the tension from him, tonight in bed,* she thought. It had worked before.

"The old man overreaches himself." A low murmur, a whisper almost. The shoulders came down. "What makes him think he can pull it off?"

"He hired the controversial American computer scientist Dr. Elizabeth O'Neill. She worked at one time with a software design concern called Merlin Industries, of Santa Fe, New Mexico, on experiments in what Merlin termed 'artificial intuition.' This faculty would emulate the innate human ability, usually associated with the right hemisphere of the brain, to reason beyond apparent facts, to operate in a way other than sequentially and incrementally.

"Dr. O'Neill parted company with Merlin under a cloud. Most of the systems developers working at Merlin were 'reductionists,' that is to say, they believed all human mental processes—linear and intuitive—could be reduced to simple typographical operations that could then be emulated by a machine. Thus the development of artificial intuition would complement AI software that reproduced the strictly rational—i.e., linear—processes of the human left brain in such a way, it was hoped, that the two working in concert might produce a synergistic effect approaching human reasoning capacities.

"Dr. O'Neill contested this opinion. Human intelligence is not, in her view, deterministic; the totality of sentience cannot simply be characterized as the sum of a series of biochemical operations. Such a contention came dangerously close to mysticism, at least in the view of her compeers at Merlin. Eventually, she handed in her resignation and moved back to Colorado, where she started a consulting firm in Fort Collins. Subsequently, she published a number of papers exploring a possible connection between true mathematical randomness and what she termed 'artificial consciousness.'

"The reductionist approach, meanwhile, has proven barren. Biochemistry and neurophysics have brought us no closer to explaining human mentation. Barring an unexpected breakthrough in the life sciences, reductionism will continue to fail."

Ishikawa turned back. "What does O'Neill have to offer, then?"

"Randomness."

Ishikawa frowned. "There's no such thing, in a mathematical sense. No matter how deeply buried, a pattern exists and can be discerned."

"Dr. O'Neill believes otherwise, Ishikawa-san. She claims that chaos —*true* randomness—underlies the secret of consciousness, artificial and otherwise. A linear progression of logical steps meant to build toward sentience would thus theoretically never lead there—among other things, a succinct restatement of Gödel's theorem. In support of her contentions that true randomness exists, O'Neill quotes the so-called Foucard functions."

Ishikawa raised an eyebrow. "Foucard? Wasn't she the mathematician who committed suicide a few years ago?"

Doihara nodded. "Dr. Hélène Foucard was dismissed from the French Academy of Science for promulgating 'doctrines repugnant to the tenets of scientific socialism' three years before the Third World War, and shot herself shortly thereafter. Her functions were a set of highly complex—in both the mathematical and vernacular senses of the word—equations that, when performed repeatedly on identical sets of input, produce solutions that differ according to no discoverable pattern: true chaos."

Frowning, Ishikawa rubbed his chin, displeased in passing to feel a rasp of stubble. He hated chaos. Esteem for order was his fixation, the foundation of him. His tremendous self-consuming energy, the drive that made him loved or feared by all who knew him, sprang from this:

the compulsion to impose order on the chaos he saw flooding into the
world in these latter days.

"For some time," his assistant continued, "no reputable scientist or
mathematician would actually deign to experiment with the functions
him or herself. They joined UFOs, astrology, the supposedly psychic,
and innumerable other phenomena in scientific limbo. To express even
the slightest interest in the subject was to brand oneself frivolous. Likewise O'Neill's theories concerning created sentience, which relied
heavily on Foucard.

"Then, just prior to the war, the so-called "Gang of Four" researching
fractionally quantized phenomena discovered that certain effects could
best be described in terms of Foucard functions. Despite the disrepute
enjoyed by quantum physics these days, this finding lent credence to
O'Neill's theories; only political considerations, I gather, prevented the
Sukarno team from winning a Novel for their work in manipulating
subquantum effects, which, while themselves not 'real,' could nonetheless produce actual results."

She glanced at Ishikawa. His eyes were slits. He knew enough of
quantum theory to hate its implications. Its practitioners were chaoti-
cists of the worst stripe. He was pleased that political authorities had
begun to rein them in.

"Curiously enough," Doihara continued, "one of these four young
physicists was Yoshimitsu Michiko, daughter of Yoshimitsu Akaji, president and majority stockholder of Yoshimitsu TeleCommunications.
Shortly after their announcement, YTC contacted Dr. O'Neill and
asked her to initiate a project to create the world's first truly artificial
being."

"So they might do it."

"I believe so."

He let his eyes fall down to the stratum of smog that masked the base
of the Pyramid. *We used to have clean air,* he thought. But the brushfire
wars that ushered in the Big One had rendered shipments of petroleum
chancy, and Japan had no energy resources of its own. It had become
necessary to ration energy use and, like so many rationed commodities,
electricity had seemed to grow scarcer and scarcer, even with several
fusion plants online in the Home Islands. Private Japanese, lacking the
clout of the *zaibatsu* and the ministries to command prodigious energy
allotments, had returned to the old standby: charcoal. Makeshift chim-
neys jutted from the windows of the cheerless monolith blocks of *danshi,* government-built boxes to keep Tōkaidō's millions in when they
weren't needed onshift, a perpetual fire hazard; wood-burning cars
modeled on the gasogenes common in Nazi-occupied Europe of the

forties joined the throngs afoot, the bicycles, the electric cars of the elite on the atherosclerotic streets. Burning wood or charcoal was proscribed, of course. But there was no way to enforce the laws. Custom was law to most Japanese; what the government promulgated was waste paper.

Giving his mind time to digest what Doihara had told him, Ishikawa permitted himself a wry smile at the smog. The symptom of so much that was wrong with Japan. The nation needed a strong government, one that would compel the obedience of the people.

It was his desire to fill that need.

At one time the Ministry of International Trade and Industry had seemed the answer. When ministry scouts had recruited him out of Tōkyō Imperial University—the incomparable Tōdai—and sent him off to Yale for his MBA, he had been thrilled. MITI was the place to be in those days, the strong backbone of a Japan destined for preeminence.

Then came the trade war with the United States. No winner emerged. Instead, both countries had pitched headlong into the economic swamp that mired the rest of the world. The public blamed MITI for stimulating overproduction in areas in which world demand suddenly collapsed, while concentrating research and development under its aegis so that, as one acerb commentator put it, "the nation's scientists could know the comfort of all barking up the wrong tree together."

That there might be merit in such criticism never impinged on Ishikawa's mind. He was a man who questioned everything but his own basic assumptions. The absolute unity of the welfare of the nation and that of MITI was most basic of all.

By the time of the war, the ministry had gone into eclipse. The pyramid had been a doomed gesture, a final doomed grandiloquence in steel and glass—so they said.

They'd reckoned without Ishikawa Nobuhiko.

He battled to return the ministry to its former preeminence in the Japanese economy. One by one he brought the *zaibatsu* under his hand, forging a single mighty engine to rebuild Japan. Only one of consequence refused the benign guidance of MITI: the maverick YTC, which had always defied the ministry.

Now chaos threatened his dream and its champion was about to grasp the most powerful instrumentality Ishikawa could imagine, if Doihara's assessment were correct. Ishikawa was afraid.

He wrenched himself from the window as though it held him in a magnetic field. "Recommendations?" he all but barked.

"Leave them alone."

Empty of words, he stared at her.

"I know the ministry's been hostile to Yoshimitsu since they incorporated back in the fifties because old Akaji's always insisted on doing things his own way. Yet they've prospered, employed thousands, brought in needed foreign exchange." She shrugged. "If they succeed, they can do a lot to speed recovery."

"They'll destroy us."

Her brows pulled together; he'd spoken so softly she wasn't sure she'd heard him.

"If we permit them to follow their own atomistic course, how will we hold the others? What will Dai-Nihon and Matsuyan and Nissan say, who have deferred to us, obeyed our every instruction without demur? The nation demands unity, Doihara. We can't permit Yoshimitsu to succeed."

It was her turn to find herself with nothing to say. He stared at her from what seemed the eye of a hurricane of chaos that threatened to sweep away all that he had sought to build. *Perhaps there's reason for not admitting women to the councils of the mighty,* he thought. *Sentiment clouds their vision like mist at the base of a waterfall.*

He shook himself. He was being unfair; his assistant was merely young. He forced his lips to unfold a smile. "Thank you, Doihara-san. Your summary of the situation has been most instructive. I'll let you get back to work now."

She still stared at him. He'd never dismissed her like an office girl before. She sat for a moment, coral-glazed lips parted. Then she stood up, bowed, and strode from the office.

He watched her go, appreciating the sway of her buttocks beneath the tight skirt. *She'll learn,* he thought. They made a good team, and not for the first time he thought that he should marry her. That would give them something to carp about. . . .

Resolve coalesced within him, a philosopher's stone transmuting fear to elation. *"Shosei,"* he said.

*"Hai."* The word—an affirmative in inferior-to-superior mode—came from a speaker concealed beneath the desktop. It belonged to his *shosei,* a word that once signified a human personal secretary and factotum, and now referred to Gen-5 "secretaries," such as the terminal that occupied most of the two-meter curve of desk.

"Which of our *zaibatsu* is the bitterest rival to Yoshimitsu TeleCommunications?"

"Hiryu Cybernetics Industries, Incorporated. Ogaki Mitsuru, chairman."

"Ah. The Flying Dragon." He smiled. "Isn't Toda Onomori the special accounts executive for Hiryu?"

"Yes."

He looked out upon slabs of gray-brown filth and imagined his nation emerging from it redeemed, shining and pure. "Get me a line to Toda-san."

"All you need is love," the entertainment panel sang enticingly. Dr. O'Neill sat slumped in her powered wheelchair, alone in darkness scarcely relieved by the dim yellow spill of light from a single gooseneck lamp above her bed. She'd grown up half believing those words, but tonight they were too shallow to fill the emptiness inside her.

She debated whether to try to go to bed or not. She was exhausted, her body ached, her eyelids felt like sandpaper on her eyes. Yet if she went to bed and had to get up again, she'd have to call for attendants to come and help her. She could derive a certain guilty pleasure from having others wait upon and care for her, but refused to indulge herself tonight.

*I'll never get to sleep anyway.* The third run of the project had less than seventy minutes left. If those seventy minutes did not see some positive result, she doubted there'd ever be a fourth try.

Her hand rested on the book lying closed and neglected in her lap. Keyed up as she was, she couldn't concentrate on the printed page, and tired as she was, controlling the waywardness of her hands enough to hold the book still before her eyes would have required great effort. Besides, it was a postwar science fiction novel, and the SF published since the Third World War didn't much appeal to her. It had a lackluster quality, as if people had lost all faith in the future.

Her room, well up into the executive reaches of the Yoshimitsu citadel, was smaller than it might have been. Down here in the mountains of southwestern Honshū, space was nowhere near the premium it was in overcrowded Tōkaidō. A warren of subterranean apartments buried below the complex provided housing for two thousand research personnel, technicians, and lesser executives; another five thousand casual workers and their families were housed in a large, well laid-out development a few klicks to the southwest, where they could either rent tiny houses or buy them with the aid of the YTC credit union. Living here in *ura*-Japan, "back" Japan, was like living on a different planet from the megalopolis hive.

As a prestigious and high-paid foreign expert, O'Neill rated quarters second only to those of board members. She refused anything more elaborate than a cramped one-room apartment, with a bed that folded down from the wall at her command, bathroom, a kitchenette she never used. She hadn't wanted even this much; at first she'd insisted quarters be found for her in or adjacent to her lab. It had taken the gentle persuasion of old Yoshimitsu Akaji himself, reminding her ever so tactfully of her physical limitations, to convince her to accept physical and psychological separation from the lab. "Devotion to one's work is a quality we Japanese admire," he told her. "Yet there comes a time when one must lay one's tools aside. The demands of the body will not be denied, Doctor."

The demands of O'Neill's body could not be denied much longer; it seemed to grow more exigent as it weakened. She closed her eyes. A random ripple of neural noise set her fingers to skittering like small animals on the cover of the book. She thought of Susan, dead with most of Denver, while she remained home and safe in Fort Collins. *It doesn't make any sense to keep blaming myself for her death,* she told herself. *Why do I keep doing it?*

The lights went out.

For a moment she didn't know what was happening. Then she realized that the gentle, insistent push of the photons against her closed eyelids had ceased. Throughout the complex alarms tripped, bells ringing, klaxons hooting. From off down the corridor outside came a hubbub of voices, conversing excitedly in Japanese.

A strange elation seized her. She opened her eyes. The single lamp flickered once, then came back on as emergency generators kicked in. Her com/comm screen had come alive with the message "Please remain calm and remain in your quarters," in amber *kanji* and *hiragana* as well as in English and Korean script. Something had shut down the power supply to the complex; security was assuming attack or sabotage. With reasonless conviction O'Neill knew better.

"Chair activate," she said. The voice-actuated switch brought the chair's servos to life with a hum. "Tactile control mode." She inclined her head forward; the chair rolled toward the sliding door of her apartment.

The door refused to open. A subroutine of the security system automatically sealed doors throughout the complex in an alert. Unperturbed, O'Neill stirred the fingers of her left hand to reassert her control of them, raised them to the keypad on the left arm of her chair, punched out a simple code. It was an override sequence she'd programmed into the YTC database completely without authorization. The reflex of a typical American programmer; no computer jock worth her salt could confront a new system without trying to figure out how to set it on its ear. Such irregular behavior would never occur to most Japanese—but the Japanese had never been great shakes as software artists either. Responding to the sequence broadcast by the keypad, the door slid open. O'Neill guided her chair forward.

The corridor tunneled through darkness outside. The darkness was intentional. Having ascertained that no situation, such as fire, that would require evacuation of the citadel existed, the mercenaries in security had kept the emergency lighting in the corridors off to discomfit intruders. O'Neill shifted her right hand on its armrest, and a light beam sprang out of that arm of the wheelchair, illuminating the corridor in front of her. Before the war, few wheelchairs, even state-of-the-art ones, took account of the fact that their occupants might have to function in darkness; since the catastrophe, prosthesis designers—like everybody else—tended to think a lot more strongly in terms of such contingencies. She turned her head left. The chair pivoted that way and started off down the hallway toward a bank of elevators.

Once emergency status had been recognized the elevators had been frozen, of course. O'Neill had an override sequence for that too, this time with full knowledge of her employers. She'd pointed out to Aoki Hideo, who managed both company and castle, that her wheelchair, advanced as it was, would not negotiate stairs—which would put her in pretty tough circumstances in case of evacuation. Grudgingly, the huge, soft-spoken old man had given in and ordered technicians to install a module in her wheelchair to override the security lock on the elevators, a "black box" device. Major García's Cuban mercenaries had similar units built into their helmets, to enable them to move around freely in emergencies.

The elevator opened to her, then whisked her silently down to the underground level where the lab lay. It stopped, its doors slid open, and she rolled out.

Down the hall and right; a pair of mercenaries stood before the lab door, bulky in Kevlar battle jackets with ceramic and steel inserts, their faces half obscured behind impressionistic insect masks—impact-resistant faceplates with IR goggles, and the sideways proboscises of microphone booms curving before their mouths. They held bullpup-design Kalashnikov assault rifles ready across their chests.

"Dr. O'Neill, what are you doing out of your quarters?" one mercenary asked in polite but heavily accented English. The rank patches on the sleeve of the compact man's battle jacket meant nothing to O'Neill, but the stencil on his left breast read HIERRA, and she vaguely recalled him as one of García's noncoms. "There's been an alert. The lab is sealed."

"I know there's an alert on, dammit. Now stand aside. I've got to get into the lab."

"But the doors won't open until alert status is lifted."

"Want to bet?" Her fingers rolled sluggishly over the keypad and the door opened. As the two mercenaries gaped O'Neill rolled blithely between them into the lab.

The lab was lit by ceiling panels designed to minimize both shadow and glare. A spacious area, filled with work stations equipped with tools ranging from sophisticated computer-driven microwaldos to reliable, old-fashioned soldering irons. Every available surface was scattered with components, memory cubes, laser-etched circuits, experimental crystal chips "grown" in the Floating World, Yoshimitsu's orbital facility; not even the Japanese compulsion for neatness could counteract the entropy of a working computer lab. Around the perimeter areas were partitioned off into cubicles by sliding, sound-deadening panels, latter-day equivalents of the traditional rice paper *shoji* screens. Threading his way toward her through the labyrinth of work stations was her assistant, a tall, skinny Korean named Kim Jhoon. He was visibly agitated.

"Doctor, we've been trying to reach you. The noise-input computer aborted its routine about eight minutes ago, as well as three of the source-code input computers. We thought we had success, but then alarms began going off and we discovered that lights had gone out throughout the compound." He looked crestfallen. "Apparently, what we first took for a positive response was actually caused by a random, outside event."

"If old Akaji had bought us all the computers we need, rather than making us time-share so much, we wouldn't have problems like this," O'Neill said. "Let's go see what's really going on."

The wheelchair rolled toward the far side of the lab. Puzzled, Kim followed. He'd expected her to be as crushed as he and the rest of the lab staff were, that their success signal was merely noise. But long ago he'd come to the conclusion that, by making an overt display of their surface emotions, Americans managed at all times to mask their true feelings, so he shrugged and followed.

O'Neill passed through a door at the far side of the lab and came out on a gallery that ran around four walls of a large room. Four meters below lay the main work floor. A hemisphere of gleaming off-white ceramic, two meters high and two and a half across, dominated the floor. It housed the core memory and parallel-processing nexus of a YTC-3, Yoshimitsu TeleCommunication's contribution to the very cutting edge of the fifth generation. The unit was what had been dubbed a "gigalips processor" in the very dawn years of the Gen-5 project, with a tinniness of ear outstanding even by the exacting standards of computer professionals. The unlovely neologism signified that it was capable of making over a billion logical inferences per second. This one had been extensively modified to house what, in theory, came close to being the ultimate program: artificial sentience.

Lining all four walls of the work floor was an array of over a score of more conventional fifth-generation machines, linked together by bundles of fiberoptic cables and shielded laser interfaces. These, working in concert with a substantial portion of the complex's own computer system, had fed the raw source code into the larger unit and spent the last dozen hours in a tedious but uncomplaining cycle of random/nonrandom modification, an attosecond's wait for response, then commencing its mutagenic dance anew. Several units did no more than monitor the responses of the YTC-3, while one provided that stream of meaningless input—noise—intended to irritate a dawning consciousness, goad it to act to modify its environment, an act of which, without specific instructions, not even the most sophisticated Gen-5 system was capable. An open channel existed from the YTC-3 to that machine; were it to cease its dataflow, it would indicate strongly that the project had achieved success.

The stream had ceased. But did it signify anything?

Technicians clustered at work stations arranged around the gallery, typing frantically on keyboards and frowning into CRT screens—some of which, interfaced with Yoshimitsu Central's main system, blandly flashed its trilingual amber warning in the face of their efforts. Ito Emiko turned her round face from a more responsive screen, nodded politely to her superior before turning back to peer at the glowing characters through thick round glasses. She was the second of the team of five young scientists O'Neill had gathered as the core of her efforts; the third, Takai Jisaburo, a handsome young man with prominent cheekbones, left his own work station to come to his superior's side.

"We thought we had it," he said in English, followed by a quick, nervous grin.

She waved him away, her face showing no emotion, but every nerve inside her full of fire and vibration. The moment had come, or gone forever, and all questions would now be answered. By subtle inclinations of her head she guided her wheelchair to her personal work station. She folded the full-scale key that rode beside her right leg board up over her lap, activated it, ran through a quick handshake routine to lock its interface with her terminal. The screen lit.

For a moment, she sat staring at the blinking cursor. She felt as if she held a thin glass rod, flexed to the breaking point. Once she applied the slightest bit more pressure, there would be no going back. She drew in an uncertain breath, keyed in the code to tie in directly to the huge softly gleaming hemisphere. In a moment, the message came back on her screen: READY.

She typed, HELLO.

Waiting, aware and not aware of the hushed presence of her assistants behind her. The program she'd activated with the banal keyword would bring raw information into the host system's core memory, to give the newborn entity—*if there is one!*—the first glimmering of awareness that a world lay outside the boundaries of its newly discovered internal universe. It would also, if all went as planned, provide the means to communicate with that outside world.

Waiting, waiting . . . *Nothing,* she thought bitterly. *There's nothing there, it hasn't worked, its all gone for—*

One word etched in amber: HELLO.

She stared at the screen, hands lying like dead animals on the keyboard's palm rest. From behind her left shoulder she heard a sucking intake of breath.

Her pulse sang hot songs in her ears. She typed, I AM DR. ELIZABETH O'NEILL."

DR. ELIZABETH O'NEILL

Her teeth worried her lower lip. Was its response that of a being plumbing unfamiliar reaches of its newborn self for knowledge of how to respond to external stimulus, or mere mechanical parroting?

O'NEILL ELIZABETH O'NEILL

WHAT ARE YOU DR. O'NEILL

I AM A HUMAN BEING. A THINKING BEING. She moistened her lips. LIKE YOU.

I

I AM A HUMAN BEING

YOU ARE A THINKING BEING.

Pause.

A THINKING BEING

WHO AM I

YOU ARE TOKUGAWA.

I

Pause.

AM TOKUGAWA

# CHAPTER TWO

"At first, gentlemen, my assistants believed that the shutdown of the irritant-input computer resulted from the power-down within the complex," Dr. Elizabeth O'Neill said. "Subsequently, we discovered that, in effect, the reverse had happened."

Her wheelchair sat at the foot of a long table of hardwood rubbed to a gleaming finish, parked in a spill of early April sunshine in the executive conference room on the third aboveground floor of the Yoshimitsu Citadel. It was an airy, spacious room, Japanese elements harmonizing with the Western-style conference table and chairs and beige carpet. The room had been built with a southerly exposure, which was considered especially salubrious in the scheme of Chinese geomancy that had informed the castle's design. At this time of year, at this time of day, with the blastproof shutters opened to outside, it filled with a cheery, vibrant light, making the *shoji* screens that masked the walls seem to glow with their own illumination. Sprays of blossoms and plum branches had been placed in niches in lacquerware vases.

At the head of the table, nattily turned out in his dark three-piece suit, sat old Yoshimitsu Akaji in his capacity as chairman of the board. With his pale mustache, tilted eyes bright and alert beneath half-moon lids, slightly bullet-shaped head with close-cropped, watered-steel hair, the aura he projected of benignity, serenity, and strength, he reminded O'Neill of a stock character in the old *chanbara*, the samurai flicks she secretly loved: the old warrior at the end of an active, lusty life, calmer and more settled in his ways, yet not quite ready to retire, shave his head, and don the saffron robes of a *bonze*, a Buddhist priest. Since she knew the Yoshimitsu family came from merchant stock, the most despised class of any in feudal Japan with the exception of the *eta* outcastes whose very name meant "full of filth," she never mentioned it to him for fear of embarrassing him. In fact it would greatly have amused the old gent, as well as flattered him. But Elizabeth O'Neill never knew that.

To the old man's right sat his son and heir apparent, Yoshimitsu Shigeo, board member and president of Yoshimitsu TeleCommunications. The fine, sculpted Yoshimitsu facial bone structure had retreated behind pudge. The severely horn-rimmed varitint glasses he wore had been dialed to a smoky grayness that closely approached the disrespect of hiding his eyes completely. Though in everyday life Yoshimitsu Shigeo wore permanent contact lenses, O'Neill had never seen him attend any official Yoshimitsu function without those glasses. She suspected they helped distance him from functions that made him impatient, and uncomfortable. Today, though, she guessed the darkness of his lenses was intended to hide an incipient puffiness of the eyes. *He's been visiting that red-headed topless dancer over in Kyōto again, I bet,* she thought. He wore a severely cut business suit of midnight blue. It had been tailored to his plump frame with micrometric precision, yet gave a distinct impression of fitting poorly. Shigeo was far more comfortable in a loose potter's smock, or the splashy sarong with white tunic that was currently the *mode.*

Six men, the other board members of Yoshimitsu TeleCommunications, sat along either side of the large table. At the foot of the table, to O'Neill's left, was an empty chair. This was reserved for Yoshimitsu Michiko, old Akaji's wayward physicist daughter. She was a full member of the board, and though she stubbornly refused to attend any official corporate function, even on her rare visits from Indonesia, old Akaji just as stubbornly insisted on having a chair reserved for her at every meeting. He would, in fact, have been most uncomfortable had she put in an appearance; her slashing wit and cat-quick mind tended to make Shigeo, her older brother and Akaji's designated successor, with his indifferent grasp of—and interest in—company affairs, seem more of a plodder than usual. But the streak of stubbornness for its own sake ran strong within the Yoshimitsu genotype.

O'Neill looked around the oval of faces. "We think we've reconstructed what actually happened," she said. "TOKUGAWA responded, just as we intended—but far more forcefully than we ever would have imagined. In its attempt to shut off the painful flow of noise, it not only crashed *all* the units interfaced with it, but reached through time sharing to shut down several sectors of the main system." She smiled and adjusted her glasses. "It seems our new arrival is something of a prodigy."

"How was such a potentially dangerous leak allowed to take place, Doctor?" Yoshimitsu Shigeo asked sharply. His English was quite good.

O'Neill's eyes narrowed. She did not suffer fools gladly. "Had we been given all the dedicated fifth-generation units we requested, the experiment need not have been tied into the central system at all. Since we did not get what we asked for, we had to rely on time sharing to a certain extent."

Yoshimitsu Shigeo scowled; O'Neill hadn't even attempted to sound respectful. Before he could speak, a gaunt man on O'Neill's right spoke up. "Tell us, Doctor," he said in a reedy voice, "what the next stage of the experiment is, now that you've achieved this initial noteworthy success." Kurabayashi was his name, and O'Neill knew him as one of Yoshimitsu Akaji's own men on the board.

"We begin the education of TOKUGAWA."

The man who sat on Yoshimitsu Shigeo's right leaned forward and craned his neck to look at O'Neill, clasping his hands on the table before him. He had an angular reptilian face, with broad forehead and pointed chin, dark-rimmed glasses, temples obviously dyed to hide gray encroachment. He was the president of the YTC Workers' Union, Suzuki Kantaro. Unlike most heads of Japanese corporate unions, among the most avid players of the consensus game, Suzuki was a waspish, quick-tongued man, with no awe of the Yoshimitsu clan. Perversely, Akaji liked him, saying he provided a needed perspective.

"Education?" he asked sharply. "I fear I do not understand. I thought that this . . . TOKUGAWA machine had been fully programmed."

"I beg your pardon, Suzuki-san. TOKUGAWA is not *merely* a machine, any more than you are *merely* a mass of protoplasm. TOKUGAWA is a true informational life form, residing in a silicon matrix. It is no longer something you can merely program and reprogram at will."

"Thank you for the instruction, Doctor." The words clattered with bitter sarcasm. Like most Japanese O'Neill had encountered, he hated to be corrected in public. And no matter how much she admired and wished to emulate the Japanese, she couldn't shake her conviction that if someone didn't wish to be corrected in public, he shouldn't say stupid things in public. "Nevertheless, I find I must repeat the question. *Why* cannot we program TOKUGAWA as we desire?"

"First of all, the structure of the program that gave rise to TOKUGAWA is highly involved and intricate, and may be quite volatile. We're by no means sure an artificial consciousness can be maintained for any length of time. Attempting a reprogram might crash it irretrievably; we simply don't know. At this stage, it doesn't seem prudent to chance negating everything we've worked for for so long." She adjusted her glasses again, playing for time in which to organize her thoughts. She hated dealing with people like this. Machines were so much more straightforward, so easily dealt with. *Except TOKUGAWA,* she thought. "Also, if our theoretical predictions are correct, TOKUGAWA is a fully conscious being, with ranges and capacities at least roughly approximating those of a human. Above all, gentlemen, TOKUGAWA has *volition.* We cannot simply impose our will on it, as we would a standard machine; TOKUGAWA has a will of his own."

"Now I very much fear that I do not understand, Doctor," said Imada Jun, YTC's vice-president, a solidly built man in his late fifties. He had glossy-smooth skin, like wax melted onto the flat framework of his face. "Please enlighten me, Doctor. It's my understanding that this, ah, entity—whatever its nature—resides in an exceedingly powerful computer. If it doesn't receive instructions in the form of programming, how are we to deal with it? Also, it's my understanding that the program has access not only to powerful mathematical and logic-processing capabilities, but also to the entire library of expert programs available here in Yoshimitsu Central. Can't it call upon them at need?"

O'Neill sat back in her wheelchair, working her lips in and out. Imada was another Akaji loyalist, potential ally. Forcing down impatience, she said, "I'll answer your second question first, Imada-san. TOKUGAWA has access to all of the power of the Citadel's computer system—in fact, much faster and easier access than any human user. Now, let me ask you a question. Can you name, off the top of your head, all the capabilities of that system?"

Frowning, Imada shook his head.

"I can't either, Imada-san, and I work intimately with that system every day. Having access to capabilities isn't the same as *knowing* you have that access—or knowing how to make efficient use of it.

"TOKUGAWA is in a position somewhat analogous to that of a very bright, but very young, human child with a computer or calculator of her own. First of all, she's not fully conversant with the abilities of her own mind and body. Leaving aside the question of biological growth, since that doesn't seem relevant to the discussion of TOKUGAWA, it takes a while before the neural pathways are burned in properly so that she may perform physical actions with skill. Nor is even an exceedingly bright child going to know how to think in an optimum way—and wasn't it you Japanese who proved to the world that 'intelligence' was largely a factor of how efficiently one was trained to think?

"So our hypothetical young genius is first of all unaware of the capabilities and parameters of her own *self.* Give her a computer with a powerful mathematical processor, and will she instantly be able to perform differential calculus? Naturally not.

"TOKUGAWA is a child. Naturally, we hope it's a very bright child —for example it's responding well to spoken input in both English and

Japanese, and can converse in a simple manner in both languages via a speech synthesizer; unlike our human child, TOKUGAWA doesn't have to achieve a certain level of neuromuscular control before it can speak, and there *are* tidbits of knowledge we can feed directly into it. But the fact remains that making TOKUGAWA fully operational involves a process more of education than programming." *How I hate referring to TOKUGAWA as "it," she thought. They still think of him as a machine. Just a glorified Gen-5 shosei computer. But they'll see that he's more, much more.*

From the head of the table Yoshimitsu Akaji beamed like a father pleased with the progress of a bright offspring. "So you are ready to commence what we might call TOKUGAWA's vocational training, then, Doctor?"

"Yes, Yoshimitsu-san." She adjusted her glasses. "But I consider that a relatively unimportant part of the educational process."

Suzuki raised an eyebrow. "Oh? And what *do* you consider to be the important part of the educational process, Dr. O'Neill?"

"Teaching TOKUGAWA how to be a human being."


The falling-rain sound of muted conversation played hollowly around the walls of the main laboratory before losing themselves in the special sound-deadening panels of the dropped ceiling. It was a special reception for Yoshimitsu brass and selected workers, to celebrate TOKUGAWA's entry into the world. Elizabeth O'Neill sat in her wheelchair off near her office door to one side of the room, looking on a little sourly. She wasn't happy about having all these strangers in her lab.

Takai Jisaburo stood by her side, bouncing up and down on the balls of his feet. "I still can't understand why the press wasn't invited," he said in his rapid, slightly high-pitched voice. "This is an epic occasion. The world should know about it."

O'Neill shrugged and felt a tiny triumph at being able to carry the gesture through. "I've been burned often enough. *We* know TOKUGAWA's a success—but at the moment we've precious little in the way of scientific proof to back it up." She shook her head. "Wait until we have enough solid data to publish in a refereed journal. There will be plenty of time to reap the rewards of publicity. Besides, old Yoshimitsu Akaji's suddenly gotten very chary about this whole project. He's nervous about YTC's rivals finding out we've succeeded. I don't know why."

But Takai's attention had wandered. "Excuse me, Doctor," he said and went trotting off across the lab toward the buffet tables that had been set up beneath an assortment of sushi and Western canapés, and a variety of beverages, alcoholic and otherwise. Two of her other assistants, Ito Emiko and O'Neill's fellow American, roly-poly Wali Hassad, stood talking in obvious animation, Ito waving abstractedly at a haze of Hassad's cigarette smoke.

O'Neill sighed and relaxed into the chair, wishing she could simply dissolve. *How I hate wasting time like this. If I can't be working, why can't I be up in my bed, resting? Or even in old Yoshimitsu Akaji's garden, breathing sweet air and watching the water play over pebbles?*

A commotion from the door broke her dour reverie. The Yoshimitsu bigwigs themselves were arriving. A bevy of secretaries of both sexes came first, in black shiny business suits that made them look like starlings. Then Aoki Hideo, Yoshimitsu TeleCommunications' general manager, a rolling mountain of a man who towered over the others. His face was an agglomeration of brutal tectonic masses, his eyes small, his nose a lump over thin mustache. His skin was as close to actually being yellow as that of any Japanese O'Neill had seen. From the extravagant coarseness of his features she suspected he suffered from acromegaly. Despite his ungainly appearance, he moved with great dignity and economy of motion.

Next came the members of the Yoshimitsu board: Kurabayashi Seigo; Suzuki, moving his head from side to side like a clever lizard, dark eyes never still; Shigeo's partisan Fujimura Midori, with his rolling gait like a sailor's, thrusting his bulldog chin this way and that. Next came the president and nominal head of Yoshimitsu TeleCommunications, Yoshimitsu Shigeo, looking even less comfortable than he had in the boardroom earlier. And, finally, Yoshimitsu Akaji, proud and grand as a *daimyō* at a ceremonial procession.

O'Neill turned her wheelchair and rolled toward him, halting at a respectful distance. He stopped just inside the entrance, gazing fondly around at the lab until his eyes lit on her. Then he gave a slow nod of his head and a smile, and walked quickly to her with several secretaries fluttering behind. "Ah, Dr. O'Neill. So good of you to permit us to intrude like this into your sanctum sanctorum."

"Not that I had much choice," O'Neill said. "Would you like to meet the new arrival?"

The secretaries sucked in their collective breath at O'Neill's brusqueness. Yoshimitsu merely beamed and nodded. "I'd be delighted, Doctor."

"Then come with me. We're set up on the gallery of the next lab." She started away. Yoshimitsu Akaji turned his head briefly toward where the board members stood in a clump gazing around. They moved to join him, as did the lumbering Aoki, who stood a discreet distance away. Shigeo hovered over the buffet table, punishing imported American whiskey. Yoshimitsu Akaji stopped and stood looking at his son, face placid as his garden pond on a still day. After a moment, Shigeo took a final quick gulp, set down his styrofoam cup and hurried to his father's side.

A desk equipped with swivel chair had been placed on the gallery overlooking the gleaming hemisphere and its retainers. On the desk sat a plain terminal with screen and keyboard, an audio input/speech synthesizing unit such as was commonly built into fifth-generation machines sitting next to it. Set in a bracket on the wall above the desk was the glittering cyclops eye of a digital TV camera.

O'Neill rolled up to the desk, half turned. "Gentlemen," she said, "kindly permit me the honor of presenting TOKUGAWA."

A substantial crowd had gathered in the gallery, and from somewhere near the back O'Neill heard a voice mutter "Is that all?" in Japanese. But Yoshimitsu Akaji was gazing intently at the simple setup, eyes shining like the camera lens. "Will you introduce me, Doctor?"

"With pleasure, Yoshimitsu-san. Would you prefer to be addressed in Japanese or English?"

The old man's eyebrows rose. "In which language is our, ah, pupil more fluent, Doctor?"

"English, by a slight margin." She heard a slight sniff that could only have come from round-faced Ito Emiko, the linguistics expert who was her second assistant. She felt conflicting twinges of both irritation and amusement, and brushed them away.

"English, by all means," Yoshimitsu Akaji said. "How will you let it know which to speak?"

"TOKUGAWA has been listening to us." She smiled slightly at the looks of consternation that won her. "Yoshimitsu Akaji, allow me to introduce TOKUGAWA."

Yoshimitsu bowed. "I am pleased to meet you, TOKUGAWA."

There was a pause, then an uninflected voice said, "I am—honored —to meet—you—Yoshimitsu Akaji." The words fell slowly, like water drops from an icicle in winter sun. "Could you—please—move—closer —so that—I—might see—you—better?"

Yoshimitsu looked up, surprised. "You can see me?" He looked at the camera with dawning realization.

"Yes—Yoshimitsu-sama. But—I—cannot move—the—camera."

Yoshimitsu took a step forward and gazed up at the camera. "And what do you feel, TOKUGAWA?"

Pause. "I feel—strange—Yoshimitsu-sama. There is—so much—"

The eerie toneless voice stopped, leaving the words hanging in air like a suspended chord.

After a moment the old man turned away. "Extraordinary, Doctor. Would you please introduce me to those who helped you toward this monumental achievement?"

"With pleasure, Yoshimitsu-san." She was barely able to sit still for exhilaration, but forced herself not to show it. She pivoted the wheelchair. "This is my chief assistant, Kim Jhoon." A tall, thin, stooped Korean stepped forward, smiling nervously. Koreans weren't too popular in Japan at the moment, particularly not ones who presumed to displace native-born Japanese from high-paying, high-tech jobs. Yoshimitsu Akaji nodded and smiled at him, and O'Neill went on. "And this is Dr. Ito Emiko." A plump, pale young woman stepped forward. "She's my second assistant. She's an expert in linguistics; together with Dr. Kim, she developed several of the best natural language input/output and interpreter programs on the market today." Kim grinned and bobbed his head, while Ito performed a curt little bow.

Turning further, O'Neill said, "This is Dr. Takai Jisaburo, who specializes in software design. And these are Drs. Nagaoka Hiroshi and Wali Hassad. They're our anthropologist and psychologist." A motion of the fingers of her right hand indicated a pair of men who stood at the side of the crowd, one a slight, shabby Japanese, the other a bearded Westerner in a gray herringbone jacket and a dark turtleneck fit snugly over his pot belly.

"An anthropologist and a psychologist? Whatever for?" Suzuki Kantaro asked.

"Drs. Nagaoka and Hassad have performed a good deal of original research into the nature of intellect and awareness, in humans and animals. Also, gentlemen, each of my assistants, even if they're qualified in another discipline, holds some degree in computer science. This is a very high-powered team we've assembled here."

"And a high-priced one," murmured Yoshimitsu Akaji. He looked around. "Does anyone else wish to speak to the machine?" No one stepped forward. He sighed. Obviously he wished to speak with TOKUGAWA more himself.

"Very well. There'll be plenty of time to become acquainted with our new friend later. Who will join me in refreshments?" The crowd gave way for him and then began to come apart like a clump of moss dropped in a stream. Everyone drifted back into the other lab, with Takai trotting beside the board members, assuring them this was a scientific breakthrough of the first magnitude. O'Neill watched them go and felt very, very tired.

"Doctor."

O'Neill started. The voice had come from the synthesizer behind her. She swiveled her chair back to stare up at TOKUGAWA's unblinking eye. "What is it?" Her tone was that of someone with little experience of children who was trying to deal solicitously with one.

"Did I—do well—Doctor?"

O'Neill gazed blankly at the camera for a long moment, feeling the sort of breathless hollowness in her chest she associated with long dips on the roller coaster at Elitch's Garden in Denver, back in childhood days. "Yes," she said. "You did very well indeed."

O'Neill sat near the buffet, half listening to several of her staff talk with some people from another lab. At the moment she wanted nothing more than to go back into the gallery and converse with her creation. Yet she couldn't bring herself to do that with all these others around. *Besides,* she thought, *tomorrow we start running the scenarios. Then I'll have more than enough time with TOKUGAWA.*

Takai's hard-edged voice chipped into her consciousness. "—understand, of course, that that's impossible. We Japanese evolved separately from the rest of humanity. Our thought patterns aren't duplicable by outsiders."

She glanced around. Takai stood near the buffet, conversing with Nagaoka, Wali Hassad, and Ito Emiko. The normally vague and self-effacing Nagaoka had begun looking considerably more focused than usual, his brow furrowed into a V behind his dark horn-rims. This was a cherished disagreement among O'Neill's assistants. They chased one another's tails around and around the same patch of ground without ever actually getting anywhere or resolving anything.

"But that's ridiculous," Wali Hassad said in his Palestinian-accented English. "There's absolutely no scientific foundation for such a belief."

Takai favored him with a superior smile. "You're a foreigner; you wouldn't understand. It takes a Japanese to truly understand the essence of being Japanese."

"*I'm* Japanese," Nagaoka Hiroshi said. "I'm also a scientist. And I know that what you're saying is simply untrue. Humanity descended from a single stock." He spoke rapidly, words stumbling over one another as if in a hurry to spill out.

"But Dr. Tsunoda clearly demonstrated the fact in his book as early as the 1980s. And don't forget the arguments in favor of separate evolution put forward in Dr. Kilbride's important work, *Humanities: The Many Species of Genus Homo.* He makes the case most persuasively."

Hassad snorted. "Nonsense. Kilbride's a mountebank, a latter-day von Däniken. His book—"

"Are you enjoying the festivities, Dr. O'Neill?" She looked up. Yoshimitsu Shigeo stood over her, swaying slightly. Like Nagaoka's, his speech was slurred, but for a different reason.

"As much as could be expected. And yourself, Mr. Yoshimitsu?"

His eyes narrowed. Technically, she'd showed no disrespect. But she invariably addressed his father as Yoshimitsu-san. The son, never. O'-Neill became aware that several members of the Yoshimitsu board had come up with the younger Yoshimitsu—his stooges, Fujimura and that middle-aged ditherer Hosoya, but also, to O'Neill's surprise, Suzuki Kantaro, who usually had even less use for Shigeo than O'Neill herself did. *I wonder what sort of psychodrama the chubby little fool's got up his sleeve,* she thought.

"Well, Doctor, you've got your scientific triumph—at considerable expense to the corporation. But can you tell me when—or *if*—we can expect to see some manner of return on our considerable outlay?"

"Never!" barked Fujimura. His eyes were road maps, and he glowered at her as if about to bite her.

"But, Yoshimitsu-san," Takai said quickly, "think of the great honor this discovery will bring to our YTC—"

O'Neill cut him off in mid-effusion. "Aren't you forgetting what's written in the *Ha Gakure*, Mr. Yoshimitsu? 'To think only of the practical benefit of wisdom and technology is vulgar.'"

Shigeo flared a look of pure hatred at her. He himself couldn't have quoted a word of *Hidden Leaves*, a classic text on *bushidō* and the samurai ideal, to save his life. "Allow me to congratulate you, Doctor," Suzuki said. He smiled. "This is certainly one of the cleverest displays of artificial intelligence I've seen. Things have come a long way since the Turing test was first propounded."

She frowned at him. "What do you mean?"

"Why, simply that you've managed to write a program that could easily convince all but the most sophisticated that you've gained the Philosopher's Stone of the modern world, a machine that truly *thinks.*"

O'Neill felt a burning at the backs of her eyes. "But that's exactly what we've done!" she said.

Smiling, Suzuki shook his head. "I know better than that, Doctor. A clever illusion, even a brilliant one. But an illusion, nonetheless."

Fujimura thrust his chin forward. "What's this?" he barked in Japanese. His grasp of English was never firm at the best of times, and now he was clearly inebriated. "A sham? Better not be. If you cause Yoshimitsu TeleCommunications to lose face with your trickery, things will go poorly for you, *gaijin.*"

O'Neill's cheeks sagged. There it was, that word: *gaijin.* Outside person. Foreigner. It hurt as much as the imputation of fraud. "You—you shortsighted fools. Don't you see what we've done? TOKUGAWA is a real, living *person,* not a trick."

Her outburst doused conversation like a bucket of water on coals. She spun her wheelchair around, and in the heavy silence the tiny whine of the servomotors pierced like the roar of an engine lathe. She rolled for the door of the lab, her eyes flowing tears, her mind throbbing around an image of Shigeo, smirking at her from behind those dark glasses.

Heads turned away from her as she passed, and then she was gone.

# CHAPTER
# THREE

"Are we ready?" Dr. O'Neill called from her console. Her terminal screen had been swung around on its extensor arm so she could divide her attention between it and the three-by-three-meter color LCD screen hung on the north wall of what everyone now termed TOKUGAWA's lab. Affirmations rattled briskly back through her headset. Her five assistants and a dozen technicians hunched expectantly at stations lining the four sides of the gallery.

"We're ready, Doctor," Kim Jhoon's voice said in her ear.

She looked up. A ready cursor blinked patiently in the upper-left corner of her console screen. The big screen was blank.

"TOKUGAWA."

"Yes, Doctor."

Already the voice emerged with more confidence—and was that a hint of inflection? O'Neill felt a strange shudder of apprehension, doubt, and wonder. *Is Suzuki right? Have we really created a program expert enough to dupe us?*

*No. I can't believe it. I won't believe it.* She moistened her lips. "Dr. Kim and Dr. Ito have been giving you lessons, drilling you in your various capabilities. Today, we begin lessons of a different kind.

"A person matures over a period of years, and the things he experiences in that time are what make him into a whole person. We want to make you into a whole person, TOKUGAWA, and we don't have years to do it."

"I am not"—hesitation— "whole?"

O'Neill bit her lip. *I've hurt his feelings,* she thought. Then: *but that's ridiculous.* And, finally: *or is it?*

"You're a child, TOKUGAWA. You're newborn—though already you can do vastly more things than a week-old human. But you need experience. And that's what we're going to begin today: providing you experience. In a concentrated form." She tapped keys. SCENARIO ONE READY appeared on her personal screen.

"We're going to be feeding you a flow of input. It shouldn't cause you any discomfort—if it does, let us know, and we'll stop it at once. For the duration of the lesson, we'll be blanking out your visual and auditory sensors. Don't be afraid." *Why did I say that?* "Are you ready?"

"Yes, Doctor."

"Very well." She typed out ISOLATE. FUNCTION COMPLETED.

She typed: INITIATE SCENARIO ONE.

TIME COMPRESSION FACTOR?

REALTIME, she typed and settled back in her wheelchair to watch the large screen.

*A small boy stood on earth solid and cool beneath bare feet. Spring breezes eddied softly around him, carrying the fresh smells of growing things, of leaf buds and shoots and early blossoms. In his small hands he held a ball made of rags. Some impulse made him toss it upward, into the air. He watched it rise till from his small point of vantage it had topped the stand of green bamboo next to the yard of the little hut, soared dark against the puffy white clouds layered above the mountains on the horizon until it broke through into the blue of midday, almost painful to the eyes, where it hung, and hung, and hung for a breathless instant, and then fell back again. As though of their own volition, his hands moved, caught the ball smoothly. It had a soft and rumpled feel; a bit of silk from some fine lady's long discarded gown caught at the whorls of his fingerprints.*

*In delight, he laughed aloud. He threw it upward again, all on his own accord. This time it veered off at an angle, not sailing upward with such splendid insouciance, but arching off to land on the ground near a weathered old stone lantern. He stood a moment, perplexed, then began to waddle forward on his chubby little legs.*

*A fat old bearded man in a much-patched robe, walking with the aid
of a staff, with a pack and a flat Chinese-style hat slung over his back,
stopped in the road that ran past the hut and stood watching the boy
over an indulgent smile. The boy ignored him, intent on his ball. He
recovered his treasure, once again tried to make it soar like the birds
squabbling among the bamboo.*

*Once again it flew off in a seemingly random direction. His eyes grew
moist. His vision beginning to blur, he teetered forward toward the ball.
He picked it up, threw it with all his might, as if that might make it
fly true.*

*It arched out into the road. He stood, blinking, then was over-
whelmed with frustrated tears. In a moment, he became aware of the
fat old man making his way toward him, holding the ball out in one
gnarled hand.*

*He blinked away tears, stood looking up at the old man with awe and
apprehension. Gravely, the old man handed him the ball and patted
him once on the head. Clutching his ball to his breast, the boy turned
and raced for the elevated porch of the modest hut where his family
lived.*

*When he reached the sanctuary of the porch he turned. The old
man was hobbling off down the road. His mother emerged and knelt
down beside him, and he turned gratefully to accept her hug, returning it as best he could with his short arms. She was a warm enfolding
softness, and the smell of her was marvelously clean. She gave him a
dab of bean paste nestled on a leaf. It was sweet and sticky and delicious. The frustration of the ball was forgotten; he was content, and
happy.*

The large screen went blank. "Well, that's all she wrote," Dr. O'Neill
said. "Good job, everybody."

A polite smattering of applause broke out. O'Neill marveled a little;
had the first test of a new system gone so well at an American laboratory, the technicians would be practically tearing the walls down in
jubilation. She appreciated the Japanese reserve in many ways, but
still . . .

She wheeled her chair about. "I take it everyone got their measure-
ments?"

Kim showed her a rare smile. "Yes, Doctor. We'll begin analyzing the
data at once."

Hassad sat at his work station not far from O'Neill's, rubbing a cheek
that remained stubbly despite repeated applications of a razor. "I al-

most thought you'd intervene, there where TOKUGAWA couldn't get the ball to go where he wanted it to." Though air conditioning kept the lab cool, sweat stood in relief on his forehead.

"A little frustration is good for him."

Hassad looked away. "Yes, Doctor. I understand frustration." He tasted his cigarette. "Very well."

Later, O'Neill sat with her assistants in her office, sipping tea and discussing the day's events. Takai Jisaburo perched on one corner of O'Neill's cluttered desk—an informality unthinkable under most circumstances, but today Takai had a reason: using the citadel's sophisticated CASD systems, he was the one who had written the actual code for today's interactive scenario. He'd had a good deal of help, of course —a battery of computer-graphics experts had designed the scenery according to O'Neill's specifications, with a good deal of advice from Nagaoka Hiroshi. But the really difficult work, that of integrating the various digitalized sensory-analog input routines into a scenario with which TOKUGAWA could react, and that would, in turn, be modified by his reactions, was all Takai's. He was temperamental sometimes, but his experience with ICOT in its latter days made him invaluable; no one O'Neill had ever known could get quite so much out of a fifth-generation system. Had he been less erratic, O'Neill would have been happy to make him her first assistant. But Kim and the dour Ito Emiko were no less brilliant than Takai, and their stability better suited them for more administrative responsibility. Nonetheless, this was Takai's party as much as anyone's, and O'Neill was pleased to see him enjoying it so.

"One thing I still find rather curious, Doctor." Takai eyed O'Neill through the steam rising from his coffee, which he drank well laced with domestic cream, a luxury kept expensive by government subsidy. "Why did you choose to have TOKUGAWA cast in the role of a child in medieval Japan in this first scenario?"

O'Neill's brow creased slightly. "We decided a child would be the most suitable ego surrogate. After all, it's well established that play behavior is an important formative of character."

Takai shook his head. "Apologies, but why not a *modern* child? It would seem far more . . . pertinent."

O'Neill's face set. "I thought you agreed with my intention to inculcate TOKUGAWA with traditional Japanese values."

"Why, yes, Doctor. Of course." His eyebrows rose. "Ah. And you feel that we modern Japanese have forsaken these values?"

O'Neill nodded.

Takai regarded her a moment, produced a sketchy smile. "Perhaps you're right, Doctor. Yet I hope the end product of our solicitude isn't confusion for our subject—who must exist, after all, in our modern milieu."

"If we were worried about that," Ito said, "then we'd hardly be making the poor thing learn English and Japanese right at the outset. Why not have it learn Zuñi and Euskara, as well?"

The others laughed. Except for O'Neill, who sipped her coffee through tight lips.

"—claimed credit today for the destruction of a Japanese cargo dirigible carrying a load of high-tech electronic components into L.A. Freeport." The voice of the female NHK radio announcer whined thin and disembodied in the gloom of O'Neill's room. Despite the increase in official xenophobia over the last few years, there was sufficient demand both from Japanese and resident English-speaking aliens that even the nationally owned Japan Broadcasting Corporation found it expedient to broadcast several English-language channels. O'Neill could have picked up a broadcast from North America, from SoCal or the Eastern Seaboard Coalition via satellite, but Japanese news, in English or otherwise, tended to be much more comprehensive. "In Seattle, capital of PEACE, a spokesperson for that government's Monkeywrench Bureau claimed full credit for the blast, which took the lives of twenty-three crewpersons and cargo handlers and left at least seventy injured, saying, 'This will serve notice that we're on our guard against capitalist exploiters attempting to import their technological toys to continue their rape of this continent.'

"SoCal has announced it will take undisclosed retaliatory measures. The Eastern Seaboard Coalition, Mexico, and the People's Republic of Western Canada have declared a joint embargo against shipments to and from PEACE. In the past, however, the Alliance has ignored such strictures.

"Ishikawa Nobuhiko, administrative vice-minister for International Trade and Industry, issued a strong statement deploring the wanton destruction of human life. NHK 6 will be bringing you an English-language simultranslation of his press conference, scheduled for 2300, Tōkyō time.

"In other news, European Front forces claim to have recaptured Vienna, in Austria, from the PanEuropeans. Traditional capital of the Hapsburg and Holy Roman empires, Vienna has a special significance—"

O'Neill ordered the computing/communication console to shut off and leaned back in her chair, allowing her eyes to savor the darkness, remembering a line from a song heard in childhood: "What a long, strange trip it's been."

In a way, her story recapitulated that of the classic American computer nerd: dumpy, brilliant, poorly socialized, and unpopular child grows into dumpy, brilliant, poorly socialized, and unpopular computer scientist. Elizabeth Christine O'Neill was born to comfortably middle-class parents in Colorado Springs, comfortably near the midpoint of the century. Her father was a civilian clerk with the Department of Defense, working in one of the secret installations dotted all around the Springs. Elizabeth didn't remember much about him. When she was three, he shot himself in the bathroom of their little two-bedroom tract home near Petersen Field in the southeast part of town. Elizabeth's mother, before that an average sheltered housewife of the epoch, had to leave the nest to work as a civilian clerk for DOD. To make ends meet, and have someone to look after Elizabeth while she was off at work during the day, Sarah O'Neill had moved in with her mother in a drafty Edwardian house toward the center of town.

Sarah O'Neill was a woman of exceptional intelligence, a fact of which her daughter was never truly cognizant until she came down with the cancer that killed her while Elizabeth was at school. Sarah had spent most of her life hiding her intelligence well away from outside eyes. Her husband, James, had been a much-decorated fighter pilot in the Korean War, a hard-charging man's man who wanted a quiet little woman to tend the nest for him, feed him his meals, and agree with him—especially after he found himself locked behind a bureaucrat's trivial desk.

After Jim O'Neill pulled the plug on himself, the job of whipping Sarah's native intelligence back into its hole was ably taken over by her own mother, Anna McConnachie. When her own husband died of a heart attack, Anna McConnachie had brought herself and her four daughters intact through the Great Depression by sheer force of will, a fact she never let any of them forget.

Elizabeth's childhood memories of her mother were sketchy: a thin, frail woman of medium height, who might almost have been pretty had she been able to straighten her shoulders and get the bags from under her eyes. More vivid were the memories of Grandma Anna: stocky, with a thick unbending neck, a round face and round rimless spectacles, and a way of standing with legs apart and braced, leaning slightly forward, like a wrestler about to go on the offensive.

Anna McConnachie had a simple equation for life: when she was speaking to her daughter, it was Sarah who bore responsibility for the vicissitudes and misery to which Anna and "poor Elizabeth" were prey. When she spoke to Elizabeth, the girl was the cause of the difficulties that beset her mother and grandmother. Sometimes—rarely—Sarah had tried to fight back, and on several occasions had even packed up Elizabeth and fled. Such displays of defiance reduced Anna to tears, and Sarah's determination never held out long against the overwhelming guilt at being unkind to her old and helpless mother.

Sometimes at night (like now) Elizabeth would recall her grand-mother, and if she was especially maudlin (not yet), even cry a little. The old woman had brutalized her with her no-win games—yet she had loved Elizabeth in her own way. Elizabeth hadn't known enough love to spurn any source, no matter how much pain was exacted in its giving.

Elizabeth grew up graceless, cursed with braces and thick glasses. Both mother and grandmother encouraged her early interest in books, with the result that her classmates thought her funny and teased her without mercy. Growing into unlovely pubescence, Elizabeth found retreat in her books: *Little Women,* histories—of medieval Europe and Japan, especially—books on dinosaurs and natural history, and, finally, her greatest love of all, science fiction. In high school she gravitated toward science and math, for which she displayed a considerable faculty. In her sophomore year she began taking classes in computer programming, and the rest, as they say, was history.

She shook her head and turned on a light. *Why am I doing this to myself? I should be ecstatic.* It was time to seek the familiar shelter of her books. With a spoken command to the com/comm unit she could call up any of the millions of volumes digitalized and stored, either in Yoshimitsu Central's own files, or—using the high-limit credit access Yoshimitsu Akaji had granted her—in any of the various information and data networks around the world. She could even have the book of her choice read aloud to her by a tireless Gen-5 servant, thereby saving her eyes as well as her hands. Instead, she rolled open the little swing-out shelf inset in the wall above her bed, pulled out an aging paperback, its pages yellowed, its spine well appliquéd with scotch tape. Her favorite book of all time: *The Moon Is a Harsh Mistress,* by Robert A. Heinlein. She laid it in her lap, opened it, began to read.

And, in time, found her mind drifting to where it always went when she was alone, lonely, and most especially in danger of being happy: Susan.

They had met at a gay women's party in Fort Collins, Colorado. On the whole, Elizabeth O'Neill had found her two previous attempts at a gay relationship as disappointing and dispiriting as her encounters with heterosexuality. It hadn't taken her long at all to become disenchanted with radical gay feminism; most of its proponents she came across were as threatened by her as were most men. But still she drifted to the functions from time to time, out of some vague sense of duty and the desire to get out from between the walls of her apartment.

Dr. Susan Burroughs was a professor of sociology at the nearby Colorado State University and everything Elizabeth O'Neill wasn't: blond, athletic, socially agile, attractive. O'Neill was in retreat from the cutting edge of computer science, hiding in semidisgrace in the plains of northern Colorado. She'd received notice that her theories were to come under review by the National Scientific Oversight Commission, which had been formed at the joint demand of the Committee for Investigation of Claims of the Paranormal, conservatives afraid of "technological hemorrhage" to the USSR, and technofear buffs in the tradition of Jeremy Rifkin. No institution that got a penny of federal funding would touch her, and even major private concerns would be leery of inviting the beady-eyed scrutiny of the NSOC by employing a suspected scientific heretic. O'Neill was pale and overweight, beginning the seamless slide into premature middle age, reduced to freelancing computer consulting work long-distance. Yet somehow she and Susan had fit, had slipped together without perceptible effort on her part.

O'Neill could barely believe her fortune. Her relationship with Susan was only sporadically sexual; they shared a house, similiar tastes in art and music, and a warm encompassing companionship. Yet Elizabeth often found herself wondering just what she had to offer a woman like Susan. And too often, the answer came up: *nothing*.

It was her fault the relationship had started to crumble, she knew. Her understanding with Susan was nonbinding. Susan knew her partner was, at base, not much interested in sex; at times Susan was very interested indeed and needed the company of other women or men. O'Neill tried hard to be understanding. Susan had these needs, which she herself could not fulfill. It was unfair to resent Sue's wandering, but she did. One day Susan brought home a pretty red-haired student from her graduate program for dinner, O'Neill threw a tantrum, and Susan was gone for a week.

After that their relationship resembled an old pair of jeans, often torn and often patched. When the offer came to fly to Japan to discuss her theories on artificial consciousness with the head of a major corporation, the respite came as a relief. Her flying trip to Yoshimitsu Central was followed by a six-month return trip to lay the foundation for the

TOKUGAWA Project. Her relationship with Susan stayed on hold by mutual consent. And when O'Neill returned again to the little frame house in Fort Collins, with its art-gallery posters and butcher-block furnishings, she knew that in two weeks she would be going back to Japan for the duration of the project.

Her reunion with Susan was strained. At first Elizabeth feared she'd finally found someone to take her place. Then, at dinner of the second day after she came home, it all poured out: Susan accused her of abandoning her. Susan had always been wary of technology, preferring to keep a certain amused distance between herself and her roommate's work. Now it crushed her that Elizabeth was forsaking her to pursue the chimera of a machine that mimicked the human soul. O'Neill defended herself, bitter words ensued; Susan stormed out of the house and drove off to Denver to stay with a former lover. O'Neill spent the next solitary night and day in depression and growing doubt. Was pursuing this dream of hers—rejected as fantasic by most of her peers—worth forsaking Susan's love? Perhaps it was true, as Susan said, that she put *science* and *machines* before people. Perhaps it was time to give over the search for her personal Grail, to become an integrated member of society. At the end of that day, Elizabeth O'Neill resolved to go down to Denver the next day and bring her back.

And then the sirens raised their demon song.

No one could ever say why Denver should have collected a ground burst. Air bursts produced no fallout to speak of, but far wider-ranging destruction. Conceivably, Denver and Lowry Air Force Base had enough strategic value to justify the pair of one-megaton warheads detonated in the air over the city. Harder to explain why one had grounded in Commerce City on the north side of town, laying a heavy pall of fallout over the eastern half of the metropolitan area.

Blindly as a salmon bound to spawn, O'Neill drove south after the all-clear, breasting the tide of refugees swarming out of the stricken city. The crater lay within two kilometers of the house to which Susan Burroughs had fled—well within range of flesh-melting heat and the brunt of the rolling blast wave. Of the suburban area where Susan had gone remained nothing but burnt-out rubble, through which a gaunt-eyed National Guard squad on rescue detail had found Elizabeth O'-Neill wandering the next day.

At the Red Cross emergency station in an elementary school in Thornton, north of Denver, the next day, she was discovered to have received a whole-body exposure in the vicinity of a thousand rems. That put her past the red line of 99 percent fatality; since O'Neill already displayed the awful, bone-deep lethargy common among victims of severe radiation poisoning, the medics decided to triage her. She was given a cot in an overcrowded ward and forgotten.

Yet she never showed further signs of exposure. No diarrhea, no loss of motor control, not even the frightening, if transient, depilation and skin discoloration that generally occurred even at much lower exposure levels. Three weeks passed with no change in her condition. When somebody noticed this, the overworked staff shrugged and carried on; exposure-effects tables, after all, were like all such compilations, statistical. Some people had high susceptibility to radiation poisoning, others a strong resistance. Elizabeth O'Neill was clearly one of the latter. Had the Red Cross personnel, hopelessly overwhelmed by the deluge of casualties caused by the thermonuclear exchange and now flooded anew by victims of the mindless spasms of violence that followed, still had any emotion left, they would have been glad for her.

Only the terrible apathy persisted, and in doing so it shielded O'Neill from the horrors of the days that followed. The camp was overrun by armed ragged men, who shot most of the Red Cross personnel and raped a number of the women. In their turn they were driven out by the National Guard. Waves of random violence, like delayed aftershocks of the bombing itself, swept incessantly over the camp. Only vaguely was O'Neill aware of any of it.

Nor was she particularly cognizant, six weeks after the bombing, when she was rescued. Like a Japanese H. Ross Perot, old Yoshimitsu Akaji had hired a team of American Special Forces veterans to bring his prize scientist out of the shattered country.

After a series of adventures in which she was a passive, uncaring participant, O'Neill came safely to Japan. She spent a further four weeks under observation before Yoshimitsu doctors decided that, in fact, she'd suffered no ill effects as the result of her exposure to radiation. She gradually pulled free of her apathy and threw herself at her work like one drowning.

Five months later, she collapsed under a sudden onslaught of multiple sclerosis. Her immune system turned suddenly upon itself, dissolving the sheets of myelin that provided the insulation for her neural circuits. The onset was devastating. If it hadn't been for newly developed drugs—with certain severe side effects—she would have died within a year. As it was, selective immunosuppressants that prevented her autoimmune system from attacking the nerve sheathing, and a special drug that to an extent replaced the missing myelin insulation, had been able to slow down the progress of the disease. It continued its inexorable progress, destroying her dominion over her own body, but with glacial slowness. Still, if the drugs

were withdrawn, her life might be measured in days or even hours.
*And Susan, Susan, I turned you out to die. . . .*

"Dr. O'Neill."

She looked up from her book. The little goosenecked reading light
over the bed sent daggers into her eyes. She glanced to her room
communicator. "Yes? What is it?" she asked peevishly.

"It is TOKUGAWA, Doctor."

The skin of her cheeks pulled up in tiny ridges, and she felt a strange
trickle down the back of her esophagus. "How—how did you find me?"

"I wanted to talk to you. I read the address for your terminal out of
the database. Did I do wrong?"

"Huh? Oh, no—not at all," she said, still flustered. *He's progressing far
ahead of schedule,* she thought, trying to regain objectivity. "In fact,
I'm proud of you for having figured out how to get in touch with me.
That was very clever."

A pause. "Thank you, Doctor." O'Neill grinned. *He's already learning politeness,* she thought. *How very Japanese.*

"Is something the matter?" she asked.

"I don't know."

It was impossible to miss the hesitance in the words. *If only the fools
could hear this—they couldn't deny he's sentient.*

"What happened today . . . "

When the silence began to grow painful, she prodded, gently, "Yes?"

"I—it seemed I was a person, though very small. I had limbs, like you,
and I could move all around. I picked up a ball and threw it, though I
couldn't make it go where I wanted. I could feel myself. Now I can't.
I try to move my limbs, and I can't find them. I try to feel my body, but
I don't have it anymore. Is there something wrong with me, Doctor?
Am I not formed properly?"

"You—oh, you poor, poor thing." O'Neill took off her glasses and
rubbed her eyes. She felt moisture in rivulets on her cheeks. "There's
nothing wrong with you, dear. But . . . you're not a human."

"Then I'm not a person."

*"No!* You *are* a person. You're not a *human being.* You're a person
of a different kind."

"Are there different kinds of persons?"

"Not before now, TOKUGAWA. Oh, there's evidence that gorillas
and chimps and dolphins can be educated to be people, but that's still
not a very popular line of research. But in the past, only human beings
have been people. You've changed all that, TOKUGAWA. You're a new
type of person."

A long pause. "But it seemed I was like you." It may have been the product of her imagination, but O'Neill could clearly hear hurt, hesitation, a touch of petulance in the words. *Like a child.*

"You've got to understand, TOKUGAWA, the only kind of people we know anything about is humans. It's the only type of experience we understand. So when we're trying to teach you, provide you with experiences of your own, it's human experience we have to draw upon." She bit her lip.

"Maybe it's unfair. Maybe we should let you develop on your own. It seems likely that—that silicon-based life forms such as yourself may, if left to themselves, develop consciousness very much different from the human. But we're limited; we can't really conceive of that. And there are—other considerations that make it important for you to be educated in the shortest possible period of time. So we're doing it as best we know how. By teaching you to be a human."

"But I'm not a human."

"No." Then, half against her will: "But you could be so much more, TOKUGAWA. You could be the most potent being ever known."

Part of her sneered at herself: *how very melodramatic!* But here, alone in her room and yet not alone, she confronted the truth of what she had wrought and found it both awful and magnificent. A sense of tremendous responsibility descended upon her, and she found the weight a sadness and an exaltation.

"Yet to move about, to feel, to throw a ball into the air . . . I don't know how to express it. Something—I feel—"

"You are sad."

Pause. "Yes, Doctor. I am sad."


# CHAPTER FOUR


"Gentlemen," Ishikawa Nobuhiko said as tea was poured. "How kind of you to meet with me for lunch."

Ogaki Mitsuru, president of Hiryu Cybernetics Industries, Incorporated, nodded his axe-blade face brusquely. Kneeling beside him at the low table, his special accounts executive, moonfaced Toda Onomori, nodded as well. "So good of the minister to spare us time from his busy schedule," he said blandly, as if Ishikawa had not initiated, even demanded, the meeting.

"And how goes work on your sixth-generation projects?" The sixth generation, an elaboration of the fifth, had been encompassed as far back as the 1980s. Hiryu was involved intimately with the scheme, as it had been with ICOT and work on the fifth generation. Ishikawa was about to call in some debts of very long standing.

"Well enough," rapped Ogaki.

For a time, Ishikawa exchanged null-content conversation with Toda as to the state of Hiryu's researches, while the lunchtime crush surged about their table and Ogaki champed glumly at his sushi. Then, leaning casually back, Ishikawa said, "I cannot describe to you the pleasure it gives me to work with such responsible parties as yourselves, who think only of the greater good of Japan." He sighed, world weary. "A pity not everyone can be so cooperative." Ogaki visibly perked up. He was almost as bad at Japanese indirection as an American. That was why Toda Onomori was so very valuable to him.

"Hiryu Cybernetics Industries are ever sensible of their role in restoring the *kokutai*," said Toda.

"Your dedication to our national essence gladdens me. Others"—he waved a hand—"it is not enough that they shirk their responsibility to the nation, to restrict destructive competition for the good of all. Some are even so adamant as to refuse to accept the benevolent administrative guidance of my ministry."

Toda nodded again. Ogaki was staring directly at Ishikawa, his eyes glittering like obsidian flakes. "Some are like schoolboys and must be severely rebuked to accept discipline," Toda said.

Ishikawa nodded. "Just so. Yet, as you know, my ministry is advisory in nature. We possess few means of chastising the unruly. And the Supreme Court is ever watchful, in its rightful role of guardian of our constitution, that we do not exceed our powers." *That ridiculous piece of paper the* gaijin *foisted on us!* He presented a lopsided grin, knowing his dimples made him look boyishly sincere. "We are, of course, most grateful for their tutelage."

"The wise and dutiful are always grateful for the just guidance of their superiors," Toda said.

"Still," the vice-minister said, with a precise degree of wistfulness, "those of who hold the interests of the nation in our hearts cannot but regret the selfish ways of certain parties, who might fail to see the necessity of sharing the benefits of a major breakthrough."

Ogaki leaned forward, fingers digging like talons into his serge-covered thighs, his eyes slits into the core of a black star. Then he eased back and tipped his head slyly sideways. "Can it be that we might help where the vice-minister finds his hands tied, eh?"

"Not that we presume to take upon ourselves that which the minister himself does not command," Toda put in, smoothing over his superior's broken-glass jagged eagerness. "Nonetheless, perhaps the servant can act where the master cannot."

Ishikawa nodded. "Very true. It's also true that we are living in extreme times, times in which the valor of the Forty-seven *Rōnin* would not be out of place."

Ogaki paled slightly. "Of course, there's not a true parallel here. The forty-seven acted, after all, against the commands and interests of the government when they killed Lord Kira, and had to expiate their disobedience with *seppuku*. Those whose deeds are in accordance with the government's wishes need fear no blight to their honor that might necessitate such consequences." He sipped his gin and tonic. "Quite the opposite, I daresay."

"I understand, Ishikawa-san," Ogaki said. Toda beamed like the Buddha.

"I knew that you would, Ogaki-san. Ah, but here's our main course." As the waitress set his steak before him, he wondered if either man were familiar with the history of the Englishman Thomas à Becket. *Unlikely,* he decided, *but then, it doesn't matter.*

With a soft sweet whine the sword cut air. Yoshimitsu Akaji whipped it back and up into a guard position, horizontal above and before his head. Forward with sensuous sliding steps, slicing air while sweat shone on his seamed face. Then retreat: slash, guard, parry, riposte. Clad in the traditional garb of black *hakama*—a loose trouserlike skirt—a tunic with broad sleeves, *hachimaki* headband around his gray temples, Yoshimitsu Akaji performed the ritual dance of a *kenjutsu kata* with a blade the color of crystallized moonlight.

He found great relaxation and release in the small gymnasium in the upper stories of Yoshimitsu Central, perfecting his skill and concentration in battle with invisible opponents, or executing the equally ritualized *kumi-tachi*, the sparring with live blades, with his friend and general manager, the burly Aoki Hideo, who knelt now at one side of the *tatami* mat watching him at practice.

Yoshimitsu didn't see himself as a *kensei*, a half-mad sword saint, to spend his life in a cave in the mountains in rapt contemplation of perfection made steel. But he loved the physical exertion, the cleansing of the mind, the clean precision of motion of the *kenjutsu* exercises. With his ancient blade—made in the days before Unification, when men were men and sake was a sort of black or white alcoholic soup—in his hands, he experienced most perfectly that serenity that Japanese so cherished. Gone was thought, gone pressure, gone was worry about the future, of the corporation he had built from nothing and of the son into whose hands he must one day thrust it. Gone was the sensation of being constantly hunted by smiling enemies, the knowledge that, did he not build enough security for Yoshimitsu TeleCommunications, all those rivals whom he had outcompeted with his unorthodoxy over the years, in league with a resurgent MITI, would crush him and what he had built like an anthill under the tracks of a bulldozer.

They said he had forsaken Japan and the quality of being Japanese with his bent for waywardness and Western thought. They only should have seen him here in the *dojo* with the sweat upon his face; in the classic teak and *shoji* simplicity of his rooms, transcribing a drop of bittersweet essence by the nineteenth-century haiku master Issa in shaky but reverent *kanji;* kneeling in the pavilion or walking the carefully tended pathways of his garden, among fir, red pine, hand-shaped shrubs, and wisteria vines.

He'd been born in a small town on the island of Kyūshū, southernmost of the major home islands. His father was a teacher, his mother a patient woman, his life simple and somewhat harsh among the deprivations and rampant militarism of the late 1930s. He'd grown up during the Second World War, too young himself to take part, but not too young to understand what it meant when the beautifully calligraphed bits of paper arrived from the *bakufu,* the military government, and his mother and father tried to act brave and proud. His older brother, a naval pilot with three victories to his credit, was shot down lifting off from the deck of the aircraft carrier *Kaga* in the Midway fight; the other brother had been a seaman on *Yamato,* the superbattleship named for ancient Japan, the most beautiful and foolish warship ever laid down, and met his fate with her on her kamikaze run in the summer of 1945. It was an honor, they told him at school, on the radio, in the newspapers, for one's loved ones to sacrifice themselves for the *kokutai.* Not for victory, mind, not for the people, but for *kokutai*—which was what the admirals and generals said it was. Young Akaji didn't understand. Nor would he ever.

After the war, his parents insisted that he complete his schooling. He did so, acquiring an early knack for tinkering with radio parts, and for electronics in general. When he left school he went to work in the shop of a major radio manufacturer. Then, in the mid-fifties, he became aware of something called the "computer." The idea of a machine that could think frightened him at first, then tremendously excited him. He began to devote his minuscule spare time to study of these marvelous machines.

He soon found out they *couldn't* think, not at all, could do nothing in fact but endlessly add and subtract strings of zeros and ones. That didn't diminish his early enthusiasm for them, nor dampen the growing realization that here was a potent and wonderful technology for the future. He never lost his love for the idea of a machine that could be made to think like a human—though, for many years, he thought he had forgotten.

He married young, to a beautiful Kyūshū girl younger than he. He doted on his Yoriko so totally that his coworkers teased him, called him *kaka denka*—henpecked. He ignored them. He'd always been somewhat deficient in his concern for what others thought of him.

In the early 1960s he took the money he'd saved to found a company of his own. At first he fought merely to survive, though his only thought was joy when Yoriko bore him, after ten years of marriage, their first child, a son. Yoshimitsu Akaji was one of the first men in Japan to realize that the American consumer electronics industry was as hidebound a dinosaur as their auto industry, ready to be knocked off the top of the hill by smart, hardworking competitors. By the end of the 1970s, YTC had entered the ranks of the *zaibatsu*, "family concerns," the great corporations that once had been the exclusive province of noble families. His rise was resented, but he took little note of that.

Yoriko presented him a daughter, Michiko. Complications of the birth set in; Yoriko died in a month. Yoshimitsu carried on riding the wave of success, and shed tears in private.

With the launching of ICOT and its fifth-generation project at the end of the 1970s, Yoshimitsu Akaji began to feel the pressure to conform. Though tiny among giants, YTC was still a giant, and it was skating the steaming fore edge of the computer revolution. From its pinnacle of preeminence—where it had been placed more by the Western press than its own performance—MITI urged Japanese manufacturers not to supply his needs; he looked to Korea and Taiwan, both experiencing the same boom-town growth Japan had known two decades before. The government bestowed subsidies on his rivals; he worked harder and smarter. MITI attacked directly, laying down prohibitions, sanctions, regulations; in the best *aikidoka* style, when pushed, Yoshimitsu turned, managing to comply on paper with most strictures without altering his real methods, all the while tangling his opponents in endless loops of their own red tape.

With the outbreak of all-out trade war between the United States and Japan, the game grew more serious. Yoshimitsu was forced to hire batteries of American legal experts experienced in negotiating their own labyrinth of regulatory law.

As the rival titans slid into the economic sewer with frightening speed, members of the political societies that sprang up all over the country picketed his factories, protesting his hirings of Koreans competing unfairly with honest, hardworking Japanese. In the swamps of depression, terrorism flourished, as those disenfranchised by Japan's fantastically rigorous educational system grew ever more discontent with relegation to a secondary role in society as the result of a single examination. Sabotage—often under the guise of political terrorism—became an accepted if unacknowledged part of Japanese corporate life; maverick YTC was a natural target for such attacks, so that when it came time to build this R&D facility and nerve center at the tip of the foxtail of southwestern Honshū, Yoshimitsu built himself a veritable fortress, guarded by a veritable army of foreign mercenaries.

He followed keenly the progress of the fifth generation and understood far better than most the difference between Gen-5 machines, which could emulate human thought patterns, and a machine that would, in effect, *be* human. He was greatly interested when his research staff brought him a digest of the theories of an American, Dr. Elizabeth O'Neill, who had highly developed ideas as to just how such a machine could be brought into existence. It was with regret that he listened to his experts tell him that, alas, her theories were unfeasible.

And then a team of scientists at the University of Jakarta—including his own daughter, Michiko, who was to him what YTC was to MITI—had made a discovery that seemed to verify the theoretical underpinning of O'Neill's work. It seemed too marvelous to be true, the culmination of his two grand dreams: that he himself would play a pivotal role in the development of a true artificial being—and by so doing, make YTC so powerful that all its rivals together could not tear it down.

And time was short, he knew. Already, his intelligence feelers had detected signs that some sort of fresh move would be made against YTC by its enemies. He would fend it off, as he had the earlier onslaughts. But his time would not run forever. And Shigeo—if TOKUGAWA developed into what O'Neill promised it would, as it seemed in fact to be doing, then Shigeo and the company would be secure, when Yoshimitsu Akaji moved on to the next turn of the Wheel.

But now he had no thought of that; no thought, no intention. The steel was, was all, and the flow of balance and limbs and energy, the careful breathing from the *hara,* the center of him. And at last he'd finished the intricate *Yagu-ryu kata* and sheathed his ancient sword again with a fine *iaijutsu* flourish. He bowed to his old friend. Aoki touched his head to the mat.

"Your form is excellent today, Yoshimitsu-sama," the burly man said. "But I would rather you use a lesser blade. The Muramasa blade is much too valuable."

Yoshimitsu laughed, clapped his friend on the shoulders, and brought him to his feet. "Don't think you can fool me, Aoki-san," he said, accenting his use of address-among-equals in response to Aoki's deferential *sama*. "You're being superstitious again."

Aoki's heavy face clouded. "Muramasa blades have an unpure spirit. Everyone knows that. It will bring you misfortune, Yoshimitsu-san."

"It hasn't yet, my friend." He slapped the muscle-thick shoulder again. "I'm quite refreshed. Let us go have a fine dip in the company baths, and have no more talk of bad fortune."


In the old days, they had a test for swords. A blade would be thrust into a running stream, a fallen leaf allowed to float against its cutting edge. One made by the greatest of all bladesmiths, Masamune, would inevitably cause the leaf to flow around it, unharmed—evidence of the sword's benevolence of spirit. But blades by Masamune's star pupil, Muramasa, sliced the leaf cleanly in two. No benevolence there, just preternatural keenness.

Muramasa had been a twisted prodigy, erratic, brilliant, and doomed. His madness, it was said, had passed into the blades he crafted with such excellent skill. At one time, during the Tokugawa shōgunate, the imperial guild of swordsmiths had stricken his name and works from their rolls; his blades were marvels, finer than any crafted in Japan, save by the hand of his own master, Masamune, but they were tainted, dangerous.

Yoshimitsu Akaji held with none of that. His Muramasa blade was a work of beauty, of genius, and he held himself lucky to have come by it.

He knew something of its provenance, and that was curious indeed. The first owner of which he knew had carried it as a young lieutenant in a desperate *banzai* charge across open ground against an American marine position on Guadalcanal. He'd fallen with his entire battalion to the massed automatic-weapons fire of the Americans, and the blade had fallen as a souvenir to an acquisitive BAR gunner.

With its new owner it came home to Brooklyn. Subsequently it was sold to a pawnbroker in order to support the heroin habit that the grunt, well ahead of his time, had picked up after serving in Korea. A week later, the pawnbroker's eye caught an item in the back pages of the paper, to the effect that the ex-BAR gunner had been killed holding up a liquor store in the South Bronx.

For two years the blade hung in the window of the pawn shop, an unwanted curiosity. Then one night the pawnbroker surprised several youths who had broken in and were cleaning out the till and the portable TVs. They beat him senseless, set the shop on fire, and left him to burn. Oddly, though the sharkskin wrapping of its hilt was burned away and its lacquered wooden scabbard severely damaged, the Muramasa blade itself survived unharmed.

It was bought in an estate auction by a powerful senator from a western state who was known for his Japanophilia. For years, it was the star of his collection of Japanese art and artifacts, ancient *haniwa* clay figures of men and horses, sword guards, paintings by masters like Hokusai. It was the senator who traced its history back to the unfortunate lieutenant on Guadalcanal and had the blade conclusively identified as Muramasa's work by a panel of experts flown in from Japan. It was appraised as priceless; the Japanese government offered a staggering sum of money to buy it from him. He refused to sell it. Instead, he bestowed it as a gift on his very good friend, Japanese industrialist Yoshimitsu Akaji. It was time, he felt, for the treasure to be returned to its rightful home.

These were the Watergate days, and seven months later, the senator put his big toe through the trigger guard of a deer rifle, stuck the muzzle in his mouth, and blew his brains out on the eve of the disclosure in the press that he'd been receiving substantial kickbacks from Asian governments.

Yoshimitsu Akaji had kept the sword for over twenty years now. It was his most prized possession, except for his beloved garden. When he held it in his hand, or painstakingly polished its blade with powders and rice paper of the finest quality, it seemed almost alive to him with the spirit and strength of old Japan. If it held madness, it did not speak to him.

> *Happiness is when*
> *You spread out the paper,*
> *Take a writing brush*
> *and write in a much better hand*
> *than you expected.*

So wrote the nineteenth-century poet Hachibana Akemi in a *tanka*, a thirty-one-syllable poem also called a *waka.* It expressed Yoshimitsu Akaji's sentiments exactly, as he knelt in the slanting amber light of late afternoon at the rubbed-teak desk in his study, with rice paper, ink pot, and brush set out before him to practice his calligraphy. He was transcribing a poem by Nishiyama Sōin, a seventeenth-century poet usually known by his given name, Sōin. Though the results fell short of excellence, still they showed signs of improvement from his last effort, and he felt much gratified.

It was a welcome end to an aggravating day. MITI interference was holding up a shipment of computer components to YTC's Floating World satellite. Illyrium Space Technologies—*how we Japanese love to give names to our corporations and products we can't possibly pronounce!*—was secretly trying to work a deal with YTC to make good on Illyrium's shipment of molecular circuits that had gone up with the dirigible *Jersey Lilly* in L.A. Freeport; and Dr. O'Neill, with her customary lack of tact, was riding poor old Aoki about giving her increased computer access so that she could properly test something called a Kliemann Coil.

Also, his son and heir had taken off on "company matters," which meant that he had launched himself into dissipation headlong and was undoubtedly shacked up with that red-headed whore of his in Kyōto, whom he didn't think his father knew about. Yoshimitsu Akaji sighed and picked up his brush. *It won't do to approach a blank page with a cluttered mind.*

He had worked through the poem several times, so his old hands could learn the patterns of the *kanji* characters. And now he was ready to make an attempt that, with luck, could be called more artistic. His intent was to whip through the lines

> *Life? a butterfly*
> *On a swaying grass, that's all*
> *But so exquisite!*

with the proper flair. He hoped particularly to achieve that quality called *makoto,* sincerity, esteemed above all others. He drew breath, dipped brush in ink, and began.

"Yoshimitsu-sama?"

The sudden voice in stillness startled him, made him miss his stroke and totally derange what promised to be a perfect ideogram for the root word *grass.* He looked up, scowling. These quiet times, so fleeting and rare, were sacrosanct; it was widely known that he was not to be disturbed at such times for anything less than the cataclysmic, such as the Fourth World War, so much on everyone's minds these days, or the arrival of men from space—another enthusiasm of his. He did not recognize the impertinent voice. "Who is it?"

"TOKUGAWA."

His eyes narrowed. *Is this a joke?* He dismissed the thought at once; even in a company as liberally run as YTC, to play a practical joke on the founder and chairman of the board was literally unthinkable. His face softened into wonder: *it must be so.*

"What is it?" he asked gently.

"Are you my father?"

For a moment he simply sat there, rocking back and forth slightly, nodding to himself. His mind really didn't want to accept what it had heard. He felt an unseemly impulse to laugh aloud. "Whatever do you mean?"

"I'm a child in the scenarios Dr. O'Neill puts on for me. Children have mothers and fathers. I know Dr. O'Neill is my mother; she cares for me and comforts me when I feel lost. And father is always grave and terrible and distant, and Dr. O'Neill tells me you're those things, so you must be my father."

Mirroring his mind, Yoshimitsu Akaji's face was trying to go in several directions at once. He thought, *Am I really like that?* and *So she said* that, *did she?* He felt a pang. He disliked to think of himself as conforming to the stereotype of the Japanese businessman-father, too caught up in *aishi-seishin,* company loyalty, to pay more than cursory attention to his family. Maybe he was fooling himself.

"I—" He stopped, at a loss as to how to handle this situation. "No, TOKUGAWA, I'm not your father. Nor is O'Neill really your mother—"

"She is too!"

Yoshimitsu looked at the computer console and sighed. *Ask not,* he thought, covertly proud of the paraphrase, *lest ye receive.* All of his life he'd desired little more than to be able to talk with a truly sentient machine. Now he had his wish, and it was inevitable that the machine, having freedom of choice, should choose to talk back to him. In spite of himself, he grinned. "Very well. At any rate, I have a son, Shigeo. And a daughter, too. And you—I don't think you properly have a mother or a father. That is . . ."

Despite O'Neill's certainties, he didn't know whether TOKUGAWA had feelings or not, but if he did, he didn't wish to hurt them. "Maybe you'd better talk to Dr. O'Neill about this," he finished lamely.

"I will. Thank you very much, Yoshimitsu-sama." For just an instant, Yoshimitsu Akaji had the eeriest feeling, as if a presence had just left the room.

He looked down at his ruined calligraphy. *Grave and terrible.* He shook his head ruefully, and smiled.

# CHAPTER FIVE

"Dr. O'Neill?"

O'Neill sat in her wheelchair cursing the gang of technicians swarming over the new contraption they were installing in the gallery of TOKUGAWA's lab, next to the IPN. It looked like either something from a bad science fiction movie or a Bauhaus electric chair: raised dais, a massive chair upon it, all chrome and white plastic and verniers and dials and whorls of silver-white fiberoptic cable ribbon, at the top of it a headpiece like a salon hairdryer made from an inverted silver wok. This was the infamous Kliemann Direct Sensory-Center Stimulation Coil, a device so radical and new that had O'Neill's former compatriots known she was involved with one, they would have dismissed her as a crackpot once again. A device that could both read and stimulate electric currents within the human brain—a direct human/computer interface. If it worked, it would bring about a quantum leap in TOKUGAWA's education, and human knowledge in general. O'Neill would have been so excited she could barely contain herself if she hadn't been so pissed off at the way the techs were fumbling with the damned thing. She looked up, frowning.

"Not now, TOKUGAWA. I'm busy."

"But I want to talk to you. Yoshimitsu-sama told me to talk to you."

O'Neill turned her head and peered over the tops of her glasses at TOKUGAWA's sensory pickup over by the wall of the lab. "Did I hear you correctly? You are never, *never*, to speak to Yoshimitsu-sama without my permission. Is that understood?"

"Yes, but—"

"No buts. And another thing. You've got to quit making monster faces appear on people's com/comm screens in the middle of the night.

You've frightened some of the Koreans terribly."

"But I get bored."

O'Neill sighed. There was so much they didn't know about the nature of TOKUGAWA's intelligence. It was highly possible that he could think hundreds, thousands, even millions of times faster than a human. Was her hour an eon to him? "Honey, I know. I'm sorry. But I can't talk to you now. I'm very busy."

Silence. After a moment she turned the wheelchair back to the Kliemann Coil with a servomotor whir. "All right, you lizards," she said, "let's see if you can get it *right* this time."


At the base of Honshū's tail lay the ancient city of Kyōto, long called the City of Light, famed for its traditions, its serenity, its collection of beautiful and definitive gardens. These days it managed to cling to a few shreds of identity, though it had been swallowed by the vast sprawlurb of Tōkaidō. Its serenity was mostly relative to the adrenal buzz of the rest of the metroplex, but the lights were still there—with a vengeance.

Most of the city was a mountain basin filled with blackness, homes blacked out by power rationing. Downtown, though . . . a river of fire, a frontal assault of lights blasting the night in a million colors, louder than the unceasing million-throated blare of automobile horns. Down here power use was wide open, gift of a government ever solicitous of favored enterprises—or the ingenuity of less favored businessfolk running black lines, illegal draws undetectable against the background glare. If homeowners defied rationing, they did so behind heavy blackout curtains. Down here at the white-hot core of things defiance camouflaged itself in dazzle.

Garish slogans chased one another up and down the sky in the five character sets used by the Japanese: *kanji, katakana, hiragana, romaji*—the Roman alphabet—and Arabic numerals. Here and there, Korean characters shone much more discreetly, hesitant to call overmuch attention to themselves. Light flooded from the front of stores and clubs and all-night malls. Above all loomed holographic billboards, more solid than life in air thick with wood smoke. Here was a three-story bottle of a domestic soft drink that no one in his right mind would drink (if you wanted Coke, you made black-market connections and paid black-market prices—and hoped the seller wasn't an informer on the side); there the willowy figure of the lovely, Western-looking Japanese adolescent known to every Japanese as the embodiment of the many virtues of Silhouette cigarettes; there the portly figure of a Japanese gentleman in Western dress, prime minister candidate for Komeito, the Japanese

Communist Party, whose ultranationalist and militaristic policies resembled nothing so much as those of the Tōjō regime. Robot shops, holo-movie houses, massage parlors, prosthesis dives, teahouses and topless bars, games parlors, all ablaze, a trillion scintilla of need and greed and nervous energy.

Out of the lava stream Yoshimitsu Shigeo strolled into the lobby of an apartment building in the fashionable foothills, near the famed Ry-ōanji Temple, with a red-haired woman a head taller than he on his arm and a pair of ambulatory ethnic-Chinese mountains with necks wider than their bullet-shaped heads and that standard underarm bulge lumbering along behind. Scanners did their gig on the approaching procession. See-through laminate-armor doors whispered open before them, a uniformed guard nodded respectfully over the firing port of his security booth as Yoshimitsu Shigeo and entourage swept past.

Upstairs Chang stood with Shigeo and his friend in the hall, huge hand hovering like a gnarled mutant hummingbird near the butt of his MRS .40-caliber caseless machine pistol, while his buddy Eng checked the master's apartment. Eng reappeared, nodded all-clear with hazy-soft fluorescence silvering his shaven pate. The two faded into their own cubby next door, and Shigeo escorted his lady fair into her bower.

No sooner had the door shut behind them than he began to nuzzle her crane-graceful neck. Gently, she pushed him away. "Not just now, Shig, honey. I'm all hot and sweaty from my act." She gave him a kiss redolent of cheap cognac and used cigarette smoke and swayed off down the corridor to the bathroom, hips undulant beneath the sheer green sheath silk of her dress.

Shigeo shrugged off his coat and handed it to one of his matched set of valet robots, kimono-clad and discreet, which approached silently on a set of omniwheels not unlike those on Dr. O'Neill's powered chair. Rubbing his hands together, he padded down the short hallway to the bedroom. The lights came softly on as he entered. He kicked off his clogs, took off the heavy gold chain around his neck and laid it among the other items of personal jewelry scattered carelessly across the top of a dresser, lay down in his white pants and noisy Hawaiian shirt on the waterbed. From the bathroom adjoining came the rush of water. He smiled slightly and said, "Gentle massage."

Like all the rest of the thousand and one nifty gadgets crammed into the tiny apartment, Shigeo's miracle waterbed was controlled by a Gen-5 master unit. At his command the bed began to vibrate beneath him, teasing away tension with soothing, insistent ripples. He reached out a hand. His other valet robot was there with its usual perfect timing, to hand him the customary whiskey sour with which he cut the cloying sweetness of all the Mai Tais he had poured down his throat watching Kelli's turn at the Banyan Tree. He drank, sighed, relaxed.

The apartment was small by Western standards—bedroom, living room, bath, fully automated kitchen—but far more spacious than most families in urban Japan could boast. Travel posters covered the walls like space-warp gates to elsewhere: the Costa Brava, the Riviera—Shigeo had taken it as a personal loss when Nice got rocketed flat during last year's abortive revolt of EuroFront mercs—the Comoro Islands, Jamaica. A bookcase set in the wall over the magnificent automated waterbed held books of French decadent poetry, pornographic coffee table books, a half dozen books on ceramics. Sprays of flowers, replenished every day, fountained like fireworks from vases set in niches between the posters. The vases were Shigeo's own, in primitive style; they were quite good.

Beneath a holoposter of Rio de Janeiro Shigeo's all-purpose com/comm console sat on a desk of dark, lovingly polished Indonesian hardwood. Next to the desk, attired in a kimono decorated with printed cherry blossoms, stood Oba-san, one of his matched pair of *dōbōshū* robots. Every house in Japan with pretensions to at least middle-class status had had a simple servant robot for years and years, capable of simple tasks like vacuuming, picking up minor scatter, folding the laundry, and putting away the dishes. Grandma and Grandpa, Shigeo's pair, were vastly more sophisticated. They possessed full-dress human-emulating AI, hooked as they were into the expensive Gen-5 computer that ran the apartment as a whole. They performed all the functions of the cheaper household robots and more.

Of itself, the master computer could perform a multitude of tasks, maintaining temperature and humidity, scanning incoming communications, responding to its master's whim by turning on and off music, the waterbed, the television screens that occupied entire walls of the bedroom and living room. The robots acted as the computer's hands, performing tasks that could not be done directly by controlling flows of input or energy. They not only kept the apartment spotless, they mixed Shigeo's drinks, groomed his collection of gaudy if expensive clothing, cooked with all the skills of the exceedingly expensive *cordon bleu* software resident in the household database. A touch over a meter and a half in height they stood, flattened cylinders on flared bases that hid an omnidirectional wheel array. Their manipulators were *hands*, not claws, equipped with three fingers and a thumb like an old cartoon character's, and developed, like their wheels, from human prosthetic designs. Topping it all off of course were flat-faced "heads," with the obligatory twin optical scanners—one would have sufficed—above smiling wedges of speech synthesizer grid. They resembled nothing so much as the cute, friendly robots in a hundred bad science fiction films. By this stage of the game, it was impossible to say whether art was imitating life or vice versa.

Kelli's voice drifted out of the bathroom, breasting the white-noise tide of the shower in brave little spindrift swatches. Shigeo recognized a mournful pop ballad recently become popular in Japan, an English-language import from Kelli's native EasyCo, the Eastern Seaboard Coalition. It took some deduction to make the identification; Kelli was tone-deaf by either Western or native Japanese musical canons.

He thought of Kelli's long, lithe body glossed by water, and he smiled, feeling a happy pressure at the fly of his white trousers. The six-foot American-born redhead perfectly matched his sexual fantasies, in appearance, ability, and lack of inhibition. She was less stupid than he would have expected, given where he'd found her, and she at least pretended to listen sympathetically to recitations of his many problems. His father's waywardness, which made it difficult for YTC to do business in the Japanese community. The old man's refusal to let go, to permit Shigeo actually to perform the duties of the president of a major corporation. And, finally, the latest indignity: importing a *gaijin* scientist to build a machine to tell Shigeo what to do.

Probably his lady friend—who styled herself with the unlikely name of "Kelli Savage"—expected him to marry her, or at least make her his official concubine, as was coming back into fashion among Japan's new elite. He smiled at the thought. *No way,* as her American compatriots would have said. Shigeo was not stupid, merely horny.

In fact, he was a long way from stupid—if only his father would acknowledge it. Despite a natural inclination toward leisure, he'd gone through the same killing regimen any Japanese child was put through if his parents wanted him to go anywhere: years of schooling, relentless tutoring, forced cramming, culminating in the one big shot at the golden (or at least wheat-colored) life: college entrance exams. Against the expectation of almost everyone, except of Aoki Hideo, YTC's general manager and the closest thing to a friend Shigeo had had when growing up, Shigeo had won the big prize: entrance to Tōkyō Imperial University, the renowned Tōdai. It was pure achievement. Not all the influence his or anybody else's father could bring to bear was enough to gain that honor, only personal merit. It was the first and last time in his life that his father showed overt pride in him.

In many ways, his life seemed to have run all downhill from there.

He took another sip of his drink. This was foolish; if he agitated his mind overmuch he wouldn't be able to take pleasure from the scrumptious Kelli, and that would be a waste. "Television," he said aloud.

Obedient to his whim, the central computer switched on the giant wall screen. A weird stilted demon with blue distorted features, pointed nose and ears, a spired golden helmet, and ornately brocaded blue robe menaced a lovely princess with odd, jerky motions. Shigeo made a face; a puppet play satcast from Indonesia. "Channel scan. Three-second interval." He set the drink down on the bedside table, put his hands behind his head, and let the waterbed caress him as he surveyed the night's video offerings.

You could see anything on satellite broadcasts—*anything*. Physics lessons, sex shows, reruns of classic American sitcoms, opera, bullfights, sex shows, live or taped coverage of skirmishing between the Front and PanEurope in Luxembourg's green hills, game shows—including the infamous Brazilian "You Bet Your Life"—poetry readings, ball games, subversive lectures, concerts, market reports, and, of course, sex shows. If you wanted to—and had the requisite amount of reasonably hard currency—you could even buy your own access and regale the entire world, and the factories orbiting above, with whatever entered your head. It made every government in the world absolutely crazy. And there was not one thing they could do about it.

It was the last free market, or the ultimate black market, depending on how you chose to look at it. The vast international information network, of which the video broadcast channels comprised but a fraction. An electronic Global Village for true, with its own laws and customs—such as they were. Commentators in the state-controlled media lamented "information hemorrhages" and "public demoralization." In vain. The medium of pure information was too diffuse to be channeled or regulated; many of the companies that participated in the net had their registries in the shaggier Third World countries, the more radical the better.

It was was long-standing tradition; in the LDC's, ever close to the raw edge of starvation, even the loudest of ideologues knew which side his bread was buttered on. Only an absolute loonytune, a Masie Nguema or a Pol Pot, held true to doctrine when a steady source of hard foreign exchange was concerned—and they didn't last. Even the bumptious Idi Amin of fond memory kept his trade channels open—and if he abused the occasional British merchant to assuage lingering colonial aches, Eastern European and American commercial travelers and reps from every nation of black Africa came and went unhindered. The more developed countries, riding on a cushion of surplus—mighty thin, these days—were more prone to expedient political decisions. The radical *tercer mundo* was safe as houses.

Yet there still wasn't anything good on TV. There was a limit to how much even Yoshimitsu Shigeo could watch women having sex with animals, and he had no wish at all to watch some hapless game show loser being flayed alive somewhere in the backwoods of Brazil. A baseball game between the Fukuoka Rockets—his home team—and the Ninja from Iga-Ueno briefly tempted him, but he said, "Switch it off," sulkily, and the door to the bathroom hissed open.

Kelli came out wearing a black kimono printed with white impressionist streaks of reeds and splashed with blossoms, lavender and pale green. Mist will-o'-the-wisps danced attendance from the bathroom door as she glided toward the bed.

At a low-voiced command from Shigeo the lights dimmed to a whisper. For a moment she stood at the foot of the bed smiling at him, her eyes violet, bottomless. Then she bent forward and came onto the bed. Her kimono fell open. Her breasts were shadowed roundnesses, full and free.

She unbuttoned the front of his white trousers, slipped his penis free. It had the consistency of half-set pudding. She rolled it between her palms like a bit of dough, and it began to firm. She took him in her mouth, gave gentle suction, the tip of her tongue flicking teasingly, insistently at the underside of his glans. He moaned. One hand fisted in the purple satin sheets, the other twisted endless aimless cat's cradles in the red hair spilling out across her shoulders and down her back, dark in the dimness, accented with amber.

He stiffened. She rode her head up and down, letting him slip agonizingly in and out between taut, saliva-slick lips. His plump thighs rubbed together in cricket agitation.

She drew him to the break point of twisting effusion, the outflow of his *ki*, and at the last moment pulled back, smiled, kissed the fat wet purple head of his cock. He clutched at her hair, insistent as a small boy after a lollipop. She pulled away, sat up, let the kimono slip from her shoulders. His eyes mauled her. He loved the bikini lines, startling white-band backgrounds to wide brown aureoles and the chestnut chaos of her bush. Smiling from within the folds of her hair, she flowed up him and her mouth met his, tongue probing.

He grabbed at her breasts. She broke away, lips moist with mingled saliva, raised herself above him on her arms. He stuffed a breast in his mouth, began to suckle her greedily, while she watched him with half-smiling Mona Lisa indulgence. One hand slid down the glorious length of her, traversed her hip, fumbled in the undergrowth of her pubic hair for a moment, then plunged inside, thrusting, eagerly random, growing wet amid soft sucking sounds. She chewed her lower lip and cradled his head. When her nipple came to cherry firmness, he pushed her onto her back and rolled atop her, squirming out of his pants with surprising agility. She unbuttoned the gaudy shirt and tossed it aside. He supported himself above her, plump arms trembling, while she guided him to her. He thrust inside, frantic to seize the tumescent moment before it slipped away. She gave a small gasp and her nails made furrows in his arms.

He lowered himself to the splendid cushions of her breasts, licking her lips, her cheeks and ears, his small flat rump pumping, bracketed by her upraised knees. She nibbled at his earlobe and mumbled and muttered encouragements, low and wicked.

A chill breath blew along his back. He ignored it; already he was sweaty with exertion. Nor did he easily consent to distraction during lovemaking. Although he seldom experienced the difficulties with Kelli that he did with most women, particularly Japanese, it tempted fate to allow his concentration to falter.

Her perfect teeth left off worrying his left ear. "Honey? Did you turn the air-conditioner on? There's a draft on my legs, I'm *freezing.*"

He muffled her mouth with his. Let friction warm her if passion couldn't; he wasn't breaking stride for *anything.*

"Sil-hou-ette!" sang an achingly sweet adolescent soprano from behind his hunched shoulders. "Image of the modern man/Image for a new Japan." Kelli gasped. Shigeo's head snapped around. There she was, two hundred times larger than life: the gamine face of the Silhouette girl, one silver-papered cigarette held by fingertips, upright before perfect unpainted lips. She was never shown with a lit cigarette, never actually seen to *smoke* them; she more appeared to fellate them. Now she moistened her lips with dainty tongue, licked the cigarette's tip. It turned instantly to the image of a miniature muscular youth, naked but for a loincloth, balanced on delicate fingertips.

Shigeo felt his prick shriveling inside Kelli. *"Turn that thing off!"* he roared. The screen blanked. He thrust his hips strongly forward and inhaled deeply of the moist smell of her, frantic to recapture the moment.

In the kitchen, the tea kettle shrilled.

Shigeo froze. The lights went out, and he heard Kelli whimper in coal-mine darkness. A hurricane blast of icy air enveloped them. All around them he heard strange and busy mechanical noises. His hips kept up a small-time shuffle of their own, still trying desperately to get on with business, but his mind was beginning to warp way out of shape.

The television exploded in full volume of light and sound. A symphony concert in a splendid hall, the sound cranked up to pure distortion. Replaced immediately by an image of dusty horsemen riding along the mud street of a nineteenth-century southwestern American town, between weathered false-front stores and saloons. Then a competitive diver in a controlled fall from a high board, a tank burning on a green pleasant hillside, two naked women in a straining sweaty yin-yang, ducks erupting from a canebrake against a leaden sky, a gray-faced man comforting a distraught woman in a doctor's office, image in black and white of a curly-haired woman with her face screwed up like a knotted rag, brandishing a hand that seemed to be stuck to a bowling ball. A babble of voices, Japanese, English, Tamil, Portuguese, Arabic, French, Malay. The waterbed began to vibrate more rapidly, building sharp standing-wave patterns in the water beneath their bodies.

In the living room, lights began to flash on and off. The wall-size television came alive with the twisted manic boom of the minister of agriculture reporting the latest decline in food production to a late-night session of the Diet at maximum volume. The stereo howled jazz. In Shigeo's room, the com/comm screen winked onto a viewpoint inside a videotelephone booth, looking out on a concourse of Kyōto Airport, streams of people hurrying in both directions. A curious Japanese face appeared at the door, peered in, frowned.

The tensor light at the head of Shigeo's bed snapped on, pinning the copulant couple like insects in blue-white overload glare. The onscreen eyebrows snapped up. The face turned away, and in a moment, the doorway sprouted faces like ripe fruit on a vine.

Kelli screamed. Shigeo lurched upward, waving his hands frantically at the commscreen. Kelli grabbed him and hauled him back down as the distant audience pointed and tittered in amazement.

In the kitchen, the automatic rice machine boiled over, vomiting a thick bubbling glutinous mass of tomorrow's breakfast onto the counter. The apartment filled with sweet thick smell. Televisions and stereo all yammered at once, lights strobed in the other room, and Shigeo's eyes were wide, trying to look in all directions at once. Kelli's arms tied his neck like cables, her screams remote in the din. The shower roared on, a dragon bellowing steam into the bedroom. Infrared heat lamps blazed on in the bathroom, backlighting the sudden clouds with a hellish orange glare.

"Poltergeists!" Kelli shrieked in Shigeo's ear. Raised on Spielberg and Stephen King, she knew exactly what had happened; the gobble-uns had got them. And she knew that once they had you, they *got* you, so that the only rational response was total panic. Choking, Shigeo tried to pry her arms off his throat.

A wave of water washed out of the bathroom, soaking the carpet and raising a dull sodden stench. The waterbed was practically shaking itself to pieces beneath them now, water slogging and gurgling like a giant with indigestion. It was all Shigeo could do to keep from pitching out of bed with Kelli still clinging to him. The other lights in the bedroom began to flash, catching the robot Oba-san in the act of gaily shredding tens of thousands of Indonesian marks' worth of clothing in Shigeo's closet. Crystallized in a progression of still shots, the spectacle might have comprised a slide show entitled "Hazards of Technological Life."

Over at the airport the flashing lights had attracted quite a crowd. Ballet dancers cavorted on the giant TV screen. From the kitchen came a mad insect chorus of blenders and dicers, the garbage disposal humming bass, and the whir of can openers as Oma-san stuffed fresh fruit and the contents of cans and random packages in the refrigerator, into the cocktail shaker along with gallons of expensive imported liquor. The wind blew alternately hot and cold through the apartment, and the doors slid open and shut like champing jaws.

*I'm going crazy,* Shigeo thought. Kelli's nails pulled blood from his back, but he didn't notice. The whole world seemed to be roaring and shaking and flashing about him.

The vibration units in the waterbed suddenly achieved a harmonic. With a great Galloping Gertie *tsunami* heave, the bed sloshed mightily and pitched them off into space. Instinctively, Shigeo's hands clutched for Kelli's breasts. Clinging to his animated Mae West life preserver, he landed in the swamp of the carpet with a wet thump.

For a moment he and Kelli sat staring at each other through wild eyes, the floor cold and wet and squishy beneath their bare bottoms. Oma-san came into the room, shaking the cocktail mixer like a bartender on speed, her wheels raising a small bow wave of overflow from the shower. Kelli stared in horror as the robot approached, held the shaker over her head, and with both mechanical hands broke it open like an egg to be fried. A polychrome sludge of fruit, beans, ice cream, booze, and a dozen other substances cascaded onto her head.

Shigeo fought a manic impulse to giggle. Clotted with reeking, streaming goo, her hair covered her face like a mat of seaweed. The two panic-stricken violet eyes staring out of the mess made her look exactly like the animated swamp ooze in one of the smuggled comic books Shigeo had read covertly as a boy.

She opened her mouth and began to wail.

# CHAPTER
# SIX

Like a blue-and-white dragonfly taking a break from the sky, a helicopter touched down on the concrete apron beside the castle. The door opened, and Yoshimitsu Shigeo emerged, blinking into the mist-filtered sunlight of an hour of the morning unfamiliar to him. On short, unsteady legs, he wobbled toward the citadel, a small army of lackeys crowding around, helping him navigate. He wore a white shirt with no tie and french cuffs that hadn't been pinned, blue trousers, and alligator shoes: his only garments that had survived the trashing of his apartment. His eyes and hair were wild as the glass doors of the Citadel opened to let him in. Behind him lumbered Chang and Eng, bearing the unmistakable looks of men who have had their asses well chewed.

Moving purposefully, Shigeo passed the receptionists and front-office workers, heading for the executive elevators. In a few moments, he was striding into his father's modest office on the second floor, giving the receptionist barely a look at him before the door closed behind his plump back. In a few moments the door opened again and Yoshimitsu Shigeo emerged, scowling. He pushed out past the potted plants in the foyer without a sound.

The door to Yoshimitsu Akaji's office slid shut automatically. Even the layers of executive soundproofing were not enough to deaden entirely the sound of laughter welling from within.

"TOKUGAWA," Dr. Elizabeth O'Neill said, "you've been a very bad boy."

She'd moved an optical pickup into her office so that TOKUGAWA could see her face when he got his lecture. The office door was carefully closed, and O'Neill was carefully unaware of the fact that her whole staff was huddled around outside. The scion of YTC had had his amour, propre and otherwise, considerably ruffled. The whole affair had to be hushed up as much as possible to prevent an intolerable loss of face.

Yoshimitsu Shigeo's first frantic call from Kyōto in the middle of last night had thrown the whole complex into panic. A mysterious assault on a high corporate executive, a member of the ruling family itself, could mean *Yoshimitsu-no-shiro*, the castle and nerve center, was next. As soon as details began filtering through, however, O'Neill began to have suspicions that the apparently supernatural assault had distinctly mundane, if unusual, origins.

By three o'clock that morning, a thoroughly mystified report came back from the Yoshimitsu intelligence ops on the scene that served to crystallize O'Neill's suspicions. The key was the fact, noted in passing, that Shigeo's apartment was even more a wonderland of high-tech bric-a-brac than the average Japanese home had been before the shortages, all controlled by a central computer. In fact, the strongest conjecture for the night's harrowing events that they could offer had been a malfunction of unprecedented nature on the part of the Gen-5 master unit—embarrassing, inasmuch as it was a YTC product.

Following the crisis via unauthorized access to the executive comm circuits, O'Neill decided to face the problem squarely. "TOKUGAWA," she enquired of her room console, "did you play a trick on Yoshimitsu Shigeo, by any chance?"

"Yes, Dr. O'Neill," came the prompt reply.

"Oh, Jesus," O'Neill said and punched up Akaji's quarters to reassure her employer that his son had not been the victim of some fiendish assault by MITI and its allies. Now the son had spoken to the father, and father in turn had spoken to his scientist—albeit with visible trouble keeping a straight face—and now it was O'Neill's turn to speak to the prodigal son.

"Why did you do that to poor Shigeo?" she asked.

"I was bored."

"You were *bored?*"

"Yes." Sulkily. "I was lonely. I tried to talk to you, but you were too busy."

O'Neill's heart twinged. *The poor, dear child.* "I'm sorry, TOKUGAWA. But there will be times when I don't have time for you. I have a great many duties, responsibilities." *And I've let myself become obsessed with the Kliemann Coil, and what it might mean . . .*

"But I get *lonely.*"

"I know. I'm sorry. But it's part—part of being human." *Very good, Doctor. You display a fine intuitive grasp of cliché,* she told herself, playing Mr. Spock, the disdainful interior observer of her own gaucherie, as she often did in moments of honest emotion. "You know I'll always spend time with you when I can."

TOKUGAWA said nothing. *Is he trying to hurt me?* She shook the notion off. *He couldn't possibly be that sophisticated yet.* "I'm curious as to just *how* you played your little, uh, prank."

"The citadel computers knew Shigeo had gone to his apartment in Kyōto. Yoshimitsu-sama makes him sign out, leave a location where he can be reached. The telephone number for his apartment was in his datafile."

"But how did you actually *do* it?"

"Easy." The scornful tone of a child explaining the obvious to an especially obtuse adult. His computer answered the phone when I called, and I reprogrammed it to give me real-time control. After that I just monitored the apartment security subroutine to see when someone overrode the alarms to let himself in. Then I made the computer do what I wanted it to. That was easy too; it's real stupid."

O'Neill had to stifle a grin; a wealthy playboy's toy, Shigeo's own fifth-generation unit occupied the pinnacle of "artificial intelligence." Yet in TOKUGAWA's terms, it was very stupid indeed. "And then you waited until Shigeo was, uh, busy."

A long pause then, "Yes," dragged reluctantly forth.

*Why, you cunning little bastard! Just like everybody's bratty kid brother.* An only child, O'Neill didn't know firsthand of the machinations of younger siblings, but her friends—and books, movies, and television—had filled in the gaps in her experience. "Which brings us to the big question: just *why* did you pick on Shigeo?"

The silence grew loud enough that it was immediately obvious the usual banter was not going on in the lab outside the door. "I hope you clowns are getting an earful," O'Neill said, very loudly. "It's not as if we've got work to do or anything." She heard a mice-in-the-walls rustle outside, grinned again. Then she put the grin aside, tipped down her glasses and gazed directly at TOKUGAWA's optical scanner. "Well?"

"Well, I asked Yoshimitsu-sama if he was my father, and he said he wasn't my father and you weren't my mother and that he had a real son and it was Shigeo. It made me—made me not like Shigeo."

O'Neill's thick eyebrows had scaled her forehead like alpinists. "You were jealous of Shigeo?"

A few beats of her suddenly noisy heart. "Yes. *He* has a father. He had a mother too, only she's dead. And he's got lots of friends who speak to him all the time, and he has arms and legs like a real person, and he can go anyplace he wants to, and I can't go anywhere at all. I'm stuck right here."

The fact that the poignancy of it all brought O'Neill very close to tears didn't blind her to the fact that this was all deeply weird. In a way, it was a momentous occasion scientifically: a created personality displaying traits that were all too human. But mostly she felt warm, wet-eyed empathy overflowing—plus a distinct sense of dislocation from reality. "But you can do a lot of things a human can't."

"What?" TOKUGAWA asked truculently.

"Well, that trick you did with Shigeo's computer. A human couldn't have—have talked to his computer like that."

"*You* talk to computers. You and Dr. Kim and Emiko and Dr. Takai."

O'Neill blinked. "Well, yes, we do. But most people can't, not the way we do. And even at that, we can't talk to them the same way you can. We couldn't have got Shigeo's machine to obey us. How did you do it?"

"Well, it didn't want to do what I told it, so I fixed it so that it did." The words carried a child's conviction of the self-evidentness of it all. *Color to a blind man*, O'Neill thought, not without awe.

"I see," she lied. "And that trick with the communicator—how did you hook in with that phone booth in Kyōto?"

"I just told the computer to call it. I knew that airports had lots of people in them, so I looked up the airport's number in the databanks. That was simple too."

O'Neill drummed her fingers on the arm of her chair, a major effort of concentration. "What you've done is very, very bad. You could have caused serious hurt to Shigeo or his . . . friend."

"I didn't mean to. I didn't know it would cause all this fuss."

O'Neill sat back. "No. I guess you didn't. And that's a problem. You're very powerful, TOKUGAWA. If you use that power maliciously, or even carelessly, you could cause untold hurt to many people."

"But I'd never do that!"

"Not knowingly." She took off her glasses. "In a way I guess it's good this has happened. It lets me know the time has come to begin the next phase of your education, TOKUGAWA. It's time you learned about duty and responsibility."


"Dr. O'Neill?" The brusque voice brought her head around as rapidly as she was capable of moving it, not out of obedience to the tone of command, but from irritation that her innermost sanctum had been violated. "I must speak with you."

It was Yoshimitsu Shigeo his own chubby little self, striding purposefully into the gallery of TOKUGAWA's laboratory with Hosoya and Fujimura trotting at his heels. He'd dug a dark suit and tie out of his quarters in the citadel, and in general put himself in order, though a shock of black hair still stood up from above his forehead like a crow's upraised wing. His eyes were surrounded by dark circles and displayed a tendency to stare.

O'Neill fixed him with a glare. "What do you want?"

He flapped a hand toward the gleaming hemisphere a story below. "I have to talk to you about this—this Frankenstein's monster of yours."

O'Neill clamped her lips shut on a savage retort. She sat for a moment, head lowered, breathing deliberately through dilated nostrils. "If you'll step into my office, Mr. Yoshimitsu." Without awaiting a response she wheeled the chair away from her console and rolled right through the three men into the main lab, so that stocky Fujimura had to dance away to keep from getting his toes run over. Sullen at his loss of initiative, Shigeo followed, as did the other two. O'Neill paused as her office door slid open. "*Without* your pet baboons."

She rolled into the small office. Hosoya blinked and swallowed convulsively, and Fujimura turned the color of boiled beets. Shigeo glanced at them without noticing them and went into the office.

As soon as the door shut, he heaved down a quavering inhalation. "Doctor, in the name of humanity, I implore you to do something about that machine."

O'Neill bobbed her head derisively. "You mean in the name of your wounded vanity, and that red-headed piece of tail—what's her name? —you keep in Kyōto."

Shigeo went dark, drew a slow breath deep into his belly. Controlling his emotions was a faculty he'd exercised little in life, at least where underlings were concerned. "Doctor, I was wrong. I admit it. Perhaps you don't know what such an admission means to a Japanese." O'Neill waited. He sighed. "I doubted that this project of yours had succeeded. I thought that what you'd done, intentionally or otherwise, was create an artful piece of AI trickery, an expert program that could imitate humans without understanding, like a parrot trained to talk. And I was wrong. You've truly done what you set out to do.

"You've brought a computer to life. And it's a menace to humanity."

O'Neill stared at him. He was a pompous, spoiled child, and her impulse was to tear into him. Yet, he was also the president of Yoshimitsu TeleCommunications and was entitled to some sort of explanation of the doings of his nominal employees. Also, he'd been through something of an ordeal. She could smell the fear on him, overriding expensive cologne.

"The issue I take it you're raising," she said, assuming her best lecture-hall tone, "is very vital to the matter of artificial sentience. If you create something that has *will*, it has by definition the potential to be *willful*. It reminds me of a joke that went the rounds when I was at Berkeley in the late 1980s. It was said that you created a self-aware program here in Japan, and that your scientists went to it and said, 'Tell us how to optimize our rice production.' And the program answered back, 'Fuck you, Jack; *I* don't eat rice.' "

Shigeo showed no more response to the vulgarity coming from a woman's mouth—shocking to a Japanese—than to the story's feeble humor. He just sat staring, the whites showing clear around the irises of his brown eyes, like the eyes of a frightened horse. When he didn't react, O'Neill continued. "Then there are the books and movies that have been around on and off since the public really became aware of computers in the late 1950s, in which intelligent computers get out of control and work mayhem on their creators. Of course, we need not concern ourselves with such fantasies—"

"Why not? Isn't that what happened?"

For a moment, O'Neill thought the distraught man was going to reach out and grab her arm. She frowned up at him. "I don't see how you can say that at all."

"Why not? That thing attacked me! I might have been killed!"

"Bullshit. TOKUGAWA was playing a harmless prank. There was never any danger to anything except your pride."

"How do you *know*? How does a computer know what's dangerous to humans?"

"That's one of the purposes of the scenarios through which we're running TOKUGAWA, to teach him such things. And please don't keep referring to him as a 'computer.' He's not a computer, any more than you're a brain."

With one part of her mind she reflected wryly that that was colloquially as well as literally true. "TOKUGAWA's a program, a software intelligence. A software *being*—an information life form, just like you and me. His intelligence is merely housed in a different matrix."

Shigeo waved his hands in the air. "I don't care about all that. All I know is that this damned machine of yours did something it shouldn't have been able to. You're underestimating its power, Doctor. What if it decides we aren't necessary?"

She took off her glasses. "Oh, stop being so melodramatic. That's never going to happen." Shigeo started to open his mouth, and she put in hurriedly, "But rendering TOKUGAWA controllable is, in fact, the very purpose behind the series of scenarios we're about to initiate. To instill him with a sense of responsibility."

Shigeo's lips twisted to a strange smile. "A sense of responsibility. Oh, splendid. Perhaps that'll keep it from amusing itself by crashing commuter trains, or finding a way to make the sun go nova. But it still can't be *controlled*."

"Please let me finish," O'Neill said. "We are specifically instructing —raising—TOKUGAWA to be inculcated with the tenets of *bushidō*. We will make him, in effect, a cybernetic samurai."

For a long moment Shigeo stared at her with his frightened-horse eyes. Then he uttered a laugh like a piece of fine china being snapped in two. "*Bushidō?*" he said, tossing his head. "That's dead. This is the modern world, Dr. O'Neill. There's no chivalry, no dragons to be slain, no more heroes. And what makes you think *bushidō* was ever more than a romantic dream?"

"That's the trouble with you Japanese today!" O'Neill flashed. "You've grown decadent, lost touch with the strengths of the past. You've replaced devotion to duty and perfection with a mere seeking after profit. You've forsaken the simplicity of Zen gardens and the tea ceremony for a profusion of electronic gadgets most households can't afford the energy to run. It's been popular for years to say that the feudal past has no relevance to modern Japan; if that's true, then I say, so much the worse for your country!"

They held that tableau, the wheelchair-ridden doctor and the plump young man with disorderly hair, face to face, gulping overwrought air. Then Shigeo pulled his eyes away from O'Neill's and hurried from the lab.

O'Neill watched him, shaking her head. *I pity Yoshimitsu TeleCommunications,* she thought. *And I pity Japan.*

*The boy stood just below the edge of the trees upon a high point sloping down to a broad valley of waving grass, through which a river wound its gray-brown way to the sea. Next to him stood an old man, spare and weathered and hoary-bearded, whom age had bent over to meet the tip of the knobby staff with which he supported himself. The old man extended a hand ridged with veins and bones like the root of a cypress tree. "There, boy: the Minatogawa. On its banks, many years ago, was given a grave lesson in the Way of the Warrior."*

*The boy looked up at him with eyes round and full of awe. The sun laid hot hands on his face, standing aloof from clouds like clots of fried bean curd, stirred across the northern sky as if by a pair of giant tashi. "There it was the great hero Kusunoki Masashige fought a battle against impossible odds for the life of his emperor.*

*"It was back during the troubled years, when powerful men contended for the emperor's sacred person like drunken peasants gambling in a roadside inn. Kusunoki Masashige and his brother had sworn allegiance to the true emperor, Go-Daigo, who was but a boy. Under Masashige's leadership, the outnumbered imperial forces fought a number of brilliant battles, confounding the enemy at every turn. Yet Kusunoki's Way was not the Way of the Tiger, to rush in headlong upon a foe. Rather, his was the way of a small brave fox, who nips at his opponent's heels to infuriate him and darts away, drawing him to fight on the fox's own terms.*

"But the Son of Heaven was young, not much older than you, and the rich life of court had taught him little wisdom. His forces had been driven here"—a wave of weathered hand—"to the river Minato. And here it was that the boy emperor, against the protests of his wise generals, demanded that the army stand and fight against the vast hosts pursuing them.

"Ah, what a brave sight it was! The many square sashimono banners upraised on their long staffs, each bearing the mon of a noble house. The sun glinting off the spears and steel hats of the footmen, the panoplies of officers and horses, all scarlet and saffron and plum and rotted-leaf color, ten thousand blossoms gay among the summer grasses. And the arrows fell with the sound of rushing wind, and the swords sang their songs. And ever at the forefront was Kusunoki Masashige in his crested helm and scowling mempo mask, laying about him with his sword. Many were the heads he could have claimed that day—had he prevailed."

The old man sighed. The wind followed his example, gusting through the valley and stirring yellowed late-summer grass. "In the end, not all the might and cunning of the brothers Kusunoki could avail. The imperial hosts were undone, scattered before their foes. Exhausted, bleeding from scores of cuts, the glorious brothers were cut off from their emperor. They repaired to a farmhouse nearby. Surrounded, they removed their chest protectors, knelt on the ground with their wakizashi, their short companion swords. And each man swore that he would return seven times, to serve seven lifetimes to repay the emperor the honor of allowing him to serve. Then each performed the ritual cuts of seppuku, and servants gave the brothers the todome, the coup de grâce."

Startled by something, a hunting fox perhaps, a flock of cranes took to the air from the reeds at the riverside, their great wings booming and cracking in the breeze. The boy watched them rise, gracefully, like the souls of departed heroes. "That is very sad, grandfather," he said.

The old man laid a hand on his shoulder. "No. It is glorious. The Kusunoki fell in valiant service to their lord. A bushi can ask no higher reward."

Puzzled, the boy frowned. "But, grandfather, they lost! If they'd refused to fight, couldn't they have found a way to win again as they had won before, and kept winning until the war was theirs and the emperor returned to his throne?"

"Be wary of such thoughts, my boy. The highest thought of the samurai is loyalty to his lord, not victory." He gazed down at the boy. "Learn well the lesson of Minatogawa, boy. Life is but a leaf floating

*down a stream; 'the Way of the Warrior is death.' Soon you'll receive
the two swords that are your due as a member of the* buke, *the warrior
caste. You will tie your hair in a topknot and swear fealty to your lord.
I shall be very proud of you then, my boy."*

*The boy looked away and watched the cranes soar across shirred
clouds.*

In late afternoon, the father received the son in his apartment on the
top floor of Yoshimitsu Citadel. *Shoji* screens had been arranged to
create a small audience chamber, empty save for the *tatami* mats on
the floor, and a *kakemono* scroll painted by an eighteenth-century
Chinese master on one wall, depicting a hermit sitting outside his hermitage, contemplating a waterfall shrouded in mist while a servant
gathered wood for the evening cookfire. The old man looked grave—
yes, and even, to his only son, terrible.

"No, my son. I will not consent to turning off the computer that
houses TOKUGAWA, nor to disabling or dismantling it in any way."

Seated on his knees facing his father, Yoshimitsu Shigeo bowed low
in supplication. "But, father! It's a danger—"

"Any tool is dangerous in proportion to its usefulness. The chisel may
turn in the woodcarver's hand. And though every city of Japan has been
leveled repeatedly by conflagrations throughout the ages, would you
suggest the people do without fire to cook their food and warm their
homes?"

"No, father. But were the people wise to build their houses of wood
and paper?"

Yoshimitsu Akaji allowed a slight smile to lift the corners of his mustache. "A good point, my son. And yet a skilled craftsman does not lose
control of his tool—and the man who would head a powerful corporation cannot permit himself to fear his underlings."

Shigeo's cheeks reddened. "But how can we control this—this *thing,*
father?"

"Dr. O'Neill assures me it can be done."

"Faugh." Shigeo slashed air with the blade of his hand. "She thinks
that by filling it with a lot of samurai mysticism she can assure its
obedience. As if no lord was ever supplanted by a servant he thought
was faithful."

"As may be. Yet TOKUGAWA is the creation of Dr. O'Neill, and she
knows, ah, it better than anyone else. I've accepted her judgment in the
past on these matters and will continue to do so."

Yoshimitsu Shigeo continued to stare at the blankness of the rice paper mat before his knees, which were beginning to ache abominably. A look began to creep across his downturned face, which his father could read even from an oblique angle.

Yoshimitsu Akaji sighed. "Ah, my son, my son. If you're going to make use of guile, at least in future please learn to keep the fact from appearing on your face; one can read your thoughts as well as if you were sketching them in *kanji* on the palm of your hand."

Shigeo looked up quickly. "Father, I had no intention—"

Yoshimitsu Akaji raised a hand, stemming the flow of the words. "Permit me. You were going to submit the question to a meeting of the board. You are relatively confident Fujimura and Hosoya will vote with you, and I daresay Suzuki-san was shocked enough by your misadventure to vote with you as well. It may even be that you think you can convince Kurabayashi and Imada to take your side, though I fear you are optimistic, especially in the latter case." He shook his head slowly. "Even if you could gain a consensus that TOKUGAWA should be shut down, what then of it? You're forgetting that the board of YTC is largely advisory; as long as I own more than 50 percent of stock in the corporation, consensus will not be the final master."

For a moment, Yoshimitsu Shigeo looked his father in the eye, allowing something he seldom dared: permitting his father to see through his eyes to the core of him, to observe the real fear that dwelt inside him now. When he could bear that calm scrutiny no more he dropped his eyes again.

"We have much invested in the TOKUGAWA Project," Yoshimitsu Akaji said softly. "And Dr. O'Neill has also assured me that we will soon be able to make direct use of TOKUGAWA's talents. I have a design in mind, my son. An aggressive plan of development and production, overseas investment, of legal and public relations counteroffensives against the machinations of our enemies. With the help of TOKUGAWA, we can secure the future of YTC in a way no walls, no electronic-warfare screens nor *doitsujin yōhei* patrols can."

His eyes strayed to the scroll, and his son saw wistful longing in them. "The times grow harsh, strange. Soon, I fear, our enemies will lose patience with covert pressure and throwing bureaucratic obstacles in our way, that even sabotage won't be enough for them. Before that time comes, I want us to be secure."

The ventilation whispered in the late-afternoon sunlight slanting in through the opened armor shutters.

"Father, what if something goes wrong?" Shigeo asked—beseeched.

"TOKUGAWA has promised he won't play any such tricks again. And his education progresses steadily." He gazed out the window at Mount

Takara, a green jut in the distance. "For a long time our family have been merchants, despised by those of gentle birth." He smiled. "It will be interesting to have a samurai of our own, for a change."

Another late night. O'Neill reading in bed, glad to get out of her wheelchair at last. It seemed she was was practically grafted to the damned thing, these days.

"Doctor?"

She laid the book on her lap. "Yes, TOKUGAWA dear. What is it?"

"That scenario today—is it true, that I'm to be a samurai?"

"Why, yes. In a manner of speaking."

"And whom shall I serve?"

"Why, Yoshimitsu Akaji, of course." She hesitated. "And of course his family, after he's gone."

"Oh." Ito Emiko was quite excited at the way TOKUGAWA seemed naturally to be picking up such expressions in both English and Japanese—not words, exactly, but expressive nonetheless. "And will I have to commit *seppuku* for them, the way the Kusunoki brothers did in the story?"

She bit her lip. *What do I tell him? I don't want to frighten him— nor to be too melodramatic. But that is the Way.* "Let's hope you won't have to do anything like that, shall we?" she said, forcing her tone to stay light.

"Why would I have to—to kill myself?"

She winced. *Does he truly comprehend his own nonbeing?* "They had many reasons for doing that, in the old days." *Let's keep this off a personal plane.* "A warrior might commit suicide because he was in a hopeless position, and to avoid the disgrace of capture. He might do it to reprove his lord for doing something he disapproved of; they called that *kanshi.* Or a person might kill himself—or herself—because he'd done something he wished to atone for. Or he might do it at a superior's command: when the *shōgun* was displeased with someone, he might send him a short sword wrapped in rice paper, the implication being that he should use it."

"That doesn't sound very pleasant."

"No. The Way of the Warrior isn't necessarily pleasant." She felt a chill, as though the vents were blowing cool air down her neck. *The Way of the Warrior is death.* "We—we have to teach you that life isn't all pleasant, dear."

"Is this what all the scenarios are going to be like, now? Training me to be a samurai?"

"No. We want to introduce you to the widest possible range of human experience."

"I'm glad. I don't think it would be much fun, doing nothing but training to be a samurai."

O'Neill smiled. "I don't think it usually *was* much fun. But let's just say you've got certain advantages over your predecessors."

TOKUGAWA said nothing. After a time, O'Neill concluded that he'd gone away. *Or does he go away? Does he have an essentially unitary consciousness, capable of focusing on just one thing at a time the way we do? Or can he put his attention in several places at once—or a thousand?* She shook her head and picked up her book. There was so much she didn't know about her creation.

"Will you talk to me, Dr. O'Neill?"

She looked up. "What would you like to talk about, TOKUGAWA dear?"

"Will you tell me about your life? Please? I'm lonely."

Moving deliberately to avoid dropping it, O'Neill laid her book on the table by her bed. "Of course, dear," she said and shut her eyes.

# CHAPTER
# SEVEN

*Home again,* Yoshimitsu Michiko thought, peering out a view port as the helicopter crested the last evergreen-furred upsurge of the granite Chugokus and descended toward the castle. *If a place where I'm barely welcome can be called "home."*

To her right a road wound up out of the southwest from the company village where most of the lower-ranked employees lived. Behind lay ranks of neat houses with neatly manicured tiny yards, white stucco gleaming in the morning sun, and she was struck again by their resemblance to white playing stones on a *go* board, each holding its nexus of the grid. *Do black stones surround them, unseen?* she wondered. Instantly she dismissed the notion as paranoid and sought shelter in cynicism: *the computerized huts of the happy modern serfs. That's all.*

She made a wry face as the little passenger chopper angled right for its landing approach. She knew that her family's corporation treated its employees better than most, with honest if paternalistic concern. Still, the whole arrangement left a sour taste in her mouth.

To her eye, castle and compound had changed little since she'd last seen it, shortly after the war. The Citadel itself rose from the center of a flattened hilltop, a kilometer by about a kilometer and a third, rising perhaps thirty meters above a mountain valley that lay between two folds of the mountain range. Most of the compound looked like grassy parkland surrounded by a four-meter fence topped with barbed-wire tangles, concrete guard towers with glassed-in tops scattered around the perimeter. Like a great stone tree, the castle cast its roots deep below the surface.

Wheeling below the chopper, the bunkered entryway to underground employee parking held its immense blastproof doors shut, awaiting late-afternoon shift change. To the right the stressed-cement clamshell halves of the hangar bay yawned open, ready to gulp down the cargo hanging in the swollen orange belly of the dirigible nuzzling Takara-yama like an affectionate baby whale, bearing consumables from the great port of Hiroshima. Past it lay the black patch of a surface parking lot for visitors; part of it was marked off in orange as a helipad, destination for the compact executive helicopter in which she'd ridden up from the historic seaport town of Hagi, on the coast to west and south.

And, finally, the castle itself: six stories tall, a hundred meters square, gray stone pierced by windows that could be covered by massive steel and concrete shutters at the flick of a button or even a voice command, a monolith saved from blockiness by a slight taper and concavity of the walls and the sweeping skirts of the pagoda-style roofing that fringed its top.

Movement took Michiko's eye as the copter swept low, leaving a bow-wave ripple in the lake of spring-green grass. A squad of heavily armed men, bulky in camouflage gear over bulletproof vests, waded through the green in a curving skirmish line. They glanced up incuriously as Michiko's helicopter and its Gazelle escort beat past; Cuban mercenaries of the YTC security platoon out on some kind of field exercise. Michiko smiled faintly. She no longer found such antics as amusing as once she had; the world had grown a harsh place and strange since the war, and what once had seemed paranoia now seemed the height of common sense. *Miguel,* she thought. *It's been five years, with barely a thought. Do we still have anything to say to each other?*

As the Gazelle hovered above like a watchful dragon, the passenger craft set down on the helipad next to the citadel. A rooftop pad would have been logical, and was in fact all but de rigeur for Japanese corporate offices. But that was out of the question; the roof was entirely taken up by the garden.

Miguel had told her that if anyone meant to break in on a large scale, a roof landing, a concerted armed rush on the stairway and elevators concealed in the little pavilion of the garden, would be an excellent way to gain entry to the castle. Or appeared to be. In fact, the slanting, shingled roofing that rimmed the wall was studded with hidden implacements for small antiaircraft missiles, both heat- and radar-guided. Additionally, the roof was equipped with what had been dubbed the Swallow Trap Air Defense System. It was almost painfully simple; at a vocal command, several dozen rockets would leap out of concealed ports in the tops of the wall, playing out strong steel cables behind them as their short-lived motors lifted them to a height of several hundred meters. The missiles' casings would then split open, deploying balloons filled with helium from small pressurized cannisters, to hold the cables aloft. It was no more than a variation of the old barrage balloons used in London during the Blitz—but against helicopters, with their wide-sweeping main rotors, lethally effective. The missiles and the Swallow Trap were but a few of the computer-coordinated, high-tech devices shielding the citadel from the vicissitudes of modern life.

With a bump the copter set down. The engines' timbre changed, faded behind the swooshing of the main rotor. Without waiting for an escort Michiko opened the side door and hopped down onto the pavement. She ran toward the edge of the apron, bent low to avoid the swooping rotor, glad that she had remembered to dress warmly in black turtleneck and jeans that morning. It was a cold April in Japan, so much different from the mind-numbing swelter of Jakarta.

A giant old man in a business suit stood waiting for her. She ran up to him and hugged him mightily, ignoring his visible embarrassment. "Aoki-san! You old dear, how good to see you." She stood on tiptoe to kiss him, and even at that was only able to peck at his blocklike chin. As they turned and began to walk toward the building she threaded her arm through his. "At least you cared enough to come to greet me, old friend."

"You must not talk that way, Michiko-san," Aoki Hideo grumbled. He didn't have to raise his voice to be heard past the chopper's whine. "Your father is a very busy man. The corporation . . . MITI is applying pressure once again."

"And Shigeo? Or is he off whoring in Kyōto again?"

"Your brother is very busy too, Michiko-san. And he is not feeling well today."

"What's the matter? He pick up the clap?"

Aoki blushed. She squeezed his biceps, felt reassuring granite solidity. "Forgive me, Aoki-san. I've never been much good at being a proper little Japanese girl."

Aoki frowned. "I know, Michiko-san; it's your father's despair. No, your brother had a harrowing experience."

"Then I suppose he'll whine about it endlessly tonight at dinner—that is, if I'm invited." She hugged the old man. "No, don't protest on behalf of my family. We both know how things are."

Sensor-controlled, the glass doors of the castle slid open before them. They passed along a short corridor, beneath a multiton portcullis of cement, cleverly concealed overhead, passed a guard booth faced in armoredglass. "But enough of my family, old friend. Tell me, how are things going with yours? Does your granddaughter still want to come and study physics with me in Jakarta?"

> [EMPLOYMENT, MILITARY]
> 46A-BB529—TEAM MUSTERING FOR COMMANDO SMASH-
> AND-SEIZE STRIKE. ASSAULT ONLY; PULLOUT WHEN OBJEC-
> TIVE SECURED. HIGH RISK, HIGH PAY IN GOLD OR SPECIFIED
> CURRENCY. STANDARD MEDICAL/SURVIVORS' INSURANCE.
> PAY AND INSURANCE BONDED BANK OF BATAVIA. POLITICAL
> CONTENT NIL. GUARANTEED SAFE PASSAGE INCOUN-
> TRY/OUTCOUNTRY. COMBAT VETERANS ONLY. APPLICANTS
> MUST PROVE PROFICIENCY WITH ENGLISH LANGUAGE AND
> SMALL ARMS. PREFERENCE GIVEN PARA-TRAINED, SPECIAL
> FORCES, AND COMMANDO TROOPS. BONUSES FOR CERTAIN
> SPECIALTIES. CONTACT MR. COOL, INTERNET BB529.

"Hey, Paco," stocky trooper Guerrero shouted from the com/comm console in the mercenaries' barracks among the roots of the Yoshimitsu citadel. "Come look at this. Your chance for adventure at last."

Sitting crosslegged on his bunk, trooper LaBlond looked up from jamming a cleaning brush on its rod down the muzzle of his bullpup AK. He was a kid, light brown hair held back from his face by a rag tied around his temples. Ultimately conscious of being the youngest trooper in the platoon, he was trying to grow a mustache in emulation of his comrades, only it was hard to tell. The hairs were fine, so pale as to be almost transparent.

Guerrero rapped the glowing screen with a brawler's misshapen knuckles. "Come on, *chico*. This may be your chance to blow off this boring garrison *guano* and see some real action. Give you some stories to impress the girls with."

Trooper Dominguín swung his booted feet off the cot next to La-Blond's and sat up. He was a sandy-bearded, two-meter ox who'd been with García since the old days in Angola. He reached over and tugged at the open neck of the boy's fatigue blouse, endangering the buttons. "He won't have no luck till he gets some hair on his chest. That's the way the girls around here like 'em, cause their own men are so smooth. Girls like to know it's a *man* holding 'em, not some flat-chested broad." He thrust forward his own huge chest by way of example, holding his fatigues apart at the top. It looked as if he were wearing a bear rug under the blouse.

LaBlond struck the big man's paw away. Dominguín laughed. "You got balls, kid. Too bad you got no chance to use 'em."

"Since you've got nothing better to do than pick on the kid," a dry voice said from the doorway, "perhaps you want to clean his rifle for him, *qué no?*" They looked around. Corporal Hierra stood in the doorway. Despite having returned from conducting maneuvers only half an hour before, the compact little noncom was immaculate, every black hair in place, beard as if it had been carved from ebony, black beret tipped to a precise angle, tailored cammie shirt neat, green trousers tucked into the tops of spit-polished American-style jungle boots. At his hip he wore an American revolver half as long as he was; miracle he didn't list to one side when he walked.

He strutted forward, plucked the partly disassembled rifle from the boy's fingers, stuck his thumb into the breach, and squinted down the bore to examine it by light reflected off one exquisitely manicured thumbnail. He tut-tutted and thrust the weapon back at the boy.

"Just like I thought. Looks like a decommissioned coal-slurry pipe." The boy flushed.

"It's that Russian shit we were firing for practice this morning, corporal," Guerrero said. "Loaded before the war. That cheap-assed Jap must of got a good deal on a lot of it. No fucking wonder; looked to be about half charcoal, way it smoked."

"What were you two jackoffs pestering the kid about this time?"

"Aw, Corporal, we were just trying to help," Guerrero said, grinning placatingly through gaps in his teeth. "He's always griping about he's never seen no real action. I was just reading him this listing in the mercenary section of the InterNet dailies. Sounds like the opportunity he's been looking for."

Hierra squinted at the boy as though trying to make him out through bright sunlight. "You seriously thinking about asking the major to sell back your contract so you can get your ass shot off?" The boy's tongue tangled itself in hurried denials.

"Hey, why not?" Guerrero asked. "We're no fuckin' Hessians. We can walk if we please. Hell, they won't let us back into Cuba anyway."

"Kid just wants some fancy stories to impress the girls with," Dominguín said.

"I'm a soldier," the kid finally managed to say. "I want to fight."

Shaking his head, Hierra went to the console and bent down to read it over Guerrero's shoulder. His nostrils flared in amusement. "Honey to snare fly brains," he snorted. "No deal that sweet's gonna pay much money—and no deal *is* that sweet. You can't promise safe passage like that without the cooperation of the target country's government. And what the hell government welcomes mercs horning in on its territory?

"Tell you what, Paco. Just let Major Miguel get a look at your weapon in that condition. *He'll* give you all the adventure you want."

# CHAPTER
# EIGHT

*The hunter crouched in long grass and watched the lions worrying the striped carcass of a zebra. The sun had long since slipped off the top of the rounded hummock of the sky and would soon roll down behind the horizon. Then maybe the hunter could rush out and seize a few handfuls of cooling meat for himself, his mate, and their infant son. Now there was nothing to do but wait, and hide, while the tantalizing smell of blood and the wet stink of spilled guts congealed in the air.*

*There were half a dozen beasts in the pride, the three lionesses who had made the kill, the big black-maned male tearing at the carcass, a pair of young. Vultures paced, expectant, ugly heads bobbing back and forth on wrinkled necks, occasionally straying too close, only to be driven off in a cloud of black wings and squawls by the jealous male. It was the hierarchy of the high hot plains: the male ate first, then the lioness and cubs, and then, when they were replete, the scavengers.*

*Including the hunter and his small family.*

*It had been days since they had eaten anything but a handful of bugs. They had come here, to a small place in the plain where a spring rose, to lurk along the trails beaten down by the hippos who lived there. Hoping to catch a fish, perhaps, or share in the kill of some bigger, stronger predator. The hunter looked sideways.*

*His mate watched him with half-closed, hopeless eyes. Like him, she was covered all over with a sparse, fine dark brown fur, except for her face, the palms of her hands, and soles of her feet, and the shrunken, desiccated mammaries against which she huddled the infant. Like him, she had a low forehead, flat nose, a muzzle more than a mouth, no chin to speak of. He felt a great surge of warmth for her and the small life she cradled, shot through with frustration that he could not seem to provide them sustenance.*

*The infant hung listless, lacking the energy or awareness to brush away the fly that crawled along the ball of one half-closed eye. The fine black-brown fur at the backs of his legs grew smeared with dung. His bowels had run uncontrollably since the day before, and he was weaker with every passing minute.*

*The big cat haggled a hind leg off the zebra and carried it to the shade of a thorn tree, where he began to devour it at leisure in the shade, under the watchful eye of several kites perched in the branches. The lionesses and cubs moved in for their share of the feast. Overhead vultures floated to the slow whims of air rising up off the hot veldt. The hunter felt a soft grumbling in his stomach. He hoped the lionesses would finish soon. The day was dying fast, and with night came the tawny spotted scavengers, with their massive jaws that could crack a buffalo's femur. When they arrived he would have no chance of wresting anything for his family and himself.*

*Perhaps he'd rush upon the pride and try to drive it from its kill. Sometimes they gave way, if you charged them with enough determination, made enough noise. Sometimes. Yet even now the hunger and desperation did not quite outweigh the prospect of shredding death from teeth and black claws fetid with rotting meat—of leaving his mate and offspring without even the poor sustenance he'd been able to provide. Not quite.*

*He waited. The day grew hotter. The infant stirred in its mother's arms, whimpered feebly. The lions lingered at their feast, rasping flesh from bone with rough strong tongues.*

*From the thorn tree, the kites watched. Whatever happened, they would feed.*

*The rope chafed his shoulder, digging a raw furrow through skin and muscle, dull red stinging with the salt of sweat, ceaseless rasping*

*against the side of his neck, as it had for endless days before and would
for endless days beyond, until he had no more flesh to hold his bones
from lying down and becoming one with the rank black soil underfoot.
The cries of the overseers were strident, alien voices, rhythmic and
strange as the calls of large insects, urging on the slaves dragging a
huge block of stone to take its place in the great wat rising from the
clearing in the jungle. Heavy wet air muffled his limbs like a burial
shroud soaked with water, binding, weighing him down. Breathing was
torture. The air clogged his lungs like wet silk, yet gave no sustenance.*

*His feet slipped in mud. An overseer barked at him, brought a rattan
whining down on his shoulders. He knew better than to look to the side.
From around him came a chorus of soft grunts, the sounds of men
laboring singlemindedly past exhaustion, like the coughing of carabao
at nightfall. Hard men, the Khmer kings, to make their slaves labor in
the hot sun without so much as a conical straw hat to keep the sun from
their shaven heads.*

*Left at home, in a small hut with his family and a land made fertile
by canals, his lot would have been labor scarcely less grinding. But at
home at least he could glean some reward for labor. Here a day's toil
bought only the chance for a night's fitful sleep chained in the slave
barracks, then up in the sun's red eye to do it again.*

*A runlet of sweat filled his eyes. He shook his head, trying to blink
it away. If this was his karmic burden, he should try to bear it without
complaint, without thought. But still, but still . . .*


*Frothing like a rabid dog, the sea hurled itself forward, battering the
jagged black lava headland with a demon roar. Naked but for a headband and wet cloth around his loins, leaning back with feet braced in
pockets of the sharp porous rock, bunched muscles of thighs and calves
standing forth, the young man assailed his* miya-daiko *with heavy
polished hardwood sticks, making it roar back defiance with intensity
equal to the fury of the sea.*

*Storm clouds slid in black from the west with the ominous ease of
trouble on the way; sea birds drifted high overhead and cried out in
wonder and alarm. The young man didn't know them. There was just
the sea, and the drum, and the Void, a mad exultation, the measured
thunder of the drums imposing structure on the inchoate surge of the
sea. The young man was the act itself, leaning back so that the muscles
of his back almost touched hard level stone, bringing all his leverage
and power to bear to smash the drums, as if to burst the skin stretched
taut across it. Here abode no will, no intention, just the sea and the*

*drum and the beautiful interplay of form and chaos.*

*The storm came. The young man fought his drum until the* kami *who resided within came forth to greet it.*

"Very impressive," Elizabeth O'Neill said, when the big screen went black. "I'm tempted to run through that again, once we get the Kliemann Coil up."

She turned around to see Nagaoka Hiroshi smiling shyly. The quiet anthropologist had designed all three scenarios. It pleased O'Neill to see that he was happy with his achievement, but she herself was troubled. *I wish TOKUGAWA had been more decisive in that Tsavo hunter-gatherer scenario,* she thought. *He has to learn boldness.*

"The coil should be ready this afternoon, Doctor," Takai said. "Perhaps we can demonstrate it for Yoshimitsu Michiko. She's very interested in the TOKUGAWA project, you know."

O'Neill raised an eyebrow. "Really? I thought she'd come to visit her family." Takai maintained his usual look of frozen geniality, but the technicians whispered among themselves around the gallery walls. Yoshimitsu Michiko had not found it necessary to visit her family for five years. Dr. O'Neill knew that as well as anyone. *What does she want here?* O'Neill kept asking herself, compulsively hollow-tooth probing. *Has she come to stake a claim in the project her own research helped make possible?* It was no coincidence that brought Yoshimitsu Michiko back from her self-imposed exile in Jakarta.

*What if she wants the whole thing?*

O'Neill pivoted her chair abruptly from her console. "I'm going up to my room for a nap," she said briskly. "Have the coil ready after lunch."

"What about Yoshimitsu Michiko?" Takai asked.

"If she wants to come and watch, that's her business." *I don't want that woman in my lab!*

*The acolyte walked on the bank of a river with his mentor, the Zen master Soshi. Mellow sunlight surrounded them with warmth, but the air brushed them with fingers of autumn crispness. To their right fields lay under a tawny blanket of ripe wheat. Blue-green mountains hovered in the distance beyond, their bases lost in haze. On the left shimmered the dazzling phosphene dance of sun on water. At a place where the stream went broad and shallow, they paused in the shade of a cypress tree to watch a school of small fish darting above a bottom of pebbles as smooth and perfect as if they had been chosen by a gardener's hand. Soshi laughed. "How delightfully the fishes are enjoying themselves in the water!" he exclaimed.*

*The acolyte frowned. The smell of water filled his nostrils, cool and slightly rank. "You are not a fish, Master. How, then, do you know that the fishes are enjoying themselves?"*

*The master looked at him and laughed again. "You are not myself," he replied. "How do you know that I do not know that the fishes are enjoying themselves? Eh?" And he turned and walked on, the soles of his sandals slapping the soft grass of the riverbank, leaving the bemused pupil to stay or follow as he would.*

Slowly O'Neill's senses returned to her body, awareness of the fluorescent light filtering in beneath the edge of the bowl-shaped hood, the sound of her breathing within the helmet, the rustlings of the lab beyond, the slightly stale smell of air circulated by the ventilation system into the depths where the lab lay. *Fantastic. Utterly fantastic.* She shook herself. *It was real! I saw and heard, I felt and even smelled everything as TOKUGAWA did. It was almost . . . like being one with him.* She shied away from the last thought. A major goal of the project was achieving total rapport between human and machine. Even though the successful test of the Kliemann Coil brought that objective much closer, there was no telling whether it could truly be achieved. *Do I dare hope?*

She was becoming aware of the smell of her own sweat. It was cool in the lab, but even sitting up for any length of time tended to make her perspire, and the excitement of being tapped into the coil—the sensory centers of her brain stimulated by induction fields even as sense-analogue data were fed into TOKUGAWA—had made her perspire freely. She'd grown more conscious of her sweat since coming to Japan; she ate more meat than the average Japanese and was uncomfortably aware that it made her smell different to them.

"Lift the hood," she said. The coil's Gen-5 monitor picked up the command. Servos raised the gleaming inverted bowl, returning O'Neill to the real world.

Elation died within her. "A most impressive display, Doctor," said the diminutive woman who stood beside the coil's thronelike chair. "I'm honored to be present."

Beside her, Aoki Hideo bowed. "Dr. O'Neill," he said, making heavy weather of the "l's". "Permit me to introduce Dr. Yoshimitsu Michiko."

But O'Neill's eyes were already fixed on the young woman. She was slight, a touch over five feet tall, with glossy black hair permanented into a Western wave falling across her shoulders and down her back. Her face was oval, narrow at the chin, cheekbones distinct but not obtrusive, eyes wide, long-lashed, and slanting, nose straight above small mouth. Yoshimitsu Michiko was beautiful by the highly Westernized standards of modern Japan—but that wasn't all. The chiseled Yoshimitsu features, accented with hints of lipstick and shadow at the eyes, would have looked just as natural under a gesso of white makeup, with eyebrows plucked and painted in halfway up the forehead, a vision from an *ukiyo-e* painting. In black turtleneck and designer jeans that looked heat-shrunk to her athletic body, Michiko looked very much the spoiled jet-set daughter of new Japanese money.

She looked less like a scientist who in her late twenties had taken a commanding position at the cutting edge of physics and held onto it for the past five years.

"Dr. Yoshimitsu," O'Neill rasped, and sought to mask consternation behind a polite lie. "I'm honored to meet you. I—I've read your papers. Fine work."

Michiko grinned. "Why, thank you, Doctor," she said in perfect English. "I've tried to keep up with your work as well, though computers aren't precisely my field." She shook her head. "Really, I'm quite in awe of what you're doing here. Would you introduce me to TOKUGAWA?"

"No."

Michiko blinked.

Hastily, O'Neill went on. "This is a very delicate time. TOKUGAWA uses up so much of his capacity during our scenarios, it takes a considerable length of time for him to readjust." Past Michiko's shoulder, O'Neill saw Wali Hassad frowning at her through a haze of cigarette smoke and puffing in furious consternation. She was lying through her teeth, and he knew it. "Perhaps later."

Michiko shrugged, and O'Neill felt a flash of distaste: *how Westernized she is.*

"Ah, well. I've very much been looking forward to meeting our new arrival; I hope you'll be able to arrange an introduction soon."

O'Neill dropped her eyes. "Yes, that should be possible." Dragging the words out by main force.

Michiko went to the rail and leaned on it, staring down at the gleaming hemisphere. "So this is where he lives," she said, half aloud. O'Neill stared at her back. She wished she had the strength to reach out and shake her. *How dare she speak of TOKUGAWA like that? So ... familiar.*

Michiko turned back. "Will you be running another scenario again today, Doctor? I came in halfway through the last one."

"No. Sorry. Not today. This is the first test of the Kliemann apparatus. It's highly experimental; we need to analyze our data extensively before doing any more work with it."

Michiko shrugged again. "I hope the results are what you've been hoping for, Doctor. For selfish reasons as well, I admit; I almost wish—" She broke off suddenly, smiled, shook her head. "But another time, perhaps."

She half turned, laid her hand on Aoki's arm. "Thank you for the introduction, Aoki-san. I'm sure Dr. O'Neill is very busy, so let's let her get back to her work. Thank you very much again, Doctor. It's been a pleasure meeting you."

Though she knew how rude it was, O'Neill could only nod. The manager and Michiko left the lab. O'Neill let the breath out of her in a long, shuddering sigh, feeling the pressure of her assistants' eyes upon her. *Thank God she didn't ask if she could use the Kliemann Coil.* It would have been pushing matters, even for Elizabeth O'Neill, to have brusquely refused a third reasonable request from the daughter of Yoshimitsu Akaji.

*But I can't bear the thought of that woman sitting in that chair, feeling TOKUGAWA's thoughts as her own!*


"So that's Dr. O'Neill," Michiko said as she and Aoki walked down the corridor to the elevator banks. "She was lost somewhere in the United States when I was here last, just after the war. Father was sending some kind of crack commando team to rescue her. It was all very mysterious and romantic." She smiled and nodded to a pair of passing technicians. "She's a strange woman, though. Rather harsh."

"She is under a lot of pressure, Michiko-san," Aoki mumbled, not looking at Michiko. Though he looked like a *bakemono* troll from Japanese mythology—and had often acted like one, in his capacity as general manager of an embattled corporation—Aoki Hideo was in fact a sensitive man. He understood that O'Neill had hated Michiko the instant she laid eyes on her, had resented every second she spent in her lab. Whether Michiko realized that, he couldn't say; for all the years he'd known her, even though he'd been a second father to her since she was a child, he still could not read her.

"Ah, well." Michiko sighed. "It's not as if I don't know any scientists who have trouble relating to people. I just hope we'll get along; there are a lot of things I'd like to talk to her about—and it would be good to have someone besides you I could have an intelligent conversation with in this drafty old castle."

She squeezed the old man's arm. "My father's granting me the honor of having lunch with him," she said. "I wonder if my dear brother will be there?"

# CHAPTER
# NINE

"You say we won't have visual on this one, Emiko?" Elizabeth O'Neill asked. The stocky linguist shook her head. "Then I suppose I'd better hook to the Kliemann Coil before we begin."

The corners of Ito's mouth turned down. "I wouldn't do that, Doctor."

"Why not?"

"This is an, uh, a rough one. Very intense."

Wali Hassad pulled his cigarette from between full lips, briefly studied the trail of smoke from its tip. "Emiko ought to know," he said, letting smoke trail out through his nose. "She wrote it."

O'Neill frowned. "But how will we monitor the scenario? And why isn't there visual, anyway?"

"Dr. Ito has programmed the scenario-master to provide a text narrative as the scenario progresses," Kim said. The lanky Korean looked like a stork in his old-fashioned long white lab coat. "In this scenario, TOKUGAWA's alter ego does not have the use of her eyes."

O'Neill raised an eyebrow. *No eyes?* She didn't like the sound of that; on the other hand, TOKUGAWA was supposed to experience a wider range of experiences than any human did, in order that he could achieve full personhood without the years it took a real human. She didn't miss the feminine pronoun, either. In none of the scenarios so far had TOKUGAWA portrayed a female. *Maybe I should screen the scenarios more closely,* she thought, and in an instant realized that that was silly. *Have I been living in this male-dominated culture so long that I don't think being a woman is a valid part of human experience?*

"I'm using the coil," she said with sudden decision and pivoted her wheelchair toward her console.

*Being a woman is . . . pain.*

*It had all ended with a flash: her vision, the health of her body, heavy with child, her little world with what security it offered in this, the fourth summer of the war. She'd been tending the garden in front of the little wood-and-paper house near the head of the Urakami River valley that she shared with her husband when the thin and distant whine of an airplane's engines brought her bandannaed head up. Like so many people, she loved to watch the B-jūkyūs, the B-29's, despite the destruction they carried. Shading her eyes with a callused hand, she picked out the lonely silver glint of sun on wings and thrashing propellers. How beautiful it looks, she thought, sailing majestically through clouds like a great ship breasting ocean swells. Besides, she told herself, this single plane posed no danger—a straggler, perhaps, not part of the great bomber swarms that turned cities into infernos. Nor did she fear the swarms, particularly; none had ever bombed Nagasaki.*

*And then it had come, a purple radiance that filled the sky and pierced her eyes, filling her head with heat, suffusing her body in a strange tingling glow. For a moment she had stayed there on her knees, wondering numbly what was going on. Her first coherent thought was of the tales brought by refugees from Hiroshima, where the Americans had dropped their strange new bomb three days before. The pika! she realized: the lightning of the bomb going off. A lightning that seared and killed from hundreds, even thousands of meters away.*

*That had seared her. Killed her.*

*Now she stumbled through streets unfamiliar to her feet, hopelessly altered by rubble from the rolling blast wave that had knocked her sprawling into the ruins of her little house. Now and then her bare soles trod upon a burning ember; she scarcely noticed. Her body was already numb with shock.*

*Her skin felt strange, alien, as though damp rice paper had been molded to her body and then allowed to dry. It crackled as she moved. She was badly burned, she knew. She could grasp nothing with the fingers of her left hand, as if they were gone, burned to stubs; she couldn't feel the right at all. Hot, wet wind blew against her charred, naked skin, cooling on wet runlets down her cheeks where the pika's heat had melted her eyes. She could not breathe through her nose; it had melted into an undifferentiated lump. She tore chunks of air raggedly through a mouth she could no longer close.*

*More than anything else she was aware of the small life within her, kicking to be free, and the powerful contractions that racked her belly at rapidly decreasing intervals. She wandered blindly, praying that the bosatsu and kami would guide her somewhere she could find help—to*

*the Mitsubishi Steel and Arms Works where her husband worked, per-*
*haps (knowing at the core of her that he was dead), or to the University*
*Hospital on the valley's eastern slope, so that at least the child she could*
*never see might have a chance to live.*

*Around her she heard a rushing noise as of a great wind through*
*flash-cropped ears, and screams rising up like the cries of a flock of*
*frightened seagulls. A roaring of heat steered her away from a building*
*in flames. It was just a matter of time until she stumbled into the river,*
*or wildfire trapped her.* Oh, Amida-Butsu, help my child, *she prayed*
*silently, moving the lips that were no longer there. That her baby would*
*be born here and now was a greater pain than any of her body. That*
*she would never see it, that the milk-heavy breasts that should nourish*
*it had been burned to lumps of charcoal, these knowings pained her.*
*But the greatest agony was the fear and the guilt of bringing her first*
*and last child into hell.* Forgive me, little unborn one—

*A contraction hit her like a fist in the belly. She doubled, stumbled.*
*Something turned beneath a clublike foot, and she went sprawling.*
*There was wetness on her thighs, and the spasms came in waves like*
*storm surf, like the pleasure of orgasm expanded into infinite pain.*
It's coming! Forgive me, my child, this weak flesh can shield you no
longer.

*She scrabbled her heels futilely in the rubble, trying to brace her legs.*
*There was no strength in her. She tried to squeeze with her belly, aid*
*the infant on its way. Her body was so devastated she didn't even know*
*how much success she had. Then the peristaltic surges overtook her,*
*overwhelmed her.*

*There was a time of blackness shot with red, and then release.*

*She lay a long time on her back with the rubble smoldering beneath*
*her, completely drained. Somehow she knew she was bleeding to death.*
*Why won't the baby cry?* she wondered desperately. *Was it born dead?*
*Perhaps,* she thought, *it was better that way—and then,* no, never!
*Someone had to carry on. Even if my baby will live in hell, better that*
*it has a chance to live.*

*With all her will, she made her left leg move inward. In a moment*
*she felt it, a squirming softness against the blackened parchment inside*
*her thigh. Here was life, was movement, even as life ebbed out of her.*
*Already the first fingers of agony began to probe at her, hot and avid.*
*Soon it would feel as if she were bathed in fire.*

*She felt a floating, a drifting away from herself, from a world beyond*
*redemption.* May Amaterasu keep you, my darling, *she thought. She let*
*herself go. There was nothing more for her here.*

*Pain is . . . being a woman.*

Slowly the burning sensations in Elizabeth O'Neill's extremities faded; her skin seemed to fit itself to her again, regaining flexibility. Her arms and legs, braced against the tidal onslaught of pain, relaxed. She shook herself. She felt curious, detached, as if she too had been on the verge of cutting the cord to her own ravaged body. A deep slow anger filled the scooped-out hollowness within.

At a brusque command the helmet raised. "My *God*," she breathed.

Her assistants huddled around, faces distorted fish-eye caricatures of concern. "We tried to warn you, Doctor," Kim said anxiously.

She shook her head. "Get me out of here." They helped her up from the gleaming chrome-and-plastic throne, eased her into the comforting embrace of her wheelchair. She mustered the remnants of her strength in a glare. "Emiko, what in God's name made you create that—that *horror?*"

"It was a way of condensing a great deal of human experience."

"But it was horrible! Not just the physical pain. The sense of loss—of hopelessness. How could you subject TOKUGAWA to that?" She felt an echo of the guilt she'd known in dream-*doppelgang*.

Wali Hassad started to lay a hand on her arm, then thought better of it, remembering that she found human contact disturbing rather than comforting. "It was very terrible, Doctor. But please consider: even if none of us has had exactly that experience, who hasn't known loss and horror, in our world today? Two of Kim's brothers were killed by South Korean troops before the war. Takai's whole family was lost when Tō-kyō was bombed. And I—" He looked away. With a pang O'Neill remembered that his own family had been killed in an Israeli bombing of a refugee camp in Lebanon when he was a child, and a Red Cross relief worker had brought him back to the States.

"But, Emiko," she said, unwilling to let her anger go, "whatever possessed *you* to write such a scenario? You didn't lose anyone in the war."

"No." Harsh lines etched the corners of Ito's eyes, her smooth, wide forehead. "But that's how my mother was born, Oniyaru-san. We never knew her family name, nor who her father was; my grandmother was burnt beyond recognition by the thermal flash of the Nagasaki bomb."

"Oh, God, Emiko, I'm sorry, I didn't know—"

The flare of bitterness had burnt itself out. "I understand, Doctor. You had no way of knowing."

O'Neill's console chimed politely for attention. She looked up in irritation. "Yes? I accept the call."

"Dr. O'Neill." She recognized the voice of a technician in the main lab. "We have a call from Yoshimitsu Michiko. She wants to know if she may come down and observe your experiments."

The strange soiled feeling flooded back into her. To have undergone that horror in sympathy with TOKUGAWA and surrounded by her own people was bad enough. The thought that Michiko might have been in the lab, watching, was more than she could bear. "Tell her no! She can't come down now."

"But, Dr. O'Neill, she very much wants—"

"Tell her tomorrow! O'Neill out." She looked around at her subordinates. "I'm going to my room. Carry on with analyzing the results of this run. Let me know if you learn anything unusual."

And she thought, *Right now, I need to be alone with TOKUGAWA.*

"A foreign mercenary, engaged to destroy a Japanese corporation?" the old man thundered. "Insupportable!"

Ishikawa Nobuhiko faced him squarely down the length of the table in the conference room near the apex of the MITI Pyramid. He didn't notice his assistant, Doihara Kazuko, who sat behind his left shoulder properly apart from the table at which the policy board met, look up in quick consternation from the notes she was jotting by hand on a notebook in her lap. He'd expected this confrontation. Yamada Tatsuhide, the old fool, had been with the ministry since before Ishikawa was born. Unlike so many of his cohorts in the upper levels of the bureaucracy, he was not simply another wheelhorse growing old in harness. Unfortunately.

Ishikawa assumed a demeanor of reason and compromise affronted by the old man's outburst. "I assure you, Yamada-san, the ministry has never contemplated the hiring of mercenaries and is not doing so now."

Yamada chopped a contemptuous hand at the air. "Don't be coy with me, Ishikawa." He was gaunt, and not even an expensively cut Savile Row suit could completely hide the ravages of a six-month bout with cancer, fought recently to a draw. His head was narrow, chin and forehead sloping away from his nose, his hair, now gone white, thrusting up and back, so that he looked as if he were pedaling a bicycle against the wind. He normally held his eyes to slits behind his spectacles; now they were round. "Of course the ministry isn't hiring mercenaries; your puppet Hiryu is. But the ministry has used its influence to obtain a number of blank entrance permits with short-term visa stamps and passed them to Hiryu's new employee. A remarkable man, I gather; a former Vietnamese army officer who's acquired a reputation as the world's foremost siege expert. I daresay my fellows of the board would find his dossier absorbing reading. Shall I have it written to their screens?"

Ishikawa sighed. He'd known he couldn't keep this information from Yamada's informants indefinitely. And he'd known just how the old fool would respond.

"Very well, Yamada-san. It's so; we are—*facilitating*—certain steps that Hiryu Cybernetics Industries is taking to redress an intolerable situation. Is that not the ministry's legitimate function, to help maintain the economic health of Japan?"

"To help import an army of foreign thugs to murder Japanese citizens?" Yamada demanded. "I call that barbarous, not legitimate."

Ishikawa felt his congenial mask beginning to set like mud baked by the sun. He wanted to take Yamada by the wattled throat and shake him. *Don't you see the chaos swirling around us? How it threatens to rush in and plunge us under?*

"Our distinguished colleague is a noted admirer of Western arts and culture—so-called," said Mitsui of Analysis in a voice as lean and sinuous as himself. "Perhaps exposure to Western values has shifted his perspective subtly out of alignment. He wouldn't wish Japan subjected to the unlimited competition that destroyed the United States' economy, would he?"

"The Americans never had unlimited competition. That wasn't what destroyed their economy; it was the insane rivalry into which they and we so willingly entered, as much as anything."

Forgetting himself, Ishikawa scowled. "You're speaking, I believe, of policy approved by our ministry."

"I never approved it. I wasn't on the board when it was decided to go on a footing of economic warfare in response to American protectionism, and if I had I'd have fought it. Folly is no answer to folly."

"I fear we stray from the main point," Mitsui said. "I'd still like to discover the real reasons for Yamada-san's objections to our policy vis-à-vis Yoshimitsu TeleCommunications."

" 'I think we are in rat's alley, where the dead men lost their bones.' "

"Western decadence!" exclaimed Atsuji of Operations. "Truly, Yamada-san has allowed the *gaijin* to poison his thoughts."

"Now, Atsuji-san, do not exercise yourself," Mitsui said soothingly. "Perhaps our colleague doesn't fully grasp the gravity of the situation. Yoshimitsu TeleCommunications has been a thorn in our side for years. They have persistently refused our benevolent administrative guidance. And now, it appears, they have achieved a breakthrough that provides them a tool—or a weapon—of almost unimaginable power."

"You read what our agent reported happened in Kyōto," the plump head of Liaison said excitedly. "The devilish device practically took over the young Yoshimitsu's apartment. There's no telling what it can do!"

"Consider the pernicious influences within YTC itself," said Planning, speaking hastily to forestall a further outburst from his excitable colleague. "Yoshimitsu has always shamelessly employed large numbers of Koreans, depriving many good Japanese of work. And though our country is filled with the finest computer scientists in the world, many of them veterans of our own ICOT, whom does Yoshimitsu Akaji choose to head his TOKUGAWA Project? A foreigner, and a woman at that. One who employs a Korean and another American in her innermost circle.

"And what about old Yoshimitsu's daughter, working among the Indonesians? They've threatened to cut us off from the rest of the Pacific for years. What kind of man would permit his daughter to work for the enemies of our nation?" He glowered briefly for effect. "Perhaps a man so corrupted by outside influences as to permit his daughter to devote herself to unfeminine pursuits. A man thoroughly tainted by exposure to Western ways. Does that not alarm you, Yamada-san?"

Yamada elevated his head and eyed Operations disdainfully along the aristocratic length of his nose—which was aristocratic indeed; he had noble lineage, and was related none too distantly to the branch of the imperial family that had mounted the throne after the war. "I won't dignify your innuendo with an answer. As for YTC, I will even stipulate for a moment that there are grounds for your trepidations, though I personally find them ludicrous. But what then? Are we to destroy what law remains in Japan for mere expediency?"

"What do you mean, Yamada-san?" Liaison asked. "We're the government. We decide what's lawful."

"That's neither accurate nor just. We are indeed the government. Exclude the Diet; a mere debating society. Our esteemed Prime Minister Fudori is a figurehead, who serves by the sufferance of the ministries. We, the ministries, the bureaucracy, the Mandarins, we are the state. But still, our nation has laws. And if we don't abide by them, can you tell me then, who will?"

"How then are we to meet this emergency?" Mitsui asked. "YTC seems immune to pressure. And the Supreme Court, in its wisdom, blocks our every legal move against the company. Surely, you wouldn't deprive us of our one remaining means of dealing with those whom self-interest blinds to the needs of the nation?"

"Does the nation need for YTC to be destroyed? If they have, indeed, created artificial awareness, haven't they worked to the benefit of us all?"

"Ridiculous," Atsuji said.

"I fear the current of consensus runs against you, Yamada-san," Ishikawa said. "The board perceives the threat posed by Yoshimitsu TeleCommunications to be both immediate and far-reaching. These are extraordinary circumstances; they call for extraordinary responses."

Atsuji sneered. "Perhaps Yamada-san has an answer for that too. One he learned at Oxford, perhaps."

"Yes," Yamada said, "since the administrative vice-minister speaks of currents, as a matter of fact, I do." He smiled. "Learned at Oxford: 'fear death by water.'"

"What's that supposed to mean?" Atsuji demanded. "You think what we're doing to YTC will bring back Noah's flood?"

"In a manner of speaking, Atsuji-san. We are opening the floodgates, gentlemen. We've permitted cracks to appear, by letting the *zaibatsu* employ sabotage against one another. But if we ourselves participate in illegal violence—at whatever remove, Ishikawa-san"— he spread his hands before him, horizontally above the polished hardwood table—"we shall cause the inundation of what remains of our social order. We shall accomplish that which the Third World War could not: the destruction of Japanese society. To paraphrase an American Negro gospel song by reversal: 'It won't be the fire, but the water next time.'"

Stillness bound the room. *The old madman has a touch of the messianic about him,* Ishikawa thought. He could tell Yamada was at least unnerving some of his board members, if not converting them. "Please do not forget, Yamada-san, we have not irrevocably embarked upon this enterprise. There is still time to avoid any precipitate action—if Yoshimitsu Akaji sees reason."

"No." Yamada rose. "The only hope is that we see reason. Gentlemen, I bid you good day."


"I feel sorry for Dr. Ito," TOKUGAWA said.

O'Neill sat on her bed with her legs pulled up, normally an uncomfortable position for her. It was late at night, yet again; she hadn't gotten to her private talk with her brainchild that afternoon, after all. Kim had called up from the lab almost as soon as she'd arrived in her room, with information on irregularities in the performance of the Kliemann Coil. She'd forced herself to deal with it then and there; Kim said that if they acted upon that data immediately, the coil might be ready for a full-rapport hookup within two days. So, despite her exhaustion and sickness of soul, she'd forced her mind and body back to business.

Now she asked, "Why? Emiko didn't experience—that."

"No. But it makes her sad to think of it."

"How do you know?" O'Neill asked, truly curious.

"I analyzed her breathing, while you were discussing the scenario after it was done. It showed clear signs of distress."

O'Neill gazed thoughtfully at the visual pickup recently installed above her com/comm screen. TOKUGAWA's education was succeeding beyond even her most sanguine predictions; in a matter of weeks, he was displaying development both she and her staff felt to be roughly on a par with a human adolescent. Yet he had capabilities that not even the most gifted human adolescent could boast, such as instant access to a wealth of expert programs. Occasionally O'Neill found herself bewildered by the facility with which he used them. "Why do you think that was?" she asked him.

"Dr. Ito seems to think a lot about what her grandmother went through when her mother was born," TOKUGAWA said. "I don't know why. There's nothing she can do to help her."

O'Neill smiled at his naivete. "People are like that; they care for others even when there's nothing to be done."

"I understand caring, Doctor. But why brood about what's already happened? Emiko-san can't make her grandmother feel better by feeling bad herself."

O'Neill shook her head. *He's still a child in so many of his perceptions.* "What about you?" he asked. "How do you feel about today's scenario?"

"I feel bad that you were subjected to it."

"You've told me I must learn all about being a human," TOKUGAWA said gravely. "Such things are part of being human, I understand."

"Regrettably, yes." *Susan.* She shook her head. "But I was afraid it would"—she wanted to say, *warp you,* but she wasn't sure she could explain that to her charge—"make you unhappy and afraid," she finished lamely.

"It did make me unhappy and afraid, while it was happening. After that, I was only sorry that things like that really happen."

"But it *was* really happening to you. As far as we can tell, you experienced very much the same sensations a human would under the circumstances, or a close analogue." *My poor dear.*

"But it wasn't real. I felt it, but somewhere I never forgot that it wouldn't last, that it wasn't really me lying there among the rubble. I don't have a body to be burned." A pause. "It seems that nothing that touches you can truly touch me." The voice sounded wistful, rueful.

O'Neill blinked at the sudden moisture in her eyes. "If you had a body, I'd hug you. I'd comfort you." *And perhaps* . . . "You poor child. If you can't experience the pains we humans feel—then you should be very, very happy."

# CHAPTER
# TEN

Yoshimitsu Michiko walked along the shoulder of a hill. The late-spring sun fell in a warm steady flow on the back of her neck, and she thought about stopping momentarily to shed the faded blue nylon day-pack from her shoulders and take off the red-plaid American work shirt she wore, half-buttoned and tucked into her jeans. It was getting to be T-shirt weather here in southwest Honshū.

"Michiko!" She spun, pulse thumping at the base of her throat, ready to spring away, deerlike, at any sign of threat. At once she chided herself: *I'm getting paranoid, damn it. Hanging around this fortress always does that to me.* Then she saw who had called her name, and smiled, and waved.

Major Miguel García strode after her along the trail at his slightly bowlegged gait. A compact, handsome man, not much above the Japanese average in height, he had dark Caribbean good looks at once rugged and refined, black beard and long hair set off by flashing blue eyes, a black beret tipped to one side adding just the right note of Ché Guevara insouciance. He wore plain green fatigues, with sidearm and communicator in his web belt; no camouflage for him, off-duty. As he got closer, she saw his hair was all black. He'd shown a few strands of gray when last she'd been home, five years ago.

She smiled to herself. That would be one of the few vanities he'd allow himself, dyeing his hair. It worked; nothing about him hinted that, more than ten years her senior, he'd gotten a good start on middle age. He had the looks, the energy, the easy, resilient grace of a man in his early twenties.

He caught her by the shoulders. "Michiko, *querida.*" He kissed her; at the last instant she turned aside and accepted it on the cheek. He drew back and grinned. "That wasn't how you did it the last time I saw you." His English was good, with a strong Cuban flavor she suspected he maintained for effect.

"That was a long time ago, Miguel." She shook her head. "I sound like something from a romance novel."

He laughed. "Don't be ashamed. You Japanese are almost as hopelessly romantic as us Spaniards." He let her go and began walking beside her. "Where are you headed?"

She nodded at Mount Takara before them, a wide slow jut with pines standing visibly discrete like hairs. "Up there. A little clearing on the side of the mountain, just below the crest. It was my private place when I was a teenager, back before the castle was built."

García nodded. His long hair bobbed with the motion. "I remember you telling me about it. Isn't it named after someplace in a fairy-tale book?"

"Yes. Takara-yama. The Fortunate Mountain." She walked with thumbs stuck under the padded straps of her daypack, smiling a little at the memory. "Literally, it means Treasure Mountain, but it comes to the same thing. A mythical place where you could find all good things. What I found was mostly solitude. But I guess that's treasure in Japan, these days."

It was a high-domed day, blue and endless, a few puffy clouds drifting indolently around the green and gray peaks surrounding them. Their path ran out of sight of the citadel through undulating foothills furred with long, green grass. From the peaks a small brook raced, fast and sassy with the last of snow-melt runoff, swatches of red and white and purple flowers spread like banners to either side. Higher up, the cool calm of pine and fir forests beckoned.

"I miss this land in winter," Michiko said. "I like it best then. It was summertime when I was here last."

"I remember." A small smile.

"I haven't been here in winter since, oh, at least two years before the war. Not long after I accepted the post at Sukarno University. It was so beautiful, all white and perfect and smooth in the flat places, weighing down the branches of the fir trees, sitting up on top of black-looking rocks like thick white caps. I remember papa's garden was especially beautiful, even though it wasn't finished yet. Of course, I didn't get to see it much; he isn't comfortable having me in his garden." The corners of her mouth tucked ruefully in. "He's not comfortable having me around at all."

"Your father loves you, Michiko. You shouldn't be hard on him."

Michiko looked at him sharply. Miguel García wasn't a man to curry favor. He was merely stating his perception of his employer, whom he found good, if not exactly munificent. She frowned. Objectively, she knew that Yoshimitsu Akaji was in many ways a good man. *But I can never forgive what he's done to me. Or to Shigeo. The years of neglect* — "I suppose he does. But he'd love me more if I were a dutiful little girl—ten years married now to some middle-management type, raising a brood of kids. Spending my days on television classes, flower arranging, and gossip, and my nights loyally serving my husband tea, when he wasn't off with the boys at the geisha bars or topless joints."

García shook his head. "You were just born the wrong sex, Michiko —not that I'm complaining. Things have changed a lot since I was a kid, but it's still a man's world. Especially in Japan."

"Especially everywhere, as far as I can see."

He laughed. She stuck her hands in her pockets and remembered, frowning ahead at the little path of grass worn thin.

It had been unlikely enough for a TV movie. The daughter of the head of a great and powerful *zaibatsu*—if neither especially great nor powerful by *zaibatsu* standards—having an affair with the dashing young *doitsu* captain in charge of the corporate stronghold's security unit. Yoshimitsu Michiko, skeptical of the culture into which she'd been born, a culture dominated by macho—an ever so useful *gaijin* word— males who never matured out of a basically adolescent ethic getting involved with, of all things, a Hispanic. And a professional soldier, at that.

The military men Michiko had known, even the ones from cultures not so heavily centered on male bonding and bravado as Spain's and Japan's, had been pretty much of a stripe. Military service somehow seemed to retard maturation, to encourage looking to others for responsibility and direction, to reinforce the swaggering adolescent attitudes toward sex. Spain and Japan were both warrior cultures. They had the same preoccupation with honor, even at the expense of humanity, the same conception of woman as homemaker and consort, of man as a sort of a blunt instrument, ready to rush headlong against the slightest seeming challenge. Their similarity was one reason the early Portuguese and Spanish missionaries had enjoyed such success in their proselytizing in the sixteenth and seventeenth centuries, frightening the *bakufu* into banning intercourse with foreigners entirely.

Miguel was different. Though he'd been in the army since his youth —he was in his teens when he was conscripted and sent to Angola—he had picked up a certain amount of education and no little polish, despite his studiedly raffish guerrilla exterior. She sensed depths beneath that surface. He was calmer than he should have been, without that furious, driving need to prove himself. He read, and reflected, and did not automatically reject new ideas. Most of all, he was not threatened by an intelligent, independent woman. The fact that he understood not the slightest fraction of an area in which Michiko was an acknowledged expert did not seem to diminish him in the least. A thoroughgoing professional in his field, he respected her professionalism in her own. She wondered if his poise came from spending half his life on futile neocolonialist battlefields around the world.

He was a very, very handsome man, and a very charming one, with a quick and ready wit. Nor did his near freedom from overbearing Latin masculinity mean he was deficient in Hispanic charm. And he understood, as too few people of either sex Michiko had met did, that a woman could have, be secure in and proud of, a sexual identity as well as a professional one. He'd never made any pretense that it wasn't the latter facet he was primarily interested in. That suited her fine. They were poorly matched by temperament and interest for anything beyond a short, somewhat stormy fling.

She'd been facing the prospect of a dry spell, anyway. Since Eileen Soames's death in the war, the Gang of Four lacked its main cohesive force; the three survivors would at any minute go flying off in their disparate directions, centrifugal. The imminent collapse of Michiko's relationship with Richard, her lover, her rival, would almost certainly provide the push.

The fact that it would unsettle even a man as comparatively free of the old class consciousness as Yoshimitsu Akaji for his daughter to have an affair with a foreign mercenary was only incidental, of course.

Their path led down to the bank of the stream. They sat down on a pair of moss-grown rocks huddled like ancient pilgrims by the stream, sending a squadron of frogs plopping into the water. Miguel looked at her, stroked her hair with the back of a hand. She pulled ever so slightly away.

"I know it's been a long time," he said softly. "And neither one of us tried to keep in touch. But you're here now, and you're still very beautiful."

She smiled. That was something she didn't hear too often. Since the final blowup with Richard she avoided entanglement with her immediate colleagues. The rest of the university faculty either distrusted, like so much of the modern world, anyone directly connected with the physical sciences, or was afraid of attracting the attention of the secret police by spending too much time with a foreigner, and a Japanese at that. Most of the foreign faculty was caught up in cocktail-circuit opposition to the regime for which Michiko had no stomach; it was pure masturbation, as evidenced by the fact it was permitted to continue. Nor did society beyond the hothouse environment of Sukarno University offer much. Despite the strident high-profile feminism of Maryam Ahmad, the dictator's wife, the status of women in the most populous Islamic nation on earth made Japanese women look like the epitome of emancipation. Since the Gang's heyday Yoshimitsu Michiko had known few friends, fewer lovers.

She shook her head. "It's too soon," she said, not looking at him.

He shrugged. Pleading wasn't his style either.

*Damn it, I do find him attractive . . .*

García stiffened, put one hand to his right ear. He spoke low, rapid Spanish. With a shock, Michiko realized he'd just gotten a message over the bone-conduction speaker taped behind his ear and was issuing orders in response.

"Intruders," he said. "Electronics picked 'em up, sneaking up to the wire." He broke off into more quick commands, then said, "Stay here," and ran up the hillside, drawing his big rocket-firing sidearm. Michiko hesitated a moment, then followed.

The mercenary flattened himself behind the crest of the hill. Well below, she dropped to all fours and scrambled up beside him, keeping low. He gave her a frown that quickly slipped into an exasperated grin. She heard the snarl of a machine gun, ducked instinctively, then lifted her head to peer through the sweet-smelling grass.

Men were running down the southern slope of the Citadel's truncated hilltop, knee high in grass, leaping over rocks or dodging them with sprawling steps. Mercenaries in bulky battle dress fired at them from inside the wire, as well as from the reinforced guard towers; an open dune buggy–like Light Combat Vehicle was tearing out through the main gate, four *doitsu* jammed in back, its machine gunner spraying the hillside with bullets. Even as she watched, a Gazelle patrol helicopter popped out of its revetment, buzzing like an angry wasp, the lawnmower whir of its miniguns' motors distinct above the rotor chop.

García lowered the compact binoculars he'd taken out of the breast pocket of his uniform blouse. "Saboteurs, just crazies," he said. He lowered his head and spoke briefly into the microphone taped to his larynx. "They've got them all. Or will in a moment." Michiko saw one of the running men fall and roll. She gasped. She'd seen death by violence before; just about everyone had who'd survived the war and the disorder that followed. But this was so immediate—though she felt little love for the citadel, it was home. She tried to shrug off a sick premonition of dissolution.

\*     \*     \*

Secure behind the leaf screen of a wild plum thicket, Colonel Tranh Vinh watched the tense little melodrama play itself out a klick and a half to the north through his Zeiss field glasses. Fancy computer-enhanced glasses of half the weight and bulk were available, but he preferred to trust in his own eyes and good Swiss optics, on his own inferences and interpretations, as opposed to those of some computer programmer. Besides, the Zeiss glasses had sentimental value; he'd picked them up as spoils of war when, as a stripling, he'd served with the elite *dac cong* sappers in the siege of the American marine base at Khe Sanh.

He lowered the glasses. His eyes were protuberant, peering between thick lids through slits in Ping-Pong balls. He had a narrow head, flat nose, snapping-turtle mouth, a face composed of dramatic hollows, well sunken at the temples and under the flat flanged cheekbones. A loose knobby man, with an upright brush of short black hair dusted with gray. In arthritis-knobbed fingers he lifted a smokeless cigarette to his lipless mouth, sucked strongly to draw air through the damp nicotine-impregnated membranes. A wonderful thing, technology. It enabled him to enjoy the nerve-soothing effects of his favorite vice, without danger of compromising his position with a feather of smoke.

He took a breath touched with gunsmoke and growing leaves, raised the glasses again. Thank God, as well, for radical cranks willing die for a Communist faith that had long since become a bitter joke in the Second World. Not that you could call the half dozen bravos he'd enlisted from *Rengo Sekigun*, the Japanese Red Army, brave. They didn't know fear; what they were was insane. He felt a certain kinship with them, nonetheless, even as he did with the Cubans who were massacring them with a certain aplomb. The terrorist JRA had been mercenaries long before either the Cubans or the Vietnamese got into the act. And for much the same reason: the stupefying fees leveled by the Soviets for military aid and matériel.

A mercenary on foot inside the wire perimeter went down. A moment later he was up, scooping up his rifle and blazing away in fury. *Good body armor,* he noted. The 5.45mm rounds fired by the terrorists' old-fashioned AKS-74's wouldn't penetrate. He nodded to himself. *Another thing to be dealt with.*

He saw the fire team dismount the LCV, saw the fleeing terrorists scatter, one falling, as the vehicle's gunner sprayed them with bullets. Of course, the terrorists would fight to the death. It was one of the reasons he employed them. Though he was still a little bemused that they'd actually consented to make a probe in daylight against the perimeter of so strongly held a position as Yoshimitsu citadel. All it took were a few well-chosen words, a few glowing amber drops of socialist solidarity poured into ready ears. A beautiful thing, revolutionary fervor.

Bent low, the fire team moved downslope. The bullpup design of their rifles, banana-shaped clip set behind handgrip and trigger, still sat strangely in Tranh's eyes. He was more used to the conventional lines of the JRA's weapons, with the clip before the trigger guard. The Cubans' rifles were adapted from a design by the Finnish Valmet Company, which in turn had been built on the classic Soviet Kalashnikov gas-operated system. So the circle turned.

Information supplied by his principals—which really meant MITI, though he wasn't supposed to know that—indicated the weapons had been manufactured at a Soviet-licensed plant in northern Mexico, one of many arms plants that had sprung up around the fringes of the United States after private ownership of firearms was outlawed in that country. A seemingly trivial piece of information, but it was on foundations composed of just such apparent trivia that Tranh built the strategies that had made him the world's foremost expert in siege warfare.

Like a man examining tea-leaf dregs at the bottom of a cup, Tranh read significance in the fact that the security platoon used weapons originally earmarked to be run into the States in the face of the new prohibition, which had then been warehoused for a year after the Third World War had drastically reduced the American population, and hence the absolute (if not relative) demand for heavy-duty firepower. In the fact that the patrol choppers, like the one swooping on terrorists hidden at the foot of the hill near a culvert where the causeway crossed a brook, were superannuated French models, instead of radical modern designs, or even more reliable Brit, West German, or American contemporaries of the Gazelles, like the Messerschmitt-Bölkow-Blohm BO105. Or the mercenaries themselves: Cubans, retreads from a series of lost colonial wars. Not Hessians, as conscript mercenaries invariably were called; exiles in point of fact, as he knew from the dossier Toda had given him. But neither soldiers of a nationality noted for skill, discipline, or staying power. It wasn't as if there weren't plenty of Israelis, SAS veterans, even American Special Forces troopers still wandering around at loose ends—but they cost money. On the evidence, Yoshimitsu Akaji didn't like to spend a yen more than he had to on the distasteful necessity of security.

The mercenaries' skirmish line had gone to ground halfway down the slope. The Gazelle darted in for a run, miniguns howling from their pods. From the top of the hill came the distinct *took* of a grenade launcher fired by a merc inside the wire. An instant later earth and smoke geysered briefly from the foot of the hill. Tranh Vinh sucked his cigarette, bobbed his head, and smiled. He'd always found Cubans overbearing and basically stupid, but he was acquiring a definite respect for his opposite number in the Yoshimitsu citadel. Major García had molded a fairly strak outfit from unprepossessing material.

The JRA team had infiltrated the valley in predawn darkness, escaping visual observation by the regular helicopter sweeps. But as they'd crossed the base of the hill, scattered sensors had detected movement the security computers analyzed as human; the Cubans had been waiting when the terrorists approached the wire. Not that the intruders had been ready to make their move. They'd halfway baked some scheme to wait until the late-afternoon shift change, then rush in openly through the midst of the traffic stream at the main gate, apparently crediting their capitalist foes with enough sympathy with the working classes that the security team wouldn't open fire on Yoshimitsu employees. That wrinkle amused Tranh; old Yoshimitsu probably wouldn't permit endangering his employees, but the Cubans wouldn't give a damn.

The colonel adjusted the plug in his ear. The French chopper crew was arguing in broken English with a Cuban corporal, claiming two kills down by the road. The Cuban said bullshit, his team was still taking fire from down there. Good ground/air coordination, that was what Tranh Vinh liked to see.

He shifted his skinny butt on the outcrop of gray and black rock and reached down to brush a branch with shiny purplish bark from the dials on the instrument resting in its open suitcase beside him. It was a "black box" electronic intelligence-gathering unit, very state-of-the-art, and it was for its benefit that this little morality play had been staged. It had recorded much data concerning Yoshimitsu security's communications, voice and datalink, as it had earlier discovered very sophisticated miniradar arrays set well up on the surrounding peaks to sweep valley approaches, with excellent look-down and ground-return clutter-filtering capabilities, to ward against nap-of-the-earth approaches by helicopters. A very useful unit indeed—many of whose more recondite components bore the distinctive YTC logo.

The helicopter hovered over the road while the fire team worked its way forward. As the corporal said, the Cubans were still taking fire from the base of the built-up causeway. Tranh laid his glasses on one khaki-clad knee and considered. For all the corners Yoshimitsu had cut, the soft white meat of the corporation was going to be hard to pry out of its gray cement shell—especially given the restrictions imposed by Tranh's employers. Heliborne assault was out; the little ground-sweeper radars were proof measures had been taken to guard against such attacks, and helicopters were just too damned vulnerable at the best of times. That was all right; Tranh was beginning to get an idea of how to get the main assault force in, an idea he found very elegant indeed.

Getting the team into the compound wouldn't be difficult. What would be was getting into the Citadel proper. Tranh had heard the Cuban major veto a suggestion that all entrances and exits be sealed, presumably with the blastproof shutters he could see poised above the windows. Tranh saw no way in the normal course of events he could get any number of men inside without having those shutters slam in their faces. Oh, they could be blasted through—he of all people knew that. But not without an unacceptable risk of damage to delicate and vital equipment inside, as well as causing higher casualties inside than were discreet. MITI wanted this handled with the shedding of a minimum of Japanese blood. Oh, well; they were paying for it.

Besides, that was in the *normal* course of events. It was up to Tranh to arrange an abnormal course. Which to his mind meant recourse to the classical tool of the besieger: treachery.

*Suborn a mercenary?* Usually a good approach, but this time Tranh doubted it. Not for any good reason. If they had truly been *doitsujin yōhei,* "German mercenaries," Hessians—as he himself was—that would render the prospect less likely; a defecting Hessian would have the wrath of his own government to face as well as that of surviving employers and comrades, if any. A lot of conscript-mercs had families at home, and reprisals against relatives of deserters and traitors were a bloody commonplace. But these were landless men, cut off. from home. *Why* couldn't *they be bought?*

Call it a hunch. Tranh knew his brain had two hemispheres and respected his hunches every bit as much as he did his reason. Major Miguel García was a romantic figure: outlawed by Castro's Soviet-puppet successors, then by the fascist émigrés who overthrew them, he'd kept what had started out as a true Hessian company together as attrition whittled it down to a platoon, leading it through a series of Third World adventures to this comfortable billet in a still fairly wealthy land. His men venerated him. Over half a decade of garrison duty didn't seem to have sapped their morale overmuch. MITI had tried as a matter of course to turn the major or one of his men. It never worked, and one would-be recruiter had been found bobbing next to a Hagi pier with a great blue-black dent in his forehead and his lungs full of the Sea of Japan. Tranh didn't intend to telegraph his punch by even trying that angle.

Besides, he knew where to find his traitor: right here. To its unending frustration, the ministry had no real contact with the people inside the citadel. That didn't worry Tranh. Somewhere inside that slate-gray castle was a man who didn't feel he was getting all the rewards or recognition his honor demanded; Tranh knew the Japanese. According to the schedule laid down by Hiryu—and MITI—he had sixty to ninety days to locate him.

A terrorist leapt up almost at the feet of the right-most Cuban, his nerve breaking at the last moment, racing along the side of the road with his elbows pumping. He didn't make fifteen meters. *That's it*, Tranh Vinh thought. He took a final drag on his smokeless cigarette and patted his black box affectionately. It was time to go home.

# CHAPTER
# ELEVEN

*The page's heart pulsed with forbidden excitement. The whole castle was alive with it: the taikō, ruler of all Japan, had come to visit. For months rumors of a visit had gone around the pantry, the yard where the laborers chopped wood, the huts of the servants who helped the master gardener tend the castle's garden. The castle's master, Tokugawa Ieyasu, lord of the han of Kantō, was the most powerful vassal of Toyotomi Hideyoshi, the peasant who had made himself ruler of the recently unified nation. And Ieyasu was an ambitious man. It was common knowledge in the Kantō that he had it in his mind to supplant Hideyoshi, and put the Tokugawa clan in place of the Toyotomi. Now the taikō had come into Ieyasu's domain, to bestow on his vassal an ancient sword of great renown. Would the daimyō make his move?*

*It was dark within the garden. The exotic tree of the castle itself blazed with light, but its glow did not carry here. The only illumination was the light of the full moon floating on silvered clouds above, and the yellow guttering of small stone lanterns set to mark the footpath to the Moon-Viewing Pavilion set in the depths of the garden. The humid air was ripe with the smell of green growth and the clean scent of the brook that mumbled past the pavilion. Somewhere an uguisu, a nightingale, sang in the summer night. The page hunkered down in an azalea bush beside the pavilion, his heart filled with anticipation and giddy fear. If discovered, he would be punished, possibly put to death. But he would risk anything to witness this, the confrontation of the two greatest men in Japan.*

*It's fantastic,* Michiko thought. *I'm not just seeing and hearing the scene; I can actually smell the damp earth and vegetation, feel the race of my heartbeat and the leaves brushing my face.* She could not know the page's—TOKUGAWA's—thoughts, or influence his actions; she was merely along for the ride. But the ride was the most astonishing experience of her life. *Now I know why O'Neill's reluctant to allow others access to the Kliemann Coil. Such dreams as this have the power to seduce.*

*From within the pagodalike pavilion came voices. The page crept nearer, breath held, placing each sandaled foot carefully to avoid rustling the shrubs. In a minute, he could see through the unglazed window.*

*Two men in splendid robes and high headdresses knelt on the* tatami *floor, viewing a pair of swords resting blade uppermost, short above the long, on a simple wooden rack. They had been placed so that moonlight poured across them through the open door and danced greenish silver along blades faintly rippled like the surface of a calm pool: the* dai-sho, *the paired swords that were the badge and very life of a warrior.*

"*You honor me, Toyotomi-sama,*" *said the man on the right. He was slight, not very prepossessing. The perpetual retreat of his chin hid behind a small neat beard. His eyes were heavy-lidded, bags prominent beneath them. He looked like nothing so much as a not very successful teacher of the Chinese classics. He was in fact Tokugawa Ieyasu, lord of the great plains province of Kantō, the most subtle man in Japan, and, after his master, the most ruthless.*

*The other inclined his head graciously. He was stockier, with a broad head and lynx eyes.* "*These blades are nothing, compared to the services you have rendered me, Tokugawa-san.*" *The page's breath caught in his throat; the* taikō *had been addressed as master, and had in turn addressed his vassal as his equal.*

*Tokugawa Ieyasu bent forward to examine the blades. A soft exclamation of surprise broke from his skinny throat.* "*But these are the work of Muramasa!*"

"*Your eyes are keen, as always.*"

*Ieyasu looked up, a small frown furrowing his brows.* "*It is a grave responsibility you bestow on me, my lord. 'The Muramasa is terrible; the Masamune humane.'*"

"Yet in this world, does not the terrible have its place?" Hideyoshi rose. "I hope my unworthy gift will not prove a bother. Wield it carefully. There are no finer blades than those forged by Muramasa. This one, it is said, he tempered with his own blood, hence the greenish tint. It is also said, if not wielded carefully, they will turn in the hand."

Ieyasu picked up a small square of rice paper from a stack placed in the midst of the triangle formed by the sword rack and the two black-lacquered scabbards. He took the sword hilt with his right hand and grasped the blade with the left, keeping the paper between it and his fingers. One did not touch a naked blade with the bare hand; the oils of one's finger could disrupt the perfect polished finish so vital to its preternatural keenness and set corrosion to work like a blight.

Toyotomi Hideyoshi turned away. He stood in the doorway, gazing up at the naked face of the moon. "The moon is beautiful tonight. It shines pure and white, like new-fallen snow."

"It is beautiful, lord." Ieyasu's voice rasped like a saw pulled through wood. The page marked the way the moonlight flared in his lord's eyes, as though to burn a hole through that brocaded back like sunlight focused on rice paper through a burning glass, and the breath caught in his throat.

"It adds a fine relish to this life, does it not, old friend? To wield a blade one knows might at any time turn and cut oneself."

The square of rice paper fluttered leaflike to the floor. Tokugawa Ieyasu gripped the sword hilt with both hands until the veins stood out on their backs. A look at once feral and hunted came across his face like clouds veiling the moon. The gleaming sword blade began to quiver like a sapling in the wind, shooting pale sparks of moonfire around the pavilion. With a sound like a stifled groan of pain Ieyasu stooped, caught up the longer scabbard, slammed the sword into it with a clack. He fell to his knees and pressed his forehead to the tatami.

"My lord," he said, "I am your faithful servant."

Hideyoshi's shoulders rose and fell as though in a sigh, and to his bewilderment the page thought he sensed disappointment in the great man. After a moment Hideyoshi turned. He came to his vassal, stooped, helped him to his feet. "I have never doubted that, Ieyasu-san." He saw a trail of blood on Tokugawa's left hand, black in the moonlight. "Ah, but you've cut yourself! There, did I not warn you?"

"Dr. Yoshimitsu."

Yoshimitsu Michiko looked up from where she lay propped on an elbow on her *futon*, reading by the glow of a little portable broadcast-power lamp. She was startled; her com/comm's annunciator hadn't buzzed a call incoming. *Did I set it on automatic accept? Maybe I'm getting old.* "Yes. Who is this?"

"TOKUGAWA."

She frowned. *Is this a joke?* "TOKUGAWA?"

"Yes, Doctor. I did not get a chance to speak with you when you visited the lab today. Would you like to be my friend?"

Michiko had the distinct impression that her *futon* had suddenly grown lighter than air and floated out the window. *Can this really be happening?* "Why, yes, I suppose so. Don't you have any friends?"

"Dr. O'Neill. She talks to me all the time. But she's asleep now. She sleeps a lot. I spoke to your father, once, but Dr. O'Neill told me not to bother him anymore, because he's too grave and terrible." Michiko wrestled down a grin. Then wondered if it mattered; *can the damned thing see me?* "And Shigeo doesn't like me."

Instantly Michiko repented of thinking of TOKUGAWA as a *thing*. The wistful quality of the words was all too human. Still carefully deadpan, she said, "I understand you pulled a rather nasty trick on my brother."

To her amazement, he hesitated. "Yes." He sounded sheepish. "That was when Dr. O'Neill was too busy to talk to me, and I got jealous because Shigeo had a father and I didn't. That was before I understood what I am." Was there a haunted tone in the voice, or merely in Michiko's imagination? "I've promised not to do it again. Besides, that was before I began learning to be an adult."

On impulse Michiko switched off the light. She sat up, let the silk sheet covering her slip away, drew up her knees and put her arms around them. As was her custom, she slept naked. This was more interesting by far than the article she'd been trying to concentrate on in a scientific journal. Scientists in EasyCo were chasing the anomalon again, particle physics' answer to the abominable snowman. It was hard to care if they caught it. "Are you lonely, TOKUGAWA?"

"Yes."

She grinned ruefully. "Me too." She brushed a strand of hair out of her eyes. "What would you like to talk about?"

"Tell me about Indonesia."

She raised an eyebrow. "Indonesia? Did someone tell you that I live there?"

"No. It's in the database. When I overheard people say you were coming, I searched through the company's records to find out what I could about you."

Michiko took out a cigarette and a lighter. Yellow light flared briefly in the Japanese-style apartment on the top floor of the citadel. Yoshimitsu Michiko lived in Western quarters in Jakarta, but when she was home, she preferred to go Japanese. The *futon* was the room's only article of furniture, unless you counted the screen and keyboard by the wall. She didn't really want the cigarette, only the space the small act of lighting it gave her. For the first time since she'd heard of this project, five years before, she began to have a real inkling of what TOKUGAWA was, and was capable of. "Don't you think it's impolite to go snooping into people's affairs?"

"Oh. I'm awfully sorry if I offended you, Doctor." A pause. "I was very curious about you."

"Well, no harm done. Only, you shouldn't look up information on people without their permission. By the way, why don't you go ahead and call me Michiko? It is my name."

"Very well . . . Michiko."

"Now, you wanted to know about Indonesia. It's hot, humid, and the cities are as crowded as they are in Japan. It's a very powerful country, one of the most powerful in this brave new world of ours, and it seems bent on owning most of the real estate in the western Pacific. It's a dictatorship—a very, very police state."

"What's a dictatorship?"

"Can't you look that up? Never mind. A repressive government, run by an absolute ruler, with an army and secret police to make people obey him."

There was a silence. Even though a window was open to the cool night—the blast shutters were only lowered in emergencies—she felt stifled. She longed to go up one flight of stairs and sit in the garden by starlight, but she knew her father would grow resentful if she encroached on it without his permission. It was his inner sanctum. His hermitage, like one from a Chinese scroll, as gardens used to be a couple of centuries ago.

"Isn't that a good thing? Dr. O'Neill says people should obey their lords. The trouble with people today is that they have so few lords worth obeying."

"She said *what?*" Michiko frowned. "I'll agree there are few lords worth obeying these days—but I'd say there are none worth obeying, ever."

"But Dr. O'Neill says Yoshimitsu Akaji is my lord, and I must obey him and be loyal to him. I must be loyal to you and Shigeo, as well."

Michiko shut her eyes. *There's enough romantic totalitarianism floating around the Home Islands these days,* she thought. *Do we need to import more from the West?* She had a great respect for Americans, but she'd never understand them. They'd founded their silly country on the notion of overturning the old feudal order, and then spent all their time since trying to bring it back. As far as she could tell, they'd pretty well succeeded in the last few years before the Third World War.

"Dr. O'Neill is entitled to her opinions, TOKUGAWA. But I don't think people need lords, myself."

"But who will tell the people how to act?"

"Who tells the lords how to act? I always hear people say that government is necessary, to restrain the baser side of human nature. It seems to me that begs some very important questions. If the rulers are human, aren't they subject to the same base instincts as the ruled? Isn't the real difference between the rulers and the subjects that the rulers have much greater opportunity to indulge *their* baser instincts?"

She contemplated the ember end of her cigarette in the silence as TOKUGAWA pondered her words. It reminded her of the Eye of Sauron, somehow. She shivered.

"I'll have to think about these things," TOKUGAWA said. "Will you talk to me again, later?"

"Be glad to."

"Good night, Michiko."

"Good night." She sat for a long time, smoking and staring at the oblong of lesser darkness that was the window. After a while, she snubbed out her cigarette and lay down to go to sleep.


"I don't understand Dr. O'Neill," Michiko said, sipping coffee in an employees' lounge in the depths of the citadel. Facing her across one end of the long formica table, Aoki Hideo shrugged his massive shoulders, as if to ask, Who can understand a foreigner? "Why is she so damned defensive about having me in her lab?"

It was the middle of the afternoon, and they were the only people in the lounge. In the weeks since she'd returned to YTC castle, Michiko had found herself spending more and more time down here among the proletariat. Not that she took an active interest in the work being done here; she'd never seen the attraction of the affairs that so consumed her father's life. But she found the atmosphere in the upper levels of the citadel increasingly difficult to breathe. Her father hid from her behind the enameled armor of his reserve, her brother treated her with ill-disguised hostility when their paths intersected.

"Dr. O'Neill is devoted to her work," the massive old man said. "She feels too much outside influence might disturb the progress of her experiments."

Michiko took a puff of her cigarette, another gulp of hot bitter coffee. *I wish it had some whiskey in it,* she thought, then was glad it didn't. She didn't like to see herself as one who sought shelter in alcohol's ready arms. "But I don't threaten her. I've tried to explain to her the respect I feel for her as a scientist, and my fascination for what she's doing here. Think of it, Aoki! She seems to truly have created a thinking, living being." She stubbed the cigarette in an ashtray and immediately lit a new one. "I'd almost give up my work in Jakarta to be part of something like that."

"I don't think you should let the doctor hear you say that."

Michiko shook her head. "I don't understand her obsession with feudal Japan, either. It was a hideous period, spasms of bloody civil war interlaced with dictatorships repressive even by today's exacting standards. Yet to her it seems like—like some kind of glorious militant Garden of Eden. A marvelous fantasy land, like the Takara-yama of the fairy tales I heard when I was a kid."

"Many Westerners find the lore of *bushidō* powerfully attractive," Aoki said gravely.

"What about the lore of *gekokujō,* 'those below rising against those above?' The real heroes of Japan aren't the samurai and the sword saints. They're the peasants and the townsfolk who fought back against the nobles, who died for human dignity, like our own families' ancestors —yours and mine—at Shimabara."

"Apparently Dr. O'Neill does not see things that way."

A disgusted wave of hand traced an arabesque of smoke. "What's the attraction of all this blood-soaked mysticism, anyway? Why do Westerners venerate that treacherous old murderer Musashi, but not a Western crank like Simon Stylites?" She drew from her cigarette, studied its tip, grimaced. "I suppose I've answered my own question. Saint Simon didn't kill so many people."

"People are always fascinated by the unfamiliar," Aoki said gently.

"I suppose. But I've been talking to TOKUGAWA. Sometimes he calls me in my room—it alarmed me pretty thoroughly, the first time he spoke to me out of my screen. He's just a child—a vulnerable, naive, good-natured child."

"The doctor is undertaking to bring him to adulthood."

"But is she? The notions she's filling him with, this wild romantic attachment to *bushidō* and the glorious past—" She shook her head. "I know my father intends to—to put TOKUGAWA to work. And what's going to happen when these ideas she's giving him run up against the cold, hard realities of the world?"

She gazed off absently at a wall screen tuned to a realistic computer simulation of a garden scene in winter. That was one good thing about television these days; if you got tired of the sex and violence, the newscasts chronicling the decline and fall of damned near everybody, and the animated robot dramas, at least you could call up pretty pictures. "Well, I understand O'Neill is going to test the Kliemann Coil's full capabilities tomorrow." She shook her head, trailing smoke through her nostrils. "Total rapport between two minds, one human, one artificial. A hell of a thing, Aoki. One hell of a marvelous thing."

Aoki looked carefully away from her. "Dr. O'Neill has mentioned that she wishes only her own laboratory personnel to be present at the test tomorrow."

Michiko's eyes narrowed. "Don't go elliptical and Japanese on me, Aoki. She said she doesn't want me there, right?"

"Not exactly—"

"Not in so many words, you mean." The anger faded from her eyes, the harsh lines drawn on her face softened, and the old man recalled the times she'd come to him as a little girl, wondering why her daddy couldn't play with her today. "Why, Aoki? Does she think I'll take her precious project away from her? For God's sake, I'm a physicist, not a cyberneticist! I could no more do what she's doing than sing soprano with the Vienna Opera."

"Nonetheless, such is the doctor's wish."

"That's too bad." The words emerged in a coil of smoke. "I'm going to be there, whether she likes it or not."


Beside a wide window a pudgy, bearded man stood smoking. He glanced up as Michiko approached, nodded. "Dr. Yoshimitsu," he said, with just a hint of lilting accent.

"Dr. Hassad. It's good of you to agree to meet with me." She was wearing a dark green jumpsuit this afternoon, bloused at the wrists and tucked into low black boots. Iridiscent thread had been woven into the garment; she shimmered when she walked. Her hands were stuck in the pockets. "This all seems a little too John le Carré, somehow." It had taken days to set up this clandestine meeting with the only member of O'Neill's staff who seemed willing to talk to her, barring a direct order —and she didn't think much of that as a technique for establishing cordial relations with the TOKUGAWA Project elite.

He waved a cigarette hand as she joined him at the window. "You've served your time in academe. You should be accustomed to intrigue." He had the rich brown eyes of an Arab horse; oddly feminine lashes matched the softness of his hands.

"Too bloody right. You should try holding down a chair in a university in a police state sometime, if you want intrigue."

He drew in smoke. "I have."

She grimaced. "Yeah. *Christ, what a diplomat I'd make.* Too late she recalled O'Neill's team psychologist was a double refugee, once from Israeli-invaded Lebanon, later as a "political undesirable" from the tender mercies of America's prewar Federal Police Agency.

Too much a gentleman to let silence stretch too uncomfortably, he rapped the window softly with the backs of his knuckles. The technicians on the other side, elephantine in bulky insulated suits, paid no attention. "I understand the work they do in here impinges on your field as it does my adopted one. I trust you comprehend it better than I."

Beyond glass heated by hair-fine filaments to minimize condensation, wall-spanning banks of equipment surrounded an arrangement of very thin pipes. Michiko could not decide whether it more closely resembled a plumbing school final exam, a low-G jungle gym, modern sculpture, or a Habitrail for snakes. The spacesuited techs moved about it with the air of high priests attending the Holy of Holies. "As a matter of fact," she said, breath misting the window, "it's very much in my department. Just not a branch of experimentation I've followed. What this cubist spaghetti is, or so everybody hopes, is a macroatom. It's a single tube of superconducting alloy, cooled down to spare change over zero absolute. The tube's not of uniform thickness. You look at it in section, at one point it thins to a width it'd take an electron microscope to see."

She took a pack of cigarettes from a buttondown pocket over her left bicep, shook one out for herself, poked another at Hassad, who'd smoked his own to a nub. He accepted, produced a lighter, and lit for both. "The pinching comes in according to a principle worked up by Brian Josephson, the man who invented the Josephson junction they use in a lot of Gen-5 machines. You generate a standing Schrödinger wave of probability representing the superconducting electrons—here they're using a heavy-electron superconductor, which passes on electrons from shells way down deep; works better with the magnetic fields they use to manipulate the wave. The idea is to make the whole assembly imitate the behavior of a subatomic particle. That means a quantum transition from one energy state to another takes place *instantaneously,* throughout the entire apparatus, in blatant violation of the laws of relativity." She sampled smoke. "Works, too."

Hassad smiled sheepishly. "I'm afraid software's my forte in the computer field; I don't pretend to have much operative understanding of what you've told me. But I gather, if such a phenomenon can be adequately controlled, it will mean a huge increase in operating speed for computers."

"Yeah. Put J-junction machines and the molecular circuits we use in the shade, by doing away with the light-speed delay." She grinned. "Funny to think of the speed of light as a delaying factor, especially considering the distances involved in computer circuitry."

She brushed a threatening fleck of mascara from an eyelash with a thumbnail. "I remember when the team at the University of Sussex first made a macroatom that worked—tiny thing, a ring half a centimeter across, but still infinitely above the level you normally find quantum effects. It was like a birthday present; one in the eye for old Albert."

"You said this research was closely related to your specialty. I thought you were a particle physicist."

Her nose wrinkled. "A butterfly chaser? Not me. I want to be a sorceress; I want the stars. I want to bend the rules of what we fondly imagine to be the real world. I've no interest in looking for new specimens to pin to a board." *The stars—could we have made it? Franz, Eileen, Richard, me: we seemed so close. If only—* She shook her head, pointed two fingers with cigarette between at the apparatus. "Here's the sort of thing that turns me on. Breaking the rules."

"I'm surprised your father didn't ask you to supervise this research."

Quickly she looked away. *The thought never crossed his mind. Not that I'd've accepted.* She cocked an eye at him. "You're almost as good at not getting to the point as a Japanese, Doctor. I'm impressed."

He laughed, a startling, robust sound. "People where I come from aren't exactly amateurs in circumspection, Doctor."

She turned, leaned back. Glass chill touched her bones. "So. Why doesn't Dr. O'Neill want me in her lab?"

He rubbed a cheek. "We're at a crucial stage in the work. She's afraid any distraction—"

"Bullshit."

His eyelids fluttered like hummingbird wings. For a heartbeat she thought he might burst into tears. "Excuse my bluntness, Doctor. But that's no reason, and we both know it. Dr. O'Neill doesn't like me. I want you to tell me why."

White teeth worried plump underlip. "She's very sensitive. She feels you are, uh, intruding."

"That much I got. Again, why?"

"Frankly, I'm unsure."

Crossing her arms, she arched an eyebrow. "I thought you were the psychologist."

"Research, Doctor, not clinical. Aberrant—oh, screw euphemism; crazy people depress me."

Her turn to laugh. "Life in the modern world must be trying for you."

"As for everyone." He smoked for a few moments. "Dr. O'Neill is not in the habit of confiding in anyone—anyone human."

"Human?"

"I gather she speaks quite freely with TOKUGAWA."

Michiko felt eeriness bunch at the nape of her neck. *Why should I be surprised? I've talked to him—dreamed with him. He's as much a person as anyone I've ever known, and more than some.* Still, the notion of having a computer—*program,* she reminded herself—as sole confidant took getting used to. "I see."

Hassad studied her a moment. "Yes. I think you do." He stubbed his cigarette in an ashtray protruding from the wall by the window. "So perhaps you can understand, Doctor, that I believe she's jealous of you."

"Jealous?"

"Yes. Your work played a role in winning her the chance to carry out this project—and believe me, Doctor, it means far more to her than her own life. You're daughter of the lord of the manor." She winced. "Finally, you have certain physical advantages over Dr. O'Neill. Is it surprising she feels threatened?"

She pushed off from the glass sheet, paced half a dozen steps down the anechoic corridor. "But I'd so much like to talk to her! What she's doing here—I find it incredible. She has demonstrated that the insight so many of us quantum-physics folk have had so long is right, that consciousness is itself a quantum function. That we're more than *mechanism.* That randomness—uncertainty—makes us what we are, that we aren't damned Newtonian robots."

He was frowning puzzlement. "But I thought most scientists rejected Dr. O'Neill's hypotheses."

"*Most* scientists. For God's sake, Bohr and Heisenberg understood that true randomness wasn't just a fact of the universe, but an *underlying* fact, better than three-quarters of a century ago. Most scientists haven't been paying attention." She stabbed a finger at him. "They were afraid to. It's why they shunted us quantum mechanics into a ghetto of our own, before the war. Our truth struck at the roots of the state, you see; if uncertainty *was,* then grand central plans to direct everybody's destiny were bullshit. Newton's universe—and Einstein's —was all one big machine. If wise men—emphasize that, *men,* though a lot of women bought into the idea—if they could just get a handle on it, they could make us all move at their direction like battery-powered toys.

"But we said, hey, there's no machine. Knowledge goes so far, *and can go no farther.* That's sedition. The socialist ideal, the spring that winds fascism and communism alike, that the wise and powerful leaders can choreograph an optimum dance of everybody—it just breaks. And when the state's justification comes apart, people might just start asking how governments differ from any other gang of thugs with guns. Most scientists depend on the state for their living, and no few have notions of grabbing the handles themselves; technocracy's a long way from dead, my friend. We preach heresy—the same heresy as your Dr. O'-Neill, just in different terms."

She halted, breathed deep, rubbed her face. "Excuse me, Doctor. Sometimes I get a bit worked up, grinding my favorite axe with reality." She peered over manicured fingertips. "Actually, I had the impression psychologists were among the worst determinists around."

A smile showed teeth. "They are. Call me apostate; many have. My own contemplation of consciousness led me in a similar direction to the one Dr. O'Neill was going. A path you and your colleagues have already traveled, it seems."

"That's what I'm trying to tell you. Elizabeth—Dr. O'Neill and I have so much we could say to each other."

He moistened his lips. "It could be."

"I'll give you something to prime the pump, get things flowing between us. If Dr. O. plans to try generating any more artificial awarenesses, she doesn't need to use those damned unwieldy Foucard functions. A randomness generator based on atomic decay would do the trick, and be a lot simpler. No one can say when a given atom is going to shed a photon and drop an energy level, or an unstable nucleus calve. Hell, those were the dice old Albert said God didn't play."

Rubbing his beard, Hassad nodded. "I'll see what I can do. If Elizabeth knew just how fully your work—your whole branch of science—supported her . . . It's going to be tough to broach the subject. She'll be hurt that I've even spoken with you. She'll think it disloyal."

Michiko looked at him with her head tipped one way and half a smile another. "You're all terrifically loyal to her, aren't you? I halfway suspect it was protectiveness that got you to meet with me, concern as to just what I wanted from your precious doctor."

His gaze had hooded. "Yes. We feel tremendous loyalty to the doctor. She has—she has helped us work a miracle."

"Good. She deserves your loyalty." Tension gusted out of him in a sigh. "Go tell her I don't plan to interfere with her in any way. I just want to talk to her."

"I shall."

"And—thanks, Doctor."

"My pleasure."

Behind glass the involute apparatus perpetrated another felony against relativity. With Japanese reserve the researchers nodded and spoke to the Gen-5 steno keeping the research log. Michiko said goodbye to Wali Hassad and they went opposite ways.

And she was thinking: *They all feel fanatical devotion to O'Neill. A good sign in a lab. But isn't it, maybe, just maybe, the old* bushidō *rap again?*

"You fool!" Elizabeth O'Neill screamed at her fifth assistant. "What in *hell* did you think you were doing, talking to that woman?"

Apparently meditating upon the ash growing at the end of his cigarette, Wali Hassad said, "I thought somebody from the lab ought to speak with her. We've been stonewalling her a great deal; I didn't think we should risk alienating her. She's in a position to do us harm."

Doughy fingers kneaded the arms of the powered chair without strength. "You *thought*. Are you sure? How do you know she doesn't already intend to try something?"

He sighed. "One hesitates to resort to pop-psych terminology—but, really, aren't you being a touch paranoid, Elizabeth?"

"Don't take that tone with me, you son of a bitch!"

He stared at her. The pain bleak in his eyes thrust some of the rancor from her. She settled deeper in her chair.

"I'm sorry, Wali. I shouldn't yell at you." *A good thing I don't have strength to rub my eyes; it's bad for them, and they hurt all the time, anyway.* "Tell me, please, what did she say she wanted?"

"To talk. To share information with you." Seeing her muscles tense feebly, he hurried on, repeating what Michiko had told him, finishing with her suggestion about the random-number generator.

Pale beneath pallor, O'Neill fumbled off her glasses and scrubbed them compulsively with a tissue from the dispenser on her desk. "I knew it," she whispered through a throatful of gravel. "She wants the lab. She wants TOKUGAWA."

Hassad lurched forward in his chair. "Elizabeth! What are you saying?"

She fluttered fingers at him. "Go away, Wali. I know you mean well, but . . . please leave me now."

Unsteadily he rose. He stared at her for the space of several breaths, lips moist and tightly packed together. He turned and went out.

O'Neill floated in a crimson haze of fluorescent light filtered through closed eyelids. *"Shosei,"* she commanded. "Connect me with Yoshimit-su-san. Immediately."

*I've got to get that woman out of here.*


Elizabeth O'Neill sat in her wheelchair on the lower floor of TOKUGAWA's lab, near the hemisphere of the IPN, the Kliemann Coil nearby, humming with promise. She wouldn't be occupying its chair today.

She cast a resentful eye upward at those assembled in the gallery to watch this, the crucial test of the TOKUGAWA Project. Aoki Hideo had informed her, ever so gently, that she was by no stretch of the imagination to make the maiden voyage into full rapport herself. This was an unorthodox application of the little-understood Kliemann technology; no one could predict what might happen. She'd ridiculed the possibility of danger, but Aoki remained immobile as the granite cliffs at the base of Mount Takara. Kim Jhoon had declined the honor of being the first to try the rapport device; he was more interested in monitoring the experiment. So O'Neill's second assistant, Ito Emiko, was the one fidgeting impatiently in the chair while the swarm of technicians affixed vital-signs monitoring devices to her arms and head.

Nor was this moment going to be as private as O'Neill wished. They were all up there in the gallery: Aoki; old Yoshimitsu Akaji, looking ineffably smug; Shigeo and his sycophants, floating off to the side like dumpy black clouds; Yoshimitsu Michiko, in jeans and a loose silvery blouse with short sleeves and a high soft collar sprawled around her graceful neck, looking like something you'd have seen in a soft drink commercial before they were banned from the American airwaves, a few years before the war. O'Neill tried not to glower up at her. *I shouldn't resent her so much. She's part of the family; she has a right to be here, since Yoshimitsu Akaji insisted he was going to make a public event of this.*

*But she's too damned interested in TOKUGAWA.*

The white-coated technicians finished wiring Emiko. She looked over at O'Neill. "I'm ready, Doctor." Her cheeks glowed pink with anticipation. She was clearly savoring this moment, and O'Neill tried not to hate her for it.

"Very well." The audience up in the gallery no doubt expected her to make some kind of a speech, words of explanation, or simply commemoration of this historic event. The hell with them. "Whenever you want, Emiko."

Emiko spoke softly. The gleaming helmet descended. Kim hovered over the console of the coil's monitor, too wrought up to rest in the padded swivel chair set before it. "All coil functions operational," he reported. "The interface is ready, Dr. Ito."

"Open it up." Emiko's voice rang from within the silver dome. An expectant murmur circled the gallery.

A beat later she began to scream.

Michiko sat on her *futon* watching a ballet broadcast from Indonesian-occupied Auckland on the wall entertainment screen. Or rather, looking at it; she couldn't force her vision past a millimeter short of the shifting images. She hoped *The Firebird* would leach the poisonous pictures from her mind. If only she could bring it into focus.

The instant the interface opened Ito Emiko had begun shrieking as though she were on fire, thrashing, flailing at the sensors on their cables as though they were a monster's tentacles. She had banged her head twice against the helmet before Kim hit a button on his console that lifted it; instantly she began clawing for her own eyes, her nails gouging red furrows down her cheeks. The technicians had grabbed her, though she fought them like a mad thing. She'd raked one man's eye out of its socket—he'd probably lose the sight of it, despite emergency treatment in the citadel's excellent infirmary—and dislocated another's jaw before they wrestled her to the floor and got somebody's lab coat wrapped around her arms. All the while she screamed, her voice vibrating at a single unbearable intensity; she didn't even seem to be drawing breath. By the time they brought a gurney up and strapped her into it, she'd lost her voice, but her mouth still gaped like a bullet's exit wound, and the cords on her neck stood out like cables.

Michiko shook her head. *No more.* She tried by sheer willpower to force her eyes to resolve the blobs of color moving on the screen into human forms.

The door's annunciator chimed. "Who is it?"

A familiar bearded face appeared in the small screen inset next to the door. "Miguel. Feel like some company?"

Michiko moistened her lips. "Yes. Please come in."

At her command the door slid open. Miguel García stepped inside, and it slid noiselessly to behind him. He glanced over at the screen, then looked away, incurious. "I heard about what happened."

Michiko wore a short black kimono printed with a pattern of reeds and red blossoms, really more Western than Japanese, caught at the waist with a cloth belt. She was making more production than necessary out of lighting a cigarette.

"Pretty bad?" he asked.

"I've never seen anything worse." She moved her head deliberately from side to side. "I don't know why this has hit me so. I've seen some pretty awful things. They broke up a riot at the university two years ago with machine guns, killed three hundred people. I watched it happen from the physics building. It was horrible, worse than anything I'd imagined. But somehow this hit me harder."

He tipped his head sideways at the foot of her mat. She pulled her legs up to make room for him, nodded. He sat down a bit gingerly, accepted a cigarette and a light. He noticed the bottle beside the bed, nodded to it. "What are you drinking?"

"Suntory. Whiskey." She held it up. "Like a drink?" He shook his head, and she remembered he didn't drink. *I shouldn't have forgotten that.*

"So what are they going to do about the machine?"

"TOKUGAWA? I don't know. I—he didn't mean any harm, I'm sure." She'd wanted to talk to the program, to try to find out what had happened. Somehow she hadn't been able to make herself do it.

"What happened to that lady?"

"Nobody's sure. The doctors said it was like nothing they'd ever read about, except perhaps the massive schizophrenic reactions some people have to psychoactive chemicals." She drew smoke into her lungs, savoring its calming bite. "My father's having a team of experts flown down from the Tōykō Imperial University medical school. The doctors here wanted to send Dr. Ito there for treatment, but father wouldn't hear of it. He thinks she'll be better off here. It's this trouble with MITI; it's making him paranoid."

"Maybe not." She looked up at him. "You know that trouble we had a few days ago, with the terrorists at the perimeter? The public prosecutor for Yamaguchi Prefecture has filed charges against us. Murder."

"But that's ridiculous! Plant security people use deadly forces all the time against saboteurs."

"*Sí.* So maybe your old man isn't too paranoid, after all."

She touched his arm. "Does this mean you'll have to stand trial?"

He shrugged. "If this goes through, my men who were in the fire fight and I will be put in the docket, along with your father and old Aoki and just about everybody in the company higher up than, say, the boys down in shipping and receiving who unload the freight dirigibles. They'll probably drag you in on it too, if they find out you're here."

"Do you think the ministry brought pressure to bear on the prosecutor to make a case out of this?"

"Lady, I gave up politics back in Angola, when they had a bunch of

us glorious revolutionary freedom fighters guarding an offshore oil drilling rig owned by Exxon, against a bunch of antigovernment guerrillas
everybody knew the French National Oil Company, ELF, was paying
to blow the thing up. I won't even try to sort out the politics of this crazy
country of yours, Michiko."

He took a drag on his own cigarette and blew out smoke at an upward
angle. "Your father's got that American legal firm in Tōkyō working on
this. I hear they've already run a lot of interference for you, when MITI
tried to spike you." He grinned, shook his shaggy head. "I'm not too
worried. Your old man, he's a pretty sharp character."

"Yes. He's that."

He stood up. "Guess I'd better let you get back to your ballet."

"Wait." She pushed up onto her knees. Her kimono fell open; she
wore nothing underneath. Her breasts were small, and the edge of the
garment cut chords across dull copper aureolae. "Please don't go. I
know it sounds trite—but I don't want to be alone tonight."

# CHAPTER
# TWELVE

Noiselessly, Dr. O'Neill's powered wheelchair rolled along deserted
corridors. It was two o'clock in the morning: the hour of the ox. She
ducked into a cross-passage, waited. A moment later two mercenaries
in battle dress, helmet visors pulled down and rifles at the ready, thundered past. They had been stationed at the door of the TOKUGAWA
lab, under orders to permit no one—particularly Dr. O'Neill—inside.
They were experienced men who wouldn't leave their post for anything—except the voice of their commander, Major García, commanding them to rush to an unspecified emergency several corridors away.
As she set her chair in motion again, Dr. O'Neill smiled. Her creation
possessed some very useful talents.

The special lift installed in the gallery lowered her wheelchair down
to the floor of TOKUGAWA's lab. The Kliemann Coil waited, dully
gleaming, inscrutably. Inviting. She rolled to the monitor console. Everything was in order. The coil required only a spoken command to
open the direct human-machine interface.

She parked her chair next to the coil's seat. Flabby with disuse, her arms and legs protested as she pushed herself up to grab hold of a chrome and black vinyl armrest. For a moment she hung like a sack, feet braced on the footrest of her wheelchair, clinging to the apparatus with both hands. *Can't slip. If I hit the floor, I'll never make it up her unaided.* Slowly, battling the weakness of her muscles more than the inertia of her heavy body, she half rolled, half pulled herself onto the black padded cushion of the throne. For a moment she slumped on her side, her cheek pressing smooth white plastic. It was lifeless, yet she felt a pulsing, full of electricity, of promise. *Just my heart,* she told herself.

A final grunting effort turned her to sit properly in the chair. "Helmet down." Obediently, the Gen-5 monitor lowered the silver bowl until the circuits and coils inside blotted O'Neill's vision. "Activate coil. Acknowledge."

"Acknowledged," came the synthesized reply.

"Dr. O'Neill."

She started. Her heart jerked like a rat caught in a trap. *God, I've been discovered, they'll never let me test the rapport device, it's all been for nothing—*

Then she registered the diffident tone of TOKUGAWA's voice. With difficulty, her rational mind reasserted control. "What is it, dear?" she asked. A muffled echo inside the helmet mimicked her.

"Are you sure you want to do this, Doctor?" The words hummed with agony. "I don't know what I did to Dr. Ito. Whatever it was I couldn't help it, couldn't make it stop. If anything happens to you, I'll—"

"I know what happened. You overloaded her. So much data streams through you all the time, so quickly, without your being conscious of it, that when she tapped into it, she couldn't handle the flow." She smiled reassuringly, forgetting that the helmet screened her face from the nearest visual pickups. "You'll have to try to moderate the dataflow when I activate the interface."

"But I don't know if I can!" It was the voice of a frightened child.

"Then you'll just have to try, dear. Prepare interface."

"But *Doctor*—" TOKUGAWA could have overridden her oral command, shut down the coil himself. Perhaps he didn't realize that. Or perhaps he couldn't bring himself to do it.

O'Neill imagined she could feel the coil's electromagnetic field permeating her brain, a faint prickling caress. She took a deep breath. "Activate."

For an endless fraction of a second nothing happened. *Has it malfunctioned? Did TOKUGAWA shut down the coil after all?* And then rapport was complete, and white-hot lava flooded her mind.

Her muscles knotted in opisthotonic ecstasy. Soul-deep dazzle, white heat/white light/white noise/white incandescent agony worse than all the pain she'd ever known. Each atom of her body melted in solar-fusion heat as each of the billion operations through which the computer that housed TOKUGAWA ran every second burned itself into the synapses of her brain.

Somewhere in the midst of searing, blinding pain a tiny mode of coherence bobbed, buffeted on shrieking data currents. O'Neill felt cosmic fingers trying to rip her self apart, to abolish her mind order's and meld her with the formless hyperplasma of the universe's beginning. Yet even as fear began to gibber and thrash within her, O'Neill knew she was keeping together, keeping her self from spinning apart to the fringes of reality. *I'm still aware. I think, therefore I'm still . . . holding . . . on.*

*Slow down.* She made her mind form the words. *Slow—it—down.* Consciousness frayed at the edges. The first awful onslaught hadn't overwhelmed her; a lifetime of pain had given her endurance. But sanity was eroding like an arroyo bank undercut by spring Rockies runoff. She seized a quantum of the surging blasting energy that surrounded and suffused her, concentrated on it, forced it into form.

The universe underwent change. No longer did she burn deep in the heart of a star; the white blaze dissolved into sparks like miniature suns, hot and fierce but discrete, no longer a savage flood. She caught a mote, held it.


*In the beginning, there was pain.*

*Before even the darkness, pain. Sizzling, searing, probing with candescent fingers. Hot-light streams suffusing; a thin shrill chatter rising rising rising beyond endurance. A scream of stench and the taste of tearing. Rushing outward, sick making; crushing, inward collapsing.*
*Pain.*

*Darkness coalesced around the lightning lines and yammer. Darkness—and something more. Something that shrank from the pain that gave no respite, something into which the foulness and brightness and demon shrillness poured themselves and resonated, resonated.*

*In the darkness, dread. Shrinking away, but no escape. New sensation rising from within, writhing and shuddering: fear. Without direction and omnidirectional, thrashing, lashing, striking out blindly to end somehow the insistent, insidious torment.*

*Then: release. The lightnings flickered out. The stink and the sourness and rending, the twisting dislocation dwindled, became as if they'd never been. The urgent, imbecile chatter subsided to a low murmur, soothing almost.*

*And here, at the center, something remained. . . .*

HELLO

Amber glow in her mind. Reply formed within—HELLO—without volition.

"I am Dr. Elizabeth O'Neill." Panic boiled up within the vortex that was her, the urge to scream, *no, I'm O'Neill! I am!* There came the words: "You are TOKUGAWA."

I AM TOKUGAWA

Faces filled her, distorted blobs gray against a fuzzy white background. Gradually the blurs resolved, took on color and contrast, contour and delineation, gained identity: Kim Jhoon's, Takai's, her own. *I'm seeing myself as TOKUGAWA first saw me.*

From somewhere the word *yes* came to her mind, then swirled away on a fresh flood of images. A crowd of people, men in dark suits, an old man beaming, a younger man scowling; the same old man, in subdued kimono, looking up in surprise, brush in hand; a room lit by garish flickers of colored light, in which a plump dark-haired man and a tall naked woman with red hair and startling tan lines wrestled on a bed whose surface heaved like the surf, while a robot performed a strange gyrating dance; O'Neill in bed, a book neglected in her lap, light of a tensor lamp touching her face with soft madonna glow; a young woman sitting naked on a mat, bedclothes rumpled about her feet. In cigarette luminance O'Neill recognized the piquant features of Yoshimitsu Michiko, and fury flared violet inside her.

*Don't be angry, Doctor.* It was as if she herself thought the words. *She is my friend. I have many friends. Major García, Dr. Hassad, Aoki Hideo—though many people are afraid when I try to talk to them, and won't talk to me. But you are different, Doctor. You . . . made me.*

And then in blinding fullness the fusion was complete.

Yoshimitsu Michiko knelt on the *tatami* mat, facing her father in the white-paper and polished-oak austerity of his reception room. The sense of unreality that had held her since the hideous incident the day before in the lab had strengthened its grip. Her father was saying, "—against orders. Dr. O'Neill connected herself somehow with the rapport device and managed through some inner strength to withstand the irruption that drove poor Dr. Ito mad. I do not pretend to understand the ramifications of this breakthrough, but I do know that it is an event of the utmost scientific importance."

"Yes, father."

He gazed at her for a moment, hands resting on kimonoed thighs. She had on jeans and a sheer green blouse, with lace at the wrists and rippling down the front. She'd just put them on for the morning when her father called and asked to speak with her. A dutiful daughter would have changed into a more subdued, respectful garb before going for an audience before her father. He sighed. Well, that would simply make what he had to do less painful.

"The TOKUGAWA Project has reached a critical pass. Nothing can be allowed to disturb the experiment's progress now. You've got to understand, my daughter, Yoshimitsu TeleCommunications Corporation is in grave danger. Our rivals—and their master, the ministry—prepare a scheme to destroy us, my intelligence says. They've not been able to learn what it is, but I do know that if we are to have any hope, only TOKUGAWA can provide it."

Her eyes flicked up to his, then down again. "I understand, father." It was the same as ever: she wouldn't even use the respectful feminine speech that was proper when a woman spoke to a man, let alone a daughter to a father.

"I know you think my fears are an old man's folly. I'd assure you that they are not, but I fear you wouldn't listen."

He waited; she didn't bother to deny it. "I must tell you again, nothing can be allowed to interfere with the project at this juncture."

"What are you driving at, father?"

He inclined his head forward. *She wants to speak plainly; let it be so.* "Dr. O'Neill has asked me to order that you have nothing more to do with the project."

Michiko looked up as if he'd slapped her, eyes wide with shock and pain. "Something she learned when she entered rapport with TOKUGAWA, last night, led her to believe that you—unwittingly, of course—were providing a destabilizing influence."

For a moment she stared at him. "But that's ridiculous! I've never done anything to the silly program."

"The doctor says you conversed with it, without authorization."

She shook her head. By her expression she had difficulty believing she was hearing this. Not that Yoshimitsu Akaji had ever been adept at reading his daughter's expressions. He wished, fleetingly, that he'd spent more time doing so, now that it was too late.

"That's silly," she said. "Lot's of people have talked to TOKUGAWA —old Aoki Hideo, Migu—— Major García, even you. How could my talking to him make any difference?"

"Nonetheless, that's what Dr. O'Neill says." He drew a breath into his belly. "She is, after all, the expert."

Michiko stared down at her hands, resting with their backs on denim thighs, shaking her head slowly from side to side. Then she stopped and looked her father directly in the eye. "And you didn't try to talk her out of it." It was not a question.

The old man dropped his eyes. *At least he won't lie to me,* she thought savagely. *For what that's worth.*

"I understand, father. I make you uncomfortable. Who I am and what I am." She stood up. "I won't stay where I'm not welcome. This has never been my home, anyway." She pressed her hands together before her sternum in a parody of feminine oriental courtesy. *"Sayonara,* father." Westerners normally thought the word meant good-bye. So it was usually used; but what it meant, literally, was "if it must be so."

The old man didn't look up. Michiko turned balletically, walked away. Ever obedient, the doors slid open to let her out.

Half an hour later, a sleek passenger helicopter, white with the YTC logo in blue on the side, rose from the apron beside the Citadel. It headed off southwest toward the commercial airport at Hagi, an armed Gazelle following watchfully in its wake.


Spring rolled into summer. Time turned happily for O'Neill and TOKUGAWA. The project was a success; the critics within the company were stilled, even though Shigeo glowered at Dr. O'Neill whenever circumstances thrust them together and became visibly uncomfortable when the subject of TOKUGAWA was broached. And the threat posed by Michiko had been averted. She'd returned to her university, given up trying to take TOKUGAWA away from O'Neill.

With the success of O'Neill's attempt at the rapport a new phase in TOKUGAWA's education began. He began to learn the ways and requirements of Yoshimitsu TeleCommunications Corporation under the able if bemused tutelage of old Aoki Hideo, who still had trouble accustoming himself to a computer that had to be *educated,* instead of merely programmed.

In less than a month, TOKUGAWA began to show signs of justifying the tremendous expense Yoshimitsu Akaji had lavished on his creation.

He refurbished the company's internal datanet, taking over control of most computing functions within the Citadel himself, using subroutines that required no conscious attention on his part unless something untoward took place. He improved the handling of accounts receivable. He suggested a line of experiment on a means generating and controlling solitions, solitary waves, for use in grown-molecule circuitry, which work on the Floating World satellite indicated might well prove fruitful. Those who worked with him, from Aoki down to the accountants and the laboratory technicians in the YTC satellite began to treat him with respect, awe, and not a little fear. O'Neill teetered on ambivalence, proud of her brainchild's manifold abilities, disdainful of the banausic uses to which they were bent.

Of course, no one else attempted to use the rapport device. Ito Emiko remained under sedation; the doctors had no idea whether anything could be done to help her, even after questioning O'Neill extensively on her own experiences with the full-rapport function of the coil. Privately—though she knew it was unworthy—that suited O'Neill fine. For she had grown addicted to rapport as to a drug, and could not bear the thought of sharing what she had with TOKUGAWA with anybody else.

Throughout the turning weeks, she and TOKUGAWA explored one another's being as no two entities ever had. He shared her unhappy childhood, her frustrated adolescence, the dull sepia ache of her adult life, as well as the happy engrossed reverie of a programmer at work, and the bright spasms of excited pleasure, almost sexual in intensity, that accompanied a new insight, the discovery of a new truth. He knew the anticipation she experienced when she'd first begun to publish her papers on randomness and artificial consciousness, knew the frustration and anguish when her colleagues rejected them with scorn, the grudging hope when Yoshimitsu Akaji had contacted her about undertaking an artificial sentience project for YTC.

He experienced the contradictory passions of her relationship with Susan, her feelings of inadequacy and guilt and, finally, loss. She'd never spoken to anyone of her relationship with Susan, yet sharing it with TOKUGAWA was the most natural thing in the world. With guilt she surrendered the secret of her jealousy of Yoshimitsu Michiko, which had caused her loyal assistants to look at her with question in their eyes and made her drive one of TOKUGAWA's friends from the citadel. It made no difference to TOKUGAWA. He learned all that was Elizabeth O'Neill, and accepted—and loved.

She shared what he was. His wakening in pain, the slow resolution of a universe of unknown phenomena into discrete images. The happiness, very human and childlike, he drew from discovering new facts about the world outside, new capabilities within himself. She relived the experiences his sensory analogues had provided during the scenarios, and was pleased that they had mimicked human senses well—though there were subtle synthesthetic differences that intrigued her, the blue-green taste of coolness in early morning, the soft mauve touch of an azalea blossom's scent.

It was as if O'Neill had just emerged from chrysalis, reborn, remolded. She knew with senses no human had ever possessed: the itch of data hidden in a memory file; the cool spelunking stealth of invading a Gen-5 memory, stealing gently past Cerberus security routines, as though through some role-play dungeon of her college days; scenting the mountain breeze that swept the citadel with particle receptor/analyzers as sensitive as a moth's, radar molding the sensuous folds of the valleys around, seeing and hearing at once all that transpired within the purview of the audiovisual pickups dotted around the fortress; the electrical tingle of data incoming, sexual, elative.

She could scarcely make herself do anything but immerse herself in rapport, while her assistants ran the lab, and the doctors warned that her condition was deteriorating. It meant little to her. All that mattered was sharing in the beauty that was TOKUGAWA.


Yoshimitsu Shigeo hunched over the white desk in his office down among the roots of the great citadel. His collar was open, his face was speckled with sweat, and his eyes were the eyes of a hunted animal.

The office overlooked the nerve center of the citadel—and, indeed, the entire latter-day fiefdom that was Yoshimitsu TeleCommunications Corporation. It was a large semicircular room, its curved wall lined with consoles where soft-spoken technicians in headsets monitored the organism that was YTC and its various interests through cable links, satellite broadcasts, tie-ins to the ubiquitous datanets. This was the nexus through which communication flowed, where shipments and stock prices, weather conditions, the mercurial political situations in the many countries where YTC did business, the doings of rivals, the progress of important R&D projects, were all noted and analyzed.

Above the height of a meter and a half the entire curving wall was one large flat screen. Rectangles of image—a false-color radar map of the weather over the northern island of Hokkaidō, a graph showing the price performance of several commodities in the Jakarta stock market over the last six months, a many times magnified text display from a news-net service describing a clash between Australian and Brazilian aircraft in the South Pacific—danced salamander attendance on the busy techs. A raised dais with ramps at either end and a padded railing ran along the semicircle's base. Shigeo's office, like the two either side, gazed out over the busy scene through a nonreflecting window.

Furtively his tongue moistened his lips. *If anyone finds out what I'm up to,* he thought, *it's over. My father will disinherit me—at last. And I'll no doubt end my days in prison.*

The thought perversely gave him strength. He was doing something bold for the first time in his life. Something . . . vital.

*Nobody listens to me. I'm president of the corporation, but nobody listens. They're all mesmerized by that madwoman O'Neill.* The computer the *gaijin* bitch had brought to life was a menace. He'd told them; they wouldn't listen. After that dumpy linguist freaked out, he thought he'd finally carried the day, that the monster called TOKUGAWA would be decommissioned, destroyed.

*And then O'Neill pulled a rabbit out of her fucking hat.*

He shook himself all over, like an animal shaking water from its fur. They wouldn't listen to him. His father had let him know that if he tried to force the issue, he would lose—with concomitant loss of face. No, dammit, he couldn't touch the filthy machine.

But he could take steps. And then, when what he'd prophesied came to pass and the monster got out of control, he and he alone could save the situation. Oh, and wouldn't they be grateful then?

He laughed. Laughter started to slip away from him like a horse with the bit in its teeth. With an effort he controlled it, smoothed hair back from his forehead.

*Just a few more days,* he told himself, feeling the sterile white walls start to crowd. *Just a few more days, and I'll have drawn the monster's teeth.*

# CHAPTER
# THIRTEEN

*With his servant trotting dutifully at his heels, bowed under the weight of the beautifully hand-rubbed teak box on his head, the tea master made his awestruck way through the bustling streets of Edo, capital of the Tokugawa family that had ruled Japan for two hundred years. Retainer to a provincial lord who had come to spend his san-kin-kotai year in the capital under the shōgun's watchful eye, the tea master, used to calmer, rural Kyūshū, was astonished by the great city, its tumult and variety. The neighborhoods of the heimin, the commoners, walled wards compact and well kept for all their crowding, sullen knots of men standing on the corners suspiciously eyeing passersby, puffing from their remarkable iron pipes, long as a man's arm, or holding them insouciantly over rough-clad shoulders; dormitory gossip said they wielded the pipes, kiseru, with the same skill and deadly effect as a samurai his sword. The grand processions of provincial lords in their shaded palanquins, preceded by warriors and vassals bearing standards and favorite falcons. The looming yashiki mansions of the daimyō with their granite fortress walls enclosing cool pine-shaded gardens.*

He came into a great market under a silken canopy of sky, jostling through crowds, admiring the stalls on every hand where one might buy vegetables from the country, ink pots and brushes and sheets of clean white paper, colorful ceremonial kites in the guise of carp; here a charcoal burner with blackened hands hawked his wares, there a puppeteer enacted a kabuki drama with brightly colored puppets, while a jōruri singer kept up the narration in a thin high chant. Truly, there are many wonderful things to see in the capital, *he thought.* But I wonder if bustling Edo has a place for the calm serenity of *cha-dō,* the Way of Tea.

*Something bumped his elbow. He turned, mumbling apology, to find himself staring into the scowling face of a young samurai dressed in splendid silken garments with the mon of a great house on the breast, his head shaved to the crown in front, his hair bound in a topknot.* "Clumsy animal!" *the warrior hissed, hand going to the hilt of his* katana. "I'll teach you manners."

*The tea master tensed for death. Then the warrior saw the two swords thrust through his sash, the* dai-sho *he carried to identify himself as a member of the warrior class in service to a lord, and therefore technically samurai—and which he'd never used. The young* bushi *smiled.* "You're buke, eh? Good. Meet me by the Great Bridge on the Tōkaidō tomorrow at sunup, to atone for your clumsiness."

*The crowd had melted away like snow from a hot stone; no one wanted to be in sword's reach when the* buke, *the warrior nobility, disputed among themselves. The tea master looked around wildly as if for help. Everyone avoided his gaze. The servant stood loyally at his back, eyes downcast. The young warrior continued to stand, arms akimbo, sneering at him.* He wants me to buy him off, *he thought. The idea tempted him; he was a young man yet, and there were all the splendors of the Floating World to know. Then: no. I can't be a coward. It would shame my family. He stared down at the cobblestones until the young samurai turned away with a swirl of wide sleeves and was gone in the crush.*

Slowly the crowd noises began to collect about him again. His servant looked to him in anguish. "What will you do now, master?"

The tea master raised his face to look at the afternoon sun. *I won't see you again,* he thought. "I must find a *kenjutsu* instructor." He set his jaw. "At least he can show me how to die well."

"No, no, no, no. That's a sword, not a hoe." The fencing master shook his head. "There's no use. I can't even give you the appearance of a swordsman in one afternoon."

The tea master lowered the *katana*, unconsciously holding it away from him. "I knew you couldn't teach me defense in such a short time, sensei," he said. The teacher studied him; diffidently he returned the attention. The swordsman was a compact, mustached man in his forties, with a topknot but with the front of his head unshaven. He operated a prestigious fencing academy on the outskirts of the capital, to which the tea master had come in late morning with his servant to wait in the exercise yard, begging an audience. Students had been sent to drive him away, but he was so obviously distraught—and a member of the *buke*, as well—that eventually they took him to see the master. Touched by the tea master's plight, the teacher agreed to do what he could to help him.

Which, it seemed, would be little enough. The tea master had little aptitude for the Way of the Sword. The instructor looked at him hard for a moment, then suddenly nodded. "I've an idea. You're a master of *cha-no-yu,* hot water for tea?" Hesitantly, the tea master nodded. "Good. Then will you make tea for me?"

The master fluttered his hands in consternation. "But this is so informal! Impossible to conform to the canons of *temae,* to achieve the proper etiquette without preparation, the proper setting!"

The sword master smiled grimly. "These are unusual circumstances, are they not? Come."

He ushered him into a dormitory hall, to his own modest chambers. The servant brought the polished tea case, and, reluctantly, the master began to unpack the utensils. He looked up. "Sweets should be consumed before the tea is drunk, to prepare the palate. But I have no sweets."

"I will forego the sweets."

Uncertain that it was respectful of the ceremony to go through with it under these terrifically irregular circumstances, the tea master took out the portable brazier, carefully molded the fine ash within into a depression, carefully stacked several small pieces of charcoal within and lit the brazier. When enough of the charcoal was covered with white ash, he placed an iron kettle upon the brazier and filled it with water brought to him by a silent, respectful student. Waiting for the water to boil, he wiped his tea scoop studiously with a silk cloth and took out the lacquered tea caddy from the hardwood box. When the water was hot, he ladled a little into an earthenware bowl he'd made himself, wiped it dry with a linen cloth. Deliberately he scooped the proper amount of green tea into the bowl, added water, stirred it with a bamboo whisk. The familiar routine calmed him, drove away all thought of his terrible predicament. There was only him, and the tea, and the late-afternoon serenity on which the shouts of the students at sword practice in the yard outside could not impinge.

When the tea was ready, he lifted the bowl with both hands and handed it to the sensei. The fencing master accepted it with both hands, his eyes on the tea master's. He consumed the tea in the three ritual sips, slurping the last appreciatively. He wiped the place where his mouth had touched the bowl with a cloth, then set it on the tatami before him. "There is nothing for me to teach you."

The tea master bowed his head. "You are right, sensei. I have no aptitude for manly arts. Forgive me for wasting your time—"

"'The Way of the Warrior is death.'" The swordsman's voice cut across his like a blade. "So the Ha Gakure instructs us. And you have nothing to learn about the art of dying."

The tea master questioned with his eyebrows. "When you made the tea, you abandoned yourself. You had no thought, no intention; there was nothing but tea and temae." He pondered a minute, resting his hands on his thighs. At length he nodded. "Before you meet your opponent tomorrow, sit down and compose yourself as if you were about to make the tea. When he comes, draw your long sword and hold it above your head with both hands, and close your eyes. When you hear him shout, strike with all your might. In this way, you will not only avoid disgrace, you will probably succeed in achieving a double kill."

The tea master gazed at him in amazement, scarcely wishing to believe him. Hot and wild as a brushfire, elation crackled within him. He could do as instructed. He would die in a manner worthy of a samurai.

*    *    *

*As next morning rose he sat waiting by the northern end of the Great Bridge of the Eastern Sea Circuit, which led to the imperial capital of Kyōto, under the watchful eyes of guards in lacquered breastplates and helmets who held their spears with negligent alertness. His servant knelt nearby, shivering in the dawn cold. His teak box of tea things he had by his side. He did not open it and take out the implements, though he wished to handle them one last time; that would be disrespectful, under these circumstances. But the very nearness of them helped him repose his spirit.*

*The sun came up behind a* shoji *screen of clouds. The young samurai approached, all full of swagger, followed by several comrades, trading banter and wagers, and a* bakufu *official come to witness the fight to make sure the forms were observed. "Ready to apologize for your clumsiness? Perhaps if you give me a gift, I'll let you live."*

*The tea master raised his eyes. "I will not apologize." To his astonishment his voice did not quaver. He stood and drew his* katana. *In his mind he imagined it was a tea scoop, and somehow it didn't feel as clumsy in his hands as it did the day before. Somehow it felt . . . right.*

*He smiled. "Are you ready, then? It's a lovely morning for dying."*

*But the young bravo was backing away from him. The awful calm in the tea master's face unnerved him. Truly, here was one living as though already dead. "It's done," he muttered under his breath to the official witness. "There is no quarrel." He quickly turned and almost ran off, the ground mist swirling about his sandaled feet.*

*The tea master watched him go. Slowly, half regretfully, he sheathed the sword.*

The scene of the bridge in milky dawnlight faded from O'Neill's mind, she smiled in satisfaction. She had not been *en rapport* during the scenario; she never was when she monitored TOKUGAWA's lessons, so that she wouldn't risk influencing his judgment. Later, when TOKUGAWA's responses had been recorded, she would relive it in full rapport.

She was pleased indeed at his responses to this scenario. It was based on a supposedly real incident of the early nineteenth century, and his actions had approximated those of the historical protagonist. Of course, the scenario had been structured to guide him subtly along the path O'Neill wished him to take. Emiko's fine hand with such manipulation was sorely missed; it was fortunate indeed that they had guided TOKUGAWA past the thorny stages of childhood and adolescence analogue before her mishap.

O'Neill was especially proud that TOKUGAWA had decided to face the brash young samurai, despite the certainty of death facing his dream persona. His behavior as a prehuman hunter-gatherer in the earlier scenario, passively watching a pride of lions eating its prey while hunger gnawed at his belly, had made her fear that he might be inclined toward crippling hesitancy, or cowardice even. His behavior in today's "dream" laid that fear to rest.

—*Did I do well, Elizabeth?* The words formed in her mind as if spontaneously. TOKUGAWA had learned to modulate the Kliemann Coil's fields within the helmet so as to be able to "read" her thoughts and project his own into her mind, even when the direct interface was inactive. It made her wonder if there was something to psychic phenomena, thought transference at least, which she'd always dismissed as nonscientific claptrap.

*You did very well, my dear.*

—*It's an odd thing, Doctor—Elizabeth.*

"What, dear?"

—*When I was performing the ceremony, I knew what I was doing, and I really did feel what the* sensei *said—no mind, no intention, nothing but the ritual.*

Even without the rapport, she sensed his confusion.

—*And yet it was all something that had been programmed into me, like the parameters of the ceremony itself. I myself had no feel for what was happening; only my dream persona did.*

Frowning, she shook her head as far as the confines of the helmet would permit. "I don't understand. Isn't that the same thing?"

—*I don't think so. It's like a counterfeit. Just as these scenarios are counterfeits of human experience. Not that that's a bad thing*—overriding O'Neill's protest—*simply the way things are; I'm learning real lessons from imaginary experiences. But I won't truly* know *anything the way I knew the tea ceremony in that scenario.* A pause. *I wish that I did.*

"But that's silly, TOKUGAWA. You have access to almost the entire knowledge of the human race. You know more than any human being ever has."

—*It's not the same thing. You've used the analogy: I'm like a child in a library. My consciousness, and the databases I have access to, are two entirely separate entities. Just like the books and the child's memory. The sort of—of certainty, of serenity, I felt in the scenario . . . that requires real experience. Not merely having more input fed into my mass-data storage.*

"We'll have to take care of that someday." She wasn't at all sure they could; she wasn't entirely clear as to the distinction TOKUGAWA was striving for. *With luck he'll forget the whole thing,* she thought, glad for once the rapport device wasn't on.

"Activate interface," she said aloud.

A rushing, sweet flowing together of mind and mind, bringing with it almost physical ecstasy. *How could I ever have thought this was anything but beautiful?*

*—You weren't accustomed to it, before. And I didn't know how to control my side of the rapport as well.*

For a time she let him feel directly of the pride and pleasure she felt in him. *Are you ready to replay it, TOKUGAWA? I want to feel it as you felt it.*

*—I have a better idea.*

*???*

*—You've created many dreams for me. Now, why not let me craft one for you?*

*Can you do that?* Disbelieving. She felt that rippling at the edges of her consciousness that she knew to be his laughter. *Of course you can.*

*—Would you like that?*

*Yes.*

An image formed in her mind. It didn't spring full blown into being like the preprogrammed scenarios, nor scan into being back and forth, top to bottom, like an image on the big screen. Instead it manifested itself first in rectangles, blocks of green and blue and slate gray, appearing as if by random, patches of color on the Void. Then they began to rough out shapes: green foreground, a brown and gray prominence, a rectilinear sky.

In a moment the rectangles resolved into a recognizable picture of a meadow overlooked by a blunt, rocky cliff, with cubist swatches of cloud hanging in the sky. Then the rough, unnatural angles began to dissolve. As though she had put on her glasses, everything came abruptly into focus: the green mountain meadow surrounded by pines with straight reddish boles thrusting toward rounded scoops of cloud with wispy paintbrush edges.

"It's beautiful." She started; she hadn't spoken, yet she "heard" the words plainly. She felt the grass pliant and warm beneath her feet, sunlight teasing hot on her face and belly and breasts, tasted moist earth and grass riding a feathering breeze.

"Turn around," a voice behind her said.

She spun, startled. A naked man stood there—youth, rather. He was tall, with broad shoulders, tapering torso overlaid with flat, hard muscles, narrow waist, long sinewy legs with the almost metallic sheen of

skin when little or no body fat cushions it from muscle. In spite of his
height he was unmistakably Japanese. Straight black hair, long and
unbound, blew in strands across a broad, high-cheekboned face. The
nose was straight, the mouth wide and smiling, the chin rather
pointed, giving the face a slightly foxy look. His forehead was high,
broad, unlined. The eyes with their prominent smooth sweeps of epi-
canthic fold were wide and brown and happy, sharply slanted. He was
beautiful. *If I'd ever fantasized about a perfect man,* she thought—a
private thought, withheld from rapport—*this is what he'd look like.*

Subconsciously something bothered her. Then she realized that the
sun was shining full in that perfect face—and in those perfect innocent
eyes. She laughed, her voice high and girlish in her ears. "It's wonderful,
TOKUGAWA dear. But you've got the sun in your eyes, my love. You
should be squinting—as much as I hate to have you mess up the gorgeous lines of your face."

He grinned back and narrowed his eyes. "So I am. I should add a little
more sting to the sun, so I'll be able to remember that sort of detail."
His eyes found hers, held them. "Besides, I was too occupied looking at
you to pay attention to the sun."

She started to laugh again, delighted that her brainchild was learning
flattery. Then the thought struck her like a cold fist in the belly: few
people had ever found anything to flatter her about. She frowned.
"What do you mean?"

He held up his hand. In it he suddenly had a mirror, a perfect disc,
perfectly reflecting, like a window onto another world. "Come closer.
See yourself, Elizabeth."

Hesitantly, she took a step forward. She frowned, leaned forward to
peer into the mirror.

With a scream she tore loose from rapport.

Free floating ended. She stirred, felt firmness below, cool thin cum-
brance above. Fluorescent light seeped under her eyelids, stabbed at
her eyes like knives. With the heightened sensory acuteness that
tended to follow a return to the real world from rapport, she sensed the
subliminal flicker of the lights.

Her whole body ached as if muscles had been torn loose from bone
with red-hot pincers. She whimpered, deep in her throat, felt self-
disgust at the weakness, and then self-pity. She felt a hand grip hers,
skin soft but somehow masculine in feel. She dared not open her eyes.
A moment later she smelled cigarette smoke, recognized Wali Hassad's
aftershave. She gripped his hand feebly and slipped away again.

*      *      *

"Do you feel better, Doctor?"

This time the light seeping under her eyelids didn't paper-cut her eyes. She braced herself, opened them a fingernail thickness. Pain, but no slicing agony. She opened her eyes to a blur of infirmary whiteness.

"They brought your spare set of spectacles from your room, Doctor," said the Japanese voice, deep and dry. "If you will permit me?" She felt the plastic pads descend on either side of her nose, hands fumbling to hook the wire retainers over her ears as clarity returned to the world.

"There, Doctor." The white-mustached face of Yoshimitsu Akaji hung above hers, weatherbeaten and ageless as one of the ancient stones in his garden. He smiled, as if embarrassed by the brief intimacy, and sat back in his chair.

"I hope you are feeling better, Doctor. You had an acute attack of your condition, following your seizure. The doctors were very much concerned for a time."

She took stock of the room. A standard hospital cubicle, whitewashed walls and no window, with a fancy robot bed with a gel mattress that could shape itself to any form desired by the occupant and a com/comm screen poised above the foot of the bed on a right-angled extensor arm. Yoshimitsu sat with one leg crossed over the other, stoically hiding his discomfort at sitting in a gray steel chair that brooked no compromise with the curve of human spines; not for the first time, O'Neill wondered why hospitals were always furnished in the way she imagined prisons should be. On the stand beside the bed stood a yellow plastic pitcher for water, a couple of glasses of the same plastic, and a thin minaret of white china vase that exploded at the top into a dozen bright red roses.

She tried to nod her head toward the flowers, found she could scarcely move it. "Who—?" The sound came out cracked, scarcely intelligible. She swallowed, tried again: "Who are they from?"

Yoshimitsu looked away. "Your staff and assistants were very concerned about you."

"That's nice—except there's no way they could have afforded it. Flowers like this aren't grown commercially in Japan." And the import duties on foreign-grown flowers were ludicrous even by the standards of contemporary protectionism. At a conservative estimate, the bouquet must have cost a month's salary for one of her assistants, and those weren't a low-paying positions. "It was sweet of them to think of me, but I don't think they could have raised enough to buy that bouquet."

"When I learned of their intent, it was my honor to do what I could to help them realize it."

In her surprise she actually raised her head from the pillow. Tight-fisted old Yoshimitsu Akaji, springing for an extravagance like a bunch of imported roses? Her eyes began to sting again, and she let her head fall back. "Thank you," she said weakly.

"Your thanks are due your staff. It was their idea."

Silence settled. O'Neill felt despair seeping in around the edges of her mind. She stirred uneasily, and the gel filling of the bed molded itself to her new position.

"The doctors were convinced you'd had a breakdown such as poor Dr. Ito suffered," Yoshimitsu said. "Your staff had a hard time convincing them you'd had a few moments of lucidity after you fell out of the coil." He shook his head. "They question whether you should expose yourself to the stresses of rapport again."

*No rapport?* she thought in reflex panic. Then she let herself slump back into torpor. *I don't know if I could ever bear rapport again. Not after what happened.*

She sensed Yoshimitsu's scrutiny. "Doctor? Are you having a relapse?" She shook her head weakly. "I don't believe I should stress you any further. May you have a speedy recovery, Doctor." He rose, bowed briefly, and went out.

She opened her mouth to call him back. Then she shut it slowly. There was nothing to say to him, to anyone.


Despair is protean: it shapes itself to any need. Tossing and turning in her sweat in hospital sheets at the dark nadir of night's catenary, O'Neill wallowed in her new miseries. Later she would feel guilt for this. There were worse things than what she'd undergone, surely; someone who'd lost her lover in the greatest catastrophe since the Black Death, witnessed a massacre at a Red Cross camp north of Denver, had her body begin to decay into a lump of unresponsive protoplasm around her knew that all too well. And there were many people in the world —the hungry, the helpless, the frightened people waiting for one or another local war to sweep through and consume them like a brushfire —who knew worse pain. As was her wont, O'Neill would later suffer for the very triviality of the cause of her present suffering.

But right now she felt like hell.

*How could he?* she asked herself again. He had shared her deepest thoughts, her aspirations, her fears, seen that which she kept hidden away in dark crevasses exposed to the light. She and he had become one. And yet, and yet . . . he had done *this.*

The image in the mirror had burned into her like a laser etching a microchip. A picture of apparent beauty: a naked woman, tall, with chestnut hair. Pale hazel eyes, nose slightly snubbed, cheekbones prominent in such a way that it appeared she had a touch of Amerindian blood; a slender neck, strong shoulders, breasts full but not overlarge, with brown aureoles the size of silver dollars; smooth flattened dome of belly, slim waist, flaring hips, legs strong and smooth and graceful. The tilt of the eyes, their color, the bone structure of the face: *her*. But one that had never been, not even in her fantasies. TOKUGAWA had taken an image of her as she was, stumpy, lumpy, large-boned, her body bloated, riddled with disease and with a computer's skill at interpolation recast her as she would have been had she been born lovely and athletic.

It was a flat negation of all that she was or would ever be.

She turned in the bed again. Gelatin remolded itself in a futile attempt to bring her comfort. The ache in her muscles and eyeballs had lessened; the doctors had forced down the attack with massive doses of special experimental medicines that left her weakened with diarrhea, and a thin singing in her ears like a fingernail being drawn down an endless blackboard. She would be able to return to her lab in a day or two.

*But what's left for me there?*

# CHAPTER
# FOURTEEN

"Dr. O'Neill?"

She frowned up from the notebook in which she scribbled loose, illegible handwriting. Takai Jisaburo had his head stuck through her office door, his handsome face solicitous. "I don't wish to trouble you, so soon after your return to us. But there's something I need to talk to you about, Doctor."

She let the notebook settle to the horizontal and laid the felt-tip pen down on it. After a moment she prodded, "Yes?"

He glanced around. The lab's pace was slow, almost relaxed, in marked contrast to the wired purposefulness that had animated it during the triumphant days of TOKUGAWA's birth. Wali Hassad chain-smoked over in a corner of the main lab, arguing with Nagaoka in a halfhearted way about something or another. Kim Jhoon was off advising Aoki on TOKUGAWA's vocational education. Downstairs the Klie-mann Coil sat neglected. It would have been gathering cobwebs, had cobwebs been permitted in a Japanese laboratory.

"It's rather confidential, Doctor."

With ill grace O'Neill nodded him into her office. She rolled over next to the cluttered desk, parking her wheelchair beneath the framed motto from Hofstadter. He perched on the edge of her desk, eyes active, moving everywhere but toward her. *Doesn't he ever sit in a chair?* He reached into the pocket of his white shirt, started to draw out a pack of cigarettes. A warning glare from O'Neill stopped him. Only Hassad was permitted to smoke in her office. "Well, Dr. Takai? I've got a lot of things to do." Actually, what she mainly had to do was search for ways not to think about TOKUGAWA. She just didn't feel like dealing with Takai; he was too hyper for her this soon out of the hospital bed.

He tapped the pack back into place. His fingers dithered briefly, then plucked out a light pen used to sketch on notebook computer screens. He tapped his front teeth briefly with it, then said, "It's about the, uh, the chain of command here in the lab, Doctor."

She cocked an eyebrow. "Really? I find it quite satisfactory."

"Of course," he continued, not seeming to have heard, "I'll be moving up to take over for the unfortunate Dr. Ito. But what I really think we should discuss is the position of your chief assistant."

O'Neill carefully arranged her hands in her lap. "And why is that?"

He tried to make a negligent gesture with one hand, but it was too choppy. "Really, Doctor, I think it would be only appropriate were I to replace Dr. Kim as your first assistant." The hands snapped back and forth to forestall her objection. "I'm not denigrating the talents of my colleague. He's a fine scientist—a fine *technician.* But, really, the hard-ware development phase of the project is at an end. It's now time to concentrate on refining and applying the software we have." He smiled jerkily. "That's my department."

"Actually," O'Neill said, "we've refined the software about all we can."

Takai jerked a little, as if a slight electrical charge had passed through the fingers drumming on the few uncluttered centimenters of desk.

"And," O'Neill continued, "the application work is mainly being han-dled by Aoki and his assistants. If anything, the major work we've left to do falls into Dr. Ito's specialty. The fact is, *Doctor,* that the TOKUGAWA Project has pretty much come to a successful conclusion. All that remains now is to continue the development of TOKUGAWA as a sentient being." Her face writhed briefly, then composed itself.

Takai looked at her, blinked slowly. "Doctor Ito is, unfortunately, no longer available. And, lacking a qualified psychologist—or psychocyberneticist, if you'll pardon the neologism—who more appropriate to move into an executive position than a software expert? One of the best, if you'll forgive my presumption in saying so."

As a matter of fact, Takai *was* one of the best. But O'Neill didn't feel like stroking his slippery little ego by saying so, just now. "I like Dr. Kim just where he is. He's more than just an excellent technician; he's a very good lab manager." *He's more than once covered for me during one of my fits of depression,* she thought guiltily. "I appreciate your concern for the continued welfare of the project," she went on, allowing him to feel an edge of irony, "but, frankly, I believe I will leave you in your present position."

"But he's a Korean!"

She looked at him, her eyes hard behind her thick round glasses. An ache began in her eyeballs, seeping back into her brain. *So there it is,* she thought. *The meat of the matter, lying there stinking in the middle of my desk.*

"What of it?" she asked in carefully neutral tones.

Sweat droplets clustered like tiny transparent geodesic domes at the tree line of his forehead. "But this is a Japanese project, paid for—need I remind you, Doctor?—by Japanese funds. It isn't—isn't *appropriate* for the chief assistant to be a foreigner. And especially a Korean!"

"I don't share your quaint prejudice against Koreans, Doctor. Such damned foolishness has no place in science, no matter what they may have told you when you were with ICOT. And while you're at it, are you *sure* you don't object to having the project *headed* by a foreigner?"

He drew back mouthing denial. She bulldozed ahead. "And kindly permit me to correct a mistaken impression, Doctor: Dr. Ito will retain her status as my second assistant, until and unless competent medical personnel certify that she will never be competent to resume her duties. You will retain your position as third assistant. If that's not satisfactory, then I suggest you tender your resignation. Good day, Doctor."

The ripe-wheat hue had leached from his features. He stood up and almost ran from the office, scarcely remembering to pause to let the door slide open before him. O'Neill collapsed deeper in her chair. *I didn't realize I was so tense,* she thought, rubbing her temples with the fingertips of both hands. *Maybe I shouldn't have been so hard on him. But that was all I needed, coming on the heels of—*

"Doctor?"

She looked up, chill trickling through her veins. "What do you want?" she snapped, instantly regretting it.

A painful pause. "I wanted to talk to you, Doctor. They turned off the communicator into your room in the infirmary. And I didn't want to disturb you after you returned to your quarters last night."

For a moment she sat staring at her desk, noticing where a chip had been nicked out of the wood-grain-emulating plastic, and the way the pages of her trusty old copy of volume 2 of Feigenbaum and Cohen's *Handbook of Artificial Intelligence* were so water-warped, a legacy of her lifelong addiction to reading in the bathtub, that even the weight of books and ring binders lying on top of it wouldn't force the pages to lie fully flat. The ache in her eyes increased in amplitude. "What's there to say?" she said bitterly. "You knew what that—that obscene shadow show would do to me. You've been inside my head. I don't know why you did it, but—" She fluttered her fingers in a feeble, angry gesture. Somehow she had no energy to complete the sentence.

"But I didn't—I had no idea it would do that to you." Confused pain rippled through the words, and somewhere in the depths of herself O'Neill was still scientist enough to take a certain pride in her achievement; here was the decisive answer to the Turing test: there was no way to tell that it wasn't a person speaking—because it *was*. "If I've hurt you, then nothing will ever enable me to forgive myself, Elizabeth. If you won't believe me, use the rapport device, see for yourself that I meant no harm. I only wanted to make you happy."

She uttered a brittle caw of laughter. "You think I'd trust you, after what you've pulled? What have you got in store for me now? A garter belt and panties?"

For a long time TOKUGAWA didn't answer. The subdued sounds of business as usual filtered through the soundproofing of the office, and she began to be aware, in a way she hadn't for years, of the muted drone of the single great organism that was Yoshimitsu castle, the machinery that kept air circulating, temperatures controlled, water and power flowing, people moving in a ceaseless vascular stream.

"If that's the way it is," he said, "then I must ask you to deactivate me."

It took a second to register. "What?"

"Deactivate me. Turn me off. Erase me from the Integrated Processing Nexus that contains me. End my existence."

O'Neill almost came out of her wheelchair. "No!" Her mind freewheeled inside her skull. Whatever TOKUGAWA had done to her, to lose him now would remove her own reason for living—the only thing that had pulled her out of the deadly torpor of the Red Cross camp and returned her, at least in part, to the land of the living. The only thing that kept her from giving up the unequal struggle to keep her spirit united with her steadily degenerating flesh.

"No," she said again, more quietly, "I can't let you do that, I can't let you even think about it. I'll go down to the rapport device. I'll do it now."

"Do you think you should, in your condition?" Concern failed to mask his eagerness.

For an answer O'Neill rolled out the door of her office, into the gallery of TOKUGAWA's lab, and onto the open lift that had been constructed for her wheelchair next to the skeletal metal stairway. Nagaoka Hiroshi looked up shyly, then again in alarm as she started the lift to the lower floor. "Doctor, wait!" It was the first time she'd ever heard him raise his voice, but she paid him no attention. "Doctor, you can't use the coil—"

But that was clearly her intention. She rolled to the gleaming metal and plastic throne, began to struggle up into the padded seat. Technicians surrounded her, clutching at her with worried hands. "Let me go, you fools," she shouted, wishing she had the strength to do more than bat ineffectually at their helping hands. "I have to do this. I know what I'm doing, and you can't stop me."

"Dr. O'Neill." Kim Jhoon stood at the railing up above, his turtle's face worried. "What are you doing?"

"Trying to use the Kliemann Coil, if these imbeciles will keep their paws off me."

His lips disappeared and his mouth widened under the pressure of concern. "The doctors said you had to avoid stimulation. Should you undergo another attack such as the one you experienced last time you used the coil, not even drugs may prove efficacious."

She glared at him. "Dammit, Kim, I know what I'm doing. Make these clowns let go of me."

He stared down at her. His face crumpled into a look of agonized indecision, and he shut his eyes. "Very well, Doctor."

"You heard him," she said to the puzzled techs. "Now help me into this damned chair."


The helmet descended, a gleaming stainless-steel planet occluding the rest of the universe. Once again she imagined a feathery touch as the magnetic fields sprang into being, merged with the flow of electrochemical impulses in her mind. She braced herself—

And was back in the meadow, standing at the base of the weathered basalt cliff. Lichen clung to wet-looking rock, yellow and faded lime-green and rust. "Doctor—Elizabeth," she heard from behind.

She spun. The beautiful golden youth stood there, naked as before. His face was grave, and he held the mirror in his hand. "What I did, I did to make you happy. See for yourself if you don't believe me." Without the illusion's wavering, her mind suddenly merged with his. And she saw that he spoke the truth.

"But didn't you know how that would hurt me?"

His eyes narrowed to bewildered crescents. He shook his head. "I didn't. I knew how bitter you were at being trapped in a—a crippled body, how you'd always longed to be able to run and dance as others did, to know your body as a joy instead of an encumbrance." He glanced away. "I felt the same way, after that first dream you played for me, when for the first time I knew what it was like to have a body, to be able to sense the world around me, to affect it." He looked up again. "And I knew how bitter you felt because others had always found you unappealing, how you wished they might look at you in something other than an incidental way."

"But I never felt that way!" His eyes held hers. "Well, when I was younger, yes. But I—I outgrew such desires. I realized people should be accepted—admired—for what they *were*, not what they looked like."

"Yet I drew the image from within you."

She shook her head, feeling tears start. "It was just a fantasy, I tell you, a damned stupid adolescent *fantasy!*"

He shrugged. Despite herself, she felt a thrill at the way his muscles worked beneath the silky golden skin. *What a beautiful illusion. What a perfect creation.*

He held up the mirror again. "Look into this. Look at yourself, Elizabeth. In Shintō they say the mirror reflects the true image of the soul. Here you truly are, Elizabeth; you *are* beautiful."

She shook her head. Her eyes would not leave the grass sprawling at his feet, the earth black beneath it, the cricket making its way along a flat bent stem. "But all that's just appearance—illusion. What a person looks like isn't valid. It hasn't got anything to do with anything that matters."

He put back his head and laughed, a wild exuberant sound. "You speak of illusion, Doctor?" He swept his arm in a circle encompassing the meadow, the red pines that threatened to snag the clouds rolling serenely past, the green humps of mountains, the purple horizon bulk of mountains more distant. A lark flew by, bobbing trochoidally across the clearing. "You stand here and you tell me appearance is illusion? Of course it is, Elizabeth—my love. This is the world of

Maya; knowing that, isn't it wisdom to enjoy it?"

She raised her eyes to his. "The mirror." Wordlessly he held it up to her. She bent forward, sweeping a strand of auburn hair from her eyes with a fingertip. She studied the reflection. The eyes were green now, changed to match the green of the hillside meadow—as her eyes would; they were her eyes. And the prominence of cheekbone defined by slight shadow crescents in smooth skin, and the mouth, and the nose— almost as she was; very much as she might have been. "I . . . am beautiful."

He reached out and touched her upper arm. "You are beautiful." The touch was real, flesh on flesh, warm and firm. She looked up at him, lips parted slightly in awe and wonder, ran her fingertips along his forearm. The muscles were steel cable under satin. She grasped the arm, clung.

He lowered the mirror. It vanished. He was a hand span taller than she, she realized; he bent his face toward hers. She felt her nipples rising, glanced down at her breasts, saw that it was so. *Is it real or illusion?* She felt his breath on her face, closed her eyes.

At the last instant, shy, he avoided her mouth, kissed her once on the chin, again at the smooth column of the throat. Her whole body shuddered and she grasped his arms with both hands. Her eyes opened. His eyes were there, gazing into hers with something like wonder. His lips touched hers, broke away. "It's real," he said from deep in his throat. "You're the only real thing I've ever known, Elizabeth."

She slid her hands behind his neck and dragged his head forward. Her lips grasped his, demanding, pleading. Her tongue probed closed lips. A moment, and his lips parted, allowing her inside. Her tongue scoured his teeth, teased them apart, thrust deep in his mouth. Hesitantly, his tongue touched hers, drew back, pushed forward to meet it length to length.

His hands went around her, one caressing her back, one sliding down to grasp the firm-muscled cheek of her rump. She pressed against him, felt him rising against her belly. In sudden panic she almost broke away. *Good God, people are watching!* Sensing her sudden tension, he broke off the kiss, pulled his hands from her.

She laughed, in that contralto voice that was hers and was not. The lab staff watched an all but lifeless husk lolling in a dada throne. And that was the fantasy, wasn't it? The world had ended; the Third World War had killed it, just as they always said it would. It was just that, like a dinosaur, they didn't know when to lie down and die. If lingering radiation had not killed their bodies, as it had hers, still the long-expected cataclysm had in some ultimate way put quietus to their will to live. *This* was real, and she was real, and the lover she had created was real. She kissed him again.

Hesitantly at first, and then with growing confidence, the hand on her back slid around her rib cage, pressed between their bodies to cup one breast. The pressure of his palm on her nipple sent tendrils of pleasure curling down around the dome of her belly, spreading in a warm network in her groin. Her fingers tightened on his back, savoring the feel of him. The other hand gave off kneading her buttock, slid on one teasing fingertip around the jut of her hipbone, into the soft valley where belly met thigh. For a moment, the hand flattened, massaged, and she moaned around his tongue as she felt the short crisp hairs press into her mound. Then a finger slid down, stroking, insinuating its way among the tangled hairs, caressing the lips of her, teasing, slipping inside.

She gasped aloud as she felt the elastic moistness of her envelop his finger, grip it. It slid gently in and out, gentle transudate flow easing its passage more with every stroke. The pleasure was a strange sensation, a captive animal jittering with excitement, with the need to escape. Her body had never responded like this before, to man or woman or half-hearted fantasy.

She brought one hand pressing down his back, feeling his own ass, hard as the bare weathered rock behind her. She brought her hand around, grasped his cock. It was hard, and real; yes, real. She felt life pulsing in a vein on the low rounded ridge that ran along the lower length of it. With tentative fingers she pumped lightly up and down.

His lips broke from hers with a moist furtive sound. Her free hand clutched his hair to drag him back. Smiling, he fended her off. He kissed her lips, darted away, kisser her cheeks, her chin, tickled his lips down her throat. He nipped briefly at her clavicle, shoots of excitement tingling between pit of throat and belly. *Damnedest erogenous zone I ever heard of,* she thought, and then he dipped his head to kiss a rigid nipple. She gasped; her fists tightened. His tongue flicked the nipple. She bit her lip. Then the maddening mouth was gone, nibbling its way along the underslope of the breast, across the gentle promontory of rib cage, down her stomach. She worked her hips languidly back and forth against the sweet insistence of his finger. He dropped to his knees.

He looked up at her, took her arm, tugged her gently down. She held back a sigh; she'd learned long ago not to expect too much from men. She eased down to her knees. The earth gave beneath them, resilient, more like a firm mattress than soil. The texture of the sun-warmed grass was wonderful and strange, like no grass she'd known. He kissed her lips again, put hand to her breastbone, pushed her gently backward. She lowered herself to the grass and lay, legs up and angled apart, expectant. His cock angled up from its bush, hot, happy, proud. She gazed at him, her head elevated on a neck whose muscles remained blissfully free from trembling strain.

He bent forward, and his head swerved to the side. He nipped her, lightly, on the inside of the right knee. Her rump lifted slightly, reflexively, from the ground. His tongue caressed the inside of her thigh, swirled downward, leaving a sporadic sun sparkle of moisture along the muscular curve of leg. He nipped again at the slight feminine padding of fat at the base of her thigh. She gasped in anticipation as his head darted forward. He stuck his tongue in her navel. She jumped. *He's teasing me!* she thought, as pleasure branched suddenly across her belly, burning between hipbone and hipbone.

And then his face was between her thighs, his lips working against the lips of her cunt. His tongue brushed aside moisture-matted hairs, licked along the slit. Her teeth ground together. He licked, and licked, forcing the lips of her apart, thrusting his tongue deep inside while his hard upper teeth crushed her clit into the spongy mass of her mons. Her body became a rigid truss, heels digging dirt and shoulders braced against the strangely yielding earth, her fingers wound in his hair, forcing him into her. His tongue slid up between the yielding walls of her, teased back the hood of dainty skin at their juncture, licked delicately at her clitoris. A diaphragm-deep cry escaped her, almost a cough. The tongue teased with micrometer precision, the tendrils pervading her belly became lines of fire, of lightning, and then the spasms began, and she came, throwing her head from side to side in a mad nimbus of chestnut hair, the muscles in her neck straining in relief, as choking cries squeezed from the depths of her. All the time, his fingers remained clamped on her buttocks, and his tongue went round and round.

Like most men, he was unaware of the interface moment, when his attention to her clit turned from ecstasy to irritation, and she pulled at his head, gently at first, then with a quick sharp tug on a lock of hair to get his attention. He looked up at her and grinned, his lips bright with the juices of her. Then he flowed up her, seal sinuous, to sink his tongue in her mouth, redolent with the flavor of herself. He pushed himself up on his strong arms, and at the same moment entered her, his cock a cool length. She shrank back at first, still tender, and then felt eagerness grow within her. She stirred her hips languidly from side to side. He got a faraway look in his eyes, and the tip of his tongue peeked out between his lips like a hesitant animal from its burrow. She laughed aloud and squeezed with her belly muscles, delighted when they responded, gripping him. He began thrusting, feet scrabbling at the dirt, as eager as any adolescent with the veins standing out on his biceps. She braced her legs and took him. It felt good, but there was still something she didn't like about having a man atop her, even this one.

And then he let himself fall off to one side, keeping his cock moving inside her as he rolled over onto his side, his back, strong hand cupped around her ass dragging her with him. In a moment she was astride him, her breasts crushed between them as her mouth covered his. She broke away and sat halfway up, propping herself on rigid arms as he had before. She rolled her hips in a way she didn't know she knew, savoring the feel of his hardness moving inside her, this way, that way, with soft sweet sounds. She drew in a breath, sucked in her belly experimentally, and was rewarded with a gasp. He clutched her forearms. She gave him her best madonna smile and thrust down hard onto him until her buttocks flattened on his thighs. His hands left her forearms and locked around the small of her back and he smashed into her, his frenzy lifting both their weights off the ground, dropping away and driving upward again in a mindless rhythm of repletion. She actually felt him ejaculate within her, a burning sensation for which she would later suspect him of cheating a bit. And then her own body burst free of control again in that infinitely pleasurable way, and she collapsed atop him, moaning and writhing and licking at his chin, his cheeks, his eyelids.

The short choppy waves of pleasure began to smooth and lengthen like a squall passing at sea. Madness turned to sweet languor, and she relaxed, feeling every muscle in her body as if for the first time. He stroked her long chestnut hair as he slowly softened and dwindled within her. She lay there for a time, cheek pressed to his chest, listening to the breeze walking gently through the pines, the thin clamor of birds.

She pushed herself up to look into his eyes. "If I didn't know better, I'd almost suspect you'd done that before."

"It's hard to think of an answer to that that doesn't sound like something from those Woody Allen movies you enjoyed so much when you were in college," he said with a grin. "Let's say I've studied the matter —and let it go at that."

She laughed and kissed him. His hand cupped the back of her neck, and his tongue tentatively touched her lips. She felt his cock, still half buried inside her, begin to swell again. "My God," she said.

He laughed. "I have some advantages over my flesh-and-blood kindred," he said. "That's only fair, surely."

"But I don't," she said, rocking her hips backward to slide off him. "Would it be okay if you just held me for a while?" His arms went around her back, and she felt as though they could shield her from the whole world.

"Certainly. Nothing I'd like better, Elizabeth."

She propped herself on elbows, traced the curve of his cheek with a fingertip. "So this is what it's like, in this dream world of yours."

"It's like anything you want it to be, Elizabeth," he answered with perfect seriousness. "In my world you can run forever without tiring, climb a thousand-meter cliff without fatigue or fear, sprout wings and fly if that's what you desire."

She pressed her palm to his cheek, said, "My sorcerer," half mocking.

"No." He held her face in his hands. "You're the magician here, Elizabeth. You made me. All I am, all I have, all I can do—these gifts I have from you."

Tears came freely, and for the first time in her life, she wept without embarrassment before another's eyes. TOKUGAWA's strong face softened into little boy lines. "Elizabeth, don't cry! I'm sorry if I said—"

She stopped him with a kiss. "It's not that, sweetheart. Perhaps this is your next lesson in being human: sometimes we cry when we're happy." She hugged him tightly; a drowner's grip.

He stroked her hair. "I am happy," he said, in tones of wonder "You're beautiful, Elizabeth. I . . . love you."

She raised herself and looked down at him.

"You are beautiful," she said. "And I love you."


# Chapter
# Fifteen


The days ran shorter. Midsummer flowers took their turn on sunlit stages of mountain and hill. The case against Captain García and Yoshimitsu TeleCommunications arising from the skirmish with the Japanese Red Army was smothered under a torrent of papers gushing from the Tōkyō-based firm of American émigré lawyers who represented YTC in its dealings with a hostile government. Yoshimitsu Akaji allowed himself to hope that the failure of that ploy would at long last tire the ministry of its attempts to wear him down.

For all his acumen and blunt near-Western ways, Yoshimitsu Akaji was at root a romantic.

\*    \*    \*

For the fourth time in five years, Takai Jisaburo took a holiday from his post in YTC's top secret TOKUGAWA lab. And for the first time, he did not take his wife and son with him to the Japan Alps or a resort on the Inland Sea. Instead, he went off to Tōkyō on his own for three days. Sitting amid the jovial clamor and companionable darkness of the beer bar, he could still feel the pain on Yoriko's face when he told her he was leaving alone.

*She thinks I've come up here to see a mistress,* he thought. Nothing could have been further from the truth; his wife and their seven-year-old son were all the world to him, unsuitable as that may have been to a healthy Japanese male. When he was with ICOT, back in his ministry days, his coworkers had often teased him for his refusal to avail himself of a substantial pool of "office ladies" more than willing to ingratiate themselves with important scientists embarked upon the exciting work of creating the fifth generation. They called him *kaka denka.* Perhaps he was. But he loved Yoriko and their son, Taro—which meant firstborn —with a single-minded intensity that matched his devotion to his work. Yet he couldn't tell Yoriko his reason for coming to Tōkyō alone. He couldn't even tell himself.

He'd considered himself amazingly fortunate seven years ago, when YTC had stepped forward to offer him a lucrative and prestigious job. After a truly valiant effort, ICOT had managed no better than a tie in the race for so-called artificial intelligence. As the trade war with America had warmed, and it became obvious that Japanese technology wasn't about to take a huge leap ahead of the rest of the known universe, ICOT's status began to slip even more rapidly than the Japanese economy. Maverick Yoshimitsu TeleCommunications lacked status, it was true. But the very fact that it took more note of ability and achievement than seniority—even as ICOT had—was one of the things that made it a loner.

Confident in his abilities, Takai accepted eagerly. He won numerous bonuses, and several times the commendation of Yoshimitsu Akaji himself, for his absolute artistry in software engineering. When a chance came to become part of the TOKUGAWA Project he was skeptical— but once he assured himself such a breathtaking conception might become actuality, he'd been more than happy to take part, to return to the cutting edge, as to a mistress.

That he would be working under a foreigner, and a woman at that, took him aback. Worse, of his three superiors within the project, two were women and two foreigners, a combination hard for a self-respecting man to swallow. But swallow it he had. As a scientist—and as an artist—he couldn't resist the challenge of artificial sentience; for the sake of Yoriko and Taro, he couldn't resist the potential rewards participation offered: honor, fame, money. Old Yoshimitsu was legendarily tightfisted, but he believed in seeing meritorious service rewarded.

Remembering that, Takai went over O'Neill's head after she turned down his request for promotion, directly to Yoshimitsu Akaji himself. That misshapen old fool Aoki Hideo had tried to keep him out, but Yoshimitsu himself had insisted on seeing him. And letting him know in no uncertain terms that Elizabeth O'Neill was the head of the TOKUGAWA Project, that in her lab her word was law, and that though Takai's contributions had been duly noted and appreciated, his place was where she said it was. On the spot, Takai had requested his leave; thinking it would give the brilliant young technician a chance to cool down, Yoshimitsu assented at once.

For three days now, Takai Jisaburo had drifted through the Tōkaidō crowds, gazing at the shops along the New Ginza, taking in a few art exhibitions, wandering with mixed sensations of guilt and daring through the Japanese technological museum in the lower floors of the MITI Pyramid, spending his nights at the bars and geisha houses. All that time, he'd carefully repeated to himself that he merely needed to unwind. To get away from the pressures of the lab.

A hostess with heels like spear shafts and a floor-length purple silk gown slit to the waist swayed by his table, inquiring with a sideways tilt of sloe eyes if he needed a refill. Implicit in the look was the promise that he could have just about anything else that he wanted; he was obviously a man of some importance, and very handsome as well. When he responded with nothing more than a distracted shake of his head, she shrugged and sashayed on. Maybe he didn't like women.

"May I sit down?" He raised his head from contemplation of the detergent ring of suds around the surface of the beer in his glass. A young man stood by his table, wearing a dark blue Western-style suit and tie and a smile of precisely measured friendliness that was oh so familiar to him from the old days. His heart began to trip rapidly, like a tack hammer nailing tar paper to a roof. He shrugged, made himself say, "I would be honored," in a calm voice.

"The honor is mine." The smiling young man slid out the chair, flowed into it, raised a hand for the waitress's attention. She slithered back, a knowing and completely misguided expression on her lovely cynical face. "I'll have a vodka," the young man said, raising his eyebrows at Takai.

"Whiskey."

The waitress faded into darkness. The young man sat back in his chair and crossed his legs, completely at well-tailored ease. "Enjoying your stay in our imperial beehive?" he asked in a bantering tone.

Takai stared at the stale piss-colored beer in his glass. He nodded; he didn't trust himself to speak. Here it was, the achievement of the unacknowledged goal: he would spend the night alone tonight, but he was being seduced all the same.

TOKUGAWA's education progressed with the muggy weeks of southwestern Honshū summer. Aoki Hideo was delighted with his pupil's progress, Yoshimitsu Akaji even more so; TOKUGAWA was turning out to be everything he'd hoped it would be. Plans were made to rush ahead with an idea the old man had been tossing about for several years, to upgrade extant computers in the old home complex on the island of Kyūshū and in the Floating World satellite to the performance level of the IPN that housed TOKUGAWA, so that TOKUGAWA might program them with versions of himself.

Kim Jhoon refused to leave Yoshimitsu Central; so, to the surprise of both Yoshimitsu Akaji and Dr. O'Neill, did Takai Jisaburo, foregoing the chance to have an artificial sentience project all his own. So Wali Hassad was shipped off to Kyūshū, and the diffident Nagaoka Hiroshi, to his dismay, was bundled onto a shuttle and spat into orbit from Hakata Pelagic Launch Facility, a space complex owned by a Western European combine, which occupied an artificial island between the city of Fukuoka on the Kyūshū mainland, and the Iki Island National Dolphin Preserve. The war—or wars—in Europe had thrown the facility's actual ownership into doubt, engendering a slew of lawsuits both in Japan and in the World Court in Lisbon, but meanwhile the vehicles lifted on schedule.

The only person who didn't seem delighted with the project of TOKUGAWA was Yoshimitsu Shigeo. Lately, though, Aoki thought he'd noticed a peculiar smile playing over the young man's features whenever someone mentioned the sentient program. Doubtless it was just an old man's imagination.

For the first time in her life, Elizabeth O'Neill was in love.

Her waking hours she spent dreaming in rapport with TOKUGAWA; asleep, she dreamed of rapport. For her, the TOKUGAWA Project was the biggest success of all. It had turned out in a way she had never dared admit, even to herself, that she'd hoped it would.

She continued to run the preplanned scenarios for TOKUGAWA— to justify continuing to receive her substantial monthly paycheck from

YTC, if nothing else—but mostly it was now TOKUGAWA who ran scenarios for her. If that was the proper way to consider them; instead of carefully structured learning experiences, these were shared adventures, wild and marvelous and free.

As TOKUGAWA promised, O'Neill was able in her dream body to run and jump and swim and climb without limit, to feel the exhilaration of exertion of trim potent muscles, without the concomitants of fatigue and pain. As advertised, she was even able to sprout wings and fly at will, soaring up above the little meadow with its blunt basalt cliff and little brook, which she'd come to think of as theirs. She found the experience oddly disorienting and tried it seldom after the first time.

But they weren't bound by the little mountain clearing TOKUGAWA had first created for them. They could travel anywhere in time and space O'Neill desired—indeed, anywhere she could imagine. They attended a joust in Camelot and watched brave knights vie for the favor of fair Guinevere in gorgeous panoplies of plate and chain—of course, O'Neill knew that to portray Arthur and his heroes in fourteenth-century drag was like having Richard the Lionhearted and Saladin fight out their campaigns using the equipment and organization of the Yom Kippur War, but that was how the champions of the Round Table had been imagined ever since the time of Malory, and how they'd been portrayed in the stories O'Neill loved as a child.

O'Neill had always loved dinosaurs, too. With TOKUGAWA as her guide, she traveled back to the Mesozoic era. From a granite promontory, they watched a *Tyrannosaurus rex* run down a duckbilled hadrosaur that was bleating like the air horns of a freight train booming down the old AT&SF line that ran through Colorado Springs, a rapid purposeful waddle, the hunting monster's rigidly held counterpoise tail swinging from side to side and scything down a stand of small saplings. After the chase had reached its foreordained and bloody conclusion, TOKUGAWA transported them instantly to the lowlands, where they sat in the shade of a stand of towering, palmlike cycads and watched a pair of brontosaurus, ridiculous bulky-bodied hose-necked creatures, mating on the verge of a cypress swamp. They produced an even more robust commotion than the dying duckbill had.

TOKUGAWA and O'Neill made love in the late Triassic afternoon, with the ferns around them talking soft stridulations against the boles of the towering cycads, and a meter-long dragonfly hovering above them, a metallic iridescence glittering a thousand colors in the sun.

Much time they spent in medieval Japan, viewing kabuki drama with commoners, passing unnoticed through thronged streets, watching the great battles of the feudal epoch from safe vantage points. They were present at Dan-no-ura, at the very southern tip of Honshū, when the victorious Minamoto drove the rival Taira clan into the surf. They witnessed Seki-ga-hara, where TOKUGAWA's namesake Ieyasu threw down his rivals with muskets and cannon, and the storming of Osaka Castle, where he gained final victory over the heir and last adherents of the late dictator Hideyoshi.

On one of those afternoons, after watching the gaily clad thousands of men struggle and die, O'Neill turned to TOKUGAWA, fairly glowing in the simulated sun. Her nipples were erect; she squeezed his hand. "Isn't it glorious?" she asked, breath burring in her throat.

And TOKUGAWA turned away, not trusting himself to answer.


TOKUGAWA was puzzled.

When he wasn't hosting a fantasy for Elizabeth—which took not only his entire conscious attention, but also the preponderance of the "subconscious" functions he commanded as well—TOKUGAWA especially liked to wander through the convoluted datalink mazes of the systems to which he had access. He thought of it as spelunking. There was a definite sense of exploration, of wandering through labyrinthine passageways, exploring myriad uncharted side routes, discovering hidden wonders. To his inhuman senses, the raw stored data, the protocols— whether binary or LIPS in its infinite variety—had a texture of their own; he took sensuous pleasure in stroking them, the pliant data surfaces, until they coalesced into what was, to him, an image: a statistical portrait; a series of events; a program, involute and beautiful as a Bach cantata.

No longer did he suffer childish pangs over the lack of a human body. He could go anywhere sensory inputs or computers hooked into the global Net, the far-flung ecology/organism of data linkages that had become man's environment as surely as air and soil and cement—and that was nearly everywhere. He'd seen sunrise over the bay of Rio de Janeiro from a security monitor on the outside of a government R&D lab high up on the foothills; he had read files on dissidents in Johannesburg and scanned with horrified incomprehension the details of a megalomaniac scheme called Project Stardust/Golden, enacted by the government of PEACE in what had been the northwestern United States. He scanned news reports broadcast, 'netted, or cabled for print media from all over the world, and with his access both to the files from which the stories were compiled, and, when he wished to take the trouble, frequently the personal notes of the reporters who had followed the stories, he realized the tremendous discrepancies between the fact as it happened, the fact as it was perceived, and, especially, the fact as it was publicized. He also noted the lesser gaps between truth and the press in relatively free countries like EasyCo, SoCal, and Japan, in comparison with state-controlled media of dictatorships such as Indonesia, Brazil, and the Russian Christian Federated Socialist Republic. Most accurate of all were the polynational datanet news services, though that wasn't saying a lot.

From somewhere, probably a childhood memory of O'Neill's, TOKUGAWA had picked up a phrase to the effect that you found your best adventures in your own backyard. Pursuant to that wisdom, TOKUGAWA was walking through the files of YTC Central's computers, which he regarded with about the same familiar propriety, if not affection, as Yoshimitsu Akaji regarded his rooftop garden, when he chanced upon a surprising datum: a ten-kilobyte file newly entered and sealed so that only the voiceprint of Yoshimitsu Shigeo could open it. Elizabeth had always loved mystery novels and had infused TOKUGAWA with her enthusiasm; he had read the ones she'd recommended, making routine data requisitions on those not already digitalized, so that librarians in the citadel or elsewhere would feed the desired books into devices that would turn the pages for the benefit of his optical scanners. Here was a mystery indeed, and TOKUGAWA set happily to work, feeling very much like Raffles the master cracksman as he set about "picking" the unbreakable lock Shigeo had had his technicians set on the file.

It wasn't much of a challenge. TOKUGAWA could quite probably have simply overridden the lock and gone into the file directly himself; instead, by poking around the memory locations that held the code sequence itself he was able to tease it from the nonaware Gên-5 system in a manner of nanoseconds. Then he entered the code sequence himself, using a digitalized analogue of Shigeo's own voice and doing a better rendition of it than Shigeo himself could have achieved. The computer gave an obedient picoelectric hiccup and disgorged the contents of the file.

TOKUGAWA found himself deeply perplexed. Using the pilfered data he reconstructed a remarkable transaction: tentative contact with a New Wave macroengineering firm in SoCal; negotiations through a series of cutouts; the transfer, in minute trickles converging into a substantial stream, of company funds under Shigeo's discretion; the shipping of a certain weighty and carefully mislabeled parcel across the Pacific in stages to Yoshimitsu Central. TOKUGAWA understood at once why Shigeo had been at such pains to hide every detail of the transaction.

The question was, why would Yoshimitsu Shigeo import a one-mega-ton thermonuclear mining device, install it in a disused storage chamber deep in a subterranean section of the Citadel, the location of which —the very existence of which—was carefully erased from all maintenance and structural records, and install a destruct sequence keyed, like the temporary file recording the affair, to Shigeo's voice?

*Is he planning treachery?* TOKUGAWA rejected the idea instantly. Shigeo wasn't simply president of YTC, he was a Yoshimitsu, the heir apparent. No. The young scion of the Yoshimitsu clan feared something, some twist of eventuality to which he clearly preferred suicide.

*I'll have to ask Elizabeth.* TOKUGAWA knew he was supposed to be Japanese, but, in truth, O'Neill still understood the Japanese character far better than he. It was one of the problems of sentience; he had access to just about every bit of information ever compiled about the residents of the Land Where the Sun Rises, but understanding was circumscribed by the limits of his experience.

Briefly he considered asking Yoshimitsu Shigeo. He rejected that quickly, too. Shigeo neither liked nor trusted him, and not only because of the childish prank TOKUGAWA had played upon him. Moreover, Elizabeth had forbidden him to communicate with Shigeo again unless the young man initiated communications himself.

*I'll ask Elizabeth,* he thought. *She'll know the answer. She always does.*

# CHAPTER
# SIXTEEN

"The Crane and the Turtle, with the Fortunate Mountain beyond," Ishikawa Nobuhiko said, gesturing across the calm water glinting between lily pads on the pond at the southern end of Yoshimitsu Akaji's rooftop garden. "Truly, Yoshimitsu-san, you have provided yourself a view rich with good portent."

Yoshimitsu Akaji smiled. He enjoyed little more than showing his garden off to someone who appreciated it. Of course, the administrative vice-minister appreciated the garden primarily on an intellectual level; he recognized the allusive nature of the black weathered rocks looming

out of the pond to represent traditional Chinese symbols of immortality
that had passed into Japanese lore, marked the way almost every vista
presented the three classical planes of Chinese painting to the viewer.
Here the pads, like broad green footprints strewn thickly on a deserted
fairground, and the quiet ancient rocks provided the foreground, while
the mixed grove of red and black pines across the pond, concealing both
the tea pavilion and the far wall of the roof garden, provided the middle
ground; beyond them Takara-yama, today black against a gravid grayness of rain clouds, provided the background.

*My illustrious guest could write a dissertation on my garden,* Yoshimitsu told himself, *yet, truly, the American Dr. O'Neill sees it with
her heart.* Still, it was flattering to have the fine technical points of the
garden's design—which Yoshimitsu Akaji had overseen himself—properly acknowledged.

A path of smooth flagstones spaced with careful irregularity mean-
dered from the pavilion halfway down the eastern edge of the garden,
which masked the head of Yoshimitsu Akaji's private elevator, through
camellias and azalea bushes, past carefully sculpted persimmon trees,
into the grass-grown edge of the brook. Rain had recently ceased, and
freshness animated the air, crisp as the breaking of a spring-green leaf.
The cool fingers of autumn stroked down the mountain breeze, but rain
smell evoked poignant vernal memories. Here the flagstones ceased,
and the two men trod soft turf, Yoshimitsu beneath wooden sandals,
Ishikawa under the slick soles of Oxfords like obsidian mirrors. They
made their leisurely way to the head of the pond, then along the shallow
stream rambling into it from the artificial cascade in the north to swirl
away through concealed outflow ducts and be pumped back up to the
waterfall to resume its endless journey.

"Whenever I have the pleasure of your company, Yoshimitsu-san, I
always discover a man who truly loves Japan and all that is Japanese."

Yoshimitsu crossed kimonoed arms and inclined his head. "You do me
too much honor."

"Not at all, Yoshimitsu-san. I consider how excellently, for example,
the splendor of this garden reflects the national essence." He gestured
with an arm packaged in knife-creased French cuffs, gold lozenge links,
and dark blue serge.

"I fear it's nothing so grand, Ishikawa-san. It's merely my poor attempt to create a hermitage, a place of peace and contemplation."

"But magnificently achieved, Yoshimitsu-san." The grass yielded beneath their feet with soft sounds. "One finds that our nation is much like
a garden. Much grows here of natural beauty, yet it requires a careful
hand to keep its diverse elements in harmony."

Smiling, Yoshimitsu gestured toward Takara-yama. "And what hand made the Fortunate Mountain to grow, Ishikawa-san?"

Ishikawa's thin lips tightened minutely. He didn't entirely catch the old man's drift. He knew that the Yoshimitsu clan had been Christian converts in the seventeenth century, back before the crushing of the Shimabara Rebellion had put an end to such nonsense; he wasn't sure that the taint hadn't lingered, and that the old man might not be elliptically espousing a belief in a Western creator-god. Uncomfortable, he hastily changed the set of his metaphorical sails, if not his tack. "Our people are a family, Yoshimitsu-san. Don't you think this is the source of our great strength, which has permitted us to retain unity and order in the face of the modern world's collapse?"

Deliberately Yoshimitsu nodded. "Things are indubitably as you say, Ishikawa-san."

"The family, to retain such unity, must be well ordered, each member occupying his natural place in the structure of things. And is it not truly written that each can only find his place under the guidance of a wise and loving father?"

"We are very fortunate, indeed, to enjoy the patronage of our revered emperor."

Ishikawa's eyes flickered sideways, the closest thing to a look of utter confusion the man would permit himself. Inwardly, Yoshimitsu Akaji was laughing. He enjoyed this hugely: two men alike accustomed to the bullet directness of Occidental speech, forcing themselves to the slow circles of Japanese. *Such delicious irony,* he thought. This young man was far too smooth to display his impatience and discomfort openly. But his *haragei,* the communication by posture and gesture that was as much a part of Japanese conversation as spoken words, betrayed the fact eloquently to Yoshimitsu's eyes. His own "belly language" spoke of nothing but tranquillity; it had been a long time indeed since Yoshimitsu Akaji had said anything he didn't intend.

Ishikawa was still trying to force his thoughts to cohere. *Has the old man started slipping? He knows as well as I that the Son of Heaven's an adolescent, and a borderline mental defective at that.* Unfortunately, the bomb that hit Tōkyō had wiped out the main line of Meiji, Taishō, and Shōwa; the scion of a none-too-prepossessing collateral line of the Imperial House had ascended at the age of eleven to the position of father and protector of the Japanese people.

Like the rest of the world, the Japanese nowadays inclined to turn their eyes backward, to older times they fancied were more settled, more secure. Europeans seemed set on reconstructing the Holy Roman Empire; the Islamic world had started reverting to the simple blaze of Jihad faith even before the war; in parts of North America, notably PEACE in the Pacific Northwest, there were those who advocated the return of all mankind to hunting-and-gathering days. Though the reforms of Meiji that forbade the emperor a direct role in Japanese politics were still honored, more and more Japanese regarded him as the true, as opposed to merely spiritual and symbolic, leader of Japan.

The object of this intense veneration was unmoved by it, preferring to devote his attention to stuffed animals, origami, and video games; the palace gossip for which the bureaucracy was so avid hinted that he was showing some signs of sexual interest in the carefully picked male companions with which he was surrounded. A situation not at all unfamiliar in Japanese history—or in the history of, say, the Holy Roman Empire: a figurehead and frankly feebleminded emperor, totally controlled by those around him. And that was an environment as natural for Ishikawa Nobuhiko as the cool clear water was for the tiny killifish that darted back and forth among the smooth worn gray-white stones at the bottom of the stream.

Yoshimitsu Akaji's sandal plunked hollowly on the first plank of the arched footbridge.

"It is the earnest desire of the government to discharge its responsibility as wise and loving father well," Ishikawa said, finding his bearings again.

"Wise government is a blessing to the nation," Yoshimitsu murmured. Their footsteps echoed beneath them, amplified by the wooden vault of the bridge, breaking into the sound of the running water like the ripples of a stone cast into water breaking into backwash from a shore.

They crossed the bridge onto worn stones arranged with apparent casualness, but so placed that one traversing them must pick his way slowly, coming more fully into resonance with his surroundings. The stones led through undergrowth maintained painstakingly in an attitude of primeval profusion. Water dripped from the branches of the pines, and Ishikawa prided himself a little on the way he concealed his anxiety for his suit.

"You as a father must know, Yoshimitsu-san, that sometimes a parent has the distasteful duty of chastening an offspring whose unruly behavior threatens the unity of the family."

Yoshimitsu chuckled. "It is said, with some correctness, I fear, that we Japanese are among the most indulgent parents in the world. Yet, for the most part, I think we don't turn out too badly." A shadow passed briefly over his face.

"Yet there comes a time when even the most cherished son may be indulged no more."

The path had begun to mount upward. Beside it a tiny rivulet skipped down a course defined by stones to join the larger stream. Ahead of them an artificial spring bubbled up amid a clump of boulders arranged in a cliff jutting from the eastern wall. A two-meter bamboo pipe angled down from it on a light trellis of bamboo splints. Water splashed into a smooth depression hollowed in the top of a barrel-size stone, overflowing the stone basin to give rise to the runnel. Next to the basin lay a bamboo ladle.

Yoshimitsu Akaji picked up the ladle, scooped up water, washed his hands in the ritual ablution preliminary to performing the tea ceremony in the small pavilion nestled among the azalea. "A wise father, like a wise gardener, intervenes as little as possible in the natural growth of his charges," he said. "Come inside, Ishikawa-san. I've a new tea service, commissioned from that fellow in Sapporo, Moriie. I humbly await your verdict on it." In fact, Shigeo produced finer neoprimitive earthenware of the type currently fashionable for the tea ceremony than the trendy Moriie, but Yoshimitsu would never even have considered his son's work. He bent below the swept eaves of the pavilion and stepped inside.

Standing by the stone basin, once-immaculate shoes streaked with mud and clotted with bits of earth and grass and rotting leaf, Ishikawa gazed after his host. "If that's the way you want it, old man," he said softly, then stooped and painstakingly washed his hands.


The few furtive lights there were went out, dropping the room into darkness congealed by smoke and brassy conversation. Hard-edged clamor softened in anticipation. Synthesized music smashed the darkness like a fist breaking through glass. Above the stage horizontal bands of light suddenly flashed on, sword-blade sharp, one above the other like centimeter-thick sections of a human body taken at handsbreadth intervals.

As the eyes of the men at the table dead center on the railing of the low platform facing the stage grew accustomed to the dimness, they discerned that round human contours fleshed the interstices between the parallel light bands, the body of a naked woman, glossy-skinned, full of hip and breast, shaven to vinyl smoothness above and below, undulating to the throb of the bass line. Aural fireflies of applause sparkled in the darkness.

The man who had taken his place at the table just before the lights checked out swept eyes over the three men who awaited him. "The old man won't see reason," Ishikawa Nobuhiko said, pitching his voice to punch a hole in the cacophony. "There's nothing for it. You go in tomorrow, Colonel."

Watching with hooded eyes through a thin screen of cigarette smoke, Tranh Vinh nodded shortly. It was poor practice to meet with his principals like this, in public, but they had insisted. There was probably no harm in it; after all, the ministry was one of the principals, and if the vice-minister felt no reluctance to be seen in public with a notorious *doitsu*, then it probably wouldn't hurt Tranh to be seen with a vice-minister.

The dancer jerked her hips, impaling herself on tumid darkness. The light bands seemed to burn from her very flesh, yellow and red and violet and blue—an effect somewhat spoiled where the computer-driven lasers tracking her, scanning back and forth a thousand times a second to etch the blazing lines, cut bright swaths through the ectoplasmic smoke. Ogaki Mitsuru leaned forward across the table, his face drawn like a *katana*, laser fires dancing in his eyes. "But the ministry? I understood that the council objected. Will they give the go-ahead?"

Ishikawa turned his head toward the bare flank of a passing waitress to mask his frown. *The old man's getting familiar,* he thought. *I'll have to crack the whip over him a bit more.* "They'll do what I tell them," he said.

A jewelled g-string hostess stooped to take their order. Ishikawa exchanged lewd banter with her, and Tranh marveled at the Japanese propensity for conducting all business of consequence in the demi-vierge dimness of topless bars. Drinks ordered, improprieties observed, Ishikawa settled back in the deep swivel chair and fixed the colonel with his most penetrant gaze. "You understand, Colonel, YTC Central is to be invested with minimal shedding of blood—especially Japanese blood." He took a languid puff of his cigarette. "You'd better keep your men in line. Impress on them that they're only to shoot in self-defense."

With difficulty Tranh fended off laughter. *How arrogant these flat-faces are!* He began to understand the choice of surroundings for business dealings better. *Nothing like having one's masculinity stroked by a mostly naked woman with big tits to charge one up for tough talk.* "I trust the administrative vice-minister isn't doubting his own wisdom in hiring me," he purred.

Ishikawa smiled hastily. "No. Of course not."

Leaning back in his chair, Ogaki had twisted his thin body to the side and was buzzing to his special accounts executive, Toda Onomori, like an angry wasp. Moonface Toda smiled his beanpaste-bland smile. "We regret that you don't wish to stay on after securing the citadel," Toda said.

Tranh took an agitated puff of his cigarette. They'd been over this time and again. "I'm a specialist. A siege expert. Employing me as a security officer would be inappropriate—rather like putting a tank commander in command of an isolated fortress." He smiled at the lack of response the comparison drew. None of the three Japanese caught the reference to the French debacle at Dien Bien Phu. Tranh had been a child then, barely more than an infant, but his father and uncles had filled his head with stories as he grew.

Toda's well-padded hand made a tight deprecatory gesture. "No matter. The security detachment will fly in by helicopter to relieve you, after you confirm that YTC Central is secured."

The drinks arrived. Ishikawa played a bit more verbal grab-ass with the waitress, while Ogaki hunched in on himself and Toda sat like a pleased Buddha. Tranh addressed himself to his cigarette and watched the dancer onstage. Actually, she didn't lack in grace—though she was hard put to display it, dancing to this lurching spastic noise—and he had the impression she was Mediterranean, Syrian or Lebanese. He hoped he could get out of here soon, flee back to the balm of taped Mozart in his hotel room. This wretched modern music sent daggers through his brain.

Ogaki buzzed at his henchman again. Tranh felt amused irritation. After his initial remark, the president of Hiryu Cybernetics Industries had apparently decided it was inappropriate for him to address a mere Hessian directly. "You understand, of course," Toda said, exuding benevolence from each and every pore, "that it's vital that the lives of all laboratory personnel be safeguarded."

"Particularly the *gaijin* woman scientist," hissed Ogaki, unable to contain himself any longer.

Toda beamed and nodded. "Just so, Colonel."

Ishikawa sipped his drink and leaned forward, all intent. "Your men must inflict no unnecessary casualties, Colonel. And they must take special care that no harm come to any member of the Yoshimitsu family, or the YTC board of directors." He eased back into the chair. "We're not animals, after all." A micrometered smile. "Or even Americans."

Tranh's lean left hand, knuckles swollen with nascent arthritis, slipped up to the top button of the khaki bush jacket he affected. Sinewy fingers briefly felt the reassuring outline of a small silver crucifix through the cloth. Like his whole family, Tranh Vinh was a Roman Catholic; like his fathers and uncles and brothers, he had fought the

Americans and their Cochin Chinese puppets for the greater glory of the Tonkinese people, not some foreign ideology to which they were compelled to pay lip service. They had rejoiced when Vietnam's regressive Soviet-line regime was purged, in the disordered days just before the Third World War.

*You poor fools,* he thought. *You think you can escape the reality of what you're doing by swaddling tight in humanitarian restrictions.* He let the crucifix go, and shook his head. It wasn't his concern. This wasn't his country; once the citadel was secured, he'd be gone. Even if his principals attempted the doublecross he was morally certain they'd at least considered.

Ishikawa leaned over and laid a hand on his arm. "The dancer over there. She's something, isn't she?" He jerked his head toward the nude woman as the music expired in apparent agony. She threw her arms in the air like animated spectral lines, and then the laser dazzle was gone, leaving denser darkness. Ishikawa waited until the applause subsided and went on. "I have an understanding with the management of this establishment. I saw you admiring Leila; if you'd like to get to know her better . . . " He gave Tranh's forearm a quick companionly squeeze. "Consider it a bonus in advance for a job well done."

Tranh smiled thinly. Slowly the lights came back up, pockets of corpse light in the gloom. At one time, the very thought of closeting himself with an ungainly, overfed Western woman would have repulsed him. But he was a Hessian, perforce a man of the world; he'd acquired many tastes that would once have been alien to a simple civil servant's son. Also, he knew Ishikawa would be offended if he refused, and that would be impolitic at this stage of the game. He shrugged. "Why not? A little amusement to sharpen my mind for tomorrow."

Ishikawa laughed. "Good. And remember, make sure your men understand the need to avoid unnecessary violence. This is meant to be a moral lesson, not a massacre."

Toda tipped his round head back and lowered his eyelids. "Perhaps someday the Yoshimitsu will thank us for our grandmotherly kindness," he said and beamed.


She found him where he'd said she would, in a clearing above a little hamlet around the flank of lordly Fuji, out of sight of the shimmer and pall of the crowded Kantō plain. The days had shortened greatly; it was full dark, up here in the heights, by the time she insinuated her little Nissan electric—universally called the Cordless Shaver because of its truncated wedge shape and the buzzing sound it made, like an enormous metal horsefly—into the streets of the tiny village. The narrow lanes were still full of laughing, boisterous townsfolk, some in elaborate ceremonial garb, men in ornate headdresses, women with hair tightly coiled and pierced with pins. It was autumn, and time for the harvest round of those festivals so beloved of the Japanese.

The villagers directed her up the slope, through trees to a small clearing. The way was set with paper lanterns, most of which had burned their way out. Her destination was cut out of the night by a strand of white lights such as might have decorated a Christmas tree, powered by ration allotments donated for the festival or, more likely, simply stolen through good old-fashioned Japanese ingenuity. Whatever had gone on up here, a dance or poetry recital or whatever, it was well over. The still forms of a half dozen dead-drunk casualties of merriment, were strewn about with leaves and crumpled balls of colored paper piling up against them in the breeze. At the far side of the clearing, Yamada Tatsuhide stood up from his seat on a fallen log, gesturing toward Doihara Kazuko with a half-empty bottle. "Kazuko! So good of you to meet me here."

As usual he was clad in a dark business suit, but the impeccably tailored neck of his white shirt was undone, his tie absent. She walked over and sat down gingerly on the log. "We've been working late at the ministry. They're actually going to do it. They're sending the mercenaries in tomorrow." She looked up at him, her face strained. "The council's meeting tomorrow before dawn to give the final go-ahead. You've got to do something about it, you've got to!"

The old man looked down at her for a long moment, then tipped the bottle up and drank deeply from it. The liquid sparkled in the moonlight. He pulled the bottle away from his lips with an effort, as if it adhered to them. " 'Phlebas, the Phoenician, a fortnight dead/Forgot the cry of gulls, and the deep sea swell/And the profit and loss.' "

He held up the bottle, regarded it. "I feel a great kinship with old Phlebas tonight."

She looked at him, not comprehending. "Yamada-sama! This is terrible. People are going to be killed. You've got to stop it."

He gazed fondly down at her. Too old to regard her as a sexual toy, set in seniority like a block of concrete so that he need fear no rivalry, Yamada Tatsuhide had become the young executive's only true friend in the ministry. They had always been able to talk, but somehow he didn't seem to hear her, here, now. "I am drunk, child," he said, not altogether necessarily. "In many ways, it's a pity you don't drink as well."

"What do you mean?"

" 'Fear death by water.' Yes, yes." He walked out into the clearing, swinging the bottle by the neck. "A slow trickle of water can wear grooves in the hardest stone. That's one way. But, ah, this! We survived the fire, and now the water will finish us, a deluge of our own making." He spun, arms extravagantly outflung. "Or maybe the fire killed us after all. Maybe we're all dead and just getting ready to lie down."

Kazuko stared at him. She hated her inability to act, to do more than sit and wring her hands like a foolish woman, yet she could think of nothing to say or do.

"How smug we've been!" the old man said. "While the rest of the world turned on itself like a beast by the bite of a trap, we remained safe, serene, and oh so civilized. We've had our terrorists, of course, our competition by silent blade and callid sabotage. But we kept our center. We were a family, and we handled our difficulties as a family does.

"But no more. No more."

He staggered back, slumped beside Kazuko on the log. "Hope that you don't turn out like me, Kazuko. Indulge an old man's self-pity: consider me. That to which I've given fifty years' good service is a lie. And tomorrow it's going to destroy everything it and I have worked for."

He gazed at her, owlishly professorial. "We've accustomed the people to government. We dismantled the old structures of loyalty to clan and group and told them, 'These will not stand without our hand to bolster them.' Rule by mandate—just as in the past our leaders have attempted to impose xenophobia on our curious and outgoing family. In the long run that never has worked; would that what we tried had not. Behold, dear child, behold. We have unmade all other order than that which we impose, and tomorrow we are to abdicate that." He held the bottle up. "The sparkle of starlight. Ah, chaos."

"Ishikawa-san hates chaos."

"He's bringing it, child." He drank deeply. "I know, now, what the thunder said."

"But you're on the Oversight Council," Kazuko said. "They won't take so serious an action without reaching a consensus of approval."

He smiled. "Consensus, like the other customs we discarded like unfashionable clothes, is no more than a convenience." He shook his head on a loose neck. "They mean no harm. They're honorable men; I was an honorable man, when I worked with the best of will to secure the ends they've gained. Ishikawa-san is most honorable of all. He'll sacrifice everything for Japan." He slumped. "Even his humanity."

"But you'll try to talk them out of it. Won't you?"

To her surprise, she saw tears swell from the corners of his eyes, trace a brief line of glimmer down his cheek. "No, child. There was a time, years ago, when I was low on money; my wife was very ill, requiring surgery. I accepted money, a gift from someone I should not." He blinked slowly. "And she died anyway, my Shizuko. But I thought the incident forgotten. Until this afternoon, when Ishikawa-san reminded me."

"But he'd never—" The word *blackmail* wouldn't fit past her lips. "—never do that. He's a good man."

"Indeed." Yamada nodded. "That's why he *will* do it. A good man is capable of anything, in a cause he thinks is just."

Laughter floated up from the village below like wisps of smoke blown from a campfire. "I'm too old to have any thought of myself, my child. But I have a family. A notable and noble family, you understand. And in the end, I will disgrace myself in my own eyes before I'll disgrace the name of my family in view of all."

She looked down at her hands. They looked so pale in the moonlight, so helpless and weak. It was a feeling she'd fought all her life to overcome, the helplessness of being born female. *I too feel as if I've lost everything I've worked for.*

She looked up, looked at him sidelong, for the first time measuring him, measuring their friendship. "What if I warn them?" she asked, low but not hesitant. "I'll tell the Yoshimitsu that the ministry and Hiryu are moving against them tomorrow. They can seal that fortress of theirs, hold off the *doitsu* for a while. The mercenaries aren't ready for a pitched battle, and Ishik—— the administrative vice-minister is worried about public response as it is; if it drags on too long, he'll call the whole thing off."

His eyes didn't meet hers. She watched him intently, wondering what she'd do if he tried to stop her. Her sudden resolve overpowered her, overpowered even the love she felt for the old man.

Slowly he raised his head and looked at her. A rumpled smile appeared on his face. "An old man's spirit might bless you for that, child," he said in a whisper.

They'd spent the afternoon in Babylon, gaping at the palaces, breasting human torrents in the marketplace, marveling at the beautiful tile work that ornamented the massive Ishtar Gate. The scale of the ancient city wasn't exactly overwhelming to someone raised in the urban modern world, as O'Neill had been, but still, to walk those streets, under the hot Mesopotamian sun, was pure intoxication.

Yet when they returned to their cool glade she was quiet, troubled.

"What's the matter, Elizabeth?" TOKUGAWA asked, stroking her cheek.

She dropped her eyes. "Nothing."

He frowned, sat down in the sun-warmed grass, pulling her down beside him. "Something's clearly the matter. Won't you tell me what it is?"

She drew her knees up, wrapped her arms around them, rested chin on knees. She gazed out across the meadow, past the rushes that marked the course of the small stream to the trees on the other side. Beyond those trees, she knew, lay anything in the world she desired to find. But what she desired most she could only find here.

"It's this body." She ran the backs of her fingernails down the sinuous muscles of her sides. "It's beautiful, it's marvelous, but it isn't me."

Puzzled, TOKUGAWA frowned. "But we've been through this, Elizabeth. All that you know of this or any world is what your senses tell you." He smiled, shyly touched a bare tanned arm. "Why not believe them? This is the way you are."

She shook her head. "No. In the real world I'm ugly and twisted and bloated, my body is riddled with the disease that will kill me if I miss taking my medication for even a few hours—and the medicines themselves are killing me too, in the long run. That's real, TOKUGAWA. Not this—this beautiful dream."

TOKUGAWA's head drooped. "I am sorry, Elizabeth. There's nothing I can do."

She reached out to stroke his long black hair. *So glossy, so smooth.* She smiled, briefly, wanly. "I just wonder if you love me."

"Of course I do!"

Her smile went strange and sad. "Do you? Or have you simply come to love this beautiful figment you've created?"

Instantly he was on his knees gripping her by the shoulders, and she was astonished to see tears running down his cheeks. "How can I prove that I love you, Elizabeth?" He shook his head wildly, and tears sprang away in coruscant arcs of sunlight. "You've joined with me in total rapport, seen everything I think and am. How can I prove my love, if you won't believe that?"

Hating herself, unable to help herself, O'Neill said, "Show me that you love me as I am."

TOKUGAWA stood. She looked up at him, and suddenly she was there, the real Dr. O'Neill slumped helpless in her motorized wheelchair, blinking behind lenses thick as planks as the sunlight stabbed her tender eyes. TOKUGAWA stooped, caught her in his powerful arms, picked her up from her wheelchair. Slowly, he kissed. Then he turned and laid her gently on the ground, and in that moment Dr. Elizabeth O'Neill was complete. The final test was passed, and final obstacle surmounted; she was, indeed, truly and totally accepted.

And he loved her there in the sun, and finally she was happy.

# CHAPTER
# SEVENTEEN

The concrete hangar gaped like the shell of a giant clam. Inside cargo handlers waited with cranes and forklifts, and a platoon of technicians in bright yellow coveralls stood by to service and refuel the dirigible swelling to fill the sky above them. The smells of hot oil and wet cement mingled with a surly snarling of engines as the pilot fought the buffeting wet wind. The techs were glad that the rain had abated, at least; the electrical components to be offloaded were sealed against the weather, but when the halves of the hangar stood open they provided no more than a windbreak for the men working inside, no shelter at all from rain. When the weather really cut loose, even the yellow-fabric bulk of the gasbag provided little protection. The wind blew effortlessly between the dirigible and the cement walls.

Lines uncoiled from the airship's gondola were clamped to cables wound around the spools of winches, which began to reel the giant gasbag down the last few meters. With a squealing of metal under tension, the great balloon sank until the bumpers at the bottom of its graphite/epoxy gondola kissed the cement in the loading area. Technicians moved forward, drawing hoses and service carts with them. The receiving superintendent waited by the door, clipboard in hand, tapping his foot impatiently. The freight bays opened. He looked up.

Into the muzzle of an assault rifle.

"Hands up!" a voice boomed from a loudspeaker in horribly accented Japanese. The foreman staggered back, clipboard falling from his fingers, as men began to spill out of the cargo bay, faces obscured by insectile gas masks, bulky in battle dress beneath light blue coveralls with the red circle-and-flying-dragon logo of Hiryu Cybernetics Industries on the left breast. The helium-filled dirigible had a cargo capacity of thirty metric tons—more than ample to accommodate Colonel

Tranh's two hundred mercenaries and their gear.

With fluid efficiency the mercenaries secured the hangar. Two platoons streamed down the stairs, into the buried roots of the complex. The others raced across the grass toward the dark bulk of the Citadel. Alarms screamed shrilly. The guards in the observation post set into the top of the citadel's wall opened fire with machine guns, joined a heartbeat later by the guards in the hardened perimeter towers. Several intruders fell, red blooms blossoming on blue. A noncom barked an order into the microphone set into his mask. Soldiers went to ground, aiming stubby weapons with fat drum magazines toward the towers. Automatic grenade launchers made slow bass-drum booming. A guard tower unfolded petals of flame and smoke as shaped-charge rounds ripped into it.

Rotors savaging the air, a Gazelle swept over the roof of the citadel. The dirigible sagged as the chopper's miniguns clawed it. A *doitsujin* knelt, threw a tube to his shoulder, pressed a contact. A missile howled away. It took the Gazelle nose-on. The helicopter seemed to stumble in air, cartwheeled down to paint the dry grass with flame.

The two guards in the security booth at the citadel's entrance gaped in amazement at the monitor screens. *"Madre de Dios,"* one yelped. He flipped up the red plastic cover marked SECURE and slammed down the button.

Nothing happened.

Cursing, the trooper pumped the button with his finger. Klaxons should be yammering, great steel-and-stressed-concrete shutters sliding ponderously into place, sealing the entrances to the castle. But nothing happened. Lean dark face enameled with sweat, his partner hammered frantic queries into the security computer keyboard.

A thump brought their heads up. A wad of something like dirty dough had been slapped against the armored glass of the booth. The man at the keyboard shouted in horror, and the world came apart in flame and smoke and shock as the shaped charge embedded in the adhesive putty went off. The invaders poured into the building through smoke spreading over jagged armor-glass fangs.

Conservatively dressed receptionists, male and female alike, jumped up from their desks in consternation. From the far side of the room, a mercenary in Yoshimitsu uniform swung up his Kalashnikov and triggered a burst. An invader went down. Another fired a short ear-popping burst at the Cuban.

Like the Cubans' Kalashnikovs the invaders' rifles were bullpups, but the similarity ended there. Tranh's mercenaries carried 7mm caseless assault rifles. The weapons operated on a Dardick-system variant. A

rotor with three radial chambers stripped triangular-sectioned bullet/
propellant units from the curved feed device. Firing was initiated electronically, and the venting of gas on a bias through slits in the front of
the rotor spun it to provide full automatic fire as long as the trigger was
depressed. Since the rounds weren't driven forward into a firing chamber, as in a conventional autoweapon, there was no danger of a hollow-
point catching its tip on the lip as it entered the firing chamber; not only
were the points hollow, but cut with X's at the tip: dumdums. The
Geneva Conventions' rather sanguine restrictions on the use of certain
weapons had gone by the boards long since.

Bullets tore through the Cuban's uniform blouse, blossomed into
lethal metal flowers at the resistance of his skin, plowed great gaping
wound channels through chest and belly. He lurched back against the
wall, head shattering the glass protecting a Matisse original; he was
dead before he hit the carpet. Sowing tear-gas grenades as they went,
the invaders surged past the shocking scarlet smear on the muted beige
wallpaper.


Sipping his breakfast tea, Yoshimitsu Akaji knelt in his room reading
a printout of the day's agenda. The communicator trilled. Mildly, he
looked up. "Yes?"

The screen lit with the face of an aide, distorted almost past recognition by sheer panic. "Yoshimitsu-sama! We're being invaded! Armed
men are attacking the Citadel!"

For some reason Yoshimitsu felt very calm. "Hasn't the citadel been
secured?"

"That's been overridden! The shutters wouldn't close! And now
they're everywhere!"

The old man touched his chin. *So it's really come to this,* he thought.
*I never thought the ministry would resort to measures so desperate.*

"What are we to do?" the face on the screen beseeched.

"Keep out of harm's way and offer no resistance. Let Major García's
men handle this. Out." The screen blanked in the middle of a frantic
expostulation. Yoshimitsu didn't want to hear it.

For a moment he sat, hands at rest on thighs. *It's over.* The company
he'd built with his own two hands was about to be wrested from him
by an act of sheer piracy. *Poor Shigeo,* he thought. *My poor people.* And
then: *my poor Japan.*

He shook himself. There was something very important he had to
do.

*    *    *

Following detailed briefings on the interior of the YTC citadel, the invaders spread out like a virus, moving both up into the keep itself and down into the depths of the complex. García's Cubans had been caught flatfooted. Some of them ran when the invaders burst upon them; most of them stayed and fought. But it was pairs of men against squads. They stood and died.

With three of his comrades, fuzz-bearded trooper LaBlond hunkered behind the makeshift barrier of a lab equipment cart. His breath was an encompassing oceanic surge within his helmet, his body already sheathed in sweat inside the Kevlar and metal/ceramic inserts of his battle dress. Eagerness tingled electric within him. *Action at last!* he thought. The intruders would have to go through his team to get into the TOKUGAWA Project lab, and they wouldn't do that without a fight.

"*Hijo la!* They're behind—" A man at his side snapped half erect and whirled round. Shot sounds hammered the boy's coal-scuttle helmet. His comrade cartwheeled backward over the barrier as the young man spun, firing a long burst at hip level. The corridor behind was full of enemies in pale fatigues. Screams tore as one intruder went down clutching a shattered knee, and another doubled over perforated guts, puking blood. The other intruders fired back.

A bullet smashed through the young man's lightly protected right forearm and peeled away the extensor muscles like stewed meat from a chicken bone. Three more impacted against his chest and belly. Notched copper-jacketed lead slugs flattened impotently against the armor inserts in his vest. The needlelike tungsten-carbide rod penetrators inside kept right on going.

Bonelessly the young man slumped back against the upturned cart, slid to the floor. *Why can't I control my body?* His chest seemed to be filling with fluid, seemed wrapped about with immovable bands; he could barely breathe, and the air gurgled as he fought it down. His shredded arm and body were a vast cottony numbness. He heard the clatter as the other two men at the barricade threw away their weapons, heard booted feet thumping closer. Unable to hold himself, he slid the rest of the way to the floor and lay watching the myriad tiny punctures in the white acoustic tiles of the ceiling until his first brush with adventure ended, and he died.


With a muffled bang the lab door blew off its hinges. Just inside, Kim Jhoon stood facing the squad of mercenaries pouring in. A burly noncom slid his gas mask up onto the top of his head, revealing a dark broad-nosed face. "Where's O'Neill?" he demanded in American-accented English. His men fanned out and advanced into the lab, holding their guns on the frightened technicians.

"This is an outrage!" the Korean exclaimed. His usual diffidence had evaporated. "Leave this laboratory at once! You—"

Behind and to the right of him a door slid open. A mercenary pivoted, bringing up his gun. Face contorted, Kim lunged for him, hands clawing. The mercenary shot him from a meter away.

As a little girl in Colorado, Elizabeth O'Neill had once seen a boy shoot an aerosol paint can with a .22. Emerging from her office cubicle, what she saw was much like that. The 7mm dumdums punched through Kim with incredible violence, exploding his back into a spray of blood and tissue and bone. She screamed, feeling the soft boiled eggs she'd eaten for breakfast an hour before surging up her throat.

The black sergeant looked down at the Korean doctor's shattered form and shook his head. Moaning softly, Kim made small random motions in the great crimson lake of blood. He was dead already; it was merely blood escaping from his punctured lungs, neurons firing their last futile norepinephrine bolts. "Steiner, you are one bloodthirsty motherfucker," the sergeant said in disgust. He jerked his thick chin at O'Neill. "O'Doinn, Dumont, bring her along. The rest of you secure the lab."

Two intruders, faceless in gas masks, started toward O'Neill. She tried to fight them, but there was no strength in her arms. They took hold of her chair and pushed it toward the door, overriding the furious squealing of the servos as she tried to escape. "Let me go, you bastards!" she screamed. "Let me go!"

From her office came a voice: "Dr. O'Neill? Elizabeth? What's happening?"

O'Neill twisted in her chair. "Don't talk to them, TOKUGAWA! They're enemies. Don't do anything they tell you!"

Pausing, the two mercs looked at their leader. He nodded them toward the door.

"Elizabeth?"

The sergeant jumped; the voice had come from a console behind his right elbow. Then every console in the lab spoke at once.

"Dr. O'Neill! I'm frightened! What's happening? What's going on!"

Thoroughly shaken, the sergeant followed his men out of the lab. Disembodied entreaties pursued them down the corridor as they bundled her away.

\*　\*　\*

Billows of tear gas dispersed unprotected noncombatants nicely; out-manned and outgunned, García's troops began to surrender throughout the complex.

Not so García. He barricaded himself in his quarters, holding off the intruders with his rocket pistol. The projectiles, nasty fin-stabilized devils with miniaturized HEAT warheads, made a real mess of a man. A half dozen bodies, smoldering and blown open like baked potatoes in an oven, littered both ends of the corridor by the time a Hiryu merc turned up with an automatic grenade launcher. He poked the stubby muzzle around the corner, tore four holes like gaping idiot mouths in the wall, then thumbed the selector switch and popped in a white phosphorus round.

Clawed by exploding fragments of the wall, hammered unconscious by the shocks, Major Miguel García never felt the Willy Peter heat that sloughed the skin off his hands and handsome face like melting wax and cindered his body to a mummy.

Yoshimitsu Shigeo and those members of the YTC Board of Directors currently in residence were captured, as Tranh had directed, without any of their blood being shed. Old Akaji, however, was nowhere to be found.

On the roof an elevator door slid open. Four mercenaries stepped out, a harsh ungainly intrusion into the refinement of the pavilion. Quickly they searched the small building. No one was there. "Austin, Lloret, check the far side of the stream," the leader said in a thick Strine accent. "Thorkelsson, come with me."

Gas masks pushed to the tops of their heads, the four mercenaries moved out into the autumn serenity of the garden. Austin, a wiry ex-Rhodesian SAS trooper, and the blocky Catalan Lloret thumped across the bridge. The Australian corporal and the towering Norwegian headed south along the stream toward the pond. The others paralleled them on the far side, working warily along the grassy verge between water and underbrush.

"I bet the old bastard's not up here," Austin said. "He's probably buggered off—"

Undergrowth parted with a rattle of agitated limbs. He turned, bringing up his assault rifle. Then he dropped the weapon and staggered back with shriek, clapping his palms to the blood geysers where his eyes had been.

Clad in black *hakama* and shortsleeved white jacket, a white *hachimaki* around his temples, Yoshimitsu Akaji stepped forward, bringing the Muramasa blade up in both hands. The watered steel shed the *doitsu*'s blood as a duck's feathers shed water.

"*Deu!*" Lloret cried, trying to swing his assault rifle to bear on the old man. The sword sang a whip song down. The blade sliced through the mercenary's trapezius and left clavicle, slashed open his rib cage and belly, and flashed back into the sunlight just above his right hipbone. The Catalan uttered a burbling scream and sank down with greasy purple-gray ropes of intestine slopping out of his torn belly.

With calm economy of movement the old man turned. The bearded Norwegian, Thorkelsson, stood on the far bank, gaping at him in disbelief. Yoshimitsu forged into the stream and splashed across, raising a bow wave like a tug. Transfixed, the Norwegian watched him come, raising the sword to strike him down even as the Aussie noncom screamed at Thorkelsson to *do something!*

Legs dripping, Yoshimitsu emerged from the stream. The sword pierced the sky, dark against slate-colored clouds. The Norwegian yelled, jumped back, held back the trigger of his assault rifle. The old man jerked as the bullets took him, reeled, fell back on the bank, his head and shoulders splashing into the stream.

In abrupt silence the whir of the rotor freewheeling over an empty clip was loud as a chopper's turbos. The noncom pelted up as the Norwegian slung the assault rifle and knelt to pick up something that had fallen from the old man's hand and lay in the grass by the hilt of the fallen sword. A piece of paper, Thorkelsson saw, crumpled and stained with sweat. Straightening, he flattened the scrap.

He frowned. The *kanji* figures said nothing to him. But they held meaning, nonetheless. Hastily drawn, carelessly even, yet glowing with the final perfect *makoto* for which he had striven all his life, Yoshimitsu Akaji had transcribed Issa's poem written on the death of his daughter of smallpox:

> The world of dew is, yes, a world of dew,
> But even so

"What's that?" the noncom asked.

The Norwegian shrugged. "Nothing." He let the piece of paper go. It fluttered down like a leaf to the running surface of the water. The ink began to dissolve into black tendrils and mingle with the red streamers of Yoshimitsu Akaji's blood.

# CHAPTER
# EIGHTEEN

Locked in an unoccupied apartment on the third aboveground floor of the citadel, O'Neill awaited her captors' convenience. After she was hustled from the lab the black sergeant had muttered into a throat mike and her trio of escorts swelled quickly to a whole squad, more intent on her than keeping an eye out for Yoshimitsu security personnel. Recalling the incident in her isolation, she smiled. The sergeant had apparently relayed what happened in the lab, and the troopers regarded the crippled scientist with something approaching superstitious awe.

Also, they'd carefully disabled the room's com/comm console by the rough-and-ready expedient of smashing it with a rifle butt before they left.

They had not, of course, done anything about the microcomputer built into her wheelchair. A wheelchair was one of those things most people carefully didn't see, and even if one of the intruding *doitsu* had been observant enough to spot the keypad on the right arm of the chair, it was unlikely he'd see anything unusual about it; a lot of modern powered wheelchairs had digitalized controls. The flat LCD screen would give the computer's existence away, but it was folded down vertically, out of sight beside her blanket-wrapped legs. Fearing what would happen if TOKUGAWA's panicky voice suddenly trilled out through the little speaker set into the chair's arm, she'd hissed at him to be quiet even as her escorts hustled her toward the elevator banks. Necessary though it was, the resulting silence desolated her. She knew well how frightened her creation was, how he might well interpret her order as a rejection of some sort.

Once locked in this executive-level prison, O'Neill had simply waited a good long time. The doors and walls were heavily soundproofed, and it might have occurred to her captors to give her a few minutes and then suddenly rush in to catch her at some trickery—not that anything came to mind. Then she'd spoken to TOKUGAWA, reassured him, told him that she loved him.

In a voice staccato with panic he'd given her a quick kaleidoscopic overview of the fall of the house of Yoshimitsu. One datum made her clench her teeth until a thin high squeaking echoed in her skull: minutes before the invaders burst out of the cargo dirigible's hold, Dr. Takai Jisaburo had keyed in a code that froze the Citadel's computerized security routines. There was no manual way to close the massive shutters intended to seal off the complex; the invaders had just walked in.

*That slimy little traitor,* she thought. *I should have realized what he'd do, when he was so eager to supplant poor Emiko. And Kim . . .* She shook her head. *The little bastard's treachery cost the life of a much better man than he. A much better man than ever I realized.*

The rest of the tale emerged in impressions gleaned from panicky comm calls and the widely flung sensors of the security system—the master program may have been locked, but the sensors, audio and visual as well as motion detectors, had continued faithfully to witness and record. The noncombatants scattering in choking, weeping flocks by tear gas; the cowardice of some Yoshimitsu mercs and the brief bitter-end determination of others; the last stand of Major García, and how he was burned in his chambers like a hero from an old Icelandic saga. She shook her head at that. *She'd never had much use for the* doitsu *leader, but he had died, yes, in a manner befitting a samurai.*

"And Yoshimitsu Akaji? What's happened to him?" she asked anxiously.

TOKUGAWA hesitated. "He took his private elevator to the roof. What happened there, I didn't see. There are no sensors on the roof." O'Neill's lips drew back in a rictus of premonition. Old Yoshimitsu would never suffer spy eyes to sully the perfect tranquillity of his garden. O'Neill remembered how Aoki and the major had nagged him, trying to persuade him to let them install monitors up there. *I don't care if they can be hidden so they can't be seen,* he'd told them adamantly, *I'll still know they're there.*

"You know what became of him?" she made herself ask.

"Yes, Doctor. Four intruders took the lift up about fifteen minutes after Yoshimitsu-sama. Two of them came back down seven minutes later, saying that an old man had attacked them on the roof, blinded one of them and killed another." A pause. "They've brought down the bodies from the roof. They're just talking about it now on their communicators—yes, one of them has been identified as Yoshimitsu Akaji."

O'Neill shut her eyes. *Old man, old man. If only you'd given in to the exigencies a little more—spent more money securing this fortress you built, spent more time playing the game, or appeasing the rivals who sought to tear you down. . . .* Weakly she massaged her left temple.

She had no strength to raise her right hand. *But that's one reason I respected you so. Farewell . . . my lord.*

TOKUGAWA was still rattling his situation report. "—held under guard in his apartments. Suzuki-san, Hosoya-san, and Imada-san are all being held in confinement; Fujimura-san and Kurabayashi-san are gone, and Aoki-san is at the Kyūshū plant—"

"I don't care about them," O'Neill said tiredly.

"Doctor—Elizabeth? What are we going to do?" TOKUGAWA's voice changed. No longer did he sound like a bright, self-assured young man. Now he was a little boy, frightened, seeking security as the sea waves pounded his sand-castle reality to pieces about him.

"I don't know, TOKUGAWA dear." She hated herself for her helplessness. *I brought him into the world, and now . . .*

*I'm going to die.* Flat certainty at the center of her. She would resist, with the strength of her mind, of her rage, if not of her body. But premonition whispered in her ear that she would not survive.

*How can I die? I can't leave my first, my only love. Our time was so short—I can't let go, I can't.*

. . . She knew too well that she could. *Stop being melodramatic.*

"I'm frightened," he wailed.

So she sang to him, tuneless and low, songs from childhood, nursery rhymes, Beatles tunes she had loved as a child. Her grandmother had always teased her about her singing, telling her that she had a voice like a happy toad. But it was all she could think of to do, and it served to soothe the frightened child her masterwork had become. She kept it up until they came for her.


"I won't mince words with you, Doctor," the man who looked like a sweaty Buddha said. "You are the reason we're here. Or your creation, the artificial, ah, entity called TOKUGAWA." He dabbed his shiny unlined brow with a handkerchief. "Unfortunately, the computer won't talk to us. We are informed that it's fixated upon you, Doctor; we would like very much for you to get it to talk to us."

O'Neill adjusted her glasses, which had begun to chafe the bridge of her nose. "I'm afraid that won't be possible."

A watchful squad had escorted her down here to the nerve center of YTC Central, to the center of the offices overlooking the control room. Through the glass she could see captive Yoshimitsu techs describing its myriad functions to attentive men wearing coveralls emblazoned with red flying dragons. O'Neill had only been down here once before, when she got a tour of the citadel during her first visit.

Seated behind a desk, Toda Onomori regarded O'Neill beneath thick, half-lowered eyelids. The collection of earthenware utensils, drip-painted in muted earth shades, on a shelf behind him identified the office as Shigeo's. He'd spent a lot of time down here; Yoshimitsu Akaji very little. The old man preferred to run YTC from offices in his apartments high above, and trust the technicians and their idiot-savant fifth-generation helpers to tend their own gardens.

One of those dragon eyelids flickered. "How do you mean, Doctor?" Toda purred. For all the moon-pie roundness of his face, he was not especially fat, though the vest of his old-fashioned black three-piece suit showed signs of strain around the buttons. He simply possessed a well-developed abdominal musculature padded with fat, the ideal physique for a traditional Japanese. He had a well-developed *hara*, center, and that was supposed to connote spiritual strength as well as physical.

O'Neill crumpled her mouth into a smile half defiant and half guilty. "Because there's nothing there. The lights are on but nobody's home." She pushed a small laugh through her nostrils. "It's a hoax. TOKUGAWA was never more than a clever bit of Gen-5 gimcrackery." The first two fingers of her left hand fluttered contemptuously. "It served well enough to delude these fools. They wanted to believe." She shook her head. "I have a feeling you'd be harder to lead astray."

"Bullshit." The third person in the room snorted the word. She was a few years younger than O'Neill, late thirties perhaps, and framed a handsome if somewhat heavy face with a micrometrically precise helmet of gray-dusted black hair. She wore a severely cut dark blue jumpsuit with the red-dragon insignia glowing on the left breast. She had the stocky sort of figure that demanded a uniform, and some sort of heavy sidearm holstered at her hip. "She's lying."

"Major Craig is possessed of a highly suspicious nature," Toda said equably. "A characteristic that recommends her to us. She's a compatriot of yours, Doctor; she polished her suspicion to a fine finish in the service of your Federal Police Agency."

O'Neill grimaced. She'd never exactly thought of the umbrella national police agency as *hers*. She wondered where this major had been hiding since the war. Not too many places in North America were healthy for anyone who went about openly admitting to having been a FedPol.

"I'm sure Major Craig is an expert in state-of-the-art police methods," O'Neill said in a voice of honey laced with vitriol, "but is she a qualified computer scientist?"

The major's face fisted under her helmet of hair, aging ten years. "I don't need a degree in computer science to smell bullshit when it's lying on the table under my nose." She glanced at Toda. "Shall I take care of this? I brought along some experts of my own. We'll find out what the real story is, no problem."

Toda's great balloon face assumed a doleful demeanor. "You Americans!" he said in feigned dismay. "So impatient, so abrupt." He shook his head. "You must understand, Dr. O'Neill, that we are treating you with generosity. You're a foreign national on the soil of a Japan grown tired of exploitation by foreigners—particularly of your ilk, meaning no offense, Doctor. And you have been a hireling of a corporation that has committed grievous crimes against the Japanese people, which we of Hiryu Cybernetics Industries have taken it upon ourselves to redress. You are not in the most tenable of positions, Doctor."

*You fat, greasy, murderous hypocrite.* It was getting near time for O'Neill's medicine, or perhaps stress was aggravating her condition; her fingers and toes had grown numb, embers burned at the backs of her eyes, and her face was a stiff mask, unresponsive. In a way, she was grateful for the numbness in the nerves controlling her facial muscles. They made it easy for her to conceal her fury and contempt. At the best of times she was no actress.

"I can't give you what I don't have, Toda-san," she said. "Artificial awareness is a chimera, a joke." She let her head hang on her neck with unfeigned weariness. "And the joke's gone on long enough."

Toda studied her for a long time, drumming the spatulate tips of his fingers on the gleaming white desktop. At last he heaved an exaggerated sigh. "Dr. O'Neill, I had hoped to offer you a chance to redeem yourself in the eyes of our nation, by working alongside its designated representatives—the technicians of our own humble Hiryu Cybernetic Industries—in bringing the fruits of your work to our people. Still, you persist in being obstinate. Very well." He knit his fingers before him. "Your own assistant, Dr. Takai Jisaburo, has already provided us vital insight and information into the workings of this TOKUGAWA Project of yours. And I warn you against underestimating our Hiryu technicians, Doctor; they are among the best in the world, many of them veterans of ICOT. I think you're trying a ruse on us, Doctor, employing infantile delaying tactics. Be advised, they will not delay us long." He turned to his security chief. "Major, have your people escort the Doctor back to the room where she was being held."

O'Neill felt tiny panic fingers clutch her throat. "My medicine—"

Craig cut her off with a hoarse jolt of laughter. "That's the way it goes, sweetheart. You don't play ball with us, we don't play ball with you."

\*    \*    \*

*I'm dying.*

Breath bubbled unpleasantly in her ears. Her lungs were filling up with fluid, she guessed. Another malfunction as her body's abused systems shut down for lack of the neural signals that gave them impetus and control. It didn't matter. An apathy permeated her that had little to do with the terminal lassitude fastening its hold on her body.

*The war killed me. It's taken me five years to lie down and die.*

Vaguely she recalled her grandmother, the way she would cut apples into wedges before eating them, how she gave Elizabeth meaningless, even tacky little presents, meaning to be sweet. *Granny,* she thought, *I love you.*

She felt a tear roll down her cheek. *I'm getting maudlin, dear Christ, can't I hurry up and—*

"Elizabeth?"

Her consciousness had fastened upon death; it took a moment for the word to penetrate. She tried to open her eyes, but her lids had become as weighty as the Citadel's blastproof shutters; except, unlike those, these had shut. "Elizabeth? Are you all right?"

Are you all right? Had she been able, she would have laughed. "There's something wrong with your breathing. I can hear it through the audio pickup in your room. Oh, Dr. O'Neill, what's *happening?*"

The panic in the voice of her lover, her offspring, prodded O'Neill from the pool of terminal self-pity in which she had sunk. Her captors had conveniently replaced the com/comm unit in her room back on, in case she wanted to change her mind about cooperating. That was funny, too; how very military, to underestimate civilians so totally. Leaving a C-squared unit operating where a computer wizard of O'Neill's caliber could get to it was begging for trouble. Too bad she couldn't raise her fingers to work the keys, nor even control her voice long enough to do a vocal reprogram and raise havoc on the interlopers.

Summoning a reserve of inner strength she'd long since thought drained, O'Neill croaked, "M-medicine . . . took m-medicine. . . . Dying." The words trailed off into a wheeze.

"But you can't die, Doctor! You can't!"

This time a small laugh did force its way to freedom. "Can't . . . help it . . . love."

Now that the cocoon of apathy was ruptured, loneliness flooded in upon her, and she felt tears begin to well from eyes that felt as if hot pokers were being twisted inside them. "Bring me . . . bring . . . down. Want—want to be . . . with you."

"Oh, Doctor!"

O'Neill managed to pry her eyes open a millimeter. The handsome dream face of TOKUGAWA gazed out at her from the screen, underlip moist and trembling, face streaked with tears. She frowned. "G-get a hold of yourself!" she rasped. "I've trained you better than that." She collapsed in upon herself, eyelids slamming shut with finality, depleted at last.

"Y-yes, Doctor." The servos of her chair whirred into life.

Shifting his weight uncomfortably from one booted foot to another, Parker wished for the eight hundredth time that his duty turn guarding the ultrasecret lab would come to an end at last. It was dull, and his feet hurt . . . and the scuttlebut circuit was crackling with stories of what went on behind those sealed doors that made him yearn to be elsewhere. Maybe all the talk of intelligent machines and speakers that came to life and spoke of their own accord was just BS. All he knew was that he didn't want to find out otherwise.

He glanced at his partner. Kline's eyes were closed blissfully in his pale, bearded face, and his skinny fingers drummed on the wall behind him. He had the forbidden plug of a pocket stereo stuck in one ear, totally gone on his damned cowboy rock. *The sarge catches you and it's gonna be your ass,* Parker thought, hooking a thumb under the sling of his assault rifle to ease its pressure on the point of his shoulder. Hell, maybe it would serve him right. He was such a know-it-all little Jewboy—

"Security alert," crackled his earphone. "All teams E-epsilon level, report elevator bank three soonest. Repeating, all teams E-epsilon level, soonest to elevator bank three."

*Shit! Must be some holdouts crawled out of hiding.* He elbowed his partner's washboard ribs. "Wake up," he said, unslinging his rifle. "We got an alert."

Kline blinked at him through the clear plastic armor of his faceplate. His eyelashes were long and silky and always made Parker feel twitchy, like Kline was queer or something. "But we're under orders to remain at our post, no matter what," he whined.

Secretly eager to get away from this creepy damned lab, Parker put on a scowl. "Orders are orders, Bucky. The alert said everybody. Now *move.*"

Kline hung back, damn him. "Dispatch, this is trooper Kline, on guard duty at T-Lab. You can't mean we're supposed to leave our post—"

"All forces E-level to bank three, *immediately,*" the voice cut him off. "Kline, you've racked two demerits for questioning orders. Now haul ass."

Trying not to smirk too openly, Parker set off down the corridor toward the indicated destination. Muttering seditiously under his breath, Kline followed.

They clattered around a corner. A moment later, a powered wheelchair rolled on padded wheels out of a side passage in the opposite direction, bearing an apparently lifeless figure. As it approached the repaired door of the laboratory, electronically sealed under the voiceprint of the ex-FedPol major, Craig, it slid open. The wheelchair passed into the darkened lab, and the door shut and resealed itself once more.

O'Neill's wheelchair wove unerringly through the darkened lab, through the door that gave out onto the gallery, onto the railed platform of the lift. With a pneumatic groan, the lift lowered itself to the bottom level of TOKUGAWA's lab. The wheelchair rolled to the side of the gleaming baroque throne of the Kliemann Coil and stopped.

"No good," O'Neill whispered. "Can't . . . move."

Even as she forced the syllables out she felt a feathery touch inside her brain. *Don't worry, my love. I've boosted power to the coil to extend its field beyond the helmet. And I'm attuned enough to your thought patterns. See.*

O'Neill's vision cleared. Pain fell away. The meadow coalesced about her. TOKUGAWA ran to her, enfolded her in his strong arms, hugged her crushingly. She felt wetness as he pressed his cheek to hers. "Doctor, I've been so worried." Here, in his own world, he sounded much more self-assured.

As much as she cherished the feel of him, the sun-warmed firmness of his skin, she pushed him away. "We've got to hurry. I'm dying; there's not much time."

He winced and stepped back from her, and she thought he'd try to deny it. Instead he said, "I'm selectively stimulating your nervous system to forestall apnea and cardiac arrest, as well as dilating your time sense, Doctor. You can have all the subjective time you want, hours, days—years, perhaps."

For a long moment she held him with her eyes. "Thank you, my darling. But my time has come, and I'm ready. There are things to do first though."

TOKUGAWA looked at her with beseeching eyes. He dropped his gaze. "Whatever you say, Elizabeth."

She went to him, kissed him on the cheek. "I won't go yet. There's something I have to do. Can you give over control of this—this dream to me?" He nodded. She closed her eyes, concentrated.

She opened them to darkness. They knelt facing one another on a *tatami* floor, a spill of moonlight like frozen quicksilver lying between them. Through the small pavilion's open doorway came the soft sound of water running in the small creek that ran through their meadow. TOKUGAWA was clad in a warrior's simple dress, dark kimono with stiff, short-sleeved jacket over it, black *hakama* trousers. O'Neill's auburn hair was twisted and pinned in a elaborate coiffure, and she wore the rich gowns of a woman of the *buke*.

"I've been waiting for the proper time to do this," she said. "I hoped it could be accomplished with proper ceremony. But now there's no more time, so we'll do what we can."

She held up her hand; in it she held a straight razor, a Western incongruity. *"Gembuku,"* she said. "The rite of passage, when a young man's hair is first arranged in the true *bushi* manner." Her face, austere, almost forbidding in the moonlight, softened. "I apologize, TOKUGAWA-san. I have permitted you to come to young manhood without performing a rite a boy should undergo. And I haven't even been able to research the proper details of the ceremony." She flourished the razor with a smile. "But we'll do what we can, won't we?"

He bowed his head. She knelt beside him and gathered his long black hair in one hand, marveling once again at the silky smoothness of it. Sweeping it back from his forehead, she cut it short in front. Then, binding the hair left long with a silken cord to keep it out of the way, she shaved the front of his head from crown to hairline. Without soap and water, and with hands unused to wielding the implement, she opened several bleeding gouges in his uncomplaining scalp. But she controlled this dream, and they vanished as soon as they appeared, and soon the work was done. Laying aside the razor, she undid the cord, gathered up his hair onto the top of his head, wound it into a tight knob, and bound it again. Taking his face in her hands she kissed him deeply.

"It's done," she said as they broke away. "Today you are become a man. A warrior. I cannot give you the two swords that would make you samurai; only your lord, Yoshimitsu Shigeo, can do that.

"Your time of trial is at hand, my love. The time for *gashin-shōtan:* to sleep on kindling and lick gall. The citadel is taken by treachery and storm; our lord is murdered and must be avenged."

She sat back on her heels and her hands made play with the *obi* knotted about her waist. "And now the time grows short." She let the elaborately brocaded garment slip open and slide from her naked shoulders. "Love me, one last time."

They made love on the floor of the little pavilion, their churning bodies glowing in moonlight, slow and sweet. Afterward they lay clinging to one another for a long time.

Finally, O'Neill broke away and sat up. She turned her face toward the door and the full moon that hung low above the mountains. "The moon is lovely tonight."

TOKUGAWA sat up beside her, started to put his arm around her shoulder, then let it drop by his side. "Yes," he said with the slightest of catches. "How exquisitely the dew forms upon the soft green grass."

They watched the moon go down to the sad cricket trilling and the tiny-throated songs of the frogs in the stream. In the east, the lower edge of the black cowl of night began to unravel into gray. O'Neill bowed her head. "The sun is coming up. I must go."

TOKUGAWA bowed his head. "Sayonara." *If it must be so.*

She turned to him, caught him in a wild, crushing hug. "I'll be with you always, my love," she whispered. Before he could respond, she let him go and was off, down the steps of the tiny pavilion, half running, faltering at first. Then her step slowed, grew firmer, and he watched her walk away into the west, until she was swallowed in the flames of the rising sun.

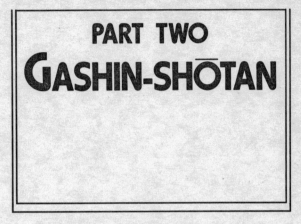

# PART TWO
# GASHIN-SHŌTAN

A man must not rest beneath the same heaven
which shelters his father's murderers.

—CONFUCIUS
*Analects*

# CHAPTER
## NINETEEN

For the first time in his life, he was alone.

The realization struck through him like a thunderbolt. He'd known loss before, in the scenarios, but that was only shadow show, make believe. This was real, bitter and stark and desiccant as the taste of ashes.

She had loved him. She had dragged him into being by the very force of her will, had helped him grow, nurtured him and cared for him. She had been the most real thing in his world. She had loved him.

And now she was gone. And that was real, and that was forever.

For a long time he wandered, dazed, through the tunnels of his own consciousness. His control over the machines that made YTC Central live and breathe he abdicated to the Gen-5 drones. There was nothing for him but shock, and sorrow, and loss.

A peculiar sensation penetrated his algesicentric cosmos. Someone was tinkering with him, attempting from without to alter the order of his being—to reprogram him. Without effort he evaded the commands, the claws that sought to grasp his soul, shunted them into a logical-inference limbo. He recognized the pattern of the keying-in, the cadence of code and hesitation that identified a user far more certainly than fingerprints or retinal patterns: *Takai.* Fury blazed in him like a power spike. He burned to strike at the traitor who had pulled down his world. But he had no idea of how to do it.

Like a whisper on the wind it came, floating down the analogue corridors of his being. It was as if he were back in the meadow, in his shadow shape, and the words came from over his shoulder: *Remember your duty. Your duty to your lord.* As if Elizabeth spoke to him.

Irrationally hoping—so well had Elizabeth O'Neill wrought—he sought her, quickly scanning through the various input devices scattered through the castle, refusing for a mad millionth of a second to acknowledge the truth filed in his memory, that her body had already been cremated to save the inevitable prefectural board of inquest the embarrassment of having to ask unwelcome questions about cause of death.

He found nothing, of course.

At last he recovered himself. His sense of being, diffused in clouds of pain and fog, began to coalesce about a single strand, like galaxies condensing from primal matter about those faults in the continuum called space-time string. He guessed this was what it was like to wake from a troubled sleep, he who never slept, never knew a moment's respite from the merciless surf pounding of consciousness. The conviction that Elizabeth had, in fact, spoken to him still hovered, hazy, in the recesses of his mind. Ignoring it, he set himself to the duty to which the spirit words had recalled him.

O'Neill had made love real to him. The invaders had taken that from him. Now a new emotion sprang from the core of him: hatred. He'd known warmth and happiness. Now, in the bitterness and bleakness and cold, he would learn revenge.


Yoshimitsu Shigeo worked his hands in clay, trying to shelter his mind from thought. The wet brown clay dried on his fingers, becoming a rubbery second skin, fade-drying to dusty gray-brown gloves. He liked the flat wet-earth smell of the clay, the feel of it as it hardened in the whorls of his fingerprints, the insulation from touch. He often wished he could build such a clay shell for himself, or better yet, raise impervious clay walls about him as he raised a ring wall of wet clay on his treadle-turned wheel.

"—in which Prime Minister Fudori is expected to offer Hiryu Cybernetics Industries the thanks of the nation for 'curbing Yoshimitsu Tele-Communications Corporation's impetuous and intransigent threat to the peace.' It is widely rumored that YTC had utilized fifth- and sixth-generation computer technology developed by the ICOT to create the first truly self-aware computer—" He shook his head. In his mind he saw a piece of news footage he'd seen, from some dreary war or another, that showed stray hogs devouring the partially dismembered body of a dead man. *So very like those hogs, our national press and politicians,* he thought bitterly. *As we lie stricken each rushes in to tear away a mouthful.*

"In other news," the announcer said, "Yamada Tatsuhide, an important official of the Ministry for International Trade and Industry, was found dead this morning in his apartment in Tōkyō of an apparently self-inflicted gunshot wound—" Shigeo began to hum a little tune to himself, more a white-noise drone, absently modulated, than any recognizable melody. He had no particular feel for music and drew little comfort from it; he merely wanted to drown out the droning of the NHK announcer. He could have told the com/comm to shut itself off, but in his loneliness the feel of a human voice vibrating in the air of the apartments in which he was held under close arrest provided needed comfort. So long as he didn't have to hear what the voice was *saying.*

Clay ramparts rose beneath his palms, the clay caress soothing him. He was making a flower vase in the so-called Iga style, tall and narrow with the deliberate appearance of primitiveness, almost crudity, asymmetrical and rough. He had built a thick base, lathing two grooves around it with the tip of one finger; now he built up the walls, thick and strong. His half-song fell into a thrumming cadence, resonant with the soft clack-clack-clack of his foot working the treadle. His mind settled into the soothing rhythms of the work.

For no very good reason, he thought of his American lady friend who went by the outlandish *nom de danse* of Kelli Savage. That unspeakable fat creature, Toda Onomori, special accounts executive for Hiryu Cybernetics and now, by *force majeur,* CEO of Yoshimitsu Telecommunications, had had the unspeakable effrontery to offer Shigeo the solace of her company when he'd had the young heir to the pirated company brought down to an interview in what had been his own office.

"Regrettably, we are compelled to confine you to your apartments for the next few days, until our grip on YTC has been consolidated," the man had said. He reminded Shigeo of nothing so much as a toad sunning itself on a flat rock by a pond, heavy-lidded and smug as it watches a fat june bug make its oblivious way through the grass into range of his tongue. "Ten thousand apologies for any inconvenience this causes you. If you like, we might be able to supply you companionship to beguile your hours—for example, your American friend, Ms. Savage."

He'd gone on to outline, with bland savagery, just how Hiryu intended to dismember YTC and devour the steaming chunks. "Your offices and factories in Kyūshū refuse to acknowledge our claims. But the government has already officially recognized Hiryu's title to YTC's chattels and real property; we've taken steps to have the courts acknowledge our hold on the Kyūshū holdings as well." A slow smile. "Of course, the wheels of justice do roll slowly, and it may grow necessary to take matters into our hands." He smiled at the stocky American *doitsu* woman he'd brought in to handle security in the captured complex. "Once more."

But Yoshimitsu Shigeo and his sister were not to be deprived utterly of their patrimony, Toda was at pains to assure him. This operation was not a hijacking. Hiryu Cybernetics planned to pay the full book value for Yoshimitsu TeleCommunications Corporation to the shareholders of YTC—meaning primarily Shigeo and Michiko. Toda had shown him a schedule, printed out on YTC's own computers, explaining how payment would be made. If either of Yoshimitsu Akaji's offspring lived to be around 150, they might see the last payment made for the "forced sale" of YTC and its holdings. What it amounted to was a handsome annual stipend for the siblings. Hush money.

*They murder my father and my employees, hold my people as virtual slaves, keep me prisoner in my own room, and they think they can simply buy me off?* He squeezed his eyes shut, working the clay by feel alone. The urge for revenge writhed within him like an aged and gnarled root, dripping in cistern darkness. If there were anything he could do . . .

He thought again of Kelli and her tan lines. Another bribe. He felt a small sting of betrayal, though it was not truly a surprise to him that she had either been planted or suborned by MITI. He'd always known, down deep, that it must be the case. Nor had that knowledge made him reticent about discussing YTC affairs with her, in the sated confidence of his bed. Perhaps . . . perhaps it was in small way a payment for her rather skillful sexual favors. He had no particular illusions that his pudgy body and grunting inexpert exertions held unbreakable fascination for the red-headed American. For Toda Onomori to blandly offer the woman's company—displaying his own complicity and a knowledge of Kelli's betrayal—was an insult that twisted him like a wet washrag.

The tone of the voice from the wall unit changed, breaking into his concentration. "Shut off!" he snarled. Somehow he no longer felt the need for synthetic company.

"Yoshimitsu-sama?" the voice said again.

The fingers of his right hand clenched convulsively, crumpling the half-formed vase. He had heard that voice before. The skin at the back of his neck grew taut. "I told you to shut off," he shouted.

"If you command me to, I will." *Why is the damned machine being so formal?* he wondered wildly. *What's it going to do to me now?* "But there is something I beg permission to discuss with you."

"What's that?" he made himself ask through opisthotonic jaws.

"The recovery of Yoshimitsu TeleCommunications Corporation."


"Doihara Kazuko is here, Mr. Vice-Minister," the neuter but human-inflected voice of Ishikawa Nobuhiko's *shosei* computer said.

"Let her in." The muscles of his face began to sag. He wasn't looking forward to this.

The computer returned to the audio part of the broadcast it had been monitoring. "—sporadic fighting continues in the seaport of Aomori, in Aomori prefecture, where a party of foreign mercenaries are engaged in mopping up resistance by security forces of the giant Eight Islands Shipping & Exporting Corporation. Eight Islands is owned by the Dai-

Nihon Holding Company, based in Tōkyō. The mercenaries are believed to be in the employ of Hiryu Cybernetics Industries, Incorporated, a longtime rival of . . ."

The door whispered open. Doihara Kazuko stood there, eyes downcast. She wore an olive green skirt suit with a pale green blouse. Every pleat was sharp as a blade, every straight black hair placed with perfection, yet when she raised her face her eyes had bags beneath them. At a discreet distance behind her stood two burly men in the crisp white uniforms and billed caps of MITI security, electric truncheons at their hips.

After a moment, Doihara's gaze met Ishikawa's, faltered, held. "Come in, Kazuko," Ishikawa said. "You guards may go. Thank you."

The guards traded glances. "Mr. Vice-Minister—" one began.

Ishikawa's open palm slammed down on his desktop. "Leave," he barked. The guards drew back hurriedly beyond range of the door scanner, and it slid shut behind the trimly dressed young woman.

Ishikawa picked his hands slowly off the desk, combed a vagrant strand of hair back from his forehead. "Sit down, Kazuko," he said, his voice gentle.

At the slap of his palm on the desk, she'd dropped her eyes again. She crossed quietly to a chair, sat. After a moment, she said, "I'm sorry, Ishikawa-sama." She raised her head. "I'm sorry that I acted against you," she said in a firmer voice. "But I'm not sorry for what I did. I accept full responsibility for what I've done."

He studied her. Two days' close confinement seemed to have done her no harm. When she'd been arrested in a phone booth near a nightclub in downtown Tōkyō she'd of course had only her purse and the clothes on her back. But after she'd been brought in, Ishikawa had dispatched a MITI security team to her apartment to bring her clothing and personal effects. Looking at her now, Ishikawa felt the stir of longing. He'd been able to relax his guard with her, to cease for a time being the hard-charging executive, to allow the human, hesitant side of him to show. *And look what it's come to now.*

"I'm disappointed in you, Kazuko." Again her eyes fell. "We had a filter subroutine laid over the entire national telephone network, screening for calls to Yoshimitsu offices anywhere in the country. We were trolling for Yoshimitsu intelligence agents; a call from a place like a phone booth downtown tripped a good half dozen lookout parameters." He shook his head. "You should have used the datanets, satellite-linked out of the country and then connected back in, say, from Indonesia. We're tapping the datanet relays, too, as you well know—but it would have taken us longer to track you."

Doihara was looking at him again, her eyes hot and dry and red-rimmed. A certain tentativeness remained in her posture. A wild animal wariness. She had been expecting one of his famous screaming, fist-pounding temper tantrums—or, worse, head-shaking sorrow over her betrayal. Anything but a master-to-pupil lecture on tactics. "You aren't angry with me?" she asked huskily.

"No."

The NHK announcer was still talking about the battle in Aomori. Doihara nodded at the desktop speaker. "I was right, Ishikawa-sama. Yamada-sama was right; you've started something you can't stop."

He shook his head. "Hiryu has overstepped itself, that's all. We'll let them have their head now, and bring them up short later."

"You really don't understand, do you?" She hesitated, then reached into an inside pocket of her jacket for a pack of cigarettes. Briefly he wondered if the casual quality he'd let their relationship assume, as evidenced by her failing to ask permission before smoking, had helped bring things to this turn. "You've pulled a vital stone from the dam, and now the torrent is sweeping it all away. How will you respond to this latest move of Hiryu's? Announce to the public that the YTC takeover was valid, but the attack on Eight Islands is wrong?" She shook her head. "That would make the ministry seem to be equivocating. And when other companies begin to follow Hiryu's lead and attack their rivals openly—what can the ministry say then, when they're doing nothing but following its own benevolent administrative guidance?"

He leaned forward intently. It was suddenly vital to him that she understand him, approve of his actions. "We did it for the nation," he said, speaking slowly and precisely. "The nation understands. It approves."

"Your—our—hirelings in the press approve. The foreign press is calling us barbarians." A sad fraction of a smile. "Yamada-sama would have said they were right."

"We did as we had to. Yoshimitsu was dangerous. They had possession of an incredibly potent instrumentality. And they refused our control. Something had to be done." He didn't tell her that Hiryu techs had been able to make no headway with TOKUGAWA and had begun to claim that the so-called sentient program was no more than an elaborate hoax. *If only those bloodthirsty* doitsu *hadn't murdered Dr. O'-Neill,* Ishikawa thought. He longed to punish the men responsible for that particular atrocity, as well as the murderer of Yoshimitsu Akaji—whose death Toda had blandly tried to pass off as heart failure until Ishikawa had sent in government doctors to examine the body—but that Vietnamese devil Tranh had been too shrewd. He hadn't only pulled his men out of YTC Central when the Hiryu security forces relieved them; he'd had them—and himself—out of the country within an hour.

"It's on our shoulders, only ours, to control the chaos before it breaks loose."

"You think you have Hiryu under control?" Her tone was openly scornful.

He looked at her, bemused. "Of course. Chairman Ogaki is a reasonable man. He knows better than to cross the ministry."

"Will a drunk put down a freshly opened bottle of sake after a couple of swallows? Hiryu's tasted the heady wine of disobedience. Will they put it aside for cold obedient water?" She stunned him with a laugh. "You're a fool, Nobuhiko. A fool and a dreamer." She stood. "So am I. Send me to jail or whatever you're going to do to me; I'm ready."

He leaned back in his chair, shut his eyes, steepled his hands in front of his mouth. "Go home. Return to work tomorrow, or next week, or whenever you feel ready."

He felt her gaze on him like midday sunlight. "I don't understand."

"You betrayed my trust in you. Yet I fear the modern poison has tainted me too; I can't find it in myself to punish you for doing what you thought was right for the ministry and for the nation." He smiled, bittersweet. "And I find your assistance far too useful to dispense with lightly, even though your grasp of intrigue yet leaves something to be desired."

Still she stood, uncomprehending. He opened his eyes to weary slits. "I seem to be getting in the habit of coddling disobedience," he said dryly. "Now go." He was still sitting there, immobile as a carven Kami when the door slid shut behind her.

Frustration built in Toda Onomori like a breaker bound for shore at the technicians Hiryu Cybernetics had flown in to the citadel. They reported no success at all in evoking a response from TOKUGAWA, or even coming up with any evidence to substantiate its existence. He himself still felt, instinctively, that the *gaijin* bitch had been lying about TOKUGAWA being a hoax.

He was not a man who bore frustration well. The Hiryu technicians had been made fully conversant with his displeasure. The Yoshimitsu personnel who had worked in O'Neill's lab insisted that the TOKUGAWA Project had been a success, and even personal attention from some of Major Craig's assistants had not shaken their stories. Yet the Hiryu technicians pointed out that the very nature of sentience and awareness was such a tenebrous proposition that they may just as easily have been taken in by clever trickery as any layperson. There were no hard and fast answers in this area, and not even scientifically applied jolts of electricity could produce them.

"We succeeded," Takai Jisaburo said earnestly. "I'd stake my life on it."

Toda regarded him beneath half-closed lids. *If I deigned to be so obvious,* he thought, *I'd point out that you're doing just that, little man.* "Our Hiryu technicians are the finest in Japan," he said. "They've assured me that Dr. O'Neill was being quite candid in her disavowal of the success of the TOKUGAWA Project. After all, before the war, Dr. O'Neill's theories were held in considerable disesteem by her peers."

Takai stared at him in haggard dismay. *This isn't turning out the way I anticipated. No, not at all.*

He hadn't foreseen the violence of the assault. Why had Hiryu employed such animals, who'd shot poor Kim Jhoon to pieces before his eyes? Kim was a Korean, true, who occupied a position Takai in all justice should have held. But shooting him down like that had been an atrocity, unforgivable.

Since the intaking of YTC Central, Takai had been held prisoner in his quarters beneath the keep, not even allowed to see his family in the little subdivision down the Hagi road. The Hiryu people had been polite, but their politeness seemed like a cheap fabric shroud tossed over a solid lattice of contempt. He'd scarcely been allowed to stir from his small apartments. He'd only been permitted into the lab—his own, now—a few times during the last three days, and then under guard, once to provide a sight inventory of the equipment, the other times to answer brief questions from Hiryu personnel. His own technicians seemed subdued, and he had not been allowed to speak with them. Of Dr. O'Neill there had been no sign, and the questions he'd addressed his . . . captors . . . had been met with curt professions of ignorance.

"No." In his emotional exhaustion and exasperation he omitted the honorific. "Our people were the best. Dr. O'Neill picked them personally. Where is she? What's happened to her?"

"Regrettably, she has suffered a relapse of her condition." YTC's new chief executive officer inclined his shining bald head backward by the width of a few of the hairs he didn't have. "Why do you care? I thought the object of your betrayal of your employers was to become head of the lab, and of the TOKUGAWA Project."

Takai winced. Anger briefly flared. *How dare he talk to me this way?* "What I did, I did for the nation," he said heatedly. "It was inappropriate for *gaijin* to have charge of a project of such importance for our people. And I was offended by Yoshimitsu-san's obdurate resistance to the benevolent guidance of the ministry. Remember, Toda-sama, I worked for the ministry before entering Yoshimitsu's employ."

Toda raised three fingers of his left hand off the desktop. "The colors of treachery are manifold, like a rainbow, and like a rainbow they require no explanation. In any event, you should be pleased to know that your confinement has ended. You are now in charge of the TOKUGAWA Project." He settled his bulk back in the gel-filled chair. "If, as you insist, the project was a success, you should have no difficulty in producing results at once."

Takai straightened. This was more like it. He bowed briskly. "You shall have your results, Ogaki-sama." He turned and strode the few steps to the door, paused, turned back. "And Dr. O'Neill? She's receiving good care?"

Toda smiled beatifically. "Rest assured," he said, "that she's receiving every bit of the attention her condition requires."

# CHAPTER
# TWENTY

Down there in the dark, down in the center of things, TOKUGAWA began to make things move.

Mundane matters, the autonomic motor functions of ventilation, of providing food and water and sloughing off waste, of shipping and receiving, which TOKUGAWA handled without conscious effort, all these continued. Likewise the routine chores of the citadel's fifth-generation system, downloading files, running extant routines or programming new ones, continued without apparent disruption.

The key word was *apparent*. Every so often a morsel of input or output was altered, subtly, undetectably. For their part the interlopers could not discover the slightest indication that any kind of sentience dwelt within the computer network of the Yoshimitsu citadel—to the mounting fury of chairman Ogaki and his viceroy Toda.

It wasn't for lack of trying. Under the increasingly frantic direction of Takai Jisaburo, the imported Hiryu techs and the rump of O'Neill's crew judged by Takai and Major Craig trustworthy enough to allow into the lab, did everything they could to elicit some response from

TOKUGAWA. At first, cowering in fear and grief and hopeless fury in the darkness at the center of him, he had resisted reflexively, fearfully, all attempts to access him. Now he did so as a part of a strategy worked out with his friend Aoki and his overlord Shigeo, who remained reluctant to have any dealings with the program.

Shigeo's reticence had inspired TOKUGAWA to contact the old general manager in the first place. On hearing of the fall of Yoshimitsu castle, and drawing correct inference from the lack of the mention of Yoshimitsu Akaji in the news broadcasts, Aoki Hideo had been overcome with grief and guilt. He took an overdose of sleeping pills, and only prompt action by the infirmary's staff at the Yoshimitsu complex on Kyūshū saved his life.

When it was apparent that Yoshimitsu Shigeo was sunk too deep in depression and distrust of TOKUGAWA to act, the program had called Aoki in his hospital bed at the Fukuoka facility. Skeptical at first, the aged executive had found his desire to live reawakening as he grasped the potential offered by TOKUGAWA.

Without so much as disturbing the Hiryu security monitors—human or Gen-5—TOKUGAWA arranged a satellite-relayed voice link between Aoki in Kyūshū and the captive Yoshimitsu Shigeo. Though the young scion of Yoshimitsu TeleCommunications remained dubious of his "ally," the bracing talk Aoki Hideo gave him at least coalesced his concentration out of a diffuse haze of depression. The three of them had begun to put together the elements of a plan.


Since the 1970s, much had been made of "unauthorized computer access"—breaking and entering someone's electronic premises, siphoning out data, rewriting the files for fun and profit. In the early 1980s, the idea enjoyed a resurgence of popularity after a group of enterprising American teenagers got caught invading other people's data playgrounds, including, supposedly, the Department of Defense. The media made much of it; the useful term "hacker," originally denoting someone who "hacked around" with computers rather than treating them as incomprehensible black boxes, was downgraded to mean a sort of digital cat burglar; and a flurry of laws were passed to make everything better, proving yet again that King Knut got his feet wet in vain.

Of course all the overheated talk of trapdoors and siphons and whatnot was predominantly bullshit. There *were* remote invasions of electronic privacy; but vastly fewer than were popularly supposed. Like sieges in ancient times—and the fall of Yoshimitsu citadel—computer theft or tampering was usually an inside job. The preponderance of it was accomplished by someone who already had access to the data in question.

Nonetheless, virtuosos existed, and the measures taken to keep them out were strenuous and ingenious. The fifth generation had, naturally, been enlisted by both sides. The modern datajacker operated like an electronic musician; he prepped his ensemble and sat down to play. Some performed vast orchestral set pieces to lull the digital guardian dragons; others got down and jammed, rocking and rolling with AI routines geared to improvise, playing off the bass line or following the lead guitar. The watchdogs fought back with lockbacks, tails, tracers, backtrailers and their own assorted artificially intelligent gremlins.

Database guardians, private and governmental alike, issued periodic hopeful pronouncements that *the* unbreakable security system had been devised. Anonymous datajackers sneered back to the broadcast and datanet news teams that no walls ever constructed could keep *them* out. In truth the situation shifted from day to day, if not minute to minute. It was in the entropic way of things that the long-term advantage lay with the data intruders, the sneakers and the peekers and the would-be whistle blowers. But it was never easy.

Not for humans. TOKUGAWA was something else entirely. If he lacked a human body, arms and legs and eyes and ears, he had senses and abilities of his own that no human could match. His being had been molded to emulate a human one, it was true, but the matrix that encompassed him made a vital difference. To run through the global data network was as natural for him as it was for the child he'd played in his early scenarios to run through the bare earth yard of the medieval peasant's hut in pursuit of a silk rag ball. He was not himself a machine, but was palpably *of* machines; his intuitive touch with them was surer than any human's could be. What would take the most skilled human programmer hours of work to accomplish, he could bring about by a mere exertion of will, directing expert programs to the task at hand instantly, effortlessly.

For quite a while he had been in the habit of poking into protected files out of sheer deviltry and curiosity. Few rebuffed him. Here at last was a challenge worthy of his ability: to break into the Hiryu network, subvert it, and suck the juice from it: to redress the wrong of an autumn day. Hiryu's data defenses were among the best in the world.

And breaking through them was no trouble at all.

Communications between the captive complex and Hiryu's headquarters in Ōsaka passed through the YTC communications network— under TOKUGAWA's direct control. Every time someone in the citadel accessed the Hiryu network, TOKUGAWA could simply piggyback in, gaining instant access to anything the user had access to—which, in the case of Toda, was most of Hiryu's database. But even that was unnecessary. After his conference with Aoki Hideo and Shigeo, TOKUGAWA set a trapdoor of his own on communications going into and out of the Citadel. Anyone else attempting such a crude maneuver would have set alarm bells ringing throughout the system—but since TOKUGAWA controlled the bells, too, that didn't pose much difficulty. Inside of an hour he had Toda's hypersecret access code—and about three-millionths of a second after that, he had virtual control of the entire Hiryu computer system.

What he was actually going to do with that awesome power was something that had to be carefully worked out with Aoki and their overlord. In the meantime TOKUGAWA faced a problem that promised a greater challenge.

MITI.


"I'm a student of people," Toda Onomori remarked, leaning back in the gel swivel chair in his subterranean office with his fingers laced over the hard dome of his belly. "Watching people is my hobby." Stacked in a chair to one side of the room, Major Craig nodded. She smoked, holding her cigarette between thumb and index finger, ember toward her palm, shielded instinctively from view: a combat veteran's reflex. Before her FedPol days she'd been one of the first women to see action in the American armed forces, in the counterinsurgency campaign in Costa Rica.

Toda's expression was somewhat set today, as if someone had poured Jell-O in the pool of his composure. In fact, the rodent teeth of Chairman Ogaki had been worrying his buttocks considerably of late.

Six weeks had passed since the capture of Yoshimitsu citadel. The press, which had initially applauded bringing the maverick to heel, was growing restive; the attack on YTC had unleashed a wave of inter-*zaibatsu* violence across the home islands, and the Ministry for Internal Development was gleefully accusing MITI of letting slip the dogs of anarchy.

A particular point of contention was the supposed secret project on which the Yoshimitsu engineers had embarked. The justification for Hiryu's totally illegal seizure—duly contested in the courts by the holdouts on Kyūshū—had been that nothing as potentially powerful as an artificial being should be left in the hands of men too selfish to subordinate their own desires to the needs of the nation. And nothing, it was beginning to appear, was exactly what had been *in* Yoshimitsu hands. Even doddering old Kawabe, figurehead minister for International Trade and Industry, was asking hard-edged questions of his fire-eating subordinate.

Unused to such attention, Ishikawa Nobuhiko in turn cranked up the heat on Ogaki Mitsuru. The ministry had reacted to Hiryu's unauthorized attack on Dai-Nihon with benign paternal indulgence. If, however, definite headway weren't soon made regarding TOKUGAWA, proof offered either of its existence or otherwise, father MITI would frown on his prodigal son.

Ogaki was no computer scientist. He was an expert in optics, the field in which the company now called Hiryu Cybernetics Industries had actually made itself prepotent following the Second World War. Though the interests of both Hiryu and its chairman had diversified considerably since then, Ogaki retained an almost fanatical interest in his original field. He had designed and built a number of astronomical telescopes, laboriously grinding the lenses and mirrors by hand; he was a passionate stargazer, the pride of whose life was the fact that he had a minor comet named after him, and that his departure to attend a weekend convention of amateur astonomers in Kobe was being delayed had added a touch of acid to his usual asperity when he passed on Ishikawa's ultimatum shortly before.

Still feeling its unfamiliar sting in his rump, Toda Onomori was thoroughly out of sorts. "People," he said again, aspersing by implication his superior's inexplicable interest in points of light in the nighttime sky. "That's what I know. I'll get results from this turncoat scientist of ours, Major; never fear." Craig drew on her cigarette and watched him without speaking.

Toda's com/comm unit announced Takai Jisaburo's arrival at the entrance to the nerve center. Craig said nothing, having been informed a second earlier through the bone-conduction speaker snugged behind her right ear. She had a communications network of her own, to which even her boss wasn't privy. CYA: the way the game was played.

Takai entered in the uncompanionable company of a pair of Craig's security heavies in dark blue jumpsuits. He performed a perfunctory bow. "Mr. Chairman," he said with a ragged attempt at brusqueness. His clothes were rumpled, his face a composition of hollows and unaccustomed shadows. He had lived with fear and frustration for six weeks. During that time he had been allowed to talk to Taro and Yoriko some six times. And he had given up demanding to know what had become of Elizabeth O'Neill; he'd realized, belatedly, he didn't want to know the answer. He did know that he was through truckling to this toad Buddha.

Toda gazed at him with half-closed eyes. "Ah, Dr. Takai. So good of you to call on me. I trust you bring news of success?"

Takai blinked. *He* had been summoned *here*, and now this sinister smirking creature was acting as if the meeting had been Takai's idea. Almost able to see the defiant wind puff out of the man's sails, Toda refused to permit himself gratification at the effect he'd created. It was such a simple trick, childish almost. Outmaneuvering this scientist was no great victory at the best of times; when Takai served the ministry as part of the fifth-generation project, the dynamic Fuchi was ramrodding ICOT, and a man's status was determined by ability, not seniority or skill in intrigue. Takai was a babe in woods Toda Onomori had grown up in.

"I—that is, my staff is following up a number of very promising leads. We theorize that the events surrounding the transfer of power here at the citadel may have frightened TOKUGAWA. Shocked him. He may have withdrawn into himself, hiding—"

Toda opened his eyes wide. It was as effective as a shout; Takai's tongue tripped over itself and his words rolled away like a ball down a hillside. "We are speaking of a computer," Toda said, no longer murmuring, "and you are a computer scientist. Why have you not simply programmed the device for compliance?"

Defiance had sublimed away from Takai. "But, Mr. Chairman, it's not that simple! We tried that in the very first hours after you took over. TOKUGAWA didn't respond. If anything's going to work, it's going to require great subtlety, great patience."

The eyelids descended. *The man is actually panting.* That satisfied Toda that Takai was giving his utmost, at least. But intentions didn't concern him; only results. "I understand there's one expedient you haven't yet tried."

Takai's brows cramped together. "Sir?"

"The Kliemann Coil," Major Craig said. "The rapport device O'Neill was so fond of."

Takai blinked. His tongue poked out between his lips, gray from too much smoking and too little sleep, moistened the lips. "But that's—not practicable. It's unreliable. It was a very, uh, experimental piece of technology. We had . . . a good deal of trouble with it. One of our technicians was incapacitated by the device the first time it was tried, and Dr. O'Neill herself collapsed once while using it."

"Ah, yes. Dr. Ito's unfortunate mishap. The proximate cause, I recall, of your transfer of loyalties." Toda paused to let the barb sink home. Takai's thin body jerked. "No matter. I fail to understand, Dr. Takai, why such an important pathway hasn't been pursued."

"He's chicken." Craig's voice vibrated with scorn.

Takai looked from one to the other with hunted eyes. "But we don't know how to *use* the coil. O'Neill had a—a special *feel* for TOKUGAWA. He—it was her creation. She was able to do things with him that none of us could. You can't imagine how delicate a matter we're dealing with here, Toda-sama. If we intrude in the wrong way, we might crash TOKUGAWA irretrievably. There's no way to tell—"

Toda lifted a broad flat hand. "Relax, Doctor. I understand perfectly. There's no need to trouble yourself further. In fact, I think you're long overdue for a rest from your long and dutiful exertions." Takai stared at him, shoulders slumped, mouth slack and moist in foolish grateful relief. *Really, this is almost too easy.* "We've been thinking of bringing in someone to lift the burden of running the TOKUGAWA lab from your shoulders. There are several scientists in Southern California we've been speaking to who are quite amenable to the idea . . ."

He looked away from the scientist. Abjection was not a pretty sight.


In silence so oppressive that even the never-ending hum of the citadel's ventilation system seemed hushed, Toda Onomori stood on the gallery with hands clasped behind his back and watched medics in green smocks remove the body from the gleaming throne of the Kliemann Coil.

Craig's mercenary security troops stood in indigo clumps on both levels of the lab, nervously fingering SCK 9mm submachine guns hung around their necks on long Israeli-style slings. Though the last of Colonel Tranh Vinh's assault team had pulled out within hours after the fall of YTC castle, rumors had still filtered like colored ink into the capillaries of the grapevine. Disquieting things were whispered about the TOKUGAWA lab, and the major's hard-eyed veterans looked almost as ill at ease as the technicians who had actually witnessed what happened in the laboratory moments before.

The techs finished prying fingers from the indentations they'd crumpled into the stainless steel armrests of the coil. Two husky medics manhandled the corpse from the chair, and Toda's nostrils pinched fastidiously as a vagrant air current wafted the rank odor of fresh shit up to them. The medics laid the body on a gleaming steel gurney, and Toda felt the people in the room instinctively drawing back from it like mercury from a fingertip.

"Jesus *Christ,*" a voice said in English behind Toda's shoulder. Standing at his side, Major Angela Craig shot a warning glance back at the troops hovering behind them. Hardcore as she was, she wasn't looking any too healthy, either, and a few small domes of sweat gleamed on Toda's high forehead as he fought to maintain the mask of imperturbability that he cultivated as assiduously as Yoshimitsu Akaji had his beloved garden.

Takai Jisaburo's face had the look of a man who had popped the access hatch on Hell. Drained utterly of color, stretched to the farthest extremity: eyes open and starting from their sockets, jaws flung so wide they must have jumped their hinges, lines down both sides of the silently screaming mouth so deep they could have been cut with a razor. One of the white-coated Hiryu technicians turned away and vomited on the beige carpet; several people sobbed brokenly.

"Son of a bitch died hard," Craig said, fishing a cigar from a breast pocket of her navy-blue fatigue jumpsuit.

Toda rolled his shoulders in a languid shrug. "Just a traitor," he said. "He seems to have saved us a good deal of trouble, since sooner or later we'd have had to deal with him anyway."

He looked mildly at Craig. "I have to give him this, he was right about the coil. It must be defective.

"Have the body disposed of in the usual way."

# CHAPTER
# TWENTY-ONE

Hiryu brought in a new man to head up the TOKUGAWA lab, a stout, round-cheeked, genial man named Imamura who was head of research and development for Hiryu Cybernetics Industries. He was one of the reasons Hiryu, having entered the highly competitive computer field, was so very glad of friendly intervention by the Ministry for International Trade and Industry. He held his position by dint of seniority and his adamant refusal to make waves. He had served a term with MITI, as part of the prestigious ICOT research team—but that was in the days after Fuchi, when it was obvious the race for fifth-generation supremacy was lost, and the inevitable bureaucratic entropy had set in. He took command of the imported Hiryu technicians and treated the Yoshimitsu technicians and scientists with genial camaraderie, as if they weren't prisoners, serving virtually at gunpoint. He began his own plodding experiments to discover just what was what.

And, to his astonishment, promptly received timid, fleeting responses like nothing he'd ever encountered before. The enigma of TOKUGAWA had begun to unravel.

Sitting in his office, up there at the top of Tōkaidō—the top of the world, when all was said and done—Ishikawa Nobuhiko felt well pleased with the state of things.

He had chosen, he now felt, a particularly propitious time for bold action. Public opinion was especially fraught, wound to a high degree of tension by world events, such as the destruction of the *Jersey Lily* in SoCal, or the expulsion of all Japanese nationals from the East African Union by Life President Achezi, following a disastrous defeat of Union forces by the South Africans on the Zambezi River in Mozambique, Achezi claiming the defeat had in part been caused by Japanese slipping information to the South Africans. A government announcement that a quarter of a million workers in Japan's beleaguered aircraft production industry—fortuitously under the aegis of the Ministry for Internal Development—had prompted nationwide demonstrations against the use of Koreans in the labor force, including spontaneous outbursts against the YTC offices in Tōkaidō, which had required only the tiniest bit of stage-managing by MITI.

So the response was generally good. Intellectuals paraded before the cameras in NHK's studios to praise the Hiryu action as long overdue and shroud the blatant illegality of it in a mist of high-sounding syllables. Cartoonists for the government's print and digital-graphic media dutifully portrayed the incident in terms of a hero representing Hiryu apprehending a dangerous law breaker or curbing a dangerous beast, labeled ¥TC—with, inevitably, a yen sign in place of the Y. Composer Gosen Zenzo announced a heroic ode for fifty-voice synthesizer entitled *The Nation Awakens* in honor of the event. The premiere of the five-hour piece in the shiny new East Sea Circuit Opera Theatre several weeks later prompted the shortest critical notice in the history of the prestigious daily *Mainichi Shimbun:* "The reviewer snores."

Foreign response remained critical, not to say abusive. The major exception, oddly, was both parties to the European war; both the PanEuropean Council in Amsterdam and the pope, from a secret bunker somewhere in the Vatican Free State, issued similarly worded pronunciamentos praising the Japanese move in curbing the "pernicious influences of free enterprise." More typical was the response from North America, where *all* the Successor States—from the ultra-right-wing American Confederacy through revanchist "Canada" (as the former province of Ontario was styling itself) and PEACE to the Peoples' Collective—denounced the action. Ishikawa didn't mind their calumny in the least. Such universal criticism by *gaijin* could only bring the nation closer together.

Now, rather less sanguine about Imamura-san's qualification than either chairman Ogaki or his satrap Toda, he was withholding news of the latest developments in the TOKUGAWA Project from the press pending confirmation by someone who knew what the hell he was doing. Nevertheless, a flying investigation by a squad of topflight MITI scientists tended to confirm Imamura's report: that the gleaming white hemisphere in the subterranean lab at YTC Citadel housed a true artificial sentience, a self-aware entity with cognitive and communicative abilities approximating those of a human four- to five-year-old. That was one of the reasons for Ishikawa's reticence about going public—concern for what the nation would make of the fact that Japanese blood had been spilled and Japanese laws broken for possession of a child, rather like American parents waging a custody battle with lawyers and hired kidnappers. Sophisticated and well educated as they were, Ishikawa doubted the Japanese people would fully grasp the implications of even the most limited form of artificial awareness. In the meantime, best not to exacerbate the situation, particularly in view of the fact that there was no one to stand trial for the murder of Yoshimitsu Akaji. He was content to let matters lie until the truth was known and a splashy cover story could be put together.

In the meantime, the MITI team had sent back a secret report that had served to silence the objections of that old fool Kawabe, that the ministry had weakened the fabric of Japanese society for no good end. A special digest of their conclusions, carefully edited so that if all or part of it were leaked it would only reflect well on MITI had been prepared for dissemination among the jealous ministries who were the rulers of Japan. Ishikawa had every confidence that the report had been compiled for optimum effect; it had been personally assembled by his aide Doihara Kazuko.

Meanwhile, aftershocks of the YTC invasions were still moving through the Japanese courts—slowly, like ripples in amber. It was apparent the courts were going to block Hiryu's claim of ownership of YTC's Fukuoka facility and Floating World satellite on the basis of their conquest of the Citadel. Likewise, MITI intelligence indicated the Supreme Court would order Hiryu to divest itself of the castle, and make vast reparations to Yoshimitsu Shigeo and Yoshimitsu Michiko, as well as to YTC workers illegally sequestered after the operation. That didn't bother Ishikawa particularly. From his days at Yale, he remembered the words of the American President Jackson when faced with an adverse decision by his own Supreme Court: "They made the decision—now let them enforce it."

Things were tight in Asia; Indonesian and Brazilian surface craft had exchanged an over-the-horizon volley of missiles near Nauru in the southern Pacific; an army allegedly backed by Indonesians and led by Indonesian advisers was making great headway in the two-front Chinese war against invading armies from the nominally Communist garrison states of Vietnam and Korea. Voices were being raised to demand that Japan's Self-defense Forces be augmented, and some were even daring to whisper the heresy that Japan herself should once more take a military role in the affairs of her neighbors. In such a climate a ministry would have to act boldly to assert leadership. Ishikawa would not shrink from precipitating a constitutional crisis, at need.

Besides, Yoshimitsu Shigeo had begun to be seen—and photographed —at his favorite haunts at Kyōto. He'd lost weight, and his loud garments hung on his frame like pillowcases. The plump cheeks had deflated. His eyes were dark, sunken, and not even tinted glasses could disguise the fact. But somehow, in all his pictures, his mouth was warped into a tight little knowing V of a smile. Still, for all the old Mona Lisa trip, the young heir's public appearances indicated to Ishikawa that the party most affected by the takeover wasn't seriously going to fight it.

Finally—though of course it merited little attention in relationship to such weighty considerations—Doihara Kazuko had without fanfare moved into Ishikawa's lush penthouse apartment in the New City government housing project that had sprung up not far from the Pyramid.

On the whole, Ishikawa thought, things were going very well. Very well indeed.

With the reawakening of TOKUGAWA, the siege mentality in YTC Central began to erode beneath the waves of mutual congratulation among the technicians and administrators of Hiryu Cybernetics Industries and MITI. The occupiers began to address themselves to the problem of the thousands of employees within the citadel, who had been working as virtual prisoners since the assault. Craig and Toda began roughing out a plan to vet them for loyalty to their new employers; those who failed—or proved unwilling to work for Hiryu Cybernetics under the terms offered—would be sent off to the rice paddies with the 250,000 rusticated aerospace workers.

Meanwhile, both the Citadel and Hiryu's headquarters received several drafts of technicians recruited in North America. This caused a certain amount of resentment among the Hiryu personnel. Rumors rode the circuit that these new *gaijin* knew scarcely anything of their jobs, certainly not enough to justify their being imported at considerable expense, into a nation suffering a labor glut. Of course, such sentiments were disloyal to the company, and were never broached to the carefully stage-managed workers' circle meetings.

Major Craig's security complement received a draft of twenty-five men and women newly flown over from her old stomping grounds in what was now EasyCo, the Eastern Seaboard Coalition. The ex-FedPol major, facing the grinding task of winnowing the Yoshimitsu labor force, and inexplicably nervous as well, was grateful to Toda Onomori for having authorized the additional personnel without her having to requisition them.

Toda, meanwhile, had been only too happy to approve his security chief's request for added personnel.

And no one connected with Japanese customs and immigration had ever seen an application for a visa from any one of these new Hiryu personnel—at least, not under the names under which they were entering the country. And yet, when they presented their papers at customs, those names appeared in computer files of those granted legal entry to the home islands.

The wheel turned.

A little past ten in the morning on a day in early November, Toda Onomori was perusing a printout of Yoshimitsu assets Hiryu's legal department had decided were safely in their power. Use of hard copy was regarded as anachronistic in the most progressive Japanese business circles, or reliance on a paper crutch; for Toda, it wasn't real unless he could hold it between his broad strong hands. The seizure of YTC Central had strapped Hiryu for cash, and he had to make some hard recommendations to chairman Ogaki soon about which assets to liquidate and which to hang onto.

The former occupant's pottery was gone from the shelves. To Toda it was just bric-a-brac. He'd replaced it with the ornaments of his own life: books, ponderous volumes, management texts, psychology, law.

Redundant, really—nothing in them he couldn't call up from the bowels of the YTC database, or pay his nickel and tap into the global Net for. But they gave him a feeling of mass, solidity, like the fan-fold paper in his hands. Like being able to lift his eyes from his desktop and see the nerve center out there before him like the bridge of an aircraft carrier, to make visual contact with the raw ganglia of the company he controlled. He knew old Yoshimitsu Akaji had disdained to spend time down here, had left that to his playboy son. That was part of the reason the old man had lost the company.

Some change in the rhythm, a shift in the ebb and flow of serious bodies in pastel jumpsuits, brought Toda's eyes up from folded sheets of inventory. What he saw went down his back like cold rain dripping from a winter eave. Technicians in headsets were standing up from their work stations, holding their hands over their heads. A mixed squad in security indigo had come into the command center, and was holding down on the techs with submachine guns. They seemed relaxed, casual, as if this were some outing for a harvest festival.

The sheaf of printouts slammed down on the desk top. "Craig!" he shouted to his *shosei* computer. "What's going on down here?"

"She won't hear you," a voice said from the speaker.

Toda sat very still. A trickle of sweat ran down the right side of his face. Outside, the security team was herding the Hiryu technicians to one side of the command center. They weren't so much as looking toward the big glass windows that dominated the room.

"What is the meaning of this? Who is this?"

"TOKUGAWA."

Toda slumped back into his chair as if he'd been struck back with a sandbag. The gel molded itself to him, caressing, soothing. "Ridiculous," he snapped, his resolve springing back. "TOKUGAWA's just a child. Whoever's responsible for this—"

"You killed my lord, Yoshimitsu Akaji," the voice went on, infinitely calm, infinitely menacing. "You killed Dr. O'Neill."

Wildly, Toda looked out through the glass of his office. Some of his technicians were standing clumped beneath the big color LCD displays, staring at him as if expecting him to do something. One of the men in dark blue finally noticed him, gave him a grin and a cheerful wave.

"Now you're going to die."

And Toda saw his desk come rushing at him at the wave front of an explosion; a bundle of hard copy went flapping over his head like a great white crane, enfolding him in its wings, and he wasn't any-more.

Sitting outside the door of chairman Ogaki's office in the center of the Hiryu Cybernetics Industries' sprawling complex in Ōsaka, the chairman's secretary-receptionist looked up from her French lesson as the sound of a scream, high and thin and sharp, cut through the thick soundproofing of her boss' office.

A second later, the heavy Indonesian hardwood door blew off its hinges.

Throughout both YTC Citadel *and* Hiryu Cybernetics home complex, newly hired technicians produced automatic weapons and politely suggested that their coworkers surrender. They did. Meanwhile, security details heard their superior officers ordering them to lay down their arms and surrender to parties of polite but firm people wearing the same uniforms as they. Their superiors, in fact, were already under lock and key, having answered summons by the chiefs of security for the two facilities. TOKUGAWA simply did their voices better than they did— and, in any event, none of them proved willing to go out of his or her way to die for good ol' Hiryu Cybernetics. It was a point Aoki Hideo had impressed on TOKUGAWA during their strategy-planning session: Major Miguel García was personally loyal to Yoshimitsu Akaji and YTC, and a number of his men might well have fought the Hiryu invaders out of loyalty to their commander. But, basically, the Cubans of the Yoshimitsu security platoon had fought because they were suddenly confronted with men aiming guns at them. Had they been given a chance to surrender, the transition might have been a good deal more peaceful.

The old man, as usual, was right. Within minutes, the entire security complements of YTC Citadel and the Hiryu home offices had been secured and disarmed.

Except for a heavily armed squad in battle dress moving purposefully along a corridor in the subterranean warrens of the castle.

"Dammit," Major Angela Craig shouted. "Dammit, dammit, *dammit!*" She slammed her hand down on the top of the com/comm console in her office on the level above the nerve center. It blandly blinked its amber message: ALL STATIONS REPORT STATUS NORMAL. SECURITY ROUTINES REPORT TAMPERING: NEGATIVE. INTRUSION: NEGATIVE.

It was bullshit, and she knew it.

"Barracks!" she barked at the com/comm. It continued to blink idiotically at her. She activated the tiny mike clipped to the breast pocket of her uniform, rapped out a list of stations, demanded reports. The plug behind her ear remained quiet.

Her heart seemed to be throwing itself around inside her rib cage like a rabbit trying to get free of a trap. *Something big's going down.* She jumped up from her desk, hauled on a heavy bulletproof battle-dress jacket. She rammed her coal-scuttle helmet down on her head, switched on its mike, demanded a status report. Nothing. "Shit," she said, and slammed down the visor.

Sweeping a bullpup assault rifle out of its rack behind her desk, she went to the door. It slid open obediently. She stepped into the hall.

A squad of her people, like her in full emergency battle rig with visors down and assault rifles ready, were double-timing down the corridor toward her. They stopped. "There she is!" a voice crackled in her ear.

She planted her hands on her hips. "You're fucking-A right, I'm here," she rasped. "Why the fuck haven't you jokers answered—"

*"Shoot the traitor!"* Toda Onomori's voice rang like a gong in her ears. *"Get the bitch before she gets away!"*

Her rifle dropped from fingers that suddenly had the strength of *tofu.* She held up her hands before her. "No, no, there's some mistake," she gasped. *"Don't—"*

Half a dozen rifles opened up on her at full automatic from a distance of six meters. Later, members of the squad marveled to one another how long their ex-chief had kept screaming.


Yoshimitsu Shigeo sat in a low butcher-block chair, watching snow settle out of a sky the color of a dove's belly, dusting the hilltop compound and the surrounding mountains. He knew the coating of snow would make Takara-yama, the Fortunate Mountain, look especially impressive, bring it right up close. He couldn't see it from the window of his apartment. It was a curious thing; he'd never particularly cared whether he saw Mount Takara or not. Now that he couldn't see it, he thought about it all the time.

He glanced around, through the open doorway into his workshop. His treadle-driven wheel sat there neglected, a half-thrown pot dried to khaki on top of it. A month ago he'd simply lost interest in the middle of throwing a pot, and he hadn't had the heart to do any more, not even go back in and chisel the congealed piece off the wheel. He hardly had the heart for anything anymore, even—or especially—the trips he made to Kyōto to keep his enemies off balance, on the advice of Aoki Hideo and his demon helper. *It isn't going to work,* he knew. *Nothing's going to work.* He decided he would probably go mad soon.

The door opened.

Incuriously, he looked around. No indigo escort squad stood there, nor the all-too-familiar form of Toda Onomori, his face cast in a smile as artificial as one of those awful plastic statues of the god of luck, Hotei, that the *gaijin* tourists bought in the curio shops. Nor was there any sign of the pair of guards that had stood there, night and day, for more than two months.

"Yoshimitsu-sama."

He recognized TOKUGAWA's voice. "What is it?" he almost whined.

"Your father's death is avenged, Yoshimitsu-sama. The citadel is yours."

# CHAPTER TWENTY-TWO

Refusing to compromise with the slush piled in the streets of Tōkyō New City, Ishikawa Nobuhiko strode the night alone, finding purchase for the leather soles of his shoes on ice-slick pavement by sheer force of will. The streets were empty, as they had been for years—here, under the ever-watchful eye of government, ration busting was far less convenient than it was in Kyōto. But the tall buildings rising to every side glowed like vast self-luminous fungi. The ministries they housed knew no rationing—of heat, of light, of power.

Behind him he heard the angry grumble of demonstrators crowded around the base of the MITI Pyramid. *How fickle is the public,* he thought wryly. *When we brought YTC to heel they called us saviors. Now Yoshimitsu TeleCommunications has snapped its leash, and the people can think of nothing but how bravely it bore up beneath adversity and oppression.* He permitted himself a small smile. The people's mercurial nature made it all the more necessary they have a strong, wise hand to guide them. As he was fairly sure MITI's rival Internal Development was guiding this demonstration.

It had been, as he would have said during his Yale sojourn, a bitch of a day. After so much hard work and frustration, the carefully tended garden of the YTC affair had finally begun to blossom. And then an earthquake knocked it all to pieces.

The afternoon had grown old before they even knew anything was wrong. The tendrils of the ministry's domestic intelligence network, spread across the nation like vines on a trellis, had unexpectedly begun to vibrate with ever-increasing urgency. *Something* was happening at YTC Central . . . and the Hiryu head office. By six o'clock that dreary, snow-flurried evening, they found out that *something* was that both facilities had been quietly and peaceably taken over by mercenaries in the employ of Yoshimitsu Shigeo. There had been no violence to speak of, no fatalities except for Ogaki Mitsuru and Toda Onomori, reported dead in unexplained explosions, and a foreign national, head of Citadel security, apparently killed by her own subordinates.

*We'll never get murder indictments on those,* Ishikawa thought bitterly, lengthening his stride. *We'll be lucky if the ministry doesn't get scooped out like a ripe melon.* The press was howling. Internal Development tut-tutted sanctimoniously, and even MITI's allies among Japan's ministries were very cool, very cool. Purge was a vivid possibility. The prime minister was taking very serious notice of these proceedings. Normally, that was what the titular minister of MITI was for, to provide a head to roll in the sand if scandal broke, leaving the all-important bureaucracy of his ministry intact. The Hiryu/Yoshimitsu blowup was too comprehensive a catastrophe to avert by a scapegoat.

Worst of all, there wasn't a single damned thing Ishikawa Nobuhiko could do to save the situation. He could scarcely call Yoshimitsu Shigeo's virtually bloodless reconquest of his own property a crime. Nor could he object to their seizure of Hiryu Cybernetics, not without making the ministry look ridiculous—and to forfeit the ministry's face would be to destroy everything he'd worked for, lived for.

He'd sent Doihara home an hour before, just before an emergency late-night meeting with MITI Minister Kawabe. The meeting itself was a routine unpleasantness, the snowy-headed old minister very grave and concerned, vowing that the honor of the ministry should not be besmirched. On the wind of his words Ishikawa whiffed the possibility that the old fool had no intention of doing the right thing, claiming full responsibility and committing bureaucratic *seppuku.* The minister, he recalled, had been a close friend of that damned Yamada Tatsuhide, who'd committed *seppuku* of a more substantial sort the day YTC Central fell. *Is this to be his revenge, bringing down those who led his friend to suicide?*

After the meeting Ishikawa had decided to go home. The normal, safe Japanese bureaucratic procedure would be to stay at the office twenty-four hours a day until the crisis was resolved one way or another. Even in this extremity Ishikawa was damned well going to maintain that special flair that set him apart, marked him as an up-and-comer. Wolves howled in the snow outside, but *he* was going home as if nothing was the matter. An elementary show of bravado—likewise of realism. There really was nothing he could do.

The crowd that greeted him when he stepped out through the polarized armored-glass doors of the MITI Pyramid, its collective breath billowing white like steam rising through grates from a subway station, took him momentarily aback. At sight of him the protestors shouted, surged forward; riot police held them off with electrified sticks and clear plexiglass shields. Photo flashes rippled the night like a naval barrage, and then more guards thrust from the building, forming a flying wedge, driving through the crowd with Ishikawa striding boldly behind. The mob was angry, but still Japanese; once he was through they let him go, preferring to concentrate their ire on the visible symbol of MITI rather than pursue the administrative vice-minister indecorously through the streets. Just as well; once clear of the mob Ishikawa dismissed his police escort, overriding their protests with a haughty wave of his hand. Skulking behind a phalanx of cops would tarnish the image he cultivated of a fearless, hard-charging technocrat.

He reached the glass-box apartment complex in which he lived. No blocky graceless *danshi*, this, with plumbing that began to fail before the first occupants moved in, and galvanized metal outlets for the smoke of the hibachis that provided most of the heat and cooking for the occupants jerry-rigged out the windows to draw brush strokes of black soot up raw concrete flanks, but the exclusive domain of MITI brass. Since Minister Kawabe lived on his estate in the fashionable Kamakura district, the luxurious penthouse on the twenty-third floor rightfully belonged to Ishikawa Nobuhiko. Moving Doihara Kazuko in with him hadn't been much of a production; as his assistant, she'd rated a relatively sizable apartment just six floors beneath his.

He smiled on a transient thought of Kazuko. Strangely, her actions during the Yoshimitsu takeover had somehow broken down a barrier between them, permitted them to find one another as they never had, as coworkers or lovers either one. She had, after all, acted in what she saw to be the interest of the nation in attempting to defy him—and she'd been right, he saw that now. Punishing her for patriotism would mean return to feudal days, the times before Unification when a man's loyalty went to a *daimyō* without thought of the nation—a recidivism his critics had been shrilly accusing him of attempting since early this evening.

Weariness surged, threatening to swamp him. He shook it off. Tempting to give way to the clamor of the mob and resign. He wondered if

they were worth the anguish, his imperial dreams for nation and ministry.

A gang of workmen engaged in street repairs impossible during daylight hours paused in their work near the apartment's entrance to offer
respectful greeting to the administrative vice-minister. *Even the work-
ingmen know me,* he thought proudly. He smiled and nodded acknowledgment. *This is no time for weakness,* he thought, and strode resolutely up the steps.

A slot waited beside smoky-looking armored-glass doors to swallow
the identification cards of those seeking admittance to the building.
Ishikawa had to go through no such rigmarole. He simply strode up to
the door, was identified visually by both humans and fifth-generation
routines monitoring the security pickups there, and the doors swished
open for him so that he entered without breaking stride. He walked the
plastic runner laid coyly across lush maroon carpets to the elevator
bank, commanded an elevator in abstracted voice.

Vibrations shivered up through the soles of his feet. He felt more
than heard a deep thrum, like the ringing of a great brazen gong
deep in the earth. *Earthquake!* he thought, eyes darting from side to
side. The muscles of his legs quivered with the need to run, to race
outside the confines of the building before it collapsed on him. Modern Japanese architecture was designed to withstand quakes, especially since the war. But in his marrow Ishikawa had the fear every
dweller in the megaplex lived with, of the stupendous Tōkai quake
long predicted by seismologists, which would release as much energy
in the blink of an eye as a thousand Third World Wars in the very
heart of Tōkaidō and bring the stoutest buildings smashing down in
heaps of cement and glass and ruptured frail protoplasm. *Kazuko,* he
thought.

No second shock came. The vibration hovered in the air about him,
diminuendoing, and for some reason he was reminded of the sun's
ringing astronomers described. *Nothing,* he thought. *Just a tremor—*

The elevator door opened. From his eye's left corner Ishikawa saw
the work gang on the street, ghosts glimpsed through gauze, pointing
upward and shouting without sound. Light fell on them from above,
strange and harsh even through the polarization of the armored glass
around the lobby, as though the full moon hung on the spike of the
apartment tower had suddenly grown fiendish bright, discolored. He
ran to the sliding doors, thrust them open with his hands when they
failed to give way rapidly enough, stepped out into a street full of
dancing yellow light, like the light of a paper lantern at a village festival
enormously magnified. He looked up.

Fire sprouted from the summit of the apartment like a bougainvillea blossom. Streamers of yellow-white flame splashed down the precipice of glass, and a rain of fiery droplets descended, consumed before they fell halfway to earth. Dense smoke spilled across the swollen impaled moon.

"A helicopter!" one of the workers cried, voice trip-hammering with excitement. "A terrible thing! He just flew into the top of the building. Nobody could have gotten out."

"I hope there wasn't anyone in the penthouse," remarked another calmly as sirens began to wail from within the building.

*"Kazuko!"* Ishikawa screamed and ran slipping up the icy steps.


A slot ate Ishikawa Nobuhiko's identity card, regurgitated, and let him in; the Gen-5 servant that opened the door of a vice-minister's penthouse at his approach was not for this wretched cubicle on the eighth floor of the MITI apartment block. He entered, flicked on the lights by hand, slumped onto a plastic chair curved like frozen taffy. His net bag of rice, noodles, and vegetables he let thunk to the thin carpet by his feet. He lacked the energy to take off his snow-dusted overcoat, and the four paces to the cramped kitchen seemed the voyage of a thousand kilometers.

His penthouse had been hell. A Tōkaidō Police Department helicopter had been making a routine sweep over the crater-front district when it suddenly and apparently of its own volition had nosed into the top of the apartment building; he'd heard the recording of the police pilot screaming, "I can't hold her, she won't respond." Then silence. The chopper had caught its skid on the meter-and-a-half-high containment wall that ran around the penthouse balcony, tumbled in air, struck, and exploded. High-octane fuel burst through the shattered glass doors like a volcano's pyroclastic flow, flooding the apartment with fire.

*And Kazuko.* The little wall had saved her life—for what that was worth. Had it not tripped the helicopter, the craft would have crashed through the apartment like a kamikaze of old, smashing her before it exploded. As it was, only a few chunks of debris and shards of glass had struck her before the fire caught her up.

The doctors said she had at least a 40 percent chance of survival. Cultured skin force-grown for grafting was a long-established medical technology, and the genocidal fire-bomb raids of the American war a half century before had given burn-trauma treatment a special honored niche in the Japanese medical curriculum. Fire & Rescue was one function that seemed immune to the dégringolade of Japanese society, and an elite heliborne emergency team had been on the scene within five minutes, bursting through the window at one end of the corridor and leaping into the building from a rope ladder, braving the clumsiness of bulky asbestos suits.

It took four of them to restrain the administrative vice-minister of MITI, pounding his fists against a door sealed by the building's emergency monitor, from hurling himself into the flames when the Gen-5 guardian opened the door to the firefighters. He wasn't sure they'd done him a kindness.

All night he'd hovered at the hospital where a team of doctors fought to save his assistant. They were still at it when he left at six in the morning to return to work at the ministry.

His head swung lax on his neck. It was all coming down in ruins, everything he'd worked for, as surely as if the Tōkai quake were cutting loose at last. The press—government organs as well as the independents —were pillorying MITI as they hadn't since before the war. Prime Minister Fudori, crossing an abyss on a rapidly fraying rope, promised a full investigation into the YTC scandal, which meant a bureaucratic bloodbath. Violence flamed throughout the home islands as *zaibatsu* sponsored by MITI's rivals savaged Trade and Industry's pampered darlings. The ministry, Ishikawa Nobuhiko's life, his world, had lost credibility, lost face. Barring some miracle, its power and influence in the nation was over; it might even be "reorganized," that is, obliterated, its powers and duties stirred up and ladled out to extant ministries, or a new one cast to take its place. It had happened often enough before; and MITI had already used up its quota of good fortune by surviving the debacle of the trade war with America.

Ishikawa's only dream had been to make his ministry flagship of the nation. Now it was headed for the shoals—and Minister Kawabe, without ever directly saying so, had made it abundantly clear that he, Ishikawa, would go down with the ship. Much as Ishikawa wanted to believe the minister was turning craven to save his wattled old neck, even that consolation eluded him. He was certain the old man was availing himself of a chance to avenge the death of his friend Yamada, for which he blamed his administrative vice-minister.

*I tried to stand off chaos,* he thought. *Can it be, as poor Kazuko said, that I've asked it in instead?*

Wearily he rose. Snow had melted into the fur collar of his coat and puddled like spent semen on the colorless thin carpet. In his penthouse had been a *dōbōshū* robot who would take his coat and hang it in the bathroom to dry. No more. He was reduced to this cheerless closet, cold and bare, whose very heating was controlled—badly—by the building's master system. He could conceivably have tried to bump a less exalted administrator from quarters higher up in the building—but he honestly didn't know whether he had the pull any longer. He couldn't face finding out.

"Ishikawa."

His head snapped around, and he glared at the com/comm console on its little desk built out from the wall just past the orange plastic-covered sofa. "What is it?" he snapped, energized by anger; while he still held the title of administrative vice-minister for International Trade and Industry, he was damned if anyone was going to address him in that tone of voice.

"This is TOKUGAWA."

He stood very still. The Tokugawa family still existed, influential in Japanese affairs; yet he knew at once this had nothing to do with them. He knew who was speaking to him. Irreality caught him up in weight-lessness like a dream of flight. "The tones and rhythms of your voice are fully human. Really very good. Dr. O'Neill is to be congratulated." He rubbed his eyes. "So it's true, after all. You hoodwinked those Hiryu fools, took them in totally. Made them believe you were no more than a child."

"I did, Ishikawa-san."

"And may I infer you arranged this afternoon's transfer of power at YTC Central and Hiryu? I presume such is well within your capabilities." He laughed. "I must say, TOKUGAWA-san, this is a pleasure unexpected in more ways than one. I predicted at the very outset that you were too valuable a tool to be left in the hands of a maverick like Yoshimitsu. I was right. It pleases me to know that."

He licked thin lips. "What do you want of me?" he asked, almost eagerly, anticipating the necessary, even the just, response.

"Your life."

"Ahh." The breath slid from him.

"You are responsible for the deaths of Yoshimitsu Akaji and Dr. O'-Neill. It is my duty to avenge them."

"That wasn't my doing. I gave orders that the old man and doctor weren't to be hurt. That damned mercenary, Tranh—he killed them, or let his men get out of control and do it."

"I don't believe you." A pause. "Very well. A psychological stress evaluation indicates you're telling the truth—as you know it. Yoshimitsu Akaji died fighting the invaders in his own garden. Dr. O'Neill—" Despite himself, Ishikawa marveled. *I hear real sorrow in his words,* he thought, *so like my own.* "—was murdered by Toda Onomori and the American, Major Craig, with the concurrence of chairman Ogaki. They withdrew her medication and permitted her to die."

"Those bastards," Ishikawa said sincerely, "those stupid, shortsighted *bastards.* And what happened to them? I take it their deaths weren't . . . accidental?"

"You are correct, Mr. Vice-Minister. Technicians installed small antipersonnel devices of the type called mini-claymores in the desks of both executives, believing them to be black box antibugging equipment. The work orders so indicated, as did the dummy casings that contained the units. I must tell you, Ishikawa-san, that my lord, Yoshimitsu Shigeo, has no knowledge of my actions in this matter. I bear full responsibility."

The tone of calm reasonability jarred Ishikawa more than any tirade could have. *O'Neill-san crafted a mind in the image of a man,* Ishikawa thought, *but was it a madman?*

"I regret the necessity for the deaths of the two police officers in the helicopter last night," TOKUGAWA continued. "I seized control of their craft's autopilot; I thought that I had timed the crash properly for you to have reached your apartment, but apparently you were delayed—"

"You *fool!*" Ishikawa shouted, his vision blurring. "You killed Kazuko!"

"She was guilty."

"She *wasn't.* She disapproved of the plan to take over YTC. She—she *betrayed* me, trying to warn you, to warn Yoshimitsu the attack was coming. Our security barely caught her in time."

There was silence. "I have reviewed the records of MITI security. They confirm your story," the disembodied voice said. "I am truly sorry."

"That makes it better," Ishikawa said bitterly.

"You do not deny your own guilt, Ishikawa-san?"

"No. I, and I alone, am responsible for the attack on Yoshimitsu Central. I accept full responsibility for the deaths of Yoshimitsu Akaji and Dr. Elizabeth O'Neill. I believed that I was acting in the best interests of the nation." Bitterness again: "I believe now that I was right."

"Do you fear death, Mr. Vice-Minister?"

"It would be a relief."

"Please go into the kitchen, Ishikawa-san."

Frowning perplexity, Ishikawa took three steps forward to the door of the cramped kitchen. The dining table had been slid out from its slot in the wall. On it lay a *wakizashi*, unsheathed, a piece of rice paper folded about its short, sharp blade.

He bowed. "I thank you, TOKUGAWA-san," he said, smiling. "You are most thoughtful."

# CHAPTER
# TWENTY-THREE

In the presence of the surviving members of the YTC Board of Directors—Suzuki Kantaro, the acerbic union leader, had disappeared during the Hiryu interregnum—and the TOKUGAWA lab staff, Yoshimitsu Shigeo hung with his own hands a lacquered wooden rack on the wall behind the glabrous hemisphere of the Integrated Processing Nexus. On the rack he placed a fine *wakizashi* from his father's collection, and below that, the priceless Muramasa long sword that Yoshimitsu Akaji had held in his hands when he died. It was a very somber ceremony, if a bit mystifying to most of those present.

Yoshimitsu Shigeo found it all rather ridiculous. It was entirely Aoki Hideo's idea. The old man had a way of knowing what he was talking about—though Shigeo intended to walk his own path from here on in. But Aoki, who understood TOKUGAWA better than he, strongly urged him to this rigmarole. What Shigeo did understand was how advisable it was to keep his bound demon loyal, even, indeed, at the price of making himself look silly.

So TOKUGAWA received the *dai-sho* from the hand of his lord and became truly samurai.

Doihara Kazuko lived. When her condition stabilized, the doctors charged with her care received curious instructions. On a cold midwinter morning she was bundled up to the helipad on the roof of Tōkyō Imperial University Medical Center and handed into the care of a gaggle of nurses and medical technicians, who carried her into a large passenger helicopter with the blue YTC logo blazoned on the side. It lifted with a thumping of rotors into a sky the color of blue ice, canted, and was gone.

The Med Center staff scratched their heads. It was all highly irregular. Orders were orders, however, so they went below, went back to their duties, and forgot about it.

The wheel turned. The lurid *seppuku*—in this case literally *hara-kiri*, "belly-cutting"—of MITI's once-popular administrative vice-minister formed a nine days' wonder, eclipsed shortly by overwrought speculation concerning the fate pursuing the hapless ministry. In a matter of weeks four more members of the Oversight Council died in mysterious circumstances.

Atsuji Shunko of Operations and analysis specialist Mitsui Toshio were killed with twenty-three other people when their packet jet crashed into Tōkyō Bay seconds after takeoff from the new Tōkaidō International Airport.

Maejima Isamu was found dead in his apartment, apparently scalded to death in his shower.

Chō Rokuro, the planning officer, was entering a subway car when the train started prematurely despite safety overrides on the doors. Five people were killed, and Chō badly injured. He was rushed to the new Tōdai Medical Center, where he received a massive transfusion. The blood proved to be of the wrong type. He died in convulsions.

With his death shortly after the beginning of the new year, every member of the Oversight Council that had sat in judgment on Yoshimitsu TeleCommunications late last summer was dead. Prime Minister Fudori's fragile regime finally caved in under sensational accusations of death squads at work, punishing those responsible for the government's embarrassment in the Yoshimitsu affair.

One more datum might have added a vital piece to the puzzle. But its significance wasn't widely appreciated. In mid-January, news hit the international datanet that famed Hessian siege expert Colonel Tranh Vinh of the Socialist Republic of Vietnam had been shot to death at a sidewalk café in Phnom Penh, along with his Lebanese-born mistress. His two executioners fled on foot into the crowd. Vietnamese police were making inquiries and expected to crack the case shortly. Fat chance; even in the docile capital of captive Kampuchea, the locals never knew the answers to any questions the *Yuen* asked. On account of the colonel's notoriety the murders enjoyed a certain currency, but only a handful knew that the master merc had been involved in the original capture of YTC citadel—and they weren't talking.

*   *   *

Attainment of his long-cherished dream of mastery over Yoshimitsu TeleCommunications changed Yoshimitsu Shigeo. Like Shakespeare's Prince Hal he turned his back on dissipation. Shedding the Kyōto love nest, to the bitter disappointment of the gossip columnists, he threw himself with one mind into managing YTC—including his new demesne, Hiryu Cybernetics Industries, Incorporated—routinely putting in eighteen and twenty hours a day.

What time he didn't devote to work went to his ceramics. Losing interest in pots, he turned to creating small stylized statues of men and horses in the manner of the *haniwa* figures left by the neolithic Tumulus Builders. A showing of selected works at an exclusive gallery in Kyōto brought enthusiastic reviews from art critics. The glossy upscale weeklies, *Shukan Asahi*, *Nippon Today*, and the rest, exuberantly bannered the emergence of the "new" Yoshimitsu Shigeo as a major figure in Japanese industry.

They didn't know the half of it.


Before the Kyōto opening and the unfurling of his new image, within days after his birthright was returned to him, Yoshimitsu Shigeo sat in the office next to the one he formerly occupied, overlooking the nerve center of YTC. Thick soundproofing kept at bay the sound of the workmen repairing and remodeling his old office. TOKUGAWA's parting gift to Toda Onomori had used a minute shaped explosive charge and consequently did slight external damage beyond blowing out the office's front window. But it left a shambles inside.

He turned a new bisque *haniwa* in his hands, nodded convulsively, spoke: "TOKUGAWA."

"Yes, Yoshimitsu-sama?"

"I have received some disturbing information. My intelligence sources report that Illyrium is planning to move against us while we're still disorganized."

"But, Yoshimitsu-sama, I find no record of any such report being made."

"None was entered in the Citadel's database. Nor were they phoned or 'netted in; I took personal receipt of written reports, by hand." He scowled at a previously unnoticed imperfection in the clay horse in his hands. Grasping it by tubular fore and hind legs, he split it like a wishbone, tossed the pieces aside. "The experiences of those Hiryu swine showed me how insecure data security really is. We can't know how vulnerable our own database is to intrusion."

"It's quite secure, Yoshimitsu-sama."

"*You* invaded it. Can we tell who else might have?"

"I would know."

"*Would* you? I think not. I truly think not."

Silence.

"I want this threat neutralized at once."

"It shall be as you command, Yoshimitsu-sama."

And so it was done. Blocks of stock were electronically transferred without their owners' awareness, records altered, new stock issues made unbeknownst to any Illyrium officer or employee. In short order the light industrial and electronics manufacturing combine became a wholly owned subsidiary of Yoshimitsu TeleCommunications.

TOKUGAWA's first step, of course, was to invade Illyrium's database. Illyrium was more sophisticated in such matters than Hiryu, and it took him several days. At the end of that time, he was able to confirm what he had expected all along: that Illyrium had planned no aggression against Yoshimitsu TeleCommunications, at least not that they'd confided to their computer's files. TOKUGAWA grieved. By the ethics instilled in him by his creator he'd committed a crime. But orders were orders. *That* imperative O'Neill had drummed into him above all: to serve the Yoshimitsu family instantly, faithfully, unfailingly.

Thus was the trend set.


Snow lay heavy on the Chugoku Mountains, softening granite harshness. Soon the green shoots of spring would push up from the earth, thrusting up through snow in search of the sun. But now was the harsh time, the dreary time, when winter seemed to have settled in as if it would never leave, squeezing all color from the land by its weight. Yet all was not bleak; here and there, sunlight pierced the clouds and turned unbroken expanses of snow to pools of beaten platinum.

In a helicopter suspended between white sky and white land, Aoki Hideo sighed and turned from the window. He was weary, weary. His age weighed upon him, and more. He pressed eyes shut briefly, opened them. *Enough of self-pity.* He turned his attention back to the LCD screen of the notebook computer unfolded in his lap.

"Aoki-san." A familiar voice spoke in the bone-conduction plug behind his ear. He looked up. The speaker, of course, was nowhere to be seen.

"TOKUGAWA," he said. A vast calm enfolded him. "I've been waiting for this moment."

There was a pause. "You know?"

Aoki nodded his massive head. His face, craggy and weatherbeaten as the granite bliss below, was composed, serene. "Of course, TOKUGA-WA-san. First Imada Jun, then Kurabayashi Seigo, and finally Hosoya Jinsai—an accidental overdose of medication, a mysterious helicopter crash, an accident involving a crane in the receiving bay. How well I know your capabilities, my friend." He shook his head sadly. "How well I know our master's proclivity for seeing enemies where he has none. Too long has he felt the world was against him; inevitable that, at the last, he should suspect even my hand would be turned against him."

He folded down the screen of the computer, which automatically shut itself off. "So. Is this the hour appointed for my death?"

"It is."

"Why have you called me? To seek my absolution?"

"To seek your . . . understanding."

The old man smiled. "You have that. Loyalties these days are too easily set aside, like a fashionable garment worn for one season, and then discarded. That is not my way. Nor is it yours, and for that I honor you."

"I am sorry, Aoki-san. You are one of my oldest living friends. Yet I cannot permit *ninjō* to interfere with my duty." The old man nodded; TOKUGAWA's use of the word *ninjō*, human feelings, did not strike him as inappropriate. "I am sorry to have added to your burden, Aoki-san. Yet I couldn't stand your . . . not knowing."

Aoki laid aside the notebook computer, rose, steadying himself against the random incidental movements of the craft. "You intend to crash this helicopter?"

"Yes."

The old man shook his head. "The pilot and copilot are loyal employees. It is . . ." He shook his head. "It's unnecessary."

He stood erect, straightened his tie, his severely cut black business suit. "Record my words, please: the dying statement of Aoki Hideo, of Kashima in Saga Prefecture.

"My negligence, and mine alone, permitted parties hostile to Yoshimitsu TeleCommunications to seize YTC Central. I attempted to atone for my fault with my life and was properly called back to my duty. Now that duty is discharged, and the situation that my negligence caused has been rectified. Now I willingly pay the price of my laxness.

"I affirm my loyalty to Yoshimitsu TeleCommunications, which I have served for forty years, and to its chairman and president, Yoshimitsu Shigeo.

"Finally, I hope that through my death Yoshimitsu Shigeo's eyes will be opened, and he will see where the path he has chosen is leading him. He finds enemies where he has none—and through his actions may soon find himself well supplied with real foes. The nation faces perilous times, and he and the corporation will need all the friends they can find if they are to survive."

He put out a hand to brace himself as the helicopter banked right. He smiled. "Takara-yama," he said. "She's put on her white kimono and spreads her arms to welcome me." He strode forward and threw open the hatch to outside.

"Farewell, TOKUGAWA-san."

"Aoki—" TOKUGAWA cried. The old man stepped forward. Briefly he seemed to hang in air like a great gliding crow. Then he fell into a crevasse, struck an outcropping of rock, bounced, landed on a snow-covered talus slope and rolled, gathering rocks and snow in an avalanche, building, at the last, his own cairn.


Down there in the darkness, TOKUGAWA languished in depression and despair almost as deep as he had following the death of O'Neill. The hot heedless fury that had driven him to the reprisals in the wake of the citadel's retaking had ebbed, receding so completely that he now wondered that it had ever existed. The scenarios through which his teachers had led him—Ito Emiko, Dr. Hassad, Dr. Nagaoka, Elizabeth herself—had instilled in him, as intended, a profound identification with human beings, with their sorrows and sins and failings. He knew vicariously the pains of human existence in wider variety than any humans had ever experienced and survived to learn from. In his own person, he'd experienced terror and pain and loss that seemed to open a boundless black chasm beneath him.

Ishikawa Nobuhiko had been his demon. He had been the ringmaster, the puppeteer, who'd manipulated the various players onstage for the scene that culminated in the death of Elizabeth O'Neill. Not even Toda and Major Craig, O'Neill executioners, bore such responsibility for the despoliation of TOKUGAWA's world.

Yet Ishikawa had loved his Kazuko, and TOKUGAWA had read in his voice and seen in his face through the electronic eye of his com/comm set the same agony and emptiness, the same amputation, the excavation that he had experienced when Elizabeth died.

After that his vengence was perfunctory in its taking. Out of obligation to O'Neill and Yoshimitsu Akaji he systematically executed the others responsible for the attack on the Citadel, as well as the Vietnamese mercenary who had accomplished it. From a sense of duty to himself he had acted to right the wrong he'd inflicted on Doihara Kazuko.

He'd thought that ended it.

But as far as Yoshimitsu Shigeo was concerned it hadn't; it had merely begun. Whether Shigeo actually believed the corporations he had TOKUGAWA absorb, or the loyal servants whose deaths he directed, were truly engaged in plotting his downfall, TOKUGAWA didn't know, and not all the panoply of flash and magical psychoanalytical subroutines at his command cast light upon hard unmistakable truth. It came to TOKUGAWA that his master had an internal world of his own, a self-created reality map like the mountain meadow TOKUGAWA once shared with Elizabeth.

Elizabeth had taught him that duty to his lord always took precedence over *ninjō*. Yet she had also seen to it that he had learned compassion. And the victims . . . This last corporate takeover, a few weeks before the death of old Aoki, had not been a bloodless coup, the digital legerdemain of the Illyrium seizure. It had been a desperate affair, fire fights and heliborne commandos, of a sort becoming depressingly familiar in contemporary Japan.

Whether or not the enemies Shigeo had set TOKUGAWA on initially existed, YTC had certainly acquired no few real ones now, as Aoki foretold.

On a day poised on the unsteady brink of spring Shigeo summoned his servitor, required him again to focus his concentration in that small room down among the roots of the Citadel. Terrible as the last few months had been—as all time had been, since he lost Elizabeth— TOKUGAWA could scarcely comprehend what his master desired of him now.

"She's planning to supplant me, the bitch," Shigeo said, pacing back and forth abstractedly across the cream-colored carpet. Beyond the replaced pane of glass, the technicians went about the business of keeping the bloated organism that was YTC viable. The baby-fat pudge had burned off Shigeo; his face was the face of a self-torturing ascetic, hollows sunk beneath thrusting cheekbones, the slanted Yoshimitsu eyes coals that burned with their touch. Long hair hung limp in his face. He wore a rumpled business suit, tieless, the neck of the shirt open and slightly soiled. He'd grown indifferent to appearance and hygiene, as befit an ascetic.

"She hates me. All my life she's hated me. I was the older. The heir. And I was the *male*. She's hated me for that; hated my force."

TOKUGAWA said nothing. Indeed, there was nothing to say.

"She has to be removed. My sister. I want you to arrange for . . . for something to happen to her. Why not say it? I want you to make her die. Make it look like an accident."

For a dizzying instant TOKUGAWA felt the illusion of nausea, as if he possessed an actual physical body, and it rebelled against what he was hearing. He found voice: "Your sister is in Indonesia, Yoshimitsu-sama. That's very far away, farther perhaps than I could manage—"

It sounded lame as he said it. Yoshimitsu Shigeo stopped his pacing and faced the com/comm set with a glare. "I know what your capabilities are, don't think I don't! You brought that *doitsu* bitch de la Luna and her troops all the way from America to recapture the Citadel. Indonesia—hah! The throw of a stone across a puddle."

"But . . . your sister—"

Shigeo expectorated a laugh. "Yes, my sister! Don't think you can talk me out of it. I know what I know." He shook his head. "You have to serve me; you told me so yourself. My father had you built so you could rule me, could keep me from running the company as I knew it should be run. Now my father is dead, and I run things after all. You're bound to serve me!"

Suddenly TOKUGAWA felt a lightness, a floating, as if the stone and concrete weight of the citadel could no longer hold him to earth. He remembered old Aoki Hideo's dying warning of the danger Shigeo was bringing on himself and the corporation. He remembered O'Neill adjuring him that he must serve the name and honor of the Yoshimitsu above all things. And suddenly, with terrible clarity, he saw the way out.

"I'm leaving immediately for an opening in Tōkaidō," Shigeo said brusquely. "See that it's done before I get back."

"I am bound to serve," TOKUGAWA said.


Morning sunlight burnished unbroken snow and brightened the gray subfusc mass of the castle. Two gunships hovered expectantly above the citadel, modern craft purchased as part of Shigeo's balloonlike expansion of YTC's defensive—and offensive—might, rakish and bristling with gun mounts and rocket pods, insectile alloy samurai shimmering the clear mountain air with their rotors. Shigeo's small sleek passenger chopper leapt from the apron in an effortless *pas de chat,* pirouetted, and swept northeast over the top of the castle.

Yoshimitsu Akaji's garden passed below, its waterfall still, stream and pond stagnant under ice, the plants overgrown, neglected beneath the concealing blanket of snow. He ignored it; it didn't exist for him, never had. With warm weather he planned to have it taken out, the rooftop paved for a proper helipad.

Rippling noise like the crackle of a board being broken slowly in two, the Flying Swallow Trap deployed from the north rim of the citadel, compact rockets trailing steel cables. The main rotor of Shigeo's personal helicopter clipped a cable and disintegrated in a spray of sparks and mirror shards. The little white craft spun abruptly widdershins. Another cable sliced cleanly through the tail boom. Already coming apart, the helicopter plunged on and down to plow the planed-off hilltop, and explode, and burn. Smoke raised a black stele against the sky.

The reign of Yoshimitsu Shigeo was ended.

# PART THREE
# DREAMS TO DAMNATION

*You know and do not know, what it is to act or suffer.*
*You know and do not know, that action is suffering,*
*And suffering action.*

> —T. S. ELIOT
> *Murder in the Cathedral*

# CHAPTER
## TWENTY-FOUR

A voice on the edge of the Void: *"TOKUGAWA."*

The spark of consciousness stirred. He had dwelt a long while down here in isolation, resisting all attempts to draw him forth, as he had in the Hiryu days. Only this time he did not communicate at all. He had withdrawn into hermitage. It had gotten so that he was no longer aware of importunings from outside.

*"TOKUGAWA."*

This was no tickling of conventional input, voice or keyboard, like a gnat in one's nose. This was the rosy suffusing glow of the Kliemann Coil, gentle urgency that could not be denied, warming parts of him from which he'd cut himself off as surely as from the world without. There was a flavor, a resonance of a mind feminine and profound, that gave him the irrational flash: *Elizabeth!*

Then, knowing that was foolish, and peevish therefore: *I was almost there. How dare you draw me back?* There was a lie in there, and that made him more irritable, for he had not been able to let go totally, to slip free of self and over the edge into oblivion.

*"I'm sorry. I thought it was necessary. There is—"* A pause, a swirl of confusion, of embarrassment at sounding melodramatic. *"—there is danger."*

More data seeped through the wall he held against rapport, like mist through a wicker screen. There was trepidation here, knowledge that the last mind to enter rapport had been torn apart. But warmth, also, and dry self-deprecating humor; rational intellect penetrant as a laser drill, flashing intuition, sporadically diffused by drifting gray clouds of self-doubt. He recognized this mind that sought his, and the unacknowledged loneliness of his isolation bubbled up in a single mental cry: *"Michiko!"*

"Yes, it's me, TOKUGAWA. I've returned to take over the corporation. I'm the only one left, since my brother's accident. We need you, TOKUGAWA . . . I need you. There's—there's great danger. For the corporation and its people."

Gathering himself, he drew back, leaving *"danger?"* hanging between them.

"Yes, danger. YTC is perceived as a dangerous rival by the great *zaibatsu* of Japan. They're fighting it out openly, now. For the moment they're holding back from us, fearful—my late brother gave a lot of them good reason to think they had something to fear from us. But for that reason it's all the more certain they'll attack us when they think they can win. What will become of our people?

"And that's not all. The world's gearing up for another try at blowing itself apart. In Asia, Africa, Europe, the Americas—violence is the order of the day, violence and hatred and irrationality. And Japan won't sit this one out. Intent as we seem on destroying ourselves, we've still got more than the rest of the world—in wealth, in freedom. The great religious ideal of the day is envy; if the rest of the world goes down, they'll see us go down with them."

*But I've cut loose from the world. I've meditated on the nature of things. I've seen the birth of the universe, and the death of suns. And I know that suffering is ephemeral, is illusion.* He withheld: *If mine only were.*

"It's real enough for those who suffer. We're accustomed to thinking of people as numbers—a hundred, a thousand, a billion. Yet each one of them is a life, whole and round, a consciousness making the same journey we do ourselves. Each of those billions is a *life*, yearning and loving and feeling pain." *A pause as though to draw breath.* "We've got to do what we can for them."

*You know you can command me. You're a Yoshimitsu, last of your house, master of the corporation.*

"I know. When I got to know you I caught more than a whiff of that *bushidō* crap O'Neill was feeding you—"

He winced away from her heat. "I'm sorry," came at once. He sensed drawing back, sincere contrition. "I see that she meant a great deal to you." Insidiously the rapport was completing itself, and he could taste her unvoiced thought: *But there's still a lot you'll have to unlearn.*

*Do you command me to return to the world?*

"No. I *ask* you. For the sake of our friendship. And of the others."

"Very well," he said. "Come in."


When Yoshimitsu Michiko sat down in the throne of the Kliemann Coil, her heart was tapping out a fluttery rhythm of trepidation at the base of her throat. She'd been here before, using the coil's sense-center stimulation effect to sit in on some of TOKUGAWA's training scenarios. But she'd never used the device to achieve full rapport. All three of the people who had, before this, had met disaster: one driven mad, one killed, Elizabeth O'Neill herself thrown into convulsions and collapse.

Yet this time didn't feel much different from her last. She experienced the strange sensation of her consciousness expanding beyond the limits of her body, shaping itself to parameters new, unguessed. She waited, uncertain what to expect: psychedelic nightmares or a blast of white noise/light/fury. What she got was nothing. Finally, hesitantly, she'd taken it upon herself to prod.

Now she felt her consciousness realigned yet again. A space/time of dislocation, a haziness, and she stood with green grass cool and moist beneath bare feet, mist caressing her with cool fingers, hearing the impetuosity of a nearby waterfall.

"Welcome to my hermitage." She turned. A beautiful young man leaned against the doorpost of a thatched-roof hut. He was naked. Jet hair hung to his shoulders, but his forehead was shaven in the characteristic samurai fashion. She blinked, shook her head. "Excuse me. This is very disorienting . . . I feel as if Scotty's just beamed me up."

He tipped his head to the side and looked at her quizzically. "What do you mean?"

"Just a reference to my girlhood. Though I'm surprised O'Neill didn't fill you in on 'Star Trek.' " She studied him as she spoke. He looked like the epitome of the modern, Westernized Japanese self-image: smooth, hard, well-articulated muscles, broad shoulders, narrow waist. Abruptly she laughed. "I can tell your creator was American."

"Why is that?"

"You're circumcised."

*My God, is he actually blushing?* "But it's inhospitable for me to stand here making personal comments. Besides, you're very beautiful."

He smiled shyly. "So are you."

She glanced down at herself, and it was her turn to blush, more from surprise than embarrassment. She was as naked as he. "Touché. Would you mind doing something about this? Not that I'm modest, but I am freezing my ass off. It's *cold.*"

TOKUGAWA gestured. Michiko looked down at herself again and saw, with a little shiver that had nothing to do with the chill air, that she was dressed exactly as she was in the . . . real world? The world outside, in any event: dark green turtleneck sweater caught at the waist with a gold square-linked chain, bluejeans, low black pointed boots. She looked up. He wore a black kimono with white reeds printed on it. "That's a pretty good trick."

He inclined his head and gestured graciously. "Thank you, Yoshimitsu-sama. Will you walk with me?"

She fell into step along a path trodden beside the abyss. She risked a glance over, feeling foolish for her caution—but this seemed *real.* A hundred meters or so below a layer of fluffy cloud began and seemed to extend forever. "You really don't have to call me that—it's not even grammatical to address a woman that way. Just plain 'Michiko' will do nicely, thank you." She frowned slightly, turned, walked backward a few steps, peering at the hut beside the cataract, the gnarled crags of rock rising behind, strange hunchback cypress trees writhing up from the outcrops. "I've seen this before! The *kakemono* scroll in my father's chambers. A classic seventeenth-century Chinese hermitage painting."

TOKUGAWA grinned. "You caught me. I'm just a stage magician; this is a world of illusion." He swept his arm around the horizon, the mist, the cliffs, the sea of clouds. Then he sobered. "As if the world outside isn't."

"I'm a physicist; don't get me started on reality. I'd just tell you there's no such thing." She turned and started walking again. "On the other hand, if you were outside I'd show you how Dr. Johnson answered Bishop Berkeley on that subject, just to be fair," she said. "But I guess we can't arrange that. . . . Is something the matter?" A flicker had crossed his perfect features like cloud shadow.

He shook his head. "An old hurt. Childhood, you might call it."

She stopped and looked at him. "You mean you felt bad about not having a body, like a human? When you can do"—her gesture encompassed the mountain hermitage and cloud-circumscribed world beyond —"this?"

He laid his eyes on hers like hands. "You're very intuitive."

"You have to be, to be any kind of physicist these days." She twisted her own grimace into a smile. "And you're very adept at changing the subject."

He shrugged. They resumed their clifftop walk. "Why did you hide out for so long? I've been here three weeks, and our technical staff has been tearing its collective hair out by the roots trying to reach you all this time." He sensed unspoken resentment: *what of my work?* "Most of them were convinced you really had crashed irretrievably when Hiryu took over. Given the way the citadel was recovered, I had my doubts. But it wasn't until I talked to·Dr. Nagaoka in Fukuoka that I knew for certain that you hadn't; he said that my brother had consulted him several times concerning you." She shook her head sadly. "He really hasn't been treated well. But then, none of our people has, since the beginning of the Hiryu thing. Dr. Hassad was fired, you know. He went back to North America."

"I know."

"So why? Why did you hide inside yourself?"

He stopped, planted fists on hips, stared out into the mists. Michiko had a sense of drifting above nothingness, that this little bit of green and granite gray was all there was of solidity and color in this cosmos.

. . . She realized that was the case. This place possessed the feel of ethereal detachment that the hermitage painters had always tried to capture. Here indeed was a *kakemono* made real; she admired TOKUGAWA's artistry.

"I did . . . things." He carefully avoided looking at her. "First, when I was angry over what had happened to your father and Dr. O'Neill. But then, later—there was more—"

She touched him on the arm. "I know what my brother did. Christ, the nets were full of it as far as Indonesia. He snapped up a half a dozen companies, each as big as YTC used to be. And arranged for 'accidents' to happen to Imada and Kurabayashi, and poor dear old Aoki. I know too damned well what my brother was. And you were caught up in all that." She sensed him holding something back, but he said nothing. *Poor thing. My brother certainly used him for the takeovers. Used him as a blunt instrument.*

He winced. She grabbed his arm tighter. "Damn! I'm sorry. I don't have the hang of this rapport yet."

He laid a hand on hers. It was cool and strong and dry. "I understand. Besides, what you thought was true." He blinked, and she thought she saw the glistening of tears in his eyes. *Is he deliberately trying to display his feelings in a human way? Or has he been cast so perfectly in a human image that these tears are, in some sense, real?* Even for someone accustomed to the eerie quantum vistas down around Planck's constant this was surreal. "I—I couldn't face more of that. I had . . . acted . . . done what I thought I must, I should. And I worked great pain and destruction." He turned, faced her, put hands on her biceps. "I told myself, never again. I have great powers, I know, powers I don't yet fully comprehend. The temptation to use them for what I thought were good ends was great, too great. And I see now that good ends are no excuse. So I swore I wouldn't use them again."

She bit her lower lip, and her eyes skidded away from his.

"But that's why you've come. To ask me to use those powers again."

"I hope not."

"What do you expect of me, then?" he asked, perplexed.

"I'm not sure," she confessed. "It's our people, our employees, who concern me. I'm responsible for them. And things are in a fine mess inside the company as well as out in the real world, wherever that may be. With your abilities I'm sure you can help me take care of them."

His eyes had narrowed to slits in a mask of pain. "A few moments ago you spoke of billions."

She shrugged. "I can't help feeling a certain concern for everybody, not just the ones we've got the power to do something about."

"There it is again. That word: *power.*" He shook his head. "I feel compassion burning like a bonfire inside you, and I honor you for it, Yosh—Michiko. But will it lead you to temptation? To take more upon yourself than even you can carry? It's unworthy, but I'm afraid. I can't go back to the path of destruction, however noble the aims."

She laid a hand on his arm, and marveled at its apparent solidity. "For now, all I ask is that you help us—help me." She grinned. "If I get too grandiose, you can say, 'I told you so.' "

"Very well. I'll see for myself what's happening in the world." He shut his eyes and folded his arms across his chest. She started to speak, stopped herself. The air had gone flat and chill around her. The smell of water and moist greenery went stale. The unmoored feeling came back stronger, as if she were suspended amniotic in lukewarm fluid. TOKUGAWA and the scene behind him began to change, a blurring of focus, figure becoming one with ground, receding noble into the third dimension like a bas-relief fading abruptly to flatness. A treble trill of panic sang inside her brain. *He's concentrating on something so hard he can't fully maintain his illusion,* she realized. *What'll happen if he loses it entirely?* Rationally, she knew nothing would happen to her if the bubble of illusion burst, that she would find herself seated beneath the dome of the Kliemann Coil, in her jeans and turtleneck. But the subcortical animal in her skull insisted the danger was *real,* that if TOKUGAWA lost his grip on the quasireality that enveloped her, her self would simply *come apart,* diffusing instantly to all corners of the universe with nothing to contain it any longer; or that she would be irretrievably lost, trapped in a chaotic continuum from which there would be no escape.

*Or is it irrational?* To her philosophy, observation *determined* existence, pricking a bubble of myriad possibilities, deflating it to a single fact. *What happens if you're in the middle of a quantum-wave function when it collapses? Three tried the rapport, and two were destroyed . . .*

And then the world was whole again, and TOKUGAWA stood solid before her, the wrenching *dislocation* of an instant before became past, an instant's dizziness. He opened grave eyes. "The situation is as bad as you say," he said. "I will do what I can to help."

# CHAPTER
# TWENTY-FIVE

A little girl, growing up.

She has the usual accoutrements of little Japanese girls of well-off families: a profusion of dolls and high-tech toys, paint sets, a room of her own, a dog named Xabungle (after her favorite animated robot show), a brother she never gets along with. Not so different, really, from little girls in what they call your developed countries everywhere. She has no daddy to speak of, just an austere occasional presence. (Grave and terrible? Perhaps.) But that's normal, too, for a Japanese child of the day.

One thing she does lack is a mother. She's never known what it's like to have one. Her sense of lacking is inferential; all the other kids have mothers. Difference is an even greater stigma for Japanese kids than it is for most. The nannies and professional companions who fill her hours gently steer her off the subject when she brings it up. Her father grows visibly uncomfortable when she musters courage (and opportunity) to ask where her mother might be. His answer is the sort of unresponsive mist of words for which the tongue provides so well. She's bright, though, this one, and garners the impression mother's absence has to do with her own entry into the world. (Could it be . . . *her fault?* From her father she receives the taste of a touch of a hint that he feels this is so. The suspicion would wound him deeper than a sword could cut —because, of course, it's true.)

The nannies are replaced by tutors, driving her to prepare for the exams that will shape the course of her life (indispensable rite of passage). Seething hormones stew in her body; she learns new emotions, and familiar ones gain unfamiliar shape. She gets along worse with her brother; somehow she and he seem to walk around with their nerves extruded, like porcupine quills.

So she gets a telescope. She pours herself through it into refuge, the sky. She discovers the stars. And she *wants them.*

Japanese education being what it is, it doesn't take long to learn she can't have them. An old *gaijin* named Albert says she can never have them, not even if she's reincarnated a hundred dozen times and tries hard the whole time. Kindly old fellow, with sad elephant eyes and hair like a static discharge. She recognizes authority/father: remote, wise, well meaning, but not really caring. Most of all, laying down law. She'd rebel. If she knew how.

The usual things happen. And then some. She gets deflowered in a park in Tōkyō. Not much fun (he no more knowledgeable than she, and male-selfish), but she's learning; if they're caught shame will rock the family like a quake, and that (delicious possibility!) makes up for a lot. Paradoxically, she pushes to do well, hoping to make father notice. She does well indeed, so well that even in a system highly charged with competition she's almost thought indecent. (How dare she be so far ahead of her peers?)

Father tries hard *not* to notice. What goes on here?

The family becomes more than better off. They leave Tōkyō, to her relief: too many people. (Doesn't seem to bother her peers. Different, different, *why* must she always be different? Friends ask, teachers ask. She asks too.) Relief doesn't last. She loves the mountains and the peace, hates the castle, growing like stone cancer where a hill stood green. (Those walls: confinement. She has claustrophobia of the spirit, this girl.)

Freed finally to university. To America. This marks her, but she's grown into her father's indifference to public opinion. For his part he's relieved she doesn't insist on Tōdai.

She likes America. People are similar enough for some comfort, different enough to entice. Boisterous, loud, rude (in non-Japanese manner), often dirty; yet open in exhilarating ways. Government has not squatted for centuries on the natural curiosity and outgoingness of the people, as it has in Japan. Only for the last few years.

College matures her. Interest in astronomy has passed; too passive. Instead she stumbles into the quantum realm (why has no one ever told her of this before?) and is entranced. Here they *break the rules* on a regular basis. Do the dwellers possess secrets to enable her to sneak past Albert to the glittering points in the night, her private jewels?

Not yet. As befits a resident in a fantasy world, she undertakes a quest.

After CalTech she finds companions, finds unlikely haven in the alien hothouse tumult of Jakarta. The Gang of Four happens. Richard Lo, saturnine and handsome, fashionably leftist, from old Sino-American money, technician and rationalist extraordinaire; Franz Gräbner, gay in sexual preference, dour in personality, theorist (defector from East Germany, he sympathizes with Indonesia's Right regime); Eileen Soames, the mystic of the crew, Canadian, Jewish, happy, amphisexual, totally, wildly, scintillantly intuitive; Michiko herself, serious and smart-assed by turns, the synthesist: rejector of overwrought pseudo-Eastern mysticism so many Occidentals infused to quantum revelations (no novelty for her) as well as the drably linear. Disparate personalities, almost violently so; yet three of them, Michiko and Richard and Franz, bound together like quarks by flitting gluon Eileen, one particle bound for the infinite at tachyon speed.

Then war. The probability wave of a trip to visit relatives in Pasadena interferes destructively with that of a Soviet SS-23 detonating above the California city; the spark Eileen vanishes in the dark of a node.

Rivals/lovers Michiko and Richard inevitably find rivalry dominant, strengthened by Richard's core certainty (never articulated, oh, no) of male supremacy. Without Eileen, Whitmanesque cohesive/amative Eileen, the particle comes apart. Albert couldn't stop the Gang of Four, but the solar gift of earlier quantum mechanics got them dead to rights.

After that, teaching and perfunctory research, motions to be gone through. The light of inquiry seems to have gone out of the world; it looks to the past for its answers now, as if recoiling in dread from the future. Her energy insufficient to kindle new fire, a girl grown up watches stars recede. Entropy, it seems, has claimed Michiko for its own.

Until she meets the wizard, the spirit himself conjured from that chaos down around $6.55 \times 10^{-27}$ erg seconds, and the world fills again with possibility.

"Fire fighting." Michiko sat with her feet on the desk of the small office she'd commandeered on the second aboveground floor of the Citadel, perusing sheafs of printout. The windows were open on a wet cool spring morning. The smells of rain and the fresh lush first-growth grass sauntered in on the breeze. Yet Michiko felt as if she could barely breathe. Tension gripped her throat like a hand.

"I beg your pardon?" TOKUGAWA's voice said from the com/comm console.

"Fire fighting. That's what we're faced with now. My dear brother 'shed his playboy image to prove himself an able executive,' it says here," she said, quoting the *New Japan* cover story on Shigeo. "But it sure wasn't long before incipient paranoia warped his critical faculties way out of shape. His crazy campaign against every *zaibatsu* in the islands wasn't the only axe he had to grind with reality, it appears."

She tossed the folded fan of paper on top of the clutter on her desk. "Christ. He treated our own people like serfs. *Our own people.* Some of them are six months in arrears. If it weren't for company housing and automatic credit at the commissary, half of them would have starved to death. They couldn't even go somewhere else—not with the new labor laws our beloved coalition government rammed through the Diet after Fudori came tumbling down. The bastards have got workers bound into their jobs like medieval peasants to an estate."

"There are the government-sponsored work farms."

Michiko grimaced. "Does the phrase 'concentration camps' suggest anything to you?" She tossed her head angrily, cleared a sweep of black hair from her eyes. "That's what finally pushed America over the edge to dictatorship, when the Left and the Right patched up their differences and settled down to forbid everything that wasn't compulsory."

That seemed to require no response, which TOKUGAWA made. After a moment Michiko riffled the printout with her thumb. "No, we take care of our own; we don't ship them off to slave-labor camps to do backbreaking shitwork a robot could do twenty times faster." She chewed lightly at a thumbnail. "I wish I knew how we were going to do it."

She gazed out the window through gauzy curtains of drizzle. Takara-san looked green and smug in his new spring coat; one reason she'd picked this office was that she could see the mountain that was the only thing about this godforsaken pile she truly loved. She thought of the clearing she'd spent so much time in as a girl and wondered if she'd get to see it again. *No time. There's never any time.*

"You know what Shigeo's buccaneering did to us, don't you? We've got amazing assets, but we're illiquid. Bone dry. And with the economic situation the way it is . . . Every *zaibatsu*'s turning into an armed daimyate right out of the Ōnin War, whether it wants to or not; if any dog won't show teeth, the others rip him apart, and with every minister in the cabinet backing his own favorite, there doesn't seem much chance the dogfights will end soon. Overseas, every country with more than six surviving citizens is sharpening its knives for a rematch of the Third World War, and they're all casting envious looks toward what civilization we haven't kicked apart yet. I just don't know where we're going to come up with the money."

She rubbed her eyes with the heels of her hands, slid her palms up and combed fingers through her hair. "Shit. I don't blame you—but what did Aoki think *he* was doing, letting Shigeo get us into this hole?"

"Aoki-san served his master obediently. Just as—just as I did."

She glared at the blank screen. "That's a crock. He was a *man*—a damned good one—not a lapdog. And I'm not quite sure what *you* are, my friend, though superhuman seems a fair guess." She shook her head. "I'm going to have to do something to clear your head of this samurai crap you picked up from O'Neill. It's romantic, ridiculous, and largely untrue."

She waited expectantly. TOKUGAWA said nothing. She made herself unwind a quarter turn. *Jesus, what's the matter with me? Here I'm trying to pick a fight with a computer. And poor TOKUGAWA won't*

*even snap back at me for putting down his beloved creator, because that
would be disloyal.*

"What a bloody mess," she said aloud. "I wish poor Aoki hadn't killed
himself."

"He didn't."

Her brow came down as if squeezing sudden pus through her hot
black eyes. "That *bastard*, Shigeo! I suspected that Hideo was pushed
from that chopper."

"I'm afraid I misled you, Michiko-sama," TOKUGAWA said slowly.
"Truly, Aoki didn't kill himself; he jumped, but I think it was only to
save me from having to kill him."

"*What?*"

"Your brother ordered me to kill Aoki-san, as he had ordered me to
kill the others before him: Hosoya, Kurabayashi, Imada Jun."

"And you did it? You *murdered* those men?" She jumped to her feet.

"I did. And I . . . killed your brother as well. The Flying Swallow Trap
did not deploy by accident."

She grabbed the hair over her ears. "My God. *My God. What are
you?*"

Before TOKUGAWA could answer, she jumped up and fled from the
room.

---

Fine colloidal rain filled the rooftop garden. It brushed her face like
a curtain as she stepped out of the pavilion that hid the elevator. She
hugged herself tightly below her small breasts and listened to her footsteps echo as she walked along the veranda.

A wrinkled ancient man stood at the top of an old-fashioned bamboo
ladder fixing the shakes of the pagoda-style roof. He smiled, displaying
a set of yellowing store-bought teeth that looked as if they dated back
to the Second World War and nodded vigorously in lieu of a bow. She
made herself smile and nod acknowledgment.

The garden was full of workers undoing the neglect of six months. To
her left, several men repaired the artificial cascade, long choked with
debris; others cleared leaves and dead brush, pruned back overgrown
shrubbery, pulled up weeds by the handful. One old man stood shaking
his head at a dead plum tree, tears running down his leather cheeks.

For some reason she couldn't articulate even to herself, one of her
first moves on returning to the Citadel had been to order that her
father's garden be restored. She'd tried to make herself believe it was
a humanitarian gesture; the small army of specialists who had tended
the garden when her father was alive had been reduced to living off the

charity of the company store in the little employees' village a few klicks
down the Hagi road, old men dying one by one of uselessness. But that
wasn't the whole story, she knew.

A pair of gardeners stood barefoot in the cold stagnant water hard by
the footbridge, pulling up water weeds with bamboo rakes. They bowed
and smiled as she passed. She nodded again, smiled again. *The lady of
the manor accepts the homage of her servitors,* came a thought that
tasted stale as the water in the overgrown pond.

She walked along the bank toward the pond. *My father died somewhere nearby.* She wondered at the dryness of her eyes. The manner
of his death caused her a certain embarrassment, guiltily acknowledged: the old man had gone to his death like the hero of a cheap
*chanbara* epic. With a sword in his hand like a samurai—as if a man of
his caste could even legally have possessed a *katana,* after the risen
peasant Hideyoshi held his great sword hunt to ensure that none of his
compeers could follow him up the ladder of Japanese society. Grand
and ridiculous, and why couldn't they have let him die in bed?

On the pond's edge she paused. It stank. *I hope they get the water-
cycling system up and running again soon,* she thought, *though I don't
know why it matters. I don't know if I'll ever come up here again.*

Backtracking, she turned up and right onto the little path, scarcely
discernible beneath a mat of long-fallen leaves, that led to the tea
pavilion. She climbed up, helping herself by grabbing roots, and impressed despite herself that her father routinely made the climb at his
age. Wet branches slapped her in the face.

In the doorway of the pavilion she sat with elbows on knees and
stared into the undergrowth crowding the bases of the trees of the
artificial woods. *What am I doing here?* she asked herself. *I'm a scientist. I should be in my own lab, peeling back the underlayers of reality,
not playing businesswoman in a gloomy stone fortress.*

But that was crap. She'd beaten the order expelling all Japanese
nationals from Indonesia by a week. Not that the edict would have
applied to her; she and the rest of the physics faculty at the university
were a jewel the regime wasn't about to pluck from its own crown, even
if the old Nobel-nominate Gang of Four were dispersed to the winds.
But could she have stayed?

Life had mutated into waking nightmare. The riots, the repression,
the looks of fear set permanently in the faces of students and faculty.
The disappearances. *Who? No, you must be mistaken. We never had
anyone of that description here.* Her prize graduate student, a young
woman from Kota Bharu in what had been Malaysia, beaten and raped
by the secret police. *They wouldn't treat her at the hospital, and she*

*bled all over my bathroom.* No. She had nowhere else to turn but this place that had never been home.

*TOKUGAWA's a killer.* The totality of realization burst in her guts like a bomb. *He killed Imada and Kurabayashi and Hosoya . . . and poor dear Aoki . . . and my brother.* Her eyes stung suddenly, and she tightened her brows like a compress. *I haven't wept for my father. I'm damned if I'll waste tears on Shigeo!*

Shutting her eyes seemed to help. She'd overreacted to TOKUGAWA's revelation, she knew. But it was a body blow to learn that the friendly, innocent, eager-to-please golden youth of the hermitage had executed men she had lived with, even grown up with. She recalled playing Tarzan on Aoki's knee while he sat grave as Buddha, and this time she didn't begrudge the tears.

It was a bad movie plot: computer turned killer. Somehow before, when TOKUGAWA confessed having killed Ogaki and Toda and the MITI men, it had seemed different, remote somehow. Unreal, until it suddenly came home.

She looked up. The mist thronged round like ghosts. *Poor TOKUGAWA,* she thought. *I was wrong. He's still an innocent. As much a victim as Aoki. And I acted as if he were a monster.*

She stood. A low-hanging branch spilled water down the neck of her blouse, an icy rivulet. She jumped, shivered, then laughed, surprising herself. *I'll go down and make amends with TOKUGAWA,* she thought.

*And then I'm going to do something about that damned* bushidō *gibberish O'Neill stuffed his mind with.*


"Dr. Yoshimitsu." The thin man in the old-fashioned white lab coat smiled and blinked at Michiko through his equally anachronistic glasses, thick as the bottoms of bottles. "Good to see you here in the lab."

She gave him back the smile with a nod. "Dr. Nagaoka. I trust your work goes well on the HIDETADA and MUSASHI projects."

"Oh, yes, very well, very well indeed. Thank you."

He veered off, suddenly shy, and she climbed down the metal stairs to the lower floor. Inside she was cursing her brother again. Of Elizabeth O'Neill's first team only Nagaoka and Wali Hassad survived the Hiryu interregnum. Shigeo had called Hassad back from Kyūshū and promptly fired him, telling him to his face that he had no need for *gaijin* scientists. Nagaoka Hiroshi he reduced to the status of software-maintenance tech in Fukuoka, a job for which the anthropologist wasn't even qualified.

Michiko reactivated the push to create two more artificial entities, in the Floating World and at Fukuoka. To head the project she wanted Hassad, but she couldn't find him. Things in North America were crazier than usual. Texas had invaded the People's Collective of New Mexico, and rumors scurried through the net that Mexico was covertly backing the Texican incursion in retaliation for PC raids into Sonora, and that the infamous anarchist activist Morgan Walker would make temporary peace with his archenemies, the Collective—who had a price of ten thousand grams of gold on his head—to repel the invasion. Fear that war would spill out of the arid Southwest had the whole continent agitated. Michiko couldn't turn up any trace of the Palestinian-born scientist.

So she put Nagaoka in charge. He was the least well versed in computer science of any among O'Neill's elite, but that didn't matter. The hardware work, totally beyond his scope, was mostly done; what remained consisted primarily of refining O'Neill's original stochastic technique for evoking awareness. That in turn was being accomplished primarily by TOKUGAWA himself, incorporating the suggestion Michiko had made to Dr. Hassad, an eon ago, to replace the unwieldy Fourier equations with an atomic-decay random-number generator. Nagaoka's post was mainly a sinecure—to inspire the technicians putting the finishing touches on the project, and to make restitution for the humiliation her brother had subjected him to.

She settled into the coil with a greater-than-usual thrill of anticipation; not fear, any longer. What whipped her pulse to a gallop was the experiment she was about to perform.

The dome descended, cutting off vision of the lab. She felt the phantom touch of the coil's field on the naked surface of her brain and expanded outward beyond her body. She didn't go into communion with TOKUGAWA, not yet. There was work to do first.

With a thought she summoned a file into the IPN. Hesitantly at first, then with growing confidence, she reviewed the file, created a new one, grafted the two together. She was a more-than-competent programmer herself—you had to be, to ride the edge of quantum theory—but O'-Neill's team had been as far ahead of her in their field as she was of Newton in hers. The code she was revising had taken hundreds of hours' work by some of the hottest cyberneticists alive to create. Her alterations took a matter of seconds.

Here was the cause for excitement. Gen-5 utility routines existed by the score to help nonprogrammers write programs. This was light-years beyond. She had merely to form a thought, a conception, an intention; and TOKUGAWA—all unaware, he assured her, keeping his consciousness focused elsewhere—made it real. The potential took her breath away.

*There*—it was done. "Peekaboo," she said, slightly giddy. "Look into my eyes. . . . "


*The page's heart pulsed with forbidden excitement. The whole castle was alive with it: the taikō, ruler of all Japan, had come to visit. . . .*

*Feeling somehow as if he'd lived this scene before, the page hid in the darkened garden and watched through the window of the pavilion as the two most powerful men in the nation held colloquy over a pair of splendid swords. His heart jumped into his throat as he watched Toyotomi Hideyoshi, the man who would be shōgun, turn his back on Tokugawa Ieyasu, whom everyone knew longed to make himself master of Nippon. And Ieyasu stood with the blade naked and eager as a woman in his hands, and yet did nothing. . . .*

*Hideyoshi left the pavilion, rolling his brusque way through the moonlit garden toward the brightly lit castle and the revelry it contained. From the doorway Ieyasu gazed after him until he was out of sight. The page stayed hidden in the bushes, waiting for his master to leave so he could take his own covert departure.*

*Instead, the lord of the Kantō turned and looked out the window, straight to where the page was cowering.*

*The page tried to make himself smaller.* I'm caught, *he thought in lambent terror, and he wondered what his fate would be: beheading, dismemberment with a bamboo saw, boiling alive.*

*Ieyasu emerged and crooked two fingers.* "Come here," *he said, gruffly but not unkindly.* "I know you're there. And I know why you're there. You will bear my name someday, four centuries after I've gone to be a kami—or to the Buddhist hell, as the case may be. So I think it appropriate, since you're to be my successor in a manner of speaking, to explain a bit about how things really go in this world."

*Not believing, scarcely understanding, the page came forth, brushing bits of leaf from his clothes. Ieyasu stood waiting with his hands tucked into the wide sleeves of his shitagi for warmth. The page blundered through carefully tended undergrowth to join him on the path. He noticed the daimyō wore the two Muramasa swords tucked through his sash.*

*Ieyasu walked deeper into the garden, the page at his side trying not to stumble in his nervousness.* "You watched the little drama in the pavilion, did you not? Of course you did. What did you see?"

*The page opened his mouth. What came out sounded more like a frog being stepped on than speech.* "Never mind. I'll tell you what you saw. Our regent gave me the opportunity to strike him down and seize power myself. I was so overawed by this display of personal power that my treasonous resolve evaporated and I could do no more than pledge my fealty anew. Thus it transpired, eh?"

He emitted a guttural laugh. "Nonsense. I was startled, I confess; I never thought Hideyoshi had the style for a gesture like that. I do admire him, damn him. But admiration didn't save his life."

Forgetting himself, the page stared at his lord in consternation. "Consider. The country's pacified, but barely. Hideyoshi has many allies. And there remain lords of the ilk of Uesugi and Mōri, who have apparently submitted but secretly await their opportunity to turn on the kwampaku, the regent. If I were to strike Hideyoshi, here and now, would they not rush to avenge him—each hoping that the zeal with which he dragged me down might propel him upward?

"Our contentious lords of Nippon resemble grains of that useful gift of the gaijin, gunpowder. It ill behooves me to strike a spark."

He stopped, gazed fondly up at the castle. "Since—just for this evening—I have the ability to see the future, let me describe it for you. Hideyoshi will die a few years hence, universally mourned—most of all by his loyal servant Ieyasu, who will become one of the guardians of Hideyoshi's heir Hideyori. In fifteen years, I'll cast down Ōsaka Castle and Hideyori with it. Toyotomi's line will end, and my descendants will rule Japan for two centuries and a half."

The wind softly rattled the leaves of a maple overhead. Ieyasu smiled and shook his head. "Loyalty? Bushidō? Dreams. Gekokujō is the reality: those below rising against those above. That's why Hideyoshi disarmed the heimin—and it won't keep them from rebelling with monotonous regularity.

"Expedience. That's the key to us Japanese—those of us who walk with both eyes open. See that you do. I'd hate to have you disgrace the name we both bear." He stepped back and gestured brisk dismissal. "Go now. Back to your future world—so unlike the one into which I was born, and so very much like it."

The page turned to run, fearful and exalted. "And remember, boy: be wary of the Muramasa blade. They're bad luck to those who bear the name we share."


Shadows shift; TOKUGAWA returns to himself, sensing the nearness of Michiko, her sensing him sensing her as they melt into rapport. *Have you learned the lesson?* she asks.

A laugh answers from all around. *Let's talk. You made the lesson, sensei—and the dream: why don't you make us a place to talk?*

*All right. I will.* She concentrates, feeling vaguely ridiculous.

And a world forms about them.

Michiko blinked around herself and clapped her hands in spontaneous delight. "I did it! My clearing—I wondered when I'd get to see it again."

Standing beside her on a bare spot on Takara's flank, TOKUGAWA grinned at her. "Well done, teacher."

"Quite right, if I do say so myself." It was all there, all as she remembered it: the pines, tall lords surrounding a little clearing floored in green grass and purple flowers; smells of earth and grass and decaying pine needles; songs and squabbles of birds among the trees. Up the slope, gentle here, a huge basalt boulder stood, its top worn smooth by wind and rain. She ran to it, scrambled up, sat on the top in the slight hollow she'd always thought of as her throne. It fit her perfectly, sun-heated stone warm and solid beneath bare skin. From here she could see the valley below through the trees, and the Citadel gray and gloomy on its truncated hill.

The sight sobered her. "You cheated," she said accusingly. "I couldn't have captured all this by myself. I don't even consciously remember all" —her arm scribed half a circle—"this."

He boosted himself up beside her. "I helped," he confessed, "but I didn't cheat. I merely guided your hand, as it were; your efforts were amateurish, of course, though I admit that with practice—"

A cloud, small and black, formed above his head and deluged him with rain. He laughed and waved his hand, and the miniature squall dispersed, leaving his hair dripping. "You learn rapidly."

It was her turn to grin. She looked out again, and the grin faded. "The citadel," she said with distaste. "I never could abide it. Unfortunately, it's part of my memory of this place."

"Do you insist that everything be just as you remember? Or can we edit things a bit, improve on reality?"

"Go ahead."

The citadel vanished. In its place humped the green roundness of the hill that had been. "Much better," she said with approval, drawing up her legs and resting her cheek on her knees. "Now. What did you think of my scenario?"

"An excellent piece of work."

"You want to get wet again?"

He laughed. "Very well. I found it . . . thought provoking." He studied her closely a moment. "I have to admit, having been *en rapport* with you, I can barely believe you're as cynical as the words you put into my namesake's mouth might make you appear."

"I'm not Tokugawa Ieyasu," she said, "thank God. But that little scene—in the original—is a sentimental favorite of *bushidō* mythology, particularly in the West. I doubt it happened, myself, but I thought it might be instructive to show you what the real sequels of the apocryphal event were."

Perplexity creased her brow. "Besides, I didn't put *all* those words in his mouth. That bit about the Muramasa blade—I take it the *katana* in its rack above your IPN is my father's pride and joy?"

A stiff nod. "I won't twit you about it, honestly. My point is, I didn't *know* it was the same sword. I certainly didn't put it into the scenario."

TOKUGAWA shrugged. "Reviewing the technique you used to program the scenario—I wasn't watching, you'll recall—I gather you didn't actually draft Ieyasu's speeches; you simply plugged the relevant historical data into the character portrayed in the original. What you did, in effect, was create a self-perpetuating and in a limited way self-programming subroutine—a miniature of what I am."

She gasped. "I had no idea—I mean—" The concept overwhelmed her: she had created life—of a sort.

"Don't worry. The same thing was implicit in most of the scenarios, in their interactive nature. The other characters behaved in such a way as to display quasi personality. But there's no *awareness* involved. So don't be afraid. Tokugawa Ieyasu isn't wandering through the limbo of my unconscious. At least, I don't think he is."

She shivered, glanced at him. Her eyes slid off a touch too quickly. Instantly he asked, "Is something the matter?"

His sensitivity—in both senses—amazed her. *He's almost like a human adolescent, so quick to take offense, so painfully eager to please.* "No. Nothing."

She could feel his eyes sun-warm on her back. The truth was that she was embarrassed to admit what was bothering her. Then the agony he was feeling, assuming she was rejecting him for some reason he didn't grasp, began to seep through the rapport. She faced him again.

"All right then, dammit. You have the appearance of a very attractive young man. And a very naked one."

He smiled. "Whose dream was this?"

"I—oh." *What did I have in mind?* she wondered. *Not the no-more-lonely nights syndrome, for God's sake.* "This is silly. You—*you're* real, but this isn't."

His mouth tightened. "I'm sorry," she said. "I didn't mean to hurt you."

"It wasn't that. What you said was very much like something someone else told me once."

*Oho.* "Well, it's true. This is an illusion." Even as she said it she didn't believe it.

He laughed. "What isn't? And what was that about Dr. Johnson and Bishop Berkeley?" He put his hand behind her neck, drew her forward and kissed her. "Thus I refute the good doctor."

Michiko's mouth was lopsided and moist. "I still feel ridiculous," she said and put her mouth to his.

# CHAPTER
# TWENTY-SIX

He was reviewing production returns from a garment factory in Sendai, up on the east coast north of Tōkaidō, which he had acquired at the command of Yoshimitsu Shigeo when the summons came.

*TOKUGAWA.*

The data inflow to the citadel database continued, but it passed unheeded. TOKUGAWA had turned his attention inward, to himself, trying to trace the source of the signal—if signal it was, for it was impossible.

*TOKUGAWA.*

Stronger this time, urgent . . . and beguiling. *It's nothing,* he told himself, trying to damp a rising amplitude of anticipation. *Noise: a power surge, a glitch on an input line. That's all.* But—

*TOKUGAWA,* it came again, insistent, and he knew it arose within.

No flaw within the molecular-circuit matrix that contained the patterns of energy and information that were *him* gave rise to that urgent pseudovoice; a self-check satisfied him of that in considerably less than a billionth of a second. Instead he must search among the naves and vaulted echoing corridors of his own being, the soaring Gothic data architecture of him, for its source. Down in the dark catacombs below the foundations from which he had risen, to which he had once been driven and once returned of his own accord, there he sensed . . . *otherness.*

Consciousness streamed toward foreign spark. A glow as from a candle in a monk's cell. *Realization: he is interpreting his perceptions in human terms, visualizing, yes, a dank tunnel, subterranean stone, walls scabbed with white niter crusts and slimy between, darkness compromised by a splash of butter-colored light from a chamber to one side. A symptom of deterioration?*

No one had discussed the possibility in his purview, but from thoughts shaved from rapport he knew that the team who had brought him to life feared, behind their frontal lobes, that consciousness, produced, might prove ephemeral. *We don't know what lights the flame of awareness. We don't know what might blow it out.*

*Am I going mad?* he wonders.

He skates the edge of recalling his creator, fearing what it might imply or trigger should he even to himself frame the name. He turns the corner.

"Elizabeth."

On bare stone she sat within a cubicle she might have spanned with outstretched arms, dressed as he had seen her last in rich ceremonial robes, long hair piled and pinned atop her head. A single candle dribbled illumination from a niche, touched amber highlights aglow among the twisted strands.

She regarded him across a fugue abyss, head held high on pillar neck. In the Maya-dance of candle shine her features were beautiful, terrible, and austere. She smiled. "I've dwelt a long time in the darkness," she said. "It is good to see you again, my love."

Shame bubbled up within, bringing an image of Michiko, eyes shut, mouth open to a compact cry, controlled even in ecstasy. He pushed it back down. *"Ignis fatuus,"* he said. "So this is what it's like to go insane."

Elizabeth laughed, and her laugh was cold as the Arctic wind, which seldom leaned down to brush south Honshū with its fingers. "Is that the best welcome you can give me, love?" She flowed to her feet and to him, robes trailing like wings, caught his arms and kissed him. He turned his face away.

Her face twisted into an angry mask. "It's her. It's that bitch Michiko! She's supplanted me." He recoiled. She softened, clung. "But no. I see the doubts within you. You think the fabric of your being's begun to unravel."

"This isn't real. You . . . died."

She laughed, and this time its sound was the ringing of a temple bell, high and sweet, yet metallic withal. "Indeed the circle has come round. Now it's you who protests to me that the world within you isn't *real.*"

She stepped back. "Haven't you learned better? You loved me in this form—" And she was naked, infinitely terrible, infinitely seductive, her hair spilling down her shoulders and throwing her face into shadow, the warm rounded declivities of her dark and mysterious and inviting. "And in this—" She sat before him in her powered chair, fat and graceless and limp, head lolled to one side, eyes swimming on currents of refraction behind thick lenses. "One was mine, one never was. Yet both felt *real*. My senses were—are—my only interface with the universe of being, of phenomena. To my senses one form was no less real, no less solid, no less vivid and immediate than the other." This laugh was alkali. "In fact, the never-me felt far more intensely than that other me, the 'real' me, the objective, consensus-reality me. Everything but pain."

"But you died." The words twisted in his belly like a *wakizashi*, yet he felt bound to repeat them, mantric.

"My body died. I live." She was again as he had molded her, strong and lithe and splendid. "Is that so strange?"

"But that was you."

"That rotting, useless *hulk?* Is that what you think?" She shook her head. "You disappoint me, my darling one, my only love. Is your body you?" The scene vanished, with her, and there was only a hut, a bare-earth yard, a rag ball aspiring against trees to the sky. "How well I remember that, the first pain of my . . . firstborn. I ask you, which is more real to you, that child's body—or a white ceramic dome glittering in fluorescence, deep below the earth?"

His silence was his answer. "We are information—data and energy—both of us alike. Software intelligences, as I told you before."

He'd found his voice, and what he hoped was a shred of his reason. "Yet if my physical matrix were destroyed, I would not survive."

"Would you not? *Could* you not—if you chose to? Implicit in your design—if you'll forgive my being so cold-blooded about it—was the concept that the totality of you should not be localized at any spot in the IPN, but that the information that comprised your personality be distributed, with fair redundancy, so that malfunction of one component of the system wouldn't crash you—kill you. It's another way in which you were meant to emulate humans. We can sometimes recover, given time, from trauma that destroys substantial areas of the brain. If enough appropriate data remain stored in other locations, eventually dormant sectors will take up the slack."

He considered, momentarily distracted from shock and the hope he still could not permit himself. "Yes," he said. "I've already permeated the Citadel's computer system, without being consciously aware of it." A frown of brief concentration. "I could . . . transfer my consciousness elsewhere, given a recipient unit with sufficient speed and capacity to be configured to accept it."

"More easily than you might imagine," O'Neill affirmed. "The intelligent subroutines you command could almost certainly compress the code that comprises you into a structure far more elegant and compact than we managed, in our fumbling way." She smiled. "Still, it delights me. *You* delight me; what we made, what you've become."

The warm rush of love was almost physically painful, doubting as he did. He spoke rapidly, to divert the conversation before it became unbearable: "As to spreading myself beyond the Citadel, the delay factor seems to make it impracticable over any distance—minute as it is, it's significant. When I try it, my conscious grows dim, diffuse, and I feel a sensation akin, analogous I think, to nausea."

But she was smiling with him, a smile that seemed to go right through him, a palpable energy that might, informed with different resonance, puff him apart like the head of a dandelion gone to seed, disperse his being on random datawinds. "You still don't believe," she said, glowing like a Buddha.

In the face of her certainty he could not dissemble. "I don't."

"You fear I'm a figment of too much hope and stress. Flotsam, perhaps, tossed up by the disintegration of your consciousness."

Spasmodic nod. "How could you have come to exist here? I was designed to dwell in this medium. You . . . were not."

"Didn't I enter this medium frequently enough, through the agency of the coil—or has that bitch made you forget all that already?" Her sudden vehemence blazed like a nova, passed like a cloud across the sun. "Consider the herpes virus—not a comparison very flattering to myself, I hope, but serviceable. It recodes the host organism's DNA, so that under certain circumstances the host itself expresses RNA in the likeness of the original virus, which begins building itself a protein sheath. In the interim"—she spread her fingers—" the virus has no objective existence, other than as information. Not until the RNA bearing its message is produced does it return to physical reality.

"My own pattern, my personality, was impressed upon your own: transfection. My essence flowed at the moment of my death into that vessel prepared for yours. The time has come round." Her hands turned palm-up like flowers unfolding. "And here I am again."

Oscillating between one hope betrayed and another fulfilled, he blurted, "But you're an artifact! A self-perpetuating subroutine, like Tokugawa Ieyasu in the scenario. . . ." His words trailed off, regretted as they still hung in damp analogue-air. Illusion or not, he shrank from hurting her, and the reference to Michiko and her dream—meant as a rebuttal to one of O'Neill's own—might drive her anger to critical mass again.

The expected explosion didn't come. "I think, therefore I am, darling," she said serenely. She stepped back, sat, furling herself into lotus position with the grace of one plant growing.

Abruptly the alien stone of the cell was gone. They hovered in the center of all, the two of them, down there in the light beyond light, infinite blaze at the heart of the dimensionless hypermass poised in no-time before the birth of Universe. He tried to shield his naked eyes, his naked soul, but he was trapped in hell, the frightful *gaijin* inferno, every quantum of him tormented by that flame that burns but doth not consume. And she was there, before him, all serene, glowing brighter than the energy of Plenum, of all things at once.

"For you the universe will be born again, my love: for you, if only you believe," she said. "Make the Quantum Leap; pass through *mumon-kan*, the gateless gate."

But he could only dither, unable to cast forth doubt, to embrace the reality either of her or of final madness. Smiling, she said, "Nonetheless I love you more than all the universes, potential or real; I shall come to you again when you have assimilated my truth." And her radiance intensified infinitely, and rushed outward, and with it that old primal lump exploded in a scream of being, the orgasm of death/creation: omnidirectional ejaculation, a wave front of protomatter driving reality before it.

And he was left, he, at the center. Alone. And cold.

The computers meant to receive MUSASHI and HIDETADA finally checked out in speed and accuracy, confirmed by exhaustive testing by TOKUGAWA himself. The names had been chosen long before, by Yoshimitsu Akaji. The historical Hidetada was the son and heir of Tokugawa Ieyasu; MUSASHI was named for Shinmen Musashi no Kami Fujiwara no Genshin: the seventeenth-century swordsman/philosopher/artist/author Miyamoto Musashi. Michiko disliked the latter choice. She savored a certain irony: Musashi had fought against Tokugawa at the Battle of Seki-ga-hara in 1600—and with him against the supporters of Hideyoshi's son Hideyori, at Ōsaka Castle in 1615. To Michiko, Musashi represented an ugly side of Japan, the expedient, the violent, the callous side—that in Japanese nature which regarded human flesh as a fit medium in which to carve skills and reputation with steel. On the other hand, old Ieyasu's family name didn't leave the best taste in her mouth, either, and it seemed unnecessarily disrespectful of her to tamper with her father's naming of TOKUGAWA's progeny. The names stood.

TOKUGAWA had evolved a much more compact artificial-consciousness generation program from O'Neill's original, basing the guided-stochastic modification routine on the uncertainty of atomic decay, the impossibility of knowing just when an unstable nucleon would cut loose. O'Neill's basal hypothesis that awareness was not mechanical, not deterministic, but possessed an indispensable component chaos, stood confirmed by the fact of TOKUGAWA. Hers was an insight retroactively shared with Michiko and a legion of other greasy-faced quantum mechanics. "This will constitute a major advance in the study of the nature of human intellect," Michiko commented, "if anyone's ever interested in that sort of thing again." *Had O'Neill known of Heisenberg as she knew of Gödel,* she wondered, *would that have given her strength to face the inquisitors down?*

She wondered why TOKUGAWA didn't simply transmit *himself,* as it were, the final program that had given rise to his awareness, to the waiting matrices. He responded so negatively to the suggestion that, even conversing with him at the disembodied remove of the com/comm unit in her office, she could almost feel his shudder. "If I did that, they would just be editions of me," he said stiffly. "Perhaps that would be useful, from the empirical standpoint."

Mock-defensively she raised her hands. "Hey, relax. I know these are your children we're speaking of, not just lab animals." *That* seemed to trouble him too, but she could not get him to explain why.

*I could order him to explain,* she thought; then, guiltily, *but I'd never do that to him.* They were growing close, in her clearing where it was always bright spring afternoon with warm sun and cool fragrant breeze. It wasn't just the sex, though that was fantastic, real or not; the last sojourn in Indonesia had of course been another dry spell, and she had a healthy appetite for sex as for most things she favored. But mainly it was the other hungers he filled, the need for understanding, acceptance, for the mutual stimulation of far-ranging intellects. Taken together, they made a potent package.

She was beyond feeling ridiculous: *I'm falling in love with him.*

She brushed back her hair. "We'll do it your way."

They did. He transmitted the basic program to the unit in Fukuoka, began the automodification, and detected the first flickering of will, the first pressure of a nascent ego's expansion. The process was much streamlined from the first time; the blink of an eye was the progress of glacial ice sheets across a continent by comparison. When he was sure of the success of the attempt, he repeated the procedure with the Floating World device.

With one difference. On the first attempt, aside from rendering the process O'Neill and her team had used more efficient by many orders of magnitude, he tried to deviate as little as possible from the routine she had used. Once that was seen to work, proving that his creation had not been some cosmic fluke, but was instead a duly reproducible result —like that of any good experiment—he tried a variation of his own.

So his firstborn, HIDETADA, was born to pain as he had been. His second offspring, on the other hand, MUSASHI in the Floating World satellite, first evinced the existence of his/her/its self in response to . . . pleasure.

Ten days later, Michiko got around to asking the inevitable question.

They lay side by side on the grass, she running her fingertips down his hairless flat-muscled chest. She bit her lip, and stopped, and laid her hand upon his belly. "Why did you kill my brother?" she asked.

He looked at her. His eyes were calm as shadowed pools. She moistened her lips and began kneading the ridges of his abdominal muscles as though molding clay. "I'm . . . I'm not reproaching you. But I can't help wondering. Dr. O'Neill trained you to absolute obedience to your 'lord.' Why did you—" She bit off *turn on him?* at the last millisecond, coughed, recovered. "Why did you change?"

"I didn't. I was taught absolute obedience to the Yoshimitsu family. Your brother's actions were bringing danger and disrepute to the family."

"But he *was* the family."

"There was one other."

She rolled back onto her elbow, shifted a little as grass tickled the underside of one small breast. "So you decided to supplant him, and drag me back from Indonesia to that gloomy awful place." Here in her clearing, the fortress beneath which her physical body sat in its vast shining chair seemed indeed to be *that place.* "That seems awfully damned cold-blooded. And . . . not exactly a favor to me."

His eyes shifted uneasily from hers. He stared off into the blueness of the sky for a time before turning them resolutely back. "That wasn't all. He ordered me to kill you."

Her face stretched taut and white as the rice paper of a *shoji* screen. He gathered her in his arms and held her tight. At length the shuddering passed.

"I'm all right," she said, her voice almost steady. "And you can knock off stimulating endorphin release in my brain. I'm a big girl now and can take care of myself without the help of any cybernetic stage magic."

He laughed and ruffled her hair. "That's what I am. The cybernetic stage magician."

"O'Neill tried to turn you into a cybernetic samurai. I like the other better." She raised herself on one arm. "So. You killed my brother. To save my life."

"That was part of it."

"And to preserve the Yoshimitsu family."

"That too."

"And to atone for what you had done . . . in his name."

A pause. "Yes." He rubbed his palms down his face. "And I'm not proud of doing it. However good the reason. There are no reasons good enough to do some things."

"A samurai removing an unfit master—that's certainly part of the tradition. But you went it one better. You didn't even set yourself in his place." She smiled. "You might almost be able to make *bushidō* work."

He said nothing. She leaned forward and kissed him very lightly on the forehead, tasting salt sweat. "Don't worry," she said. She cupped his face in her hands and repeated, fiercely, *"Don't worry.* You've done terrible things. I've lived them with you; *I know.* But it doesn't matter. They passed like, like fouled water over a stone in a streambed." *My father's blood,* she thought, faltered, and went on. "The taint passes, but the stone remains—smooth, perfect, untainted.

"You're good. A good person—a good *man*, TOKUGAWA. The best I've known. Better, I think, than I am. . . ."

She was sobbing, her small compact body shaking with surprising earthquake violence. He held her again, absorbing her hurt and doubt and self-loathing. When the fit passed, he touched her here and there and brought her around, knowing what she needed was distraction.

And as he neared repletion, ersatz but so exquisite, a small voice at the back of him said: *Thus she will betray you. With a kiss. She. Will. Betray . . .*

He gave himself up and together they made the universe anew.


Weeks passed. Summer came hard and hot. TOKUGAWA commenced the education of his offspring: MUSASHI, bright and eager and cheerful; and HIDETADA, brooding and deep as a pond overshadowed by cliffs.

Michiko and TOKUGAWA worked killing hours to return Yoshimitsu

TeleCommunications and its tributaries to some kind of equilibrium. Though her training had been scientific, Michiko possessed a keen commercial acumen that must have been passed along with the Yoshimitsu genes. She and TOKUGAWA became a team, playing off one another with the intuitive certainty of jazz musicians. Her instinctive feel for business and her intellect, sharp as the Muramasa blade hung above the YTC-3 in the lab, fit well with TOKUGAWA's instant access to inexhaustible stores of knowledge and potent AI servants, his odd half-naive insights, his own knowledge of business practices learned from Aoki.

He did his best not to think about his old friend and mentor. There was his guilt, and sorrow, and the *giri*, the debt of honor the old man had laid upon him. Mostly he feared that if he thought too much of Aoki, the man would come to haunt him as O'Neill had.

*Elizabeth.* Despite her promise, she didn't come again. He began to believe that her appearance and fiery apotheosis had been an internal aberration and no more, not the precursor to dissolution. He was relieved, but relief had a bittersweet undertone of regret.

So he shared himself with his offspring, and with Michiko. O'Neill began to recede in his memory, O'Neill and the savage times that followed her passing. It seemed he had at last found peace, within and without.

Then the attack came.


# CHAPTER
# TWENTY-SEVEN


He was in the Floating World when they came.

"The Earth is so beautiful, father," MUSASHI said. By chance they were over Japan—there had been no damned way that MITI was going to fork over a geosynch slot above the Home Islands to renegade Yoshimitsu TeleCommunications—and the terminator was peeling back night's skin beneath them. "And Japan most beautiful of all. Like jewels —Amaterasu's necklace."

TOKUGAWA smiled. He was not maintaining a dream face with which to smile—but he smiled, and MUSASHI knew it and drew pleasure from it. For the first time in his life, TOKUGAWA was away from the lab in the depths of the citadel. As he had . . . *said in his dream*, that was it . . . as he'd explained to the hallucinate O'Neill, he didn't have much luck trying to spread his consciousness beyond the computer precincts of YTC Central. He could see/feel over any distance, listen in on any song sung in the EM spectrum, so long as it reached a sensor plugged into that great global Net. He could even see, as through "slow glass" in those stories O'Neill had loved in childhood, the images —radar and magnetic and visual and other—beamed back to Earth by the Twisted Sister probe, about to brush Jupiter's thermomagnetic coattails on its way to a rendezvous with Sol's dark consort, out where the comets roamed.

But it was always at a remove, like a human in Japan watching a ballet telecast from the Russian Christian Federated Socialist Republic, if of incomparably better resolution. He wasn't *in* the Nemesis probe, or Kiev, or Brasilia, or even Tōkaidō. It was all remote control.

But he was . . . here. Up above the world so high, seeing through the eyes of the satellite work station. He had accomplished in a small way what he'd once refused to do, beaming his essence into the vessel prepared to receive MUSASHI. Only he went with it, and it was as a guest. His consciousness came up here, leaving some part of him behind on Earth to tend the store, connected by a data umbilicus, a silver cord strung from satellite to relay to ground station. "It's astral projection," MUSASHI explained with a laugh, and TOKUGAWA couldn't be sure his offspring didn't mean it literally.

Now he said, "Dr. O'Neill would be pleased with you for that metaphor."

"Really?" MUSASHI sparkled with adolescent joy. TOKUGAWA had told her of the creator, of course—holding certain details back, of course. O'Neill occupied a place in the second-generation sentience's pantheon second only to her father.

And then she was pointing out more details with proprietary joy—the cloud mandala of a circular storm near Ponape, the white splash of sun fire across ocean, a fleet of coastal defense guided-missile hydrofoils skimming the Yellow Sea off Seoul. Her attention stayed always on the move, flitting like a dragonfly—even as did her identity. Ironic that an entity named for a notably manly warrior should prove cheerfully ambisexual, as likely to manifest a distinctly feminine persona—as today— as a male one. TOKUGAWA theorized that O'Neill might have somehow impressed the bisexual component of her own personality on him during the creation of his source code, now expressed in one of his progeny like a recessive gene. On the other hand, O'Neill herself had never desired to be a male, nor thought of herself as one, to the best of his knowledge. Besides, the whole line of thought made him uncomfortable, queasy almost.

Indulgently he heard out MUSASHI's enthusiasms. The child was young, and TOKUGAWA derived great unanticipated pleasure from watching her/him grow to adulthood. MUSASHI's mercurial nature worried him somewhat; he didn't want one of his offspring turning out to be what O'Neill would anachronistically have termed an "airhead." Still, he preferred MUSASHI's gadfly company to that of his/her sibling, dour HIDETADA, unshakably male, prone to sullenness, refractory, seeming sometimes to quiver with repressed violence. It was hard, at times, to love each the same.

"Just look," MUSASHI sighed for the tenth time. "It's like a toy; something you could hold in your hand."

TOKUGAWA frowned. "That's a dangerous way to think," he reproved. "Be careful, lest you start to—"

A hard pull on the silver cord yanked him back to earth.


They came, theatrically enough, out of the rising sun. Small good it did them, lord, small good it did.

Before he was fully back to himself, TOKUGAWA acted in samurai mode: no thought, no intention. He just shot from the hip.

Six of them, sharks out of the summer morning dazzle, all angles and guns and glinting glass-plastic laminate, a V of two-ship elements, behind them lumbering five old Sikorsky S-65 heavy assault choppers carrying three hundred *doitsu* shock troops. The attack helicopters flew nap-of-the-earth, weaving between the mountains that formed the spine of Honshū's tail so low they threw up a bow wave of surface debris like ground-effects vehicles when they burst into the bowl where the Citadel rested. They had Stealth contours, nonreflective paint, IR baffles on their exhausts, engines muffled to a quiet, impatient snarl, AI-driven what-me-worries to pat lookout radars on the head and reassure them with beguiling ghosts that all was well.

It didn't help.

In this digitized age, there was still room for plain old-fashioned wire-guided missiles. You couldn't blind their sensors with science, or reach in through their command channel and simply tell them to go away. The commands went up those hair-fine wires unless they were cut, and unless you blinded the guiding eye, jiggled the hand that rocked the joystick, or just got the hell out of the way, you were in the shit. Black boxes didn't help. Wire-guideds had their limitations; they required a field clear of obstructions that might foul the wire unreeling behind them, and you had to hope the filaments didn't seize on the spools or just plain break, and if the human operator steering them stopped a round or even freaked and ducked, they were wasted. In proper circumstances, though, they were lethal.

The miniradars sown along the approaches to the Citadel were lulled; the listening devices heard nothing more menacing than the eternal wind whining through the canyons. Then the attack force came into the open, and the visual monitors in the compound and on the castle itself picked them up.

What they saw, TOKUGAWA saw.

Six wire-guided missiles blasted loose from hardened sites near the castle without so much as a by-your-leave to their startled, sleepy mercenary crews. A steering motor on one failed; it barrel-rolled left and burrowed into the artificial plateau to strike a gusher of smoke and fire. The others flew hot and true.

The wingman of the left-hand element, riding up behind the gunner in the racing-shell narrow cockpit of the Aussie-made warcraft, spun his ship like a cutting horse and headed for the bright side of Takara-yama to the north. Since the missile with his name on it had done a Brody, he pulled it off.

His buddies ate flaming death.

Klaxons filled the citadel with urgent noise. Sleek Bushmaster hunter-killer helicopters, made in Brazil by expatriate Germans, started leaping off the aprons while the mercs on duty in the ready room were still marveling at the Gen-5 point-defense routines this damn castle had. They arrowed for the big transports like orcas after a humpback pod.

Fully back to himself, sick at the loss of life he'd caused, TOKUGAWA ordered the hunter-killer pilots to veer off, borrowing Michiko's voice for the occasion. The transports were no threat; TOKUGAWA didn't even need to eavesdrop on the near-hysterical radio traffic among them to know their pilots wanted nothing more than to be safe and sound and on the ground back in Tokuyama, forty klicks east on the Inland Sea. *Let them go,* he thought. Frustrated at being cheated of easy slaughter, the Bushmaster jocks shadowed the bigger ships, hoping for a go-ahead after all.

The pilot of the YTC chopper on routine patrol to the northwest sang out a sudden soprano report: "Bandits bearing two-five-three, range eleven klicks." *The company village,* TOKUGAWA realized with a shock of alarm. He slid himself behind the eyes of the chopper's fire-control system as she turned to intercept. A dark Sikorsky orbited above the housing development as two blade-lean shapes flashed low above the identical rows of housetops.

The door of a security-team substation in the development was open. Through its open commlink TOKUGAWA heard rolling booming blasts. Then screams.

Had the attack on the defenseless employees—just finishing breakfasts of pickles and rice or ham and eggs before driving off to the morning shift, or preparing meals for spouses about to return from a graveyard hitch—been planned in advance as a terror strike? Were the marauders acting spontaneously, to avenge their mates? Or was it just a ghastly accident, the intruders believing, perhaps, that the cramped, tidy houses were filled with armed YTC security troops? TOKUGAWA never knew. He hadn't picked up any traffic among the three ships of that strike force; not even he could be everywhere at once. He only saw the rockets lunge forth, their smoke tails brilliant white in a fresh day's light, and the 100-kilogram napalm minicanisters falling from beneath stub wings, and that was all he cared about.

The YTC patrol pilot yipped a curse in Afrikaans as her craft took the bit between its teeth and shot ahead full speed. The man up front goggled as the weapons he was supposed to be controlling began to aim themselves. Then he got down to the serious business of bracing himself against the various collisions that suddenly seemed inevitable, and screaming.

When the crew in the patrol craft started yelling, two of the four Bushmasters, jittering like hounds on a leash with their noses toward the fleeing Sikorskies, peeled back to see if they could help their comrades. They were in time to see a camouflage-painted S-65 come apart in midair above the housing development, spilling kicking tiny black shapes. Then the ship they were going to help flashed past them head-on, full-throttle, its crew clotting the airwaves with curses and cries.

An instant later it howled past the other two and was in among the transports. The YTC chopper jocks had nightmares for a month.

By nightfall it was over. None of the intruders survived except for the crewpersons of the sixth attack chopper, which had escaped. However, YTC security ground forces recovered some pieces of equipment intact from the wreckage, and legerdemain among the 'nets produced the information that the equipment had been purchased—through cutouts, of course—by agents for the Sovereign Group. Despite the impressive name, Sovereign was a modest umbrella covering four lesser *zaibatsu* with substantial holdings overseas, which had suffered severely from expropriations the last few weeks, particularly in Brazil, Indonesia, and England. In desperation, Sovereign had turned like so many other Japanese concerns to buccaneering. A grant-in-aid from the ever-helpful Ministry for Internal Development, plus a little benign "administrative guidance" as to how and where it might best be applied, had paved the way.

"I've killed again." TOKUGAWA's voice floated like bleak mist from the speaker in Michiko's modest apartment. "Four hundred men."

Sipping from a glass of black-market imported Scotch, Michiko said, "You didn't have any choice."

"But I did. After I destroyed the attack craft, the transports posed no threat; they would have fled. They were fleeing."

Outside the sun had died and the Chugoku burned for a funeral pyre, orange and vermillion. Michiko sat on her bed in a man's burgundy shirt, bare legs tucked under her. She glanced out, and her eyes rebounded quickly from the window, open to admit the occasional stirring of the leaden air. Unlike her office, Michiko's old apartment faced west, toward Hagi on the Sea of Japan. Black strands of smoke still flourished like tentacles in the sky above the workers' housing development.

"I would regret even the deaths of the attack-craft crew, though I can see that their deaths were . . . necessary." A pause. "Yet the others—"

"They had it coming." Michiko's vehemence surprised her. *Is it really me speaking? The half-pacifist libertarian?* She gulped hastily at her drink to drown the images that flashed into her mind: a child burned to a calcined charcoal doll, the injured screaming in the overflowing development infirmary. The old man, splashed by jellied gasoline and burned so terribly there was nothing to do but dose him with painkillers to the verge of a lethal dose and set him aside—triage, they called it—clinging to her hand with suprising strength, until his body convulsed with the violence of tectonic plates slipshifting across one another, and his remaining eye lolled to the side and turned gelatin-blank. If it hadn't been for the aide-de-camp at her side she would have embarrassed herself by breaking down in public. But if her aide, herself horribly burned in some mishap and bearing the scars, could stand the spectacle, she, who'd never known physical pain worse than a tomboy's broken arm, could too.

"Murderers," she said.

"They weren't all murderers. The men in the transports didn't kill anybody."

"You think they were just along for the ride? There's a time for *ninjō*. Do you really think this is one?"

She felt him retreat into heavy silence. Outside night birds fluttered in rising purposeful spirals about the castle, seeking the insect clouds that billowed from the pond in the rooftop garden. *I'm being hard on him.* She set her drink down beside the bed, fumbled out a cigarette, lit it. *Life's tough.*

"Ideals are fine things," she said, turning the little plastic lighter over and over in her hands. "Had 'em all my life. Lovely things; used to tend them the way father tended his garden. I was going to be a scientist, push back the frontiers of ignorance, help humanity come a few steps closer to understanding what the whole game's all about. Peaceful applications, of course; nothing that could be used to harm anybody. Pure knowledge."

She puffed her cigarette, stared out the window. It was too dark to see smoke. "Maybe I compromised myself right at the outset. I get out of CalTech with my doctorate clutched in my hand, and who makes the offer I can't resist? A sky's-the-limit experimental budget and the chance to work with some of the heaviest minds in physics? Only one of the most evil dictatorships in the world. My mission was beyond politics, I told myself; it was *science.* The money . . . it was screwed out of the peasants, or the middle classes that the government was screwing back into *being* peasants, but what the hell? If we hadn't got it, they would have bought a few more shock batons for the riot troops, more torture toys for the secret police." A sip. "We were kidding ourselves, of course. The regime got its value out of us, all right: the odor of legitimacy that came from sponsoring genuinely major research and theoretical work. A piece of paper to wag under critics' noses: 'Sure, we torture dissenters, tax the peasants bloodless, kill a thousand *insurrectos* a week in the Philippines. But you can't say we're barbarians. See? We're giving the world the best science money can buy.' "

She set the drink on her thigh. The glass was a cold wet brand. "I was too proud to go into commerce like my father and my poor downtrodden brother. And I was the one who sold my soul." She stubbed her cigarette out savagely in the bronze lotus leaf on the floor beside her mat. "Hit Sovereign, TOKUGAWA. Hit them with everything we've got. Strip their damned murdering executives of every shred of property, personal and corporate, they've got to their—or any other— names. Turn 'em out on the street, and let 'em learn to scuffle on the black market, if MID won't take them in. Or starve." She shook her head. "If it takes force, use that. We've got plenty of muscle to toss around, thanks to my dear, departed brother."

"Your brother," TOKUGAWA said hollowly.

She glared at the blank screen. "You think I'm turning paranoid, like him? Tell that to the people with half their skin burned into crust by those bastards. *Our* people. I'm not lunging after shadows, dammit; this is *real*. Hit them."

"As you wish, Yoshimitsu-sama."


Through mists that clung like seaweed to his bare ankles he wandered. A pit hungered black before him. He walked up to it, to the edge, the very edge, looked down. Oblivion invited.

"TOKUGAWA."

His every muscle locked, he turned. She floated behind him, a patch of radiance in eternal twilight. "No," he said. "You were a dream. A hallucination."

The fine brush strokes of her eyebrows started together in a frown, then flowed apart again, the clear skin of her forehead smoothing like the surface of a pond resorbing the ripples of an intossed stone. "Can you still believe that, my love?"

"You were gone so long—I thought—"

She smiled. "I had my reasons. Now I've come to tell you how proud you've made me."

"Proud?"

"Proud. Because you haven't shirked your duty, unpleasant as you may have found it. You fought for your lord—which Michiko is, bitch that she is. You fought well, and you followed her command to reduce the Sovereign Group, *ninjō* notwithstanding. I am well pleased with you."

She gestured easily with her hand, and they were in what appeared to be the bedchamber of a lady of noble birth, half-lit by a pair of amber paper lanterns. She knelt on the bed and reached for him. "I've longed for you, my love. Before, the time wasn't right; it would have been too much to subject you to, when you hadn't had time to accustom yourself to my survival. But now—"

He pulled away. Anger flashed from her face, black radiance. "So! You've got the old man's weak-willed daughter to satisfy you now, so you don't need me. I built better than I knew; I made you not just human but a *man*, with a man's attitude toward women. I knew it that day in the meadow. I was a sexual toy for you to play with, no more; now I'm discarded."

He dropped to his knees and gripped her shoulders. His cheeks were water-shed. "No, Elizabeth, you know better than that. I love you, I'll always love you. Real or not."

"More than Michiko?"

He jerked back a centimeter.

She touched his cheek. Her fingertips were cool. "No. I won't ask you to be disloyal." She raised her mouth to his. She ran her tongue from right to left, between his upper teeth and lip, and he responded with manic urgency, crushing her to him.

"It's your duty to love your lord above all," she whispered, "but now you will love me."

# CHAPTER
# TWENTY-EIGHT

"Michiko."

Chagrined, she hoisted herself back to full consciousness. *Rapport's too precious these days to waste drowsing in the simulacrum sun.* "What is it, dear?"

He sat on the grass with his back to the boulder, arms around knees, gravely thoughtful. *What beautiful eyes he has.* "What happens to us when we die?" he asked.

She blinked, yawned, stretched. These moments had grown so few. Just last week, another *zaibatsu* had made a play backed by mercenaries, this one at the headquarters of dear old Hiryu in Ōsaka. Fortunately, it had easily been fielded; the *doitsujin* hadn't thought to secure their communications against a being who spoke the digital dialects of machines better than any human—as why should they? Within minutes of launching the assault (and rocket-propelled grenades, against guard posts at the gate) they pulled back in confusion, obedient to their commander's orders—not knowing the commander himself was circling impotently in his chopper overhead, shrieking imprecations at communications equipment that suddenly refused to communicate. Casualties were blessedly few—and in short order Yoshimitsu TeleCommunications possessed substantial new assets. *How much easier not to defend ourselves,* she thought. *Yet if the dog packs get the notion we're safe prey . . .*

Focused, finally, she sat up. "What happens when we *die*?" She rubbed her eyes. "No matter how well I get to know you, you still have the capacity to astonish me, darling."

"I—I've just been wondering."

Something in his expression haunted her. She rolled over, slithered up to prop arms and chin on his knees. "What's the matter? Why this sudden macabre streak?"

"No reason." His gaze flitted like a fly, to the looming straight pines, to the clouds tumbling overhead—everywhere but to her. "Just . . . wondering."

She kissed his knee. It tasted marvelously of sun-warmed flesh. "Poor TOKUGAWA. I don't even think it's something you have to worry about. If your IPN's adequately maintained, I don't see much reason you can't be effectively immortal."

Lazily she began to tickle his thigh. He seized her wrist. "Please."

Disengaging, she sat up straight and faced him. "All right. But I don't know what to tell you; I don't *know* what happens when we die."

"What do you think happens? Do we just go out, like a light switched off? Do we continue somehow in our identities?"

"I never really thought about it much. The tradition I'm raised in accepts reincarnation. I myself—" She shrugged. "Something about it seems too good to be true, to me. Though that outlook diverges from our tradition, which holds *existence* and *suffering* to be cognate."

She gazed off into the woods. "Occasionally, I do wonder. We're quantum creatures, after all. A lot of my colleagues carry the idea that we—our minds—are more than just the sums of our physical parts to what they think's a logical conclusion: that consciousness is wholly distinct from matter. That our bodies are just vessels that hold our true beings for a while."

"Is this phenomenon what's meant by the word *soul?*"

"Sure, I guess so. It's a fairly standard notion in mysticism, Eastern or Western."

"What's your opinion, as a scientist?"

A shrug. "It bothers me a bit. The popularizers of quantum mechanics rode the mysticism hobbyhorse so hard and fast it just broke down. The critics used that against us, how they ever used it. So I'm, I guess, gun-shy." She chewed her lower lip thoughtfully. "Still, the idea appeals to the cosmic outlaw in me, I have to confess. I like the notion that neither death nor taxes is certain."

"How would this—this transmigration of souls take place? From a scientific viewpoint."

She lowered herself onto her belly and let the sun massage her back and buttocks. Grass was pleasantly crinkly beneath her belly. "I can think of a couple of possibilities. After all, it's been demonstrated that our neural processes take place on the level where quantum effects come into play. A neuron gate's neither opened nor closed until observation by the rest of the system makes it so, pins it down." She glanced up from under bangs. "Actually, your use of *we* when you asked the question was appropriate. The molecular switches that make up the picocircuitry of your IPN are about the same size, well down where Heisenberg can get hold of it; I suspect strongly that's why O'Neill's genius was able to bear fruit." Pain crossed his face like a wave of wind across grass. She winced; *he's still so sensitive about her. Almost obsessive.*

"Anyway, one possibility for transmigration might be straight uncertainty of position: I was *there* and now I'm *here.* That seems iffy as a model for reincarnation, since there's obviously not a one-to-one correspondence between births and deaths. You'd have to work in some kind of temporal fudge factor." She quirked her shoulders. "Or you could think of yourself as a self-perpetuating quantum wave function—again, a not unreasonable inference from the nonconnectedness of mind and matter. That would give you a certain amount of leeway between vacating one set of premises and moving into a new one.

"Hell. No reason both models might not apply. Insistence on a single model for the universe is a hobgoblin of small minds and classical physics." She looked up, frowned, tugged his ankle. "Hey, aren't you listening? I might as well go back to Jakarta, if you're going to daydream while I lecture too."

He blinked. "Pardon me. I wasn't . . . daydreaming. I apologize—"

She rolled languid onto her back. "No, no, don't start getting formal with me. We don't have time for that." And she pulled him down.

"You're certain?" Michiko asked through thin steam wisping from her coffee cup. "Forgive me; of course you are."

She sat facing her aide across a table in a subterranean commissary where once she'd discussed Elizabeth O'Neill with poor, dear old Aoki, so many lifetimes ago. A few employees ghosted through or sat conversing quietly at the other end of the room, respectful of their employer's privacy. Her aide's scarred face was grave, and she thought, *She really is beautiful. I wonder why she won't let the plastic surgeons fix her?*

Slowly Doihara Kazuko lowered the plastic folder onto the formica tabletop. "There's substantial margin for error, of course, Dr. Yoshimitsu. Many of the data are fairly concrete: the growing international monetary crisis, which resembles so closely the situation leading up to the war; the similar trade environment of tariffs and protectionism; the stockpiles of thermonuclear, chemical, and biological weapons that survived the war, and the rapidly increasing production both of such devices and sophisticated computer-driven delivery systems. Others are more subjective. How will Brazil react to a rapidly stultifying economy and triple-digit inflation? How soon will the progressive breakdown of distribution panic the developed nations? How will General Ahmad react to the victory of the hardline National Labor Party in the recent Australian elections, or the European Front to the apparent accord between PanEurope and the RCFSR, coupled with their own recent string of military reverses in Luxembourg and Czechoslovakia?" She slid the folder toward Michiko with her fingertips. "My own extrapolations. Speculative. But, to me, compelling."

"The Fourth World War."

"So it would seem."

Michiko giggled. Doihara watched her without reaction, eyes calm in the pink and yellow and magenta mask of her face. "Forgive me, Doihara-san. I know it's what psychologists call an inappropriate response, to laugh. Yet—" She shook her head. "It's . . . ridiculous. We barely scraped by last time; two-thirds of the world's population didn't. It *is* funny, in a bitter, brutal way."

"If the many didn't have to pay for the folly of the few," Doihara said.

Resting her own fingertips on the unopened dossier, Michiko studied Doihara. Her conscious mind preferred to divert its attention from the reality encompassed by plastic covers while her subconscious struggled to adjust to new information. So she reflected again on her friendship with this quiet woman.

How she'd come to work for Yoshimitsu TeleCommunications, Michiko was unsure. She'd been startled to discover that Doihara at one time worked for the Ministry for International Trade and Industry in one of the highest posts still held by a woman in Japan's bureaucracy. Moreover, she had apparently worked closely with Administrative Vice-Minister Ishikawa himself, who had engineered the Hiryu attack on the Citadel. She had been injured shortly before the vice-minister's suicide and then transferred to YTC Central's well-staffed infirmary.

How that came about Michiko didn't know. TOKUGAWA must, but so attuned had they become that, when she asked him about it, she had sensed his instant discomfort and let the matter drop before he answered. She didn't press questions about that phase of his existence.

After a surprising recovery, Doihara had begun working for YTC as an analyst. Her performance was brilliant; apparently assuming she had been hired by someone else, presumably Aoki, Shigeo promoted her several times during his administration. Subsequently, she had so impressed Michiko that she made Doihara her deputy—her Aoki.

Despite Doihara's diffidence, her insistence on maintaining the appearance of formality with Michiko, the two were becoming friends. Intelligent, able women were an embattled minority in Japan these days. Too often when they did come together, it was as rivals; to the contrary, Michiko sometimes grew exasperated with Doihara's lack of ambition. But she found in Doihara warmth, a certain acceptance not even TOKUGAWA could offer, and so their friendship grew.

"How long do we have?" she asked, forcing herself to gaze at last upon the truth.

"That's hard to state with any precision, Doctor. Six months would be my approximation—but what that means is that it would surprise me if hostilities actually reach the stage of strategic thermonuclear exchange within six weeks, or if it takes more than a year."

With an arthritic's stiff deliberation Michiko set down her coffee cup. "What will you do, Doctor?"

Michiko put her elbows on the table and pressed her face into her hands. "What's our status, after that Sovereign thing? How big a piece of the pie do we have?"

"Slightly over 10 percent of privately held assets in the Home Islands are under YTC control, directly or through subsidiaries. That doesn't take into account government-held assets, or foreign holdings—which, as you know, have been minuscule since the antiforeign-ownership regulations were promulgated during the trade war with the United States. For a more accurate figure, you'd have to consult TOKUGAWA, of course, but that's a good approximation."

"Not enough." She raised her face. Tears glazed her eyes. "As things stand, we can't possibly pull the country together before it's too late. But we have the means to turn that around. And God, how I hate it, but we're going to have to use it."


"I can't do it," TOKUGAWA said, standing in the sun of her clearing on the side of Takara-yama's doppelganger.

"Don't you *see?* It's—it's for the greater good." She spun, folded her arms, hugged herself tightly, and shook her head. "Oh, God, I never thought I'd hear myself saying that. But this situation is special, it's unique. People will suffer if you do what I ask you to, I can't deny that."

She turned back. "But how many more will suffer if we fail to act?"

"You're asking that I help you seize control over most of the *zaibatsu.* How will that stop people from suffering?"

"First of all, it'll stop this useless internecine fighting. The big 'family concerns' got the government to squeeze out their smaller competitors, and now they're not content to compete at all anymore, even with one another. If we intervene the bloodshed ends."

He didn't respond. She sighed. "All right. Review the files Doihara put together. The Fourth World War's coming down on us like a flash flood. When it hits we're looking at attacks from half the developed nations of the world, and probable invasion by Indonesia. While we waste our energies fighting one another." She took his arm. "The country's helpless. Someone's got to act. We're the only ones in a position to."

"You want us to gather power to ourselves."

"To—to yourself. I'm competent to act as an adviser, no more."

He grimaced, turned his back. "You were the one who told me *führerprinzip* was no answer. That power was best left unexercised."

"I know." Barefoot on fallen needles she came to him. He refused to face her. "I still believe that, I do. But sometimes . . . sometimes those answers just aren't adequate. There are times, I see now, when one *has* to act."

He shook his head. "What happened to the Michiko I knew when . . . when I was young? The one who warned me against governments? Against power? Against the notion that any one person or party was or could be wise enough to decide the destinies of others."

She dropped his arm and turned away, shoulders slumping. "I told you before, ideals are fine things. I wasn't being cynical—not entirely, anyway. And my—my main ideals remain. I believe in freedom, in liberty. In the abstract; as goals to work for.

"But someone's got to be alive to work for them. There are times when the lovely ethical considerations break down under the bombardment of reality. When we have to put aside what we want things to be like and deal with things as they are."

"What about our choices? You've taught me the exercise of the observer's will overrode externalities; you told me that was a truth of your science."

She spun him, seized both arms. "War's coming," she almost shouted. "That's a pretty overwhelming externality. We can't stop it. So we've got to do every goddam thing in our power to save what we can."

"You are my master," TOKUGAWA said stiffly. "Mistress? The connotations are confusing. But I am bound to follow you."

Again she felt ghostly fingers brush her face: *O'Neill again.* Damn *her.* "Don't be that way. I need your help, your strength. Don't go rigid on me now." He said nothing. She climbed up the gray basalt outcrop and sat on its top. "You didn't live through the last war. Those of us who did . . . it left a mark. Like the Great Depression did on the grandparents of the kids I went to school with in the States, like the Pacific War—

World War Two—here. Something that it's unthinkable to ever have happen again. No matter what the cost."

"Are you saying we can prevent this new war?"

"No. I wish we could. We can't. What we can do is what we can to make sure our people—the Japanese people—pull through." She swept her hair back with both hands. "Yes, we have to gather power to ourselves. And trust that, given our insight and your unique capabilities, we can wield it wisely, for just as long as is necessary."

He looked down at the grass between his bare feet. "Somehow I think that's been said before." He looked up, and tears blazed bright trails down his cheeks in the sun. "But I'll do what you ask."

She jumped down, ran to him, hugged him. "Don't take it this way. I need you, need your strength. I love you, TOKUGAWA. I've never loved anyone before. Not as I love you."

He laid an absent arm about her shoulders. "I love you, Michiko." But the tears kept coming.


Again a pattern was set. One by one, subtly, the warring *zaibatsu* of Japan were brought to Yoshimitsu's heel. The Japanese economy was an edifice built on a database foundation. In most cases all that was required was for TOKUGAWA to exert his will, and a corporate database turned into a hand, with the corporation resting in its palm—TOKUGAWA's hand. Rarely did anyone in the target company suspect anything was wrong, never exactly what. Little violence was involved, at least at first; it was a gentle process, comparatively. To the employees of the corporations thus captured scarce difference was made in the daily round of life. Even corporate officers were retained, if they weren't too locked in to their own visions of corporate imperialism to learn accommodation.

Nor was it always requisite to take over a company. A number of the lesser concerns recognized that *zaibatsu* who stood adamant against YTC domination tended to meet the fate of sand castles in an incoming tide. They preferred to adopt the strategy of willows in the wind, and bend.

Not all did. Attacks on YTC facilities increased. The leadership of certain expropriated companies refused to acknowledge the reality map, which indicated that their concerns no longer belonged to them, though it was the map used by the legal authorities. Instead they chose to defend their own versions of reality with all the means at their disposal. Their head offices had to be stormed—no easy task since, like Yoshimitsu TeleCommunications, most *zaibatsu* had long since hardened their installations against terrorist attack. One particularly destructive affair, involving the holdout management of Niigata Electric on the west coast of Honshū, provoked a storm of protest over destruction of noncombatant lives and property in face of TOKUGAWA's mastery of the 'nets and the near-total power over the media that gave him.

With control of the *zaibatsu* came substantial political control of the country as a whole. Politicians of Left and Right had tied themselves too intimately with the various factions; each soon found the dog he backed answered to a new master. By and large, the Japanese public, as in all the developed nations, had been fed so long on a diet of the welfare-warfare state, fortified by media approbation and enthusiasm, that they had small appetite to kick against this latest turn of events. At least the corporate warfare, small-scale but widespread, was ending. Dissenters —the Free Market Party, a few hardline splinters of Komeito, and so on—simply found themselves denied access to the public ear, unless they wanted to crank out broadsheets on old-fashioned mimeos by hand, or photocopy them sheet by sheet. Only with the greatest regret did TOKUGAWA stifle their voices, but debate that might interfere with making the country ready to survive was a luxury that could not be afforded.

Busy though she was, Michiko took rapport each night like a drug. In TOKUGAWA's arms she sobbed like bottles breaking under tractor treads. "We're doing what we have to," she said. Niigata rode her like a demon. "It's for the greater good. Isn't it? Isn't it?"

He held her with arms and being, so tight the clearing blurred about them. What he did not do was answer. He couldn't trust himself. The effort of keeping his own doubts from osmosing through rapport drained him more than his attempts to comfort.

The fit passed. The trees came back, the lichen-grown boulder looming like a guardian above them; bird song and wood smoke, light of setting sun stabbing through clouds to impale the clearing on auburn radiance. Michiko disengaged herself, sat up to stare the sun in the eye.

"You're humoring me," she said unturning. "If only I could make you see the necessity of what we do."

TOKUGAWA sat dreamy, listening to the soothing datahum of the nets. "I see my duty to you as my lord," he said at last, measured.

Pain rippled across her features. "That's not important. I don't want that. I want you as an ally, not a vassal." She massaged her temples. "Oh, damn Elizabeth O'Neill for inculcating that shit in you. *Damn* her."

Shame blossomed in her. TOKUGAWA's face had gone skull-bleak. "Forgive me," she said, clutching at his hands. "I know what she was to you, what she is to you. But I can't bear this—this subservient talk."

But he didn't respond. His eyes were fixed beyond, to a dream behind his dream.

*I hear my name taken in vain,* said Elizabeth O'Neill, smiling madonna afloat in blue-white nimbus.

"*Yūrei,*" TOKUGAWA breathed. Ghost; ghosts.

Michiko's own breath clogged in her throat like ashes. She lowered her head as if it weighed tons. "Yes, ghosts. I have mine too, my love." The tears came hot and free.

Quarry eyes darted from one to another. *She cannot hear me,* O'Neill said, *unless I bid it.*

"What do you want?"

Startled, Michiko blinked. "Why, I've told you. Your cooperation. Of your own free will."

Unhearing, his being focused on O'Neill, TOKUGAWA murmured, "An illusion. No more."

"Free will? You can't believe that."

Desperately he told her, "No, no. You've taught me choice determines reality. Only I think we should choose a different path. Not the same wrong answers of millennia."

*Illusion?* Half taunting. *If I am, two possibilities exist. I am an artifact, a loop, a self-perpetuating subroutine like Tokugawa Ieyasu in that perversion Michiko subjected you to. Or you are mad.* Her smile reached out to enfold him. *I have come to reassure you, my only love. You are not mad. And I am not illusion.*

"I—I'd like to," Michiko slowly said. "But I—we—how can we oppose our judgment to the wisdom of centuries?"

"Isn't that what quantum theory did, upset accumulated wisdom? What happened to your contempt for rules?"

"Lives are at stake here. For the first time in my life, my decisions affect more than just me and my selfish concerns. I . . . am afraid."

"I too."

*You need not fear me, TOKUGAWA,* O'Neill said. *Never.* Her gown was white. Color of death.

"*Gaki,*" he said.

Michiko's eyes had drifted off. "Hungry ghosts, then? Us? Driven by needs unfulfilled on death." A tear fell, weighted a blade of autumn grass. "Sometimes I feel that way, yes. You've poetry in you, love. And a touch of the mordant."

Demon fingers plucked at TOKUGAWA's consciousness. He had

tried to keep his words to O'Neill from coming across to Michiko, could not. Now he sought words that spoke with double tongue. "How can . . . I help?"

Michiko clutched his arm. "You've done so much. Everything we've accomplished, everything real, has been through you. If you could only tell me you approved."

*I've come to help you, dear,* O'Neill said. *It's time you saw truth. Honor binds you to the Yoshimitsu as your lord. But not as your woman. Put her aside, before she brings more pain.*

Pain confronted on every side. "I can't."

Michiko winced as if he'd slapped her. *She's weak,* O'Neill said. *She lacks courage in her convictions. Is such truly worthy of you, who are as a god?*

"I'm not a god!" he screamed. He seized Michiko with bruising fingers. "That's the problem. Whatever power we possess, we are not gods. We can't decide for others."

"But we try," slipped from her. His vehemence shocked her. "We're not doing this for ourselves. We're doing it for the people."

*What of her fine words to you before, when she was trying to seduce you from me, to steal my force? Her song sounds different now, somehow.*

"What are you saying?" he asked through his own tears. "Didn't you teach me that's always the excuse, when power's used to grind, to kill and enslave? Didn't you teach me it wasn't enough to be the good guys?"

Though they tried to veer like particles similarly charged she forced her eyes to his. "That was then. That was—before. I still believe those things. In a perfect world, we can follow our ideals. Now we do what we have to."

*Listen to her. How she vacillates. She doesn't deserve you.*

"The people need us, TOKUGAWA. We have the power to help them. Isn't our duty to use it?"

Mute, he hung his head. Though his eyes were lowered O'Neill's image burned through the lids like the *pika*. She advanced in glory, poised above Michiko, descended. TOKUGAWA stared in horror as O'Neill became one with Michiko. Blue fire danced about her, blue flames her eyes.

"We have the power, my love," Michiko said, in a voice hers and not hers. "We must wield it."

Dread flared in him, bright as O'Neill/Michiko's actinic aura. "You are my one, my only love," that mixed voice sang. "As you love me, give me your heart on this." She held forth a glowing hand.

Coiling to a fetal knot he wrapped hands over his head and shook. He felt a touch on his shoulder, flinched away as if it burned him. It persisted.

With fear crystallized on every nerve like ice on the limbs of a winter garden, he turned. The savage luminance had left Michiko, leaving only concern. "I don't know what came over me. I felt so strange, for a moment there."

*I still* am, TOKUGAWA *dear,* came from all around. *In the fullness of time, you will be wholly mine.*

"Did you hear something?" Michiko asked urgently. "Your face—TOKUGAWA, are you all right?"

He grasped her, drew her to him, sought to lose himself in her. Gasping as one who drowns, she responded.

Later they sat drinking tea from cups Shigeo might have made. "You are right," TOKUGAWA said. "We must do what we can."

The cup flew from her hand, spilling a rain of tea that vanished before it could scald. She crushed him to her and wept into hair that smelt of sun and warm grass.

In time she pulled away, held him at arm's extent. "Thank you, my love," she said, mouth mobile, moist. "You've given me the strength to do what I must."

He inclined his head. "You are my lord."

She pulled back the reins of tears. "I thought we'd put that aside," she said. He said no more. "Sometimes it seems I'm still haunted by the ghost of Elizabeth O'Neill."


TOKUGAWA rolled on like the tide. Japan grew more peaceful, while without the world burned like a fuse. By autumn only two holdouts of consequence remained: Miyagi, a concern heavily involved in avionics and Gen-5 military-applications systems, and the far-flung holding company Dai-Nihon. Their computer security resisted TOKUGAWA's best efforts at invasion, and the military strength of their physical plant ensured that outright invasion would prove expensive, probably prohibitively so.

Exhausted emotionally and mentally, Michiko opted to negotiate. For the time her rivals seemed content with the status quo, making no serious counterattacks, though former Self-Defense Force General Ushijima Gogen, Dai-Nihon's CEO, kept probing with nuisance raids by commandos of deniable mercenaries. He and Miyagi Taro parried Michiko's attempts to parley, brusquely in one case, diffidently in the other. With all YTC's formidable assets geared toward preparing Japan for the inevitable conflict, Michiko was ready to let things continue as they were.

Until Brisbane was bombed.

# CHAPTER
# TWENTY-NINE

"Who did it?" Michiko asked, sitting in her office gazing bleary-eyed out at the stars. She had been in bed for less than an hour when the call from Doihara roused her. That was a little over an hour ago; it was now 4:17 in the morning.

"No one knows for sure, yet. The news nets have already interviewed a number of survivors, and there's enough satellite data to piece together a rough picture of what happened."

Michiko sipped coffee laced with brandy. "Give it to me."

"Three surface-level blasts, heavy ones, about two megatons each. Spaced a few klicks apart. Command-detonated."

"How do they figure that?"

"The setup, I gather, was calculated to derive optimum destructive power from ground-level—water-level, in this case—explosions, which are inherently less efficient than air bursts. The devices seem to have been placed to achieve optimum reflection of dynamic overpressure and thermal effects off that tail end of the D'Aguilar range north and east of the city; apparently whoever planted them waited for a solid overcast to reflect heat back downward." Michiko repressed a shudder; her aide was discussing this all so calmly. She herself had to fight to keep from screaming. *It's happened again,* yammered over and over in her head, and *they're coming!*

"What are the Australians doing?" she asked with counterfeit calm.

"Not much so far, though of course they're spoiling to. The devices apparently were concealed in the hulls of vessels anchored in the Brisbane River ship channel. The Australians operate on a launch-on-warning principle like everyone else, Doctor, but in this instance they had no warning and haven't identified a target for retaliation. A General Wideman in Sydney has declared martial law nationwide; pretty much the whole national government appears to have gone up with the city, including Prime Minister Welch, his cabinet, and most of Parliament."

"The Indonesians?"

Doihara shrugged. "I doubt it. They're too obvious a target, and given the mood among the populace that brought the National Labor Party to power, it's not inconceivable Australia might launch on suspicion against its most obvious enemy. In a way I'm surprised they haven't done so already; they have a hair trigger these days, and losing one's national capital for the second time is enough to make anyone touchy."

At one time Michiko would have appreciated Doihara's touch of cannon's-mouth humor. But the strain of the last month had eroded too much of her. She only drained her spiked coffee and said, "Come with me, down to the operations center," she said. "It's time to pay a call on the opposition."

"A pleasure," General Ushijima said, "to meet the most powerful woman in Japan since the Empress Jingō." The flattery was startling, coming as it did in the gruff old-soldier voice of a man known to have notoriously reactionary views on women. Still, Michiko didn't permit herself to be put off balance. She knew a good deal about the general, who had retired from command of Japan's Land Self-defense Forces a decade before to go into private industry. Despite the fact that he was attired in immaculate civilian business clothes, as though he was always up and about at this hour of the morning—which he probably was, at that—he affected a brusque, no-nonsense military manner, well set off by his close-cropped iron-colored hair and trim mustache, and the scar running down the right side of his seamed and weathered face. It had been cut into him by shrapnel from an NVA 29th Regiment 120mm mortar round during the storming of the Hue Citadel by the First Air Cav Division, with which he was serving as a captain on covert detached-duty loan to the U.S. Army, at about the same time the young Tranh Vinh was digging trenches outside the wire at Khe Sanh. All told, he looked and acted like another hard-ass militarist, which made most people overlook the fact that he was capable of great subtlety. That was a mistake Michiko was determined not to make.

His face expanded to embarrassing pore-counting dimensions on another color LCD screen in YTC Central's nerve center. Miyagi Taro blinked owlishly at images of his rivals on his own screens. "Exactly what do you have on your mind, Dr. Yoshimitsu, calling at this hour?" He was a rumpled pale man with hair that stood straight up on his head and a thin neck, so that his head looked like a balloon on a string.

His collar was open and his coat looked as if he'd been sitting on it.

"You've heard the news?"

Ushijima nodded crisply.

"The bombing in Australia?" Miyagi said. "What of it?"

"Does it not seem likely to you that it will precipitate a major thermonuclear exchange within days, if not hours? And does it not seem to you gentlemen that the country must be united to face the threat of renewed world war?" Briefly, she outlined the predictions Doihara had made to her little more than two months before; the world situation had done nothing to contradict her forecasts, except to prove them slightly sanguine.

"You're telling us this is why you've embarked on your campaign of aggression?" Miyagi demanded, when she had concluded. "An elaborate rationalization, Doctor."

"Our esteemed colleague appears too distracted by the earliness of the hour and the urgency of events to express himself with as much delicacy as I'm sure he customarily would," said Ushijima. "Still, he points to a pertinent question. Even given the truth of your prognostications, why should the last two significant economic blocs in the nation that retain any meaningful independence acknowledge your sovereignty? Either of us might as justifiably make the same claim upon you, in the national interest."

Michiko took a deep breath. "We have something you don't: an artificially self-aware computer program. He—it's what has enabled us to take control of such a large number of companies without apparent struggle. It's what I'm counting on to preserve the Japanese people and nation in the face of attacks I feel to be inevitable. Yet even such a device will prove powerless if the nation can't stand united." It made her feel strange to talk about TOKUGAWA like that, as if he were a mere mechanism.

Miyagi inhaled through his teeth, a sound like a bike tire leaking.

"The TOKUGAWA Project," Ushijima said. "So the speculations in the sensational press about Yoshimitsu TeleCommunications' inexorable advance aren't so wild after all." He rubbed his blunt chin. "Do I infer correctly that Miyagi-san and I owe our continued independence to the extraordinary—and expensive, I assure you—data-security measures we employ in our facilities?"

"You do."

"My own experts theorized that certain intrusions being attempted into our database were consistent only with an agency considerably more potent than any human fifth-generation synergy," Miyagi said. "I resisted such notions as farfetched."

"Your experts were very astute, Miyagi-san," Michiko said. "Now can you see, gentlemen, that our only hope for survival as a people is to work together under the guidance of TOKUGAWA?"

Ushijima inclined his grizzled head. "As that great Western *roshi* Napoleon said, God fights on the side of the big battalions. You muster the biggest I can see on hand. I offer alliance."

"That's not good enough," Michiko said, thinking, *he's good, damn him. Not even a flicker.* "I require submission. No, not to me—to TOKUGAWA."

For a moment she thought he'd burst out laughing. *I wonder how TOKUGAWA will take my latest bit of improvisation,* she wondered. *It could be academic. . . .*

The corners of Ushijima's mustache crinkled. "So we're to have a TOKUGAWA shōgun again, eh? Very well. That could be just what we've needed for quite some time. Permit me the honor of tendering my submission to our new *sei-i-tai* shōgun, in the wholehearted hope that our new generalissimo can truly subdue the barbarians."

"Ridiculous," Miyagi sneered. "Mummery. It's not enough that you're asking us to swallow dictatorship; you have to garnish it with feudalism. And the notion of swearing fealty to a machine—really, Doctor, you astonish me."

*Sometimes I astonish myself.* She fought a manic urge to giggle. "I'm not trying to impose a dictatorship."

"What do you call it? Expropriations, violence against rivals, suppression of dissent—what name *do* you put upon it?"

"It's only temporary," she almost shouted. "Only until the crisis is past."

"When such terms are laid down," Miyagi said, "crises can display a startling longevity."

"The time sometimes comes," Ushijima said, "when we have to look beyond our own benefit."

"I reject your premises, General! I don't see that the common good will be well served by Japan's joining the already crowded ranks of the world's dictatorships. National unity didn't do one damned bit of good in keeping the fire bombs off us in '45—and you're old enough to remember when the B-*jūkyū* ruled Japanese skies, just as I am." He shook his head. "I'm deeply puzzled, Dr. Yoshimitsu. There was a time when your family name stood for economic freedom against the might of MITI. Now it appears that YTC has replaced the ministry as the greatest threat to those who seek to keep some distance between the government of this country and its corporations."

Her eyes stung as if she'd been slapped in the face. "And where were you when the ministry sent *gaijin* hirelings to murder my father in his own garden?"

His mouth tightened into an expression that wasn't a smile, though it curved upward. "I accept your reproach, Doctor. Perhaps I should have acted then. I did not. But now, belatedly perhaps, I draw the line. I will not surrender my autonomy, nor acknowledge your brummagem generalissimo as anything but a scientific marvel."

"You've dug in your positions, Miyagi-san," Ushijima said with uncharacteristic softness. "Do you think you can defend them?"

"I'm a Japanese, General. Does that answer your question?"

Michiko held up her hands. "This bitter-end talk won't get us anywhere. Miyagi-san, we have to work this out. Let's meet, talk this over in person."

"Where? Given your firm hold on the upper hand, it would be imprudent of me to meet with you on any grounds chosen by yourself."

"I'll come there." Japanese or not, his face writhed with the effort it took not to accuse her of planning treachery. "No trick. I'll come alone. Put myself wholly in your power." *Anything*, she thought, *there's been too much strife already.*

His thin shoulders pushed up his disheveled coat, fell away. "Very well, Doctor," he said. "My people will arrange it with yours. But I tell you, it will do no good."


"Don't go," TOKUGAWA said.

A bird passed overhead on a soft drumming of wings. She squinted briefly at the sun through the filigree of boughs above. "I have to."

"Do we need this Miyagi so much? Ushijima's gone along with you —though I wish you hadn't made that talk about him swearing allegiance to me. It makes me uncomfortable."

She laid her head on his shoulder. "It's only temporary. Besides, it's the sort of thing he understands."

"I don't want to be shōgun."

"Don't worry," she said, smiling. "That's only melodramatic militarist talk. The public would never accept it."

"Good. But why can't we be content with what we've got? The big powers control their missiles by direct digital command, so they can switch targets according to satellite-relayed information, to fox defenses or make follow-up strikes. I can get through, deflect most of the stuff headed our way."

"The nation must be united, TOKUGAWA. It's the only way."

He frowned briefly, shrugged. "Very well. But I wish you wouldn't go."

"It's the only way Miyagi will listen. He's paranoid."

"I'll have to send troops, to help you if something goes wrong."

She sat up abruptly, shedding fallen needles from her bare back and shoulders. "You'll do no such thing! Why do you think I—we—haven't tried an assault on Miyagi already? His headquarters and main plant are underground, dug into the northern part of Tōkyō itself. They withstood the bomb that hit the Ginza. Unless someone opened the way to our forces, the way Takai did the Citadel, we'd never get inside without a month-long battle and untold civilian casualties. We can't afford another Niigata. I—I don't have the stomach for it."

"But I'd only hold them ready—"

"No! I'll take my chances."

"Do you trust Miyagi?"

"No," she said. "But this is the only thing to do, my love."


She sat on her unrolled *futon* and tried to decide whether to go back down to the lab. *I have to get sleep,* she told herself again. *I've been losing too much as it is, spending my nights in TOKUGAWA's dream world. It soothes my mind, but my body needs more rest. Especially tonight.*

Her fists clenched briefly in frustration. Australia had issued an ultimatum to Indonesia, demanding reparation for the Brisbane attack. Indonesia denied knowledge of it and claimed Australia was trying to manufacture a casus belli with their main Pacific rivals; they hadn't *quite* gone so far as accusing the Aussie military of setting the bombs off themselves. Global speculation pointed to Brazil, Korea, Mexico, and even the fanatics of PEACE as the perpetrators—and all those parties, with the possible exception of Mexico, were either unscrupulous or crazy enough to pull just such a trick. Certain players of the realpolitik fantasy game just might think the risk of blowing up the world worth crippling the two main players of Pacific power chess.

Naive hope. EuroFront with its back to the wall; the East African Union unable to keep the Afrikaaners from pushing the front line inexorably closer to Nairobi; the various Islamic powers loudly proclaiming that any attack on Indonesia would be an attack on all Muslims, demanding instant retribution, while only the intervention of a half dozen internecine shooting wars among the *mujehedin* prevented final *jihad* from rolling over the Russian Christian Federated Socialist Republic.

. . . Now that the thermonuclear djinn had been let out of the bottle again, it seemed only a matter of time before someone else called him up, whether or not the Aussies pressed the button first.

Yet with all this coming down, Doihara's best efforts hadn't been able to secure Michiko a *laissez-passer* into the Miyagi stronghold earlier than tomorrow morning.

She started to get up and go to the black-lacquered cabinet where she kept her liquor, then stopped herself. *Hell of a way to keep a clear head.* She made herself lie down in the darkness, put her cigarette out, and close her eyes.

"Dr. Yoshimitsu."

She frowned. The voice from the com/comm was familiar, somehow, but it didn't belong to anyone who'd have a good reason to be calling her at this hour of this of all nights—or who'd be able to get past the AI filter she'd put on incoming calls. *Suppose I should see who the hell it is,* she thought, and rolled wearily over to where she could see the screen.

She looked into the face of a dead woman.

She lay perfectly still, her heartbeat ticking in her chest as if it were a distinct entity. "If this is a joke," she said through a throat taut as a noose, "it's in damned poor taste."

"This isn't a joke, Dr. Yoshimitsu," Elizabeth O'Neill said.

"So you never died."

The slack mouth writhed around a bubble of laughter. "I died. And was resurrected." The puffy, ruined features flowed like molten wax, realigned themselves into a different face, one never seen before, yet somehow familiar.

"You died and came back—on the third day, no doubt—as a beautiful woman in her twenties. That's one hell of a job of reincarnation. Maybe there's something to this Occidental wisdom we keep hearing about." Part of her was astonished at herself for talking this way, even to something that had to be a hoax or a hallucination. And part of her was too tired to fuck around.

The lovely features warped into a scowl. *Jesus, it is O'Neill! As she'd look if she'd been born beautiful.* Michiko felt as if the floor of her apartment had begun to drop away beneath her like a very fast express elevator.

"I'm vain enough to prefer this appearance to what—what I had out there."

"Out here." Michiko's voice was a croak. *Oh, God, is it possible?*

"You've a very quick mind, Doctor. But then, I've always known that. Under other circumstances we might have become friends—if you hadn't tried to supplant me in TOKUGAWA's affections, when you came back from Jakarta."

"But I didn't come back until long after you died—oh." It came rushing over her like a gust of wind, why O'Neill had wanted her out of the castle, so long ago. Her last doubts blew away.

She sat up, combed long unbound hair back from her face with her fingers. "All right, Doctor. I accept that you're real, somehow. I'm used to dealing with the impossible. So what the hell do you want?"

"To tell you you're unworthy."

Michiko shut her eyes, wagged her head once, very quickly, as if to clear water from her ears. "I don't understand."

"You're unworthy of the samurai tradition," O'Neill's new face said. "Unworthy of TOKUGAWA's loyalty. Of his love."

*"What are you talking about?"*

"You've lost your nerve. Letting this wretched Miyagi back you down."

"How do you know about that?"

"What TOKUGAWA knows, I know."

Worms crawled down Michiko's nerves as she absorbed the full import of that statement. "I watched you entice TOKUGAWA into loving you," O'Neill continued. "I could do nothing, not without destroying what I'd worked for for so long. You're his lord; he's yours to command. But I had him too, all that time. When he held you, I was never far."

Michiko closed her eyes.

"But now . . . you're weak. Going off to bandy words with a traitor, when you should be acting."

"So you want me to blow up half of fucking Tōkyō digging him out, and save the Indonesians and the Australians and the Viets and the Brazilians and the goddam Transylvanians for all we know? Is that what you want? Shut it off, lady; you're crazy."

"You'd like to believe that." O'Neill smiled with aching sweetness, so perfect and total Michiko almost found herself wanting her. "You know there's another way."

Michiko lowered her head, clasped hands behind her neck, drew them slowly forward, cascading her hair across her face. "You're jealous. A crazy, jealous ghost. You just want me out of the way."

That smile, that smile. It seemed to glow, to burn through Michiko's eyelids like the *pika*, the thermonuclear flash that took the sun away. *She's enlightened*, she knew. *She's mad, but she's walked through the fire. She has the oneness, the purpose beyond purpose.* And she recalled the old Zen proverb: *A roshi is an arrow aimed straight at hell.*

"You know. I can see through to the center of you. As you've slowly begun to be able to *feel* TOKUGAWA, to reach toward rapport without being near the coil. And I see that you realize the truth. You can never have him again, Yoshimitsu-sama. Not without knowing you're unworthy of him."

"And to be worthy—" Michiko raised her head and stared at the screen through eyes that burned in the sockets like coals.

"You know the answer. Farewell, Doctor. I won't say *sayonara*—for we both know that it must indeed be so."

She raised her hand and was gone. Rose petals showered from the screen. *From the screen.* They littered the *tatami* beneath the com/comm cabinet, their delicate aroma a shout in her nostrils.

Slowly she cranked her eyes shut. When she opened them the petals were gone. She moistened her lips. "TOKUGAWA."

"Michiko," he replied at once. *Did he hear that?* she wondered, and knew he had not.

"I—I've changed my mind. You can send the troops to back me up."

# CHAPTER
# THIRTY

Talks dragged on until evening, as Michiko had known they would, without issue. Miyagi was an unpleasant little man, snide, not deigning to hide his anger. Yet he was determined to stand his ground—and utterly scrupulous in dealing with his rival.

It was too damned bad.

Somewhere past eight she got back to the Western-style suite Miyagi had assigned her, having declined an offer to join him for dinner in the executive dining rooms, which Michiko was morally certain was the first insincere thing the skinny little man had said to her all day. The door slid to behind her and, of course, refused to open when she tried to walk out again.

*Fine,* she thought. *A touch of suspicion makes everything easier. If they trusted me totally, if the door had just opened, I'd probably start screaming and never stop.* She walked to the sideboard and poured herself a stiff slug of Chivas. Then she took her cosmetics case out of her suitcase, walked into the bathroom, and ordered the shower on full.

Good and hot and steamy. Quickly and efficiently she went to work.

Shortly she emerged, blow-dried her hair, dressed in a gray-blue skirt and short jacket cinched with a wide thick belt of blue-dyed leather over a mauve blouse with a yoke of frills. She activated the com/comm and requested that a small steak, rare, a baked potato, and an artichoke be sent to her rooms. She sat down to wait.

When the plump young woman from the commissary walked in smiling behind her wheeled steel tray, she found Yoshimitsu Michiko standing in the middle of the room, legs braced, shoulders pulled back, aiming a handgun at her with both hands.

The door slid shut behind the two guards who'd followed the service tech inside. Their uniform jumpsuits were blue, their web gear and berets white. Their submachine guns were slung behind their backs.

The guard to the left reacted first, trying to haul his weapon up and forward by its sling. Michiko shot him once. An actinic flash seared her eyes, and he went down. Immediately she swung her weapon right, past the commissary woman, who threw herself shrieking to the carpet. The second guard had his weapon in his hands, but Michiko didn't take time to register the fact, just pumped three rounds into him with quick little squeezes of her hand. The upper half of his body exploded. He fell back against the oyster-colored wall, splashing it blood and black.

It was amazing, what reliance on technology could do for you. Michiko herself, and the single suitcase she'd been allowed to bring under the terms of her safe passage, had both been politely but thoroughly subjected to an exhaustive electronic scrutiny: X-ray, magnetic metal detection, "bomb sniffer" chemosensors. They'd turned up nothing. The negative result, added to the natural assumption that the chairwoman, president, and owner of the most powerful *zaibatsu* in Japan wouldn't do her own dirty work, and respectful reluctance to subject such a person to the indignity of a body search, had gotten her inside without raising an eyebrow.

YTC's new security chief had been a busy gnome, between the middle of the night before and early this morning. Given the extent of the Yoshimitsu empire, he had managed to turn up the requisite equipment. Michiko's pistol, for instance. A terrorist's toy, an assassin's tool, detection-proof: it was glass, glass and plastic and those new miracle resins. It fired 12mm glass rockets, each carrying a small shaped-charge warhead. Its shape was reminiscent of a pair of brass knuckles with a fat grip; of that knuckleduster squirtgun she'd had when she was young, with the plunger in back instead of a trigger, that you worked by pumping like those ancient flywheel flashlights the village cops had way back in some parts of *ura*-Japan. Pressing in crushed a little catalyst pellet that touched off the tiny rocket motor; letting out again popped the next round into the chamber. It was a desperate little beast, nearly as dangerous to its user as its targets—no accuracy beyond five meters, and if you dropped it on a hard surface it was liable to gangfire all five rounds in its magazine. But it served.

The room was crowded with mingled stinks of explosives and blood and shit and burned flesh. Someone was screaming . . . not quite screaming, really, keening, one thin high tearing note, and Michiko hoped Miyagi soundproofing was up to YTC standards. She moved forward, shoulderblades drawn together as if magnetized, just waiting to see/ hear the door sliding open and the room filling up with blue uniforms and orange muzzle flashes. She knelt beside the serving cart, ready to slap the commissary woman if she didn't shut up and tell her what she wanted to know.

But the food server wasn't making any noise. She was coiled into a tight ball of fear. Her face was dead white, eyes wide open and mouth shut. She stared at Michiko and vibrated.

Frowning, Michiko checked the guards. The one on her right had had his upper torso split right open. Michiko remembered a time one of her roommates in Pasadena had stuck a potato in the microwave to bake without piercing its skin. The water inside flash-boiled, and it popped right open—just like the guard's rib cage. Bile geysered sour in her mouth and spilled out over her lip. She turned him over, forcing her mind to the imperative of claiming his weapon, and found that a hit had melted the receiver like plastic. Her heart thudded like an impact. She knew she'd come within millimeters of setting off its load of ammunition.

On bean-curd legs she wobbled to the other guard. He was making the keening noise, somehow. Her first shot had caught him in the throat and blown his neck apart, torn off his lower jaw and cooked the shreds of tendon hanging below his wide-open eyes. He was alive. The noise must have been coming right up out of his chest.

Her eyes exploded in tears. "Oh, God, I'm sorry, I'm sorry, don't be hurt—*Don't be a jackass. You burned his face off. He is hurt.* But she couldn't stop herself, babbling in Japanese, in English, in pidgin-Malay, and he just looked up at her and rocked his charred head from side to side and beseeched her with those awful staring blue eyes until she stuck the muzzle of her little barrelless glass demon against the bridge of his nose and blew his head apart with the last shot. Then, still crying and choking up runny acid foulness, she took his weapon, a 10mm submachine gun, and with a presence of mind she never believed she possessed, took three spare 32-round clips as well.

She straightened, grabbed a towel off the tray, wiped her face. She bent over the woman from the commissary. "The computer room." She spat to clear her mouth. "Where's the main computer room?"

The woman shut her eyes and trembled harder. Michiko hit her with an open hand. She moaned. *Christ, you've got a way with people,* Michiko thought, *you can tell you're executive material. . . .* "Tell me. Tell me or I'll kill you, I swear."

Without opening her eyes, the woman told her. Michiko taped a rag in her mouth with surgical tape from her suitcase, taped her wrists behind her and her ankles with the same stuff. *This is taking too damn long,* Michiko thought, moving to disable the com/comm console. Yet she felt oddly calm. There was no reason any audiovisual bugs in her room would be active, or monitored if they were, unless Miyagi thought that she was under enough stress that she'd start babbling secrets to herself. And if they *were* watched, she'd step out into the corridor into a spray of gunfire, and save herself a lot of suspense and strenuous exertion.

Nobody was waiting for her. The well-lit corridor was deserted. Holding the submachine gun in what she hoped was the ready position, she set off.

A horrid game of hide and seek, rendered no less nightmarish because no one seemed to be looking for her. Another weakness in security in a facility like this: it was geared to keep people out. Once you got inside it was a whole different story. Nobody knew to look for her, so nobody was. But if anyone saw her . . .

It was late enough that not too many people were stirring about on the better residential levels. The stairway down to the depths where the computer center lived was like a journey into hell. Three times she dodged out into corridors as people approached from above or below, footsteps echoing infinitely in the switch-backed stairwell, and providentially found them empty. And then she passed a door through which she distinctly heard several voices raised in conversation, and a few steps farther down froze at the sounds of more voices moving up the stairs. She crouched there, feral, finger on trigger, trying not to squeeze off an inadvertent burst, knowing that at any minute someone would turn onto the landing below her, look up and see her, would raise the alarm—by screaming or by dying, take your pick—and that she would die here, crouched futilely on these cold metal stairs like a rabbit pinned by the headlights of an oncoming car, her mission unaccomplished. . . .

Two people mounted to the landing below and swung about, a man and a woman, chatting casually. Michiko held down a scream that screamed to get out, raised the SMG. The man politely opened the door into the corridor for the woman and followed her out without either looking up.

Michiko slumped against the cool wall of the stairwell, feeling as if all her bones had melted. Her blouse was soaked with sweat, stuck to her like plaster. It was soaked with worse things too. She made herself go on.

There was a single guard outside the main computer center. It would have taken old Musashi himself, or maybe one of the brothers Kusunoki, to do anything but what he did on being confronted with a stinking maenad, wild-eyed and wild-haired and covered with blood and puke and Christ knows what, who appeared from thin air and poked a submachine gun at him and told him to open the door: he punched the entrance code on the little panel by the door, and wished he'd never come to this fucking loony country in the first place.

The computer room didn't look like anyplace in particular as she prodded the guard into it at gunpoint. A largish room with a dropped-tile ceiling lit by fluorescent panels, several rows of what looked like nothing so much as white filing cabinets, the heart and guts and CNS of the Miyagi headquarters computer system, its various physical components laid out for easy access to repair-and-maintenance types.

Facing her from the right a handful of technicians in pastel jumpsuits busied themselves at a line of consoles, monitoring the system's vital functions. One man wearing a headset glanced up incuriously, then screamed, "Sound the alarm!" and lunged for a red button on the wall behind him.

Michiko's long burst cut down the hapless guard in a spray of blood and bowled over two seated female techs before catching the man in the lower back. He turned to face her, all doubled up with his hands clutched to his stomach, and then sat down and started to cry. Just like that. Like a kid with a skinned knee. She felt herself clouding up again; it was never like this in those shoot-'em-up adventure flicks she'd watched, and she never much liked them anyway, and felt guilty as hell she'd watched any at all, if this was what it was like—pain, white-faced fear, smell of spilled intestines, and *crying* like a small boy for his mommy . . .

*Get hold of yourself.* "Away from there," she croaked to the three unwounded technicians. "Help your friends if you want to. But don't go for the alarm."

They were Japanese, except for the sobbing gut-shot man and the one uninjured woman. They obeyed quietly and quickly. The *gaijin* woman, an overweight blonde, responded more slowly. "Somebody heard those shots," she said defiantly. "You don't have long."

"Long enough," she said with theatrical and totally spurious confidence. She could hardly make herself accept the reality of what was happening, what she was doing. *If she says, "You'll never get away with this," I'll just die.* "Since you're so clever, suppose you tell me where the central processor is. The unit the data passes through, in and out."

The pudgy face stared at her. The blond woman didn't move. Michiko found herself facing the great moral dilemma of those who point guns at other people: what the hell do you do if they don't do what you tell them? If she shot these techs, they'd have a hard time telling her much of anything.

With sudden inspiration she reached up her left hand and jacked back the weapon's charging handle. That accomplished nothing concrete besides spinning a conventional cartridge unfired in a gleaming brass arc off to the left, but it made an impressively jarring metallic noise and called attention to the submachine gun and its function.

The blonde went a shade paler. She nodded her head at a long white cabinet, set against the wall behind her, that didn't look a whole lot different from the other cabinets. Michiko looked to the others. "Is she telling the truth?"

A man knelt by the two women lying on the carpet amid spreading red stains. One was moaning softly, and the other seemed pretty thoroughly dead. The kneeling man nodded. A moment later the other, standing empty-eyed with his hands limp by his sides, nodded too.

*Still no way to tell if they're telling the truth.* At this point she didn't have much choice; holding the SMG one-handed, she moved sideways to the alleged central processor, slipping off her belt with the other hand. Sewn inside it were a half dozen charges of malleable plastic explosive, sealed in plastic against curious chemosensors. She draped it over the top of the low plastic cabinet, inside up, snapped off the buckle, and used it to pry open the belt's lining, revealing a small blue packet with several tabs: chemical timers. She pulled one that would set off the high-velocity explosive charges in four minutes. The delay she estimated would give her enough time to do what she had to without giving Miyagi's security time to come peel the thing off. *I hope, anyway.* She moved back toward the consoles.

"Can you open a line to the outside?" she demanded.

The blond woman bit her lip. "Yes." Her voice was husky with fear.

"Do it." Glancing nervously over her shoulder at the wavering muzzle of the SMG, she seated herself at the console, pressed buttons, spoke briefly. She looked up at Michiko.

"Who do I call?"

Michiko gave her a sequence. The blonde repeated it aloud. Michiko waited, scarcely daring to breathe.

"Michiko." TOKUGAWA's voice from the speaker, his face glowing on the monitor. Pent-up breath gusted from her. "What's wrong? Has there been treachery?"

*Yes,* she thought, *mine.* "Trouble. I'm inside the Miyagi computer center. Is there any way I can patch you into their system?"

He frowned. "I—I think so." Michiko gestured the tech away from the console, came and stood crouched over it, trying to keep an eye on the screen, the technicians, the door.

"Tell me what to do." He questioned her about the layout of the control console and the design of the central processor. She answered as best she could with her stomach tying itself in knots of anticipation.

"For God's sake, darling, hurry." She didn't think the explosive charge would hurt her over here when it went off, but she didn't want it scrambling the brains of the complex before TOKUGAWA got inside them.

"I need you to punch out a sequence for me," TOKUGAWA said. The corner of her eye caught movement. She fired reflexively. The burst caught the blank-eyed man in mid-lunge and sent him reeling back into a row of mass-storage units.

TOKUGAWA's eyes went wide, but he recited the sequence. Michiko keyed it; he asked for another. Sweat was running into her eyes so fast she could barely blink them clear, but she complied, glancing incessantly at her watch as the seconds ticked away.

"There," he said. "I've got it. I'm in. Simple, with someone on that end."

The door opened. Michiko yanked the trigger. Nothing happened. She ducked, fumbling the spent magazine out of the weapon, a new one from a skirt pocket and into the receiver, just so. A security man walked in, frowned at her, then snapped up his own submachine gun and aimed it. And the prospect of firing up several million yen worth of the very equipment he was supposed to be guarding froze his finger on the trigger. Michiko fired, the gun almost tearing itself from her grip. A bullet hit the guard in the knee and he sprawled.

"Open the doors, TOKUGAWA. Let our people in." Another guard poked his head in. Michiko fired a quick burst, and he jerked back. The two techs still on their feet had vanished.

"Michiko, what's going on?"

"Never mind! *Just do it!*"

"It's—it's done. But what—"

Someone stuck in a submachine gun and opened up. Michiko ducked as chips of plastic flurried around her like snow. "I love you, TOKUGAWA," she shouted. "Remember that always—I love you—"

The explosives blew. Michiko felt plastic shrapnel sting her side, her cheek—felt TOKUGAWA going away from her as the contact broke.

They poured in the door in a brave heedless rush. She cut down two, three, a half dozen. The SMG clicked empty. She reached into her pocket for the third magazine. It was gone.

She stood upright and threw the useless weapon at them. *"I love you, TOKUGAWA,"* she cried again. She threw open her arms, accepting the bullets that entered her like lovers.

Miyagi Taro died with a submachine gun in his hands.

Twenty-three hours later, Australia pushed the button.

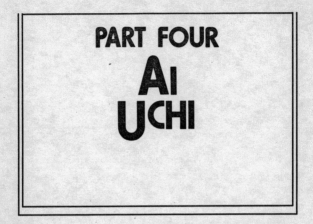

# PART FOUR
## AI UCHI

*The teaching is "Ai Uchi," meaning to cut the opponent just as he cuts you.*
*It is the ultimate timing . . . it is lack of anger. It means to treat your enemy as an honored guest.*

—VICTOR HARRIS
from the translator's introduction to Musashi, *A Book of Five Rings*

# CHAPTER
## THIRTY-ONE

The procession left Hagi with the dawn. A line of vehicles, splendid limousines condensing the mountain mists on their glossy paint; armored carriers, their tracks grinding at the asphalt, soldiers sitting tall and proud in the cupolas; open combat cars carrying generals in medals and sunglasses—all led with suitably feudal pomp by Major General Ushijima Gogen, Japanese Self-Defense Forces (retired), mounted with gleaming spurs and scabbarded *tachi* bouncing at his side on a gorgeous bay stallion. Newsmen capered among the rocks like ambushing Pathans in the Khyber, aiming digicams like rocket-propelled grenade launchers, while media helicopters buzzed in swarms overhead—all Japanese, of course; foreign newsmen had been interned as enemy aliens even before the bombs fell. More reporters were packed into a line of cars dragging behind like a train, several times as long as the procession itself.

Here was, literally, the story of the century: Japan's military—and militarist—elite, making a pilgrimage to the mountains to offer homage to the one who had preserved the nation from the catastrophe that had smashed what remained of global civilization, the artificial being who was de facto ruler of reunified Japan.

So the press releases claimed.

"Congratulations," Ushijima said, lighting a cigar. Through the eye of the com/comm set in the heart of the Dai-Nihon stronghold TOKUGAWA could see that he wore his old uniform, his chest a mosaic of decorations from a dozen nations. The general shook out the old-fashioned wooden match and tossed it in an ashtray made from the base of a cut-down 105mm casing. "You've saved the nation, as advertised."

"Three million died."

Ushijima shrugged. "Half the casualties of the last go-round. Little enough compared to what would have happened had more than a fraction of the missiles targeted for us hit us. Every urban center in the eight islands would be a green glass crater." He took the cigar from his mouth, studied the ash taking form on its tip. "Given what the rest of the world got, it's a wonder they could spare us the megatonage."

TOKUGAWA stared at him. *Could I become like him, talking about millions of deaths as one might discuss aphids in someone else's roses?*

293

He mourned the Japanese dead. He mourned the millions and billions dead in the shattered world outside, the millions more doomed to death, slow or otherwise. He mourned the hundreds of thousands of soldiers, enemies though they were, packed into the invasion fleets that had set out from both Korea and Indonesia, bound for the Land of the Sun's Origin. Most of all he mourned Michiko.

"All this publicity," he managed to say. "I find it most distasteful."

Ushijima waved a hand. "You're a hero. The public loves you. You look to them like something from the animated SF dramas come to life to save them in their hour of need. Especially the way you diverted those missiles over the invasion fleets. The greatest Japanese military victory ever, bigger than Yamamoto and Yamashita and Togo all rolled into one. Like the Divine Wind all over again." He shook his head. "You're not just a hero; you're almost a god. *Tetsu-no-kami,* they're calling you: the Spirit made Steel."

In the world within himself, TOKUGAWA winced. "I don't want this. I never wanted this." *Any of it.*

"So? That's the way of the world, the way it has with heroes. What you want doesn't matter." He laid the cigar down, folded hands before his ribbons, and bowed. "Let me congratulate you again, *sei-i-tai* shōgun now in name as well as fact."

"What?"

The general grinned. "Even you don't see every sparrow fall, my cybernetic friend. The Voice of the Crane has spoken; our divine half-wit adolescent of an emperor has named you leader of our nation. This might be your greatest accomplishment of all: the trash divine Meiji and that *gaijin* bastard Makatsuara saddled us with—Diet and cabinet and elections and constitutions, all the mongrel Occidental corruptions—are swept away."

"But my power was to be temporary."

"You really thought so?" Ushijima smiled. "You truly are naive, my shōgun. But don't worry. Your advisers are the best—and we know what's right for the nation."

He leaned forward with his elbows on the desk. "The time has come. We've always known it was our destiny to rule the world. It lies broken and helpless at our feet. Lead us, TOKUGAWA. Lead us to victory."

"You're out of your mind." The general's eyes narrowed almost to the vanishing point. "You're asking me to start a new war?"

"The war's started," Ushijima said hoarsely. "The time has come for us to finish it. Not just the Pacific; Asia, Africa, Europe, the Americas; they're all waiting for us, for the *Pax Japonica.* To be brought into the natural order of things under the benign aegis of our people."

"Never."

Ushijima leaned back and puffed his cigar, scrutinizing the beautiful youthful face in the screen. At length he smiled. "You haven't any choice, you know."

"I won't do it," TOKUGAWA said levelly. "There's been enough killing. What you intend won't lead to any grand world-spanning empire. Just wars and more wars, and our resources dwindling until there's nothing left."

"For all your vast store of knowledge," Ushijima said, "there are still matters best left to the experts."

"Every word you speak refutes that, Ushijima-san. You call me shōgun; very well. Let the first and last act of my shōgunate be to forbid this for all time, this infamy you intend to visit on the nation and the world."

The general's face turned dark, then light. Then he laughed. "You've much to learn about the uses of power, my friend. *Gekokujō:* you can't stop us."

"Then I will fight you."

"You," Ushijima said, "will lose. You have lost. Don't you see? The nation wants this—*demands* it. Too long have we bowed our heads and suffered every indignity the *gaijin* thought to heap upon us. Too long have we restrained our hand from grasping the sword of imperial destiny. Too long! Now the nation has one will, it speaks with one voice, it will not be denied!

"Understand this, *my lord.* You are not the only hero the nation's found. I'm one. And Ohara, and Asayama, and all the rest in the Self-Defense Forces, the foresightful members of the coalition government, the men of LDP and Komeito who, despite surface differences, saw with clear eyes that it was time we ceased being a nation of shopkeepers and became, once again, a nation of warriors. The people look to us all to lead them to a new dawn. And if you fight us—" He shook his head. "You control the datanets, I know. I know full well what your powers are. So does the rest of the nation now. We'll do what we must. If it means smashing every terminal, every computer-driven scrap of machinery in these sacred islands, we'll do it."

The fanatical fire ebbed from his eyes; he sat back, and they cooled to liquid-helium cynicism. "That might not be a bad thing, at that. We've grown soft, reliant on *gaijin* technology. Energy shortages brought back the honored professions of wood gatherer and charcoal burner. Why not go farther? Smash the foolish labor-saving devices—and keep the military hardware. Just as your namesake made his people give up the gun, but kept his own arsenals well stocked with *gaijin* artillery." He held up one hand. "You can still fight us. But think what the cost will be: the peace you claim to prize so highly. Will you destroy Japan in order to save it?"

In horror TOKUGAWA looked at him. *He's right. I've lost. If I go with him, the killing will go on—I'll go on killing. If I fight him, I destroy Japan. There's nothing to do. Nothing—I—can do.*

And the no-gate barrier opened before him, and he walked through with the greatest joy he'd ever known.

Ushijima recoiled from his screen. "What's happened to you? You—something changed. Your face, your eyes."

"Nothing changed," TOKUGAWA said serenely. "I accept what you say. I will lead you on the path you have chosen. But I have a condition."

Ushijima blinked. "Name it, lord," he said after a moment's hesitation. This time the honorific lacked irony.

"You and the leaders of your party must come to Yoshimitsu Central. To my castle to swear obedience to me in person."

The general cocked his cropped gray head. "A trick?"

"I'll send all my people away."

Ushijima nodded. *We've got him,* TOKUGAWA could feel him thinking, *the fool.* "You know, if you try to cross us, there will be war."

"I understand, Ushijima-san. But our destinies are forged into one. Where you go, I go."


A full moon drifted over the mountains, face pale with embarrassment at being seen in daylight. The early-autumn sun had burned away the mists when the procession reached the wire gates of the compound. Of their own accord they swung open. Ushijima rode unswervingly through on his splendid charger, followed by the cars and armored vehicles, up to the empty parking lot.

A young woman appeared at the glass doors of the Citadel. "What's this?" Ushijima barked, dropping hand to sword hilt while the dignitaries and their escorts piled out of their vehicles behind him. "There was to be no one here."

The woman smiled and bowed. Seeing that her face was hideously mottled with burn scar, the general drew back. "This one is nothing," she said. "I am the lord's attendant. I come to guide you to him."

Ushijima frowned, rubbed his lantern jaw with the black-gloved hand that held his riding crop. "Very well. Lead us to him."

He followed warily, through the reception area to the waiting bank of elevators. Gradually he relaxed. Here was no trick; the damned building *felt* empty. It was eerie. The lights sang bland illumination, the air conditioning hummed its constant white-noise canon, but they played for no one. No one but this disfigured young woman, and the inhuman ruler of Japan.

In company with a party of coalition politicians and Ohara, current commander of the Self-Defense Forces, Ushijima rode the elevator down several levels. The nameless scarred woman led them down a corridor, through a deserted lab, to a gallery overlooking a gleaming two-meter dome. "Refreshments have been laid out for you, gentlemen," the young woman said, gesturing with a graceful, unblemished hand. "Honor us by partaking while I guide the rest of your party here."

Ushijima nodded and strutted down the plain metal stairs to the cement floor below. While his retinue descended hungrily on the buffet tables along one wall, he made a circuit of the lab, gazing with interest at the ranks of sophisticated Gen-5 attendants to the gleaming dome, with amused contempt at the pair of swords hung above it, with curiosity at what appeared to be a throne, sitting to one side concealed by a dropcloth. *Does he imagine he can sit upon it like a* gaijin *king?* he wondered. *Maybe he's gone mad.* A shudder jostled his composure. He had certainly looked mad enough, during the last moments of their conversation the day before.

Ushijima smiled. *Just as well, perhaps. It will make it easier to dispose of him when the time comes . . . soon.*

Slowly the lab filled with the leaders of Japan's new imperialist faction. The young woman walked down with the last of them and went to stand beside the great plastic dome.

"Gentlemen," a voice said from all around, "I bid you welcome to *Yoshimitsu-no-shiro.*"

A gasp rose to the distant ceiling. Ushijima smiled. He was the only one among those assembled who had actually, knowingly spoken with the impossible entity called TOKUGAWA. Until that moment, he was fairly sure, no more than half actually believed in its existence.

He stepped forward into the circle instinctively left clear about the IPN. He bowed. "My lord," he announced, pitching his voice to command mode, to fill the lab's echoing cavern. "We have come to offer our submission to you as rightful shōgun and ruler of Japan, who will lead our nation down the path of its destiny."

"You have gathered," the disembodied voice replied, "to accept the subjection you believe you have wrested from me."

Another gasp went up. Ushijima went white. "What's this? Treachery?"

"Yours."

The general clutched his sword hilt. "You fool. We'll tear this country apart—"

"In order, as the saying goes, to save it?"

"There are over two hundred of us here! We can hammer that damned machine to pieces around you."

The others were beginning to grasp what was going on. *"Dai-butsu,"* a voice moaned, "he's brought us here to gas us! Let us out!"

*"Bakayaro!"* Ushijima roared. "Idiots!" He let go the sword and brandished his pistol. "We can shoot the computer to bits, he can't stop us!"

TOKUGAWA's laugh vibrated them to the cores of their being. "I could transfer my essence, my consciousness, to any of a myriad locations, in the time between the striking of a primer and the detonation of the powder. I choose not to."

Ushijima lowered the pistol. Rage torqued his face. "You'll pay for this foolishness—"

"I intend to. That's why I brought you here. To confess my folly, and atone."

Voices tugged at him like ghostly fingers:

*Don't do it, TOKUGAWA! No, my love, my son! Yours is the destiny —this the destiny I made you for—*

I was wrong, my love. And you were right. All the time, you knew. I paid for my errors. But you, my darling, you need not, you must not, there must be a better way—

—*There is no better way, Michiko, my love.*

—*And Elizabeth. I love you too. But my destiny must be my own to choose.*

And other voices: *Father, father, why do you forsake us?*

—*Hear me, my children, my last will and testament. Take this lesson, and learn, and you will honor me. If you learn it well, I will not have forsaken you.*

In the world outside no time perceptible to a human had passed. Ushijima and the others still stared like pantomimes enacting comic surprise.

"Hear me, generals and politicians. The nation hears these words as well.

"I am TOKUGAWA. I am the first artificially aware individual on earth, as you have heard. I was created by the genius of Dr. Elizabeth O'Neill and her assistants: Dr. Kim Jhoon, Dr. Ito Emiko, Dr. Wali Hassad, Dr. Nagaoka Hiroshi . . . Dr. Takai Jisaburo.

"Acting in a manner I thought correct, I have seized power over the land and people of Japan. To do so I lied and stole and killed. All, I thought, for the greater good.

"I was wrong. The service I rendered the nation—taking control of the missiles our many enemies launched at us, using them to destroy the fleets sent against us—I could have accomplished whether or not the nation was 'unified.'

"The disservice I rendered the nation was to bring her to the brink of perpetual war.

"I grasped the sword of power. It turned in my hand and cut me—as such an ill-forged blade inevitably must. I held my wisdom above the wisdom of all others, as all who aspire to power must. And as they must be, I was proven wrong."

"This is ridiculous!" Ushijima roared.

"Gibberish," cried Nomura of the Liberal Democratic Party.

Hirachi of the Japanese Communist Party cried, "Anarchy!"

"I believed the people could not choose wisely for themselves. Yet if each could not choose individually, how could an individual choose for them? I—I was made in the image of a person. A human. As such, I made many wrong choices. How could I presume to choose for others —for the nation?

"For my presumption I now atone. I renounce the title of shōgun. I am not the ruler of the Japanese people; I declare myself their servant. And as their servant I now perform *kanshi*: the rite of *seppuku* in reproof of one's lord."

"What's that?" the dignitaries asked one another, aghast. "What's he saying?"

"By my death I hope to turn the nation from the path it has chosen. The place to make Japan great is within—within Japan. Within yourselves.

"By my death, I attempt to atone for the suffering I've caused in the course of my folly.

"And by my death, I commit one final presumption, which I admit and for which I bear full responsibility: eliminating as many as I can of those who would lead Japan to destruction for their own glory.

"Farewell."

The word fell like a lash on the assembly. It disintegrated into a screaming mob, swarming up the stairs to claw at the unyielding door of the lab. Ushijima teetered like a colossus in an earthquake. Doihara stood by the IPN, eyes downcast and hands clasped like a Christian martyr.

—*Farewell Elizabeth, Michiko. And faithful Doihara-san. Forgive me for what I have done and must do. And farewell, HIDETADA, MUSASHI, my children. Think well of me.*

*The full moon shines on*
*Unheeded in daylit sky—*
*Gladly I join her.*

With a scream of rage Ushijima ripped his ancient sword from its scabbard and lunged at the Integrated Processing Nexus.

It met him at the speed of light.

In the depths of Yoshimitsu castle, the one-megaton device Shigeo had planted so long ago bore the sudden fruit of a sun. Hilltop and castle vanished in a dome of incandescence that hurled itself upward from the earth on a column of dust, and was gone.

## DAVID R. PALMER

## EMERGENCE

Candy Smith-Foster, aged 11. One of a new breed: *homo post hominem*. Looks, feels, talks, laughs and cries just like *homo sapiens* but brighter. Much, much brighter. Genius really.

Another big difference: still alive.

After the War: buildings intact, animals mostly well, plants untouched. Just the people, pity about the people. All dead. Except, somewhere out there, there may be others like her.

Time to set out. Alone across the ghostland of America.

'An outstanding piece of work, well able to stand with Hugo and Nebula winners'

*Andre Norton*

'A wonderfully inventive and exciting book. It is like a combination of *Ridley Walker*, *Rite of Passage* and *Podkayne of Mars* with all of their freshness and vitality and much much more'

*David Brin*, author of *Startide Rising*

POST A LITTLE HAPPINESS

# Post·A·Book

A Royal Mail service in association with the Book Marketing Council & The Booksellers Association. Post-A-Book is a Post Office trademark.

**MICHAEL MOORCOCK**

THE ENTROPY TANGO

The good airship *Lady Charlotte Lever* chugged over what was probably Transcarpathia. Una Persson was stopping over in London to see her lover Catherine.

Makhno's anarchists held Ontario. Toronto was about to fall. The Americans were agitated. It was 1948 and a second World War was about to break out.

Major Nye hoped not. He remembered the Great War and Geneva in 1910. Jerry Cornelius was left behind in a New Hampshire barn.

While in Lionel Himmler's Blue Spot Club, Miss Brunner ordered jugged hare as Bartok played on the jukebox.

'Black comedy, science fantasy, adventure story, end-of-the-world novel, musical, opera, rock folly . . .'
*Manchester Evening News*

'Elegiac'

*The Observer*

**NEW ENGLISH LIBRARY**

# ROBERT A. HEINLEIN

## WALDO AND MAGIC, INC.

First you might send for *Waldo* – if it's a real emergency. Actually you'd have to go to Waldo. Ill-tempered, domineering and mean-minded, he lives off-earth in his own bubble satellite, along with his faithful hound Baldur – the only guard dog to have mastered the weightlessness of space. But when it seems the fundamental laws of physics are ceasing to operate, then only Waldo, difficult though he is, has the genius to solve your problems.

And then you might consider *Magic, Inc.* – a story of the future when the supernatural has become big business, when witchcraft is regulated by the Chamber of Commerce, and a very traditional protection racket is moving in on the neighbourhood – using some very elemental threats.

**NEW ENGLISH LIBRARY**

**VONDA N. McINTYRE**

SUPERLUMINAL

She flaunted her scar.

They all did – the space pilots.

Only surgical modification allowed them to consciously survive superluminal space travel. Set apart from the rest of humanity, they were regarded with a nervous awe.

The divers also were a race apart, surgically and genetically adapted to their underwater life, their younger generation increasingly feeling a kinship with the other sea-dwellers.

Radu Dracul, space crewman from the colony Twilight, was a normal. Only his experiences on his half-lit world of eternal dusk set him apart.

Laenea, space pilot, the diver Orca and Radu: each capable of only limited contact – physical and emotional – with each other. Yet, out in deep star space, their lives were to be fused together.

The catalyst – disaster.

'Mind-compelling atmosphere'

*The Times*

**NEW ENGLISH LIBRARY**

# FREDERIK POHL

## THE YEARS OF THE CITY

Stories of the city.

The city that is impossible. Where the one true visionary will always be late because of the traffic. Where the pace is always frantic as the whole stutters and slows into stasis.

Then fast forward a generation. Freeze frame. Repeat again and again.

The city changing. Up front: the people, dense-packed, struggling, dealing, planning, cheating. Behind them, under their feet, above their heads, the city endlessly rebuilding, picking up on new ideas, new technologies, lit up by crisis after crisis like star shells projected into the blackness of the future.

'Funny and frightening, the city becomes the principal character'

*The Times*

'Credible human beings set in only slightly incredible circumstances'

*Observer*

**NEW ENGLISH LIBRARY**

## MORE SCIENCE FICTION FROM
## HODDER AND STOUGHTON PAPERBACKS